The
Motl
Mistake

The Mother's Mistake

RUTH HEALD

Bookouture

Published by Bookouture in 2019

An imprint of StoryFire Ltd.

Carmelite House
50 Victoria Embankment
London EC4Y 0DZ

www.bookouture.com

ISBN: 978-1-78681-533-0
eBook ISBN: 978-1-78681-532-3

PROLOGUE

The day was a painter's dream. Vibrant colours. Bright, cloudless sky. Green, leafy trees reflected in a sparkling river. An inviting morning, brimming with expectation of the summer's day ahead: laughter as families picnicked on the riverbanks, children screaming at the unexpected chill of the water, a line of jostling tourists, competing for the best angle to take a photo.

I felt like time should stop when I saw her. But it didn't. The birds continued to chirp as if it were any other morning.

My breath caught in my throat.

She was tangled in the reeds. They had wrapped around her pale arm, the current pulling it insistently away from her body until the shoulder had dislocated and the arm bent backwards at the elbow, like a plastic doll manipulated by a child. The rest of her was under the water's surface, bobbing.

Even if time had stopped it wouldn't have been enough. To correct things, to put things right, time would have had to go backwards. Stop me, before I started the chain of events that led me there, to the riverbank, watching helplessly as the little girl was pulled from the water.

A policeman was wading across the river, the water parting for him, the drag of the current no match for his strong legs.

He lifted her out, reached into her mouth and felt around for any debris, then tipped her upside down and thumped her on the back. Too hard. A spurt of water came out of her mouth and my heart lifted to my throat.

'Breathe,' I urged her. 'Breathe!'

His colleague reached out from the riverbank to take her from his arms. He handled her roughly as if she were little more than a doll. I fought to get closer, unfamiliar fingers gripping my forearm and pulling me back. But my anger quickly turned to despair. Her glassy eyes seemed to lock with mine. Her soul had already left her.

A scream scattered the birds and it was only when my knees sank to the muddy ground and my fingers dug into the soil that I realised it was coming from me.

'No!'

But it was too late. There was nothing I could do but watch as the police officer desperately tried to revive her, performing mouth-to-mouth and chest compressions on the riverside for a good ten minutes, before he let the paramedic take over and collapsed to the ground beside her, stroking her wet hair away from her face. As the paramedic pushed down into her small body, it jumped and shuddered at the force, her chest moving with his hands, pliant and lifeless.

I'd have done anything to hear her cry, but the only wails were from the police sirens, as car after car arrived, lights flashing with anticipation.

CHAPTER 1

The car's wheels crunch against the gravel as we pull up in front of the limestone cottage. Miles of countryside behind us and we're here. The perfect home for our little family. A shiver of excitement runs through me and I smile as I open the car door and the fresh country air engulfs me. This is the new start I've longed for.

Luckily for us, our daughter Olivia is abnormally calm. She's slept the whole two hours from our flat in London. I gently unstrap her from the baby seat and lift her out, holding her up to see the cottage for the first time. She whimpers as she wakes, squinting against the bright winter sun.

Matt gets out of the car and puts his arm around me. I breathe in the cold, crisp air, feel it tingle on the back of my throat. None of the grit of London.

'Happy?' Matt asks, squeezing my arm.

'Yes,' I say, and joy wraps around me like a blanket. Already the past seems further away, a distant memory. Now is a new beginning, the start of our life together as a family. Only the future matters.

The removal van swings into the driveway, as my mother-in-law appears from the path down the side of the building, which leads to her house at the back of the cottage.

'Claire,' she says, giving me a brief hug before taking Olivia from my arms. She presses my baby to her chest and declares that she is the prettiest little thing she has ever seen.

I grin at Ruth. We're lucky to have her. She's letting us live in her mother's cottage rent-free, so that we can save up for our own place.

Ruth looks doubtfully at the removal van. 'You've got a lot of things.'

'It's mainly baby stuff,' I say, taking Olivia back into my arms as we watch the men unload the cot onto the gravel.

'We'll have to see if it all fits.'

I laugh as I look at the cottage. It's four times the size of our flat.

'I'll open up,' Ruth says as she leads us to the front door. Weeds have taken over the garden and are starting to spread from the flowerbeds across the doorstep. I imagine Matt and me spending a day with our hands in the soil, planting seeds in the sunshine, Olivia watching from her pram.

My heart thuds as Ruth pulls out a set of keys and tries each one in turn. I can't wait to see inside.

Olivia starts to grumble and I rub her back. She's hungry. As soon as we get inside I'll feed her.

One of Ruth's keys finally fits the lock and twists uneasily.

As I step over the threshold, I cough. Damp and dust and mould. The air festers. I put my hand over Olivia's mouth.

'Oh,' I say, as I take everything in.

Shoes sit on the shoe rack, coats hang expectantly, and there's a letter on the ledge by the door, waiting to be posted. An umbrella left out long ago to dry is covered in a layer of dust. The beige stair-lift waits patiently for its owner.

Pamela, Ruth's mother, died of a heart attack three months ago.

'I haven't been in for a while,' Ruth explains, as she gathers up piles of letters into her arms from the carpet. 'Who'd have thought there'd be so much post?' she says to herself.

I hadn't expected this. I'm sure Ruth said she'd clear the house for us.

I step around her and look for a place to breastfeed Olivia. A plastic mobility walker blocks the entrance to a living room. I push it aside, go in and perch on the edge of the floral sofa. I adjust my top and put Olivia to my dry, cracked nipple. She fights at first, knocking me away. I reposition her until she eventually latches on and I wince. When she suckles vigorously, I sigh with relief. Olivia and I have both struggled with breastfeeding, but I am determined to make it work. The health visitor said it will help build the bond between us.

I look around the living room. The mantelpiece is crowded with dusty ornaments and photographs. A book lies open on the coffee table. The house is untouched since Pamela left and I feel like an uninvited guest. Matt brings me a cup of tea in a floral mug, and Ruth whisks out a mat to put it on.

'We'll have to buy some milk,' Matt says apologetically, but I sip the tea gratefully, taking care to hold it as far away as possible from my baby. It calms me.

'Full of antiques, this cottage,' Ruth says. 'I know I can trust you both to take care of everything.'

I imagine Olivia as a toddler, zooming round the cottage, causing havoc.

'We might need to move some things,' I say. I've spent the last week looking at furniture online. I'd thought we'd finally be able to choose our own.

'I don't know where you'll move things to,' Ruth replies.

I'm about to mention her huge house at the end of the garden, but I catch the look Matt gives me and say nothing.

One of the removal men comes in, out of breath. 'Where shall I put the boxes?' he asks. I look round the cluttered room.

'Upstairs?' I suggest.

Ruth leads the man away, and finally Matt, Olivia and I are alone. I let myself relax and take in my surroundings. It won't take long to clear the room and put up some pictures. We can make the cottage our own.

There's a sudden crash from upstairs, and my muscles tense instinctively. I see the teacup in my hand turning over. A scream escapes my mouth as the hot liquid splashes over my jeans. The cup falls to the carpet.

Ruth shouts at the removal men upstairs as Olivia screams. Matt rushes over, and I run my hands over Olivia, praying that the tea hasn't caught her.

'I'm sorry,' I say to Matt, tears welling up in my eyes.

I could have burned her. I could have scarred my child.

'It's OK,' Matt replies, his arm round my shoulder. 'One of the men must have dropped something. It made you jump.'

I can hear the edge of accusation in his voice. He hadn't jumped at the noise. If it had been him holding the tea, it wouldn't have spilt.

Everything makes me jump these days.

I'd hoped that would change when we moved to the countryside. But no matter how far I move, there are some things I'll never escape.

*

I cover the side of my face with my hands, peering out through my fingers as I anticipate his next blow. My cheek is cold against the kitchen tiles. I lie where I've fallen, not daring to move in case I anger him further.

Here it comes.

I feel the connection with skin, the crack of bone. The sensation is entirely physical. My mind is numb. Emotionless. But the punch is hard and I stuff my hand into my mouth to stop the instinctive scream. My daughter is sleeping upstairs.

I'm a trapped animal, frozen to the spot, as he lets out his anger, punch by punch. I deserve this. I've tried my best to please him, to be the perfect wife and mother, but I'm still not good enough. I'll never be good enough. My scars prove it. My black and blue body proves it. He can never hate me as much as I hate myself. I am nothing. No one. I lie still and let him finish, tiring himself out.

When his energy has dried up, he gives me one final, half-hearted kick in the ribs. Then he goes over to the counter and pours himself a glass of red wine, the expensive one he bought at Duty Free when he flew back from Buenos Aires last year. He leaves the room and I listen to his footsteps on the stairs.

When I hear the door of his study shut and I'm certain he's gone for the night, I stand up shakily. I wince as I put my weight on my left leg. I must have bruised it when I fell. Habitually, I check each limb still works, cataloguing my list of aches and pains in my head. The old injuries are healing, the new ones will take time. My body is in an endless cycle of injury and recovery. It's getting more and more difficult to lift my daughter without wincing.

I go to the hallway to look in the mirror. I observe my face critically, as if it's a painting. My eye is black and there is a new bruise on my cheek. An older bruise on my other cheek has faded to yellow. I'd kidded myself that it would soon be faint enough for me to cover it with make-up and go out to the supermarket or even to a mothers' group. But he's made sure that's impossible. I can't go out like this.

For a moment, I let myself imagine fresh air tingling against my skin, my face turned up to the sun. But the idea of freedom is just a fantasy that I indulge myself in from time to time. Because I haven't left the house for months.

I'm completely trapped.

CHAPTER 2

Olivia's screams get louder. All I want to do is read my book about baby sleep patterns, but I can't even manage that. I'm still only on page two. I'm never going to figure out how to make her sleep at night at this rate. Even before Olivia started screaming, I couldn't concentrate. My mind is so jumbled with thoughts of everything that needs doing, and worries about how I'm going to cope with looking after Olivia. I'd hoped that the relaxed atmosphere of the countryside would rub off on me and I'd form a better bond with my daughter. But even trying to read the parenting books is fruitless. I never get a moment to myself.

The sofa is an island amongst stacks of brown removal boxes. There's so much to unpack but nowhere to put it. Every drawer is crammed full with Pamela's things. Ruth says she plans to go through everything herself, one item at a time. But she's not emotionally ready yet. In the meantime, we stumble and trip and manoeuvre around the piles of boxes in every room. We are in transition, waiting. Everything in the house is dulled by a layer of dust. Once the house is clear of Pamela's things and we've unpacked so we can see the carpet, I'll give every inch of every room a thorough scrub.

The screams get louder. My back twinges in sympathy. My body hasn't realigned itself since the pregnancy. My spine isn't straight, my posture is off. I'm constantly leaning over, to change nappies, to comfort Olivia, to bath her. It shocks me how we all do this. Mothers everywhere. We bend down in reverence to our children, bow at their feet, as if they are the demigods we have to pray to, to keep our lives in order.

The screams have stopped. *She's dead.* The thought enters my consciousness and I know I should dismiss it, but I can't. I imagine finding Olivia trapped between the cot and the wall, unable to take a breath. Terror shudders through me.

I rush up the stairs, squeezing past the stairlift.

Olivia is sound asleep in her cot, her toy bunny next to her, in Pamela's spare bedroom. I sigh with relief. Her face is still damp from her tears and I want to touch her cheek and wipe them away, but I daren't in case she wakes.

The battered bed next to the cot calls to me. The black paint has peeled off the metal frame, and the mattress sags in the middle, but I'm exhausted and it looks like the most welcoming bed in the world. I give in and ease myself onto it, as gently as possible so I don't disturb Olivia. The spring in the middle creaks as it digs into my spine and a faint smell of damp rises out of the mattress as it gives in to my weight. I don't care. Just five minutes sleep, five seconds.

The doorbell rings.

There is a pause, a moment of stillness so complete that I have to hold my breath in order not to interrupt it. Then the doorbell rings again and Olivia's screams pierce the air.

I thump the pillow beside me and swing my legs over the side of the bed. There's no way my baby will go back to sleep now. I pick her up and hold her to my chest, rocking her back and forth.

The doorbell rings for the third time.

'Coming,' I shout. Perhaps it's Ruth, checking up on me. I must get down the stairs before she lets herself in with her key. On our very first evening in the cottage, she came in while we were putting Olivia to bed. We'd found her in the living room, rummaging through a cupboard, looking for a DVD she'd lent Pamela before she died.

The visitor is silhouetted in the frosted pane of the door. A flash of red. Too tall to be Ruth.

I open the door and a woman in a smart red coat smiles at me warmly and offers a manicured hand. In her other arm she carries a small baby snuggled up in a coat exactly the same shade of red as her mother's.

'Hi,' she says. 'I'm Emma. I live down the road.'

I manage to return the smile as I reach out my hand, juggling Olivia as she fidgets on my hip. I feel embarrassed by the dried baby sick on the shoulder of my oversized jumper and wonder how Emma manages to look so immaculate, with her poker-straight blonde hair and expensive clothes.

'Claire,' I say and Olivia screams, as if she needs to join the conversation. Emma's baby stares at the sky, oblivious to everything going on around it. I push my curly brown hair behind my ears, hoping I remembered to brush it this morning.

I'm sure Emma must think I'm a mess, but she doesn't seem to notice. 'I'm so glad someone else with a baby has moved in,' she says excitedly. 'I saw the removal van the other day and I thought I must introduce myself. You're Ruth's daughter, aren't you?'

'Her daughter-in-law,' I correct quickly.

'Oh,' Emma says, and I catch what I'm sure is a sympathetic look.

'Do you know her?'

'Everyone knows her. She's the kind of person you need to know in this village. If you're her daughter-in-law, you'll be looked after.'

I smile, bemused. There's a whole side of Ruth I know nothing about.

Emma reaches down and picks up a brown paper bag, with a logo I recognise from a shop in a nearby town.

'I bought you some cake. As a welcome to the neighbourhood. Shall I bring it in?'

I want to say no. I don't have enough energy for a conversation.

But Emma has already stepped over the threshold and into my home.

'Shall I take my shoes off?' she asks, sitting down on our dirty bottom stair, juggling her baby as she unzips her boots.

I cringe. The house is filthy. Soon the feet of Emma's pale tights will be black from the dirt and dust.

'Sorry about the mess,' I say, gesturing half-heartedly at the unpacked boxes.

Emma smiles. 'Hard to keep a tidy house with a baby.'

'What's your baby's name?' I ask.

'Lizzie. And yours?'

'Olivia.'

'How old is she?'

'Two months.'

'Lizzie's three months.'

The interaction is following the same script as all my introductions to other new mothers. The same conversation plays out at every mother and baby group across the country. Our lines are so well rehearsed it feels like we've met a hundred times before.

'Come through,' I say, picking my voice up, trying to be more friendly.

I see the cottage with fresh eyes as I lead Emma through to the dilapidated kitchen. I've been convinced that as soon as Matt and I remove the clutter we can make the house our own. But now I notice the peeling 1970s wallpaper and the unidentifiable stains on the threadbare carpet.

'This is Matt's grandmother's house,' I explain. 'She passed away.'

'I'm so sorry,' Emma says, concern in her eyes.

'It's OK. I didn't know her that well. But my mother-in-law… well, she's finding it hard to let go. I want to put some pictures up, maybe give the house a lick of paint. But Ruth…' I try to think of the best way to phrase it, so I don't sound ungrateful. 'Ruth wants the house kept as it is for now. She's still grieving.'

'It must be difficult for her.'

'Yes, I know,' I say. I lost my own mother years ago and I remember how hard it was to part with her possessions.

'It's an amazing place. So much history.'

Emma is at my kitchen counter, holding Lizzie under one arm as she rifles through a drawer and pulls out a knife to cut the cake. I put Olivia down and go over to the sink under the window to fill the kettle. I can see Ruth and Jack's house at the end of our garden. A dark, looming shadow. There's no one home.

'How big a slice do you want?' Emma asks, moving the knife round the cake to indicate where she might cut.

'A small one,' I say.

I look at her slim waist enviously and wonder why some women's bodies seem to snap back into shape after they give birth.

In the living room, I put down the tea and cake and offer Emma a seat on the antique sofa. The flowered cushions sag as we sit down.

Between mouthfuls, Emma tells me everything there is to do in the area. There's a park up the road and the local mothers run a playgroup once a week in the village.

'There's more in Oxford,' she says. 'It's only half an hour in the car. There's baby yoga, baby swimming, baby cinema. Anything you fancy doing, you can take a baby with you.'

'What did you do before?' I ask.

'Before?'

'You know. Before Lizzie. Before maternity. Before nappies and sleepless nights.'

Emma laughs. 'I was in senior management. Can't imagine it now though. How about you?'

I have a childish desire to impress her. 'I'm a journalist,' I say. It's a white lie. I *was* a journalist once. It feels like a lifetime ago.

'Local press?'

'No, one of the big national papers. In London.' I smile nervously, wondering if she'll ask for the name of the paper. I don't want to tell her. What if she looks me up and sees I haven't worked there for years?

'Gosh, a national paper. It's so hard to break into that field. You must have been determined.'

I nod, embarrassed. I don't want to talk about it. I don't want to remember how well I was doing before my career came to a swift end.

Emma's eyes search mine. 'What brings you all the way out here? It's a long commute to London.'

'My husband's a vet. He's setting up a new practice here. And we wanted to be closer to his parents, so they could help out with Olivia. So I'm less alone.'

Heat rises to my face. I hadn't meant to admit I'm lonely.

But Emma's expression is understanding.

'Where are your family?' she asks.

'My father was never around. And my mother... She passed away. A long time ago.' I pick up my tea and take a sip, hiding behind the motion. It's my mother's birthday tomorrow. It always brings everything back.

'It's so hard without the support. My parents are gone too.'

'I'm sorry.'

'It was years ago. I was a child.'

We sit in silence for a moment, before Emma turns the conversation back to babies. Sleep patterns. Feeding. Colic. The topics are comfortingly familiar. Emma's warm and easy to talk to and I hardly notice the time pass. We keep chatting as the sky begins to darken, but Emma doesn't seem to be in any rush to get home.

When Emma eventually gets up to leave it's already Olivia's bedtime and even then I don't want her to go. I hadn't realised how much I craved company. Matt has been working late every night since we moved, and I always put Olivia to bed alone.

On the doorstep, spur of the moment, I invite Emma and her partner round to dinner, later in the week.

I see the shadow cross her face and immediately regret it. It's too soon. We hardly know each other.

'I don't have a partner,' she says. 'I'm a single mother.' She seems to shrink in front of me, her eyes dewy.

'Oh,' I reply, surprised. 'I'm sorry. I didn't mean—'

She straightens up, blinking back tears. 'It's OK,' she says, with a forced smile. 'At least I have Lizzie.'

Before I can reply, she sweeps her blonde hair back behind her ears, turns and walks away, hurrying down the driveway. I feel awful that I've upset her, especially after we'd had such a lovely afternoon. I hoped we might be friends. But now I've messed that up.

I go back to the living room and feel the silence caving in on me. Without Emma's chatter it feels like the cottage itself is breathing, inhaling and exhaling as it bides its time. Even in my own living room I feel self-conscious, like someone is watching.

Olivia's eyes follow me across the room as I clear away the teacups. Maybe it's her. Maybe my own baby is making me nervous. She's always watching. I never know what she's thinking. Sometimes it feels like she's peering into my soul and judging me for all my inadequacies as a mother.

Tap. Tap. Tap.

I jump at the noise. It's coming from upstairs. A gentle rhythm. Knocking.

I pick Olivia up and go up the stairs. Only half an hour ago the cottage felt open and warm and welcoming, filled with Emma's laughter. Now the air is heavy, oppressive.

Tap. Tap. Tap.

I get to the top of the stairs and peer through the open bathroom door.

It's just the blind banging against the window frame. Emma must have left the window open when she used the bathroom.

I let my breath out and then laugh. What's wrong with me? How can I be so paranoid about every sound?

Olivia looks at me and starts to cry. I think about how Lizzie didn't cry the whole time she was here, but Olivia needed constant comforting. I grit my teeth as the all too familiar anger rises inside me. I push it back down and it's quickly replaced by the guilt that swirls around my head constantly. I want so much to love my daughter the way I should, but I just don't seem to have it in me.

Sometimes I wonder if her older sister would have been different. If she'd survived. Would she have been more good-natured? Would we have had a stronger bond?

Perhaps Olivia is taking her cues from me. The loss of her sister numbed my emotions, and now I can't love my baby the way I want to. Maybe she senses my fear and reflects it back.

With my daughter clutched under one arm, I pull the bathroom blind up and shut the window. It overlooks our garden. I stare out at the pond; a dark hole of dirty water, reflecting the moonlight. I shiver, imagining myself submerging under its murky surface, getting caught in a tangle of weeds that lurk beneath. It's not safe having a pond in the garden with a small child. One moment of inattention and a child could drown. I can't let Olivia play outside until it's drained. A cloud passes over the moon and for a moment the pond disappears, lost in the dark green grass. But I know it's out there, a deep dark hole, an accident waiting to happen.

CHAPTER 3

When I wake the next day, I have a moment of peace before I remember it's my mother's birthday. When I sit up, I feel my headache building behind my eyes and I reach for the paracetamol on my bedside table. Another birthday she isn't here to celebrate. Reality is dulled as I go through the motions of the morning, feeding Olivia and preparing breakfast. While Matt gets Olivia ready, I light a candle, filling the kitchen with my mother's favourite orange blossom scent, and stand still for a moment, eyes closed, imagining she's with me. Tears slide down my face, before I'm brought back into the moment by Olivia's cries. I wipe my cheeks with the back of my hand.

'Ready to go?' asks Matt gently, touching my shoulder lightly.

I turn and he sees my grief. He wraps his arms around me and holds me.

After a moment, I pull away. 'I'm ready.'

I blow out the candle and walk to the door. I have a second candle in my bag, that I'll light at my mother's grave. It's hard to believe a whole year has passed since I last visited.

Matt drives us to Wimbledon, where my mother's buried. We stop at a petrol station on the way and I buy flowers and bottled water. I ignore the displays of red roses and instead opt for orange and yellow chrysanthemums; her favourites.

At the graveside, I sit cross-legged on the grass, as the wind whips through my hair. The ground is hard and I can feel the February frost seeping through my jeans. I've been coming to my mother's grave on this day for the last twelve years. I fill the built-in vase with the bottled water and add the brightly coloured flowers, spreading them around evenly. They already look dog-eared and I tip in the little packet of flower food that came taped to the stems, in the vain hope they'll last a few more hours in their battle against the elements.

I put my candle on the cold, flat granite and strike the first match. It takes three before there's a spark of life. It's immediately blown out by the wind. Every year it's the same. There's only ever a flicker of light, before it goes out, but it's enough for me to have shared that light with her, if only for a second.

'Happy birthday, Mum,' I whisper. The words disappear into the air.

I close my eyes and try to bring her back. Her smell; her perfume mixed with the strawberry scent of her shampoo. I imagine her voice, her laugh, her smile when she greets me. I imagine the feel of her arms around me, strong and dependable when I was a child and then weak and fragile, bird-like, before the cancer finally took her. I can picture her with Olivia, gathering her up in a hug and then rocking her gently, gazing into her eyes adoringly.

But it wasn't meant to be.

I glance across the cemetery and see Olivia with Matt on the other side of the vast space. Matt is bending over to read the inscriptions on gravestones, Olivia close to him in her sling. I'm glad she isn't old enough to understand.

On my side of the family there is only me. My father disappeared off to his new life in South Africa long before my mother passed away. I'm glad Olivia will grow up close to Matt's parents. I hope that between us all we can give her enough love, so she won't ever feel like she's missing out on her other set of grandparents.

I chat to my mother as if she's alive. On her birthday last year I confided in her about how much I still longed for a baby. We'd been trying for over two years by then and I was exhausted by it. I was still grieving the loss of Olivia's sister and I'd lost hope that we'd get another chance.

I didn't know that just a couple of months after I visited my mother I would see the double line on the pregnancy test. Our lives have changed irreversibly since then. We've had Olivia, moved house. Everything I longed for last year, I now have. I felt I was finally being given another chance at life. My opportunity to do things right.

So why can't I be happy?

I touch the cold stone and then the words tumble out. I tell my mother how exhausted I am, how I never have a proper night's sleep. Motherhood hasn't lived up to my expectations. I just can't seem to bond with my daughter. Sometimes I feel like I don't deserve to be a parent. I'm not cut out to be a mother.

When I run out of breath, there is no answer. No reassurance or advice. Only the wind rustling through the trees. I wish my mother was here to guide me. To tell me how to love my daughter, the way I know she loved me.

I feel a hand on my shoulder and I jump.

'Are you OK?' Matt asks. 'You've been here a while.'

Olivia's fidgeting against him in the baby sling.

'I'm fine,' I say, slowly rising to my feet. 'I was just telling Mum about Olivia.'

'She finally gets to meet her granddaughter,' Matt says. Tears well up in my eyes. My mother's only time with Olivia will be moments like this, by her graveside each year, as Olivia grows.

I wipe away the tears, as I feel the warmth of Matt's embrace. He circles his arms around me, Olivia in the sling between us.

'It'll be OK,' he says.

But he can't promise me that.

*

As we start the journey back, Matt tells me he has a surprise for me. We're stopping at Richmond Park to see the deer.

When we arrive, Matt gets Olivia out of her car seat and straps her to him in the baby carrier. She calms as soon as she feels his body against hers. I love the way they look together; Olivia's deep brown eyes and high cheekbones are a reflection of Matt's. Her frame is so small against his and for a moment I see the loveable, tiny baby that others must see.

The sun shines brightly, but there's a bitter breeze and I carefully put Olivia's woollen hat over her bare head and then put my own coat on.

Matt carries the rucksack of nappies. My body is free, unencumbered. I can swing my arms, stand up straight, even run if I feel like it.

Matt takes my hand and our fingers interlock as we walk towards the deer park. I feel safe. It's so good to be out of the house in the fresh air.

'How are you settling into the cottage?' Matt asks. He's been so busy setting up his new veterinary surgery, he's hardly been at home in the last week.

I don't know how to answer. I think of the cluttered house, filled with unpacked boxes. I think of how hard I'm finding it to bond with Olivia.

'OK,' I reply uncertainly, remembering I was the one who insisted we move to the countryside. Matt wasn't keen at first, but I was determined. I was sure there'd be high demand for vets around here. I even found the premises for his surgery for him.

'Just OK?' He looks at me, concerned.

'Well, I'd expected your mother to clear out Pamela's things.'

'Me too. But she can be difficult sometimes.'

'Oh,' I say, surprised. 'She's never seemed that way to me.' Sometimes I think Matt takes his parents for granted.

'I'll talk to her about it,' he replies, brow furrowed.

'Is everything all right?' I ask.

He squeezes my hand. 'It will just take a bit of getting used to, I think. Being back. To be honest, I thought I'd never return.'

'Oh,' I say, dismayed. I desperately want us all to be happy there.

'Even my sister moved away,' Matt says. His sister used to live in the village near Matt's parents, but she moved to Hong Kong about a year ago.

'She got a new job, didn't she? A better one?'

'Yeah, she did. But I think she wanted to get away from Mum too.'

'She's not that bad, surely?' I ask, confused.

He puts his arm round me. 'Don't worry, we'll figure things out. I just need to get used to being back, that's all.'

We keep walking. Despite the bracing wind, Olivia falls asleep against Matt's body. We wander through the deer park, hand in hand. I remember how much I envied families like ours when I was desperately trying to get pregnant.

Now I'm living the life I dreamed of. I try to summon up gratitude for everything I have, but I can't. It just doesn't feel right.

Matt interrupts my thoughts. 'Do you remember when we were here last?' he asks, smiling.

'Yes,' I say. We haven't been to Richmond Park for five and a half years. But that day five and a half years ago was one of the best days of my life.

It was the height of summer. We had a picnic by the lake and fed the ducks our leftover bread. Then Matt took me to the deer. It was just after breeding season and there were lots of fawns, staying close to their mothers. Matt told me the history of the park, how the deer had always been able to roam freely.

Later, when the park was due to close, we hid in the bushes, trying not to giggle as we watched the groundskeeper patrol, locking the gates and securing the park. When we were sure he was gone, we put our blanket down by the side of the lake and drank champagne. We lay down and made love in front of sleeping ducks and reeds, picnic crumbs digging into my back as I shuddered in Matt's arms.

As I half-dozed under the stars, I felt the most secure I'd ever felt in my life. I was loved and I was in love. I wished the moment could extend backwards and forwards into my past and my future. I wanted the feeling to cocoon me forever.

In my dreamy daze, I nodded off and Matt woke me with gentle kisses on my neck. I sat up slowly and marvelled at how still the lake was as it reflected the stars.

When I turned, he was on one knee holding out a ring.

In that moment I felt everything was possible. My future flashed before me. A white dress. A wedding in a country house. My career taking off. My byline on the front page of a national newspaper. Matt waiting at home for me with a glass of wine when I'd had a busy day at work. Then later, a baby. The perfect family. The perfect career.

I've had both. The perfect family and the perfect career. I have the husband and the baby I so desperately wanted and I've won prizes for my journalism. But the stress of the city wore me down. And now, even though I have Olivia, somehow it's still not enough. I force aside the thought. Today I only want to focus on enjoying the fresh air with my husband. Nothing feels better than the wind in my face and my hand in his.

We spend another hour in the deer park and as we walk, Matt tells me about his plans for the surgery. I don't have much to say about my days with Olivia, so I let him talk. His deep, lilting voice carries on the wind and surrounds me like a lullaby. I am safe with Matt. He's always there for me. At the very worst times in my life he's been my protector. I don't want to think about what might have happened if he hadn't been there. He supported me when I felt like I couldn't go on any more, that I didn't deserve to live. I was broken. He picked me up and helped me put myself back together.

We pause by a wooded area and Matt wraps his arms around me, Olivia between us. He kisses me deeply and I remember all the longing I felt for him the day he proposed. His lips are on mine and I catch the scent of his aftershave. I can't remember the last time we had sex. We've been too busy. His arms travel down my sides, stroking my breasts as he kisses my neck. He can't quite get the angle right, Olivia's small body between us preventing a proper embrace.

I remember whole afternoons spent in bed when we first got together. I want that again. Matt and I need to reconnect, to feel part of each other again.

'Let's go home,' I whisper in his ear. 'We can put Olivia to bed, and enjoy ourselves, just the two of us.'

Matt grins at me, and we walk hand in hand, back to the car.

*

I'm ready. I'm going to leave the house. As soon as my husband comes home, I'm going to open the door and step out into the air. A bubble of anxiety rises in me. It's been so long since I've been outside, that I'm not sure if I'm even brave enough any more. But I must go to my appointment.

Thick, pale foundation masks the bruises on my face, but there are still hints of them underneath; my cheek a shade darker under the eye. I've made the rest of my face up to match with eyeshadow and thick eyeliner to distract. I don't look like myself. But maybe that's a good thing.

My husband will be home soon to look after our daughter, while I go to my consultation with the psychiatrist at the hospital. I walk around the house once more to check everything. I run my hand over the mantelpiece like I've seen him do. No dust. I check the kitchen surfaces. No stray crumbs. I straighten the tea towel hanging from the oven.

In the living room, I move my daughter along the sofa and straighten the cushions behind her. She's watching TV, staring intently at the flickering screen.

The theme tune for Postman Pat *tells me it's time to leave.*
I feel a hot flush of disappointment. Why isn't he here?
Perhaps he's not coming.

I hear the click of a key in the lock. He's home. Of course he is.
Like he said he would be. I knew I could rely on him.

I prepare a smile to greet him, and reach up to kiss his cheek.
He takes a step back, wincing away from me.

'What do you look like?' His voice is quiet, disbelieving.

I struggle to find the words. I can't tell him I need to hide his
bruises, although he must know. I need to sound casual, as if this is
an everyday thing, as if I haven't spent hours in front of the mirror
blending foundations to find the best cover for my canvas of injuries.

'I wanted to put on some make-up for a change,' I say. 'Make an
effort.'

His bright blue eyes stare through me. I fell in love with his intensity.
Before I really knew him, I thought his passion was something to
admire. But now I know that there is only a fine line between passion
and anger, and I am his outlet for both.

My words are powerless against his pure rage. I have learnt to stay
silent until he speaks.

'An effort for your psychiatrist,' he says, his voice increasing in
volume with each syllable. 'An effort for your psychiatrist, and not
for me?'

I close my eyes as I wait for the inevitable consequence of my
mistake. His hands are on my neck. Gentle at first. He likes to feel my
muscles tense under his fingers. I start to count in my head as I wait.
It's the only way to control the fear. To stop myself from whimpering.

Suddenly his fingers grip so hard I can't breathe and he pushes me
with all his strength against the wall. The crack of my head against
the plaster is a physical release. I collapse and sink to the floor as I
hear him walk away. It's over now.

I'm not going to see my psychiatrist. I'm not going anywhere.
I don't know why I ever imagined anything different.

CHAPTER 4

Matt is quiet on the car journey home, staring intently at the road ahead. I gaze out of the window, watching the terraced houses pass by, remembering my mother. I wish she was still here. Sometimes my need for her is almost a physical craving. I want her to hold me, to comfort me when things are going wrong.

'Claire!' Matt prods me and I glance over at him.

'What?'

'Olivia's upset. Can you comfort her?'

I guiltily turn around and see Olivia has tears running down her face.

'I'm sorry,' I say. 'I didn't realise…'

Matt glances over at me. 'She's been crying for five minutes.'

I must have blocked the sounds out. She cries so often.

I turn around in my chair awkwardly and wave a toy in front of her face. She calms slightly and follows the toy with her eyes.

When we're ten minutes from home, Matt tells me that he needs to go to the surgery to get some work done. Disappointed tears prick my eyes. I had imagined us curling up on the sofa in front of a romantic comedy, his arms wrapped around me.

'Really?'

'I'm sorry. I need to do some paperwork and try and identify new clients. I'm having a few teething problems. But things should settle down soon.'

'It would be nice if you were home a bit more. It's hard looking after Olivia on my own.' I've hardly seen him since we moved. He always working at the surgery.

He sighs. 'I will be soon, I promise. It's just the setting up that takes the time.'

'You could do some of the paperwork at home. Then you'd see more of Olivia.'

'You don't need me,' he says, distractedly.

'I do,' I confess quietly. 'Sometimes I feel like I'm still struggling to connect with her.'

'I thought it would be easier for you here,' Matt says, concerned. 'Away from the city.'

'I don't know, Matt. I just don't feel right. It's like I'm not cut out to be a mum.'

'You're a great mum.'

He always does this. When he doesn't want to do something, or doesn't have time, he tells me how good I am at it.

'I don't think so, Matt.'

'I'll help out more. I promise. I just need to put my all into the practice until I've gained some loyal customers. I'd expected to have a few more clients on the books by now.'

'But you're from around here. People already know who you are.' I'd imagined it would be easy for him to find customers here in the village where he grew up.

Matt's silent for a moment, thinking. 'It's not as simple as that,' he says. 'People know me too well. They remember me as a child, then a teenager. They remember my past.'

'Your past? What do you mean?'

Matt never talks about the past, and I'd assumed that was because there wasn't much to say about a happy, carefree childhood.

'Oh, just the usual teenage things,' he says. 'I think it will take a bit of time, that's all. It will take me a while to build a reputation and find new customers.'

'OK,' I reply, feeling concerned. We're relying on his income to save for a house deposit.

In the back seat, Olivia starts to cry once more, not stopping until we arrive back at the cottage.

At home, Matt takes Olivia upstairs to change her nappy, while I search around for the candle I lit for my mother before I left the house this morning. It isn't on the kitchen worktop where I left it. Matt must have moved it. I find it shoved into one of the drawers. I feel a flicker of irritation as I pull it out. Then I light it and breathe deeply through my nose, absorbing the scent and letting the memory of my mother wash over me.

Matt interrupts my thoughts as he hurries in and places Olivia in my arms.

'Have you seen the box I left in the study?' he asks, agitated.

'Which one?'

'The delivery. It came yesterday.'

'No.'

'I need to take it to the surgery.'

'Sorry, I haven't seen it.'

'I'll have another look for it.'

I hear his feet beating against the stairs, then pacing from room to room.

I hold Olivia close to me. I try to imagine my mother beside me, helping me with my baby. She would have loved being a grandmother. But she never got the chance.

As I rock my daughter, I stare out into the darkness. With the lights on in the kitchen, all I can see is my own reflection. A slightly overweight mother, holding a baby. She looks like a stranger. Behind the reflection, a shadow flits across the garden. A fox? Or a person? I'm aware that I'm backlit by the kitchen lights, exposed. I can't see out easily, but anyone can see in.

I shiver at the thought of someone out there, silently watching.

It's just my imagination, I tell myself as I turn on the kettle. Even so, I'd feel more comfortable if there was a blind over the window, and I could shut out the outside world. I must buy one.

I start to wipe the kitchen surfaces, but they're spotless. I'm sure there were a few stray pieces of cereal lingering after breakfast. Our dirty bowls have moved from beside the sink and are now drying in the washing up rack.

I know Matt and I didn't clear up.

Ruth must have let herself into the house while we were out. She's tidied up and moved my mother's candle. I frown. I don't like the thought of her being here alone, rifling through my belongings. If she behaves like that, we'll never really be able to relax here, or make the space our own. I'm going to have to speak to her and ask her to respect our privacy.

Matt reappears back downstairs, an open box in his hands.

'Did you open this?' he asks.

'No, I haven't touched it.'

'Right,' he says distractedly.

'Do you think it could have been your mother?'

'No. Why would she do that?'

'I think she's been in the house while we were out. The washing up's been done.'

'Are you sure you didn't do it?'

'I didn't. Did you?'

'No,' he says. 'Look, I've really got to go. There's so much paperwork to do. Can we deal with this later?'

'OK,' I reply reluctantly.

He kisses me on the cheek as he slips his shoes on, the box under one arm.

The door bangs shut behind him and I'm left alone with Olivia.

I don't know what to do with myself. My baby is quiet for once, staring placidly at the ceiling. Thoughts of my own mother flood my mind. I can't bear to be alone.

I remember the present I've been meaning to give to Ruth as a thank you for letting us stay in Pamela's house. It's just a token really. A framed photo of me, Matt and Olivia with Ruth and Jack. I see it as the first of many family photos, symbolising our new start.

I pick up the carefully wrapped gift, bundle Olivia into her snowsuit and go to the back door. I could do with some company and it would be nice to get to know Ruth and Jack a bit better.

When I knock on the back door of their house there's no answer. I can see the lights are on and hear the faint rumble of the television. I shift from one foot to the other, shivering in the cold.

Then I knock again.

'Hello?' I shout.

No answer. My brain starts to fill with worry. I found my own mother slumped in front of the television, her body already cold, a daytime breakfast show chattering obliviously in the background.

I knock again.

Then I pick up my phone. My finger hovers over Matt's number, undecided. There's probably nothing wrong. But what if there is? I would regret my inaction forever.

Just then, I hear a gentle plodding and Jack appears at the door. He opens it a fraction.

'Hello?'

'Hi,' I say.

I expect him to open the door wider, but he doesn't. Olivia whimpers.

He looks at me expectantly.

I hold up the present in my hands. 'I just wanted to drop this off. It's a gift for Ruth. Well, for both of you really,' I say with a smile.

'OK,' he replies, opening the door slowly, and letting me into the warm house.

He lumbers back towards the corridor and I follow.

At the kitchen door he turns, and looks at me with raised eyebrows.

'Your shoes,' he says.

I notice my footprint on the kitchen floor and look down, embarrassed.

'Sorry. I must have got a bit muddy.'

I struggle to take off my shoes as I balance Olivia, and Jack watches silently.

Then he leads me into the living room.

'It's Claire,' he announces to Ruth, and she promptly stands and smiles. She looks immaculate as always, in a blue cashmere jumper, colour-coordinated with her earrings. As she looks me up and down, I remember I haven't changed out of my jeans since sitting on the ground by my mother's grave.

'Claire! And Olivia. How lovely.'

The television is off now and when Jack reaches for the control, Ruth snatches it out of his hands.

'We have company,' she says firmly. 'Claire, do you want a cup of tea?'

'Yes, please.'

Ruth and I go to the kitchen and she puts on the kettle.

'We don't usually have visitors at this hour,' she says. 'What a pleasant surprise.' I can tell from her voice and forced smile that she's far from pleased. It's only 6 p.m.

'I can come back another day. I'm so sorry, I didn't mean to interrupt.'

'It's no bother, dear.'

In the awkward silence that follows I hold out the present towards her, almost thrusting it into her hands.

'This is for you,' I say. 'From me and Matt. To say thank you for letting us live in your mother's house.'

She eyes the present warily. 'Should I open it now?' She almost looks as if she doesn't want it.

'You could do. You don't have to though. I mean, I could come back another day?' I'm uncertain now. Olivia is heavy and I want to sit down, but I don't feel welcome. The kettle has boiled, but Ruth doesn't seem to have noticed.

When she seats herself at the table, I take that as an invitation to sit down opposite her. She opens the present and studies the photo.

'It's lovely,' she says finally. 'What a nice thought. Thank you.'

'I'm glad you like it.'

'I suppose we're your only family, really, aren't we?'

I'm taken aback. 'Well, my father's still alive…'

'But in South Africa?'

'Yes.'

'Well, it's nice to have you closer. It must be hard for you without your mother.'

'It is.' I nod, feeling too uncomfortable to confide in Ruth.

'I know the feeling. It's been hard losing my own mother. I can't imagine it happening when I was younger. It must have been awful.'

She reaches her hand across the table and touches mine.

'I'm sorry about Pamela,' I say. 'She was always kind to me and Matt.' I wonder if I should broach the subject of clearing out her things.

'It's so hard to throw away memories,' Ruth says, as if she's read my mind.

'I know.' I remember going through my own mother's meagre possessions before the council took back the flat. They'd given me a month. It had already been reallocated to another family.

'I can help you if you like,' I suggest. I don't want her to keep coming into the house when we're out, sifting through my belongings.

'I'd prefer to do it on my own.'

I sigh, remembering how she'd stuffed my mother's candle in a drawer. 'Of course. But I'd prefer it if you didn't let yourself in when we're out.'

She bristles. 'It is *my* house, Claire.'

We reach an uncomfortable silence.

'I'd better go,' I say. 'I need to get Olivia ready for bed.'

'OK,' she replies, looking at me intently. 'By the way, I'm not sure whether Matt mentioned this to you, but you're both invited round to lunch on Sunday. One o'clock sharp.'

'Oh,' I say. 'Thank you.' I'd been planning to spend the weekend trying to unpack what I could, but lunch will be a welcome break.

'I'll expect you at one then.'

I start to slip on my shoes to leave, but Ruth frowns.

'It's best to use the front door,' she says. 'We're not set up for people coming in at the back. No mat to wipe your feet. No shoe rack.'

I frown. It will only take thirty seconds to get to my house if I go out the back, instead of walking down the gravel driveway and then turning back again towards the cottage.

But I comply. It's hardly worth making a fuss about. I carry my shoes down the hall, to the front door and then Ruth holds Olivia while I put them on.

'Bye,' I say.

'See you Sunday. Don't be late.'

When I get back to the cottage, it's time to put Olivia to bed. First I need to feed her. I adjust my top and put her on my breast. She fidgets, hitting me and fighting before she eventually latches on. I wince at the pain and think longingly of the pre-prepared bottles of formula in the fridge. I've promised myself that they're only a last resort. Only if the pain gets too much.

I gaze out of the window between the gaps in the dusty venetian blinds, thinking about my conversation with Ruth. I can't work her out. She was always so nice to me before we moved, but now I'm starting to see what Matt meant when he said she could be difficult. She seemed to deliberately make me feel unwelcome at her house. Perhaps she was just tired. Sunday lunch will be a chance for us to start again and get off on the right foot.

The blinds are angled so I can catch glimpses of the outside world but no one can see in. A shadow crosses in front of the window, pauses, and then moves on. I freeze, my arm tightening around my daughter.

It's nothing. Just someone walking past the house. Perhaps a rambler. Ruth has told us that a walking path cuts directly through our driveway. Despite her attempts to keep them out, they have a right of way.

I take my baby off my breast, ignoring her screams as I pull my top down, go over to the window and twist the lever to close the blinds completely. I sit back down on the sofa but neither Olivia nor I can settle. I know she's hungry, but she seems unnerved now, reluctant to suckle. The health visitor told me earnestly that Olivia picks up stress from me, that I just need to relax.

I take her upstairs and fill the bath, checking the temperature on the floating children's thermometer that's shaped like a flower. It's one degree too hot. I add more cold water, but now the water level is too high and the plastic baby seat disconnects from the bottom of the bath and bobs upwards. I pull the plug, let the water go down a bit and then gently place Olivia in the bath seat.

She screams. I pull her out quickly, her wet body soaking my T-shirt. I check the thermometer again, certain I've made a mistake, but the temperature is well within the range. I put my daughter back in and wipe a flannel over her bald head. I hear a faint knocking sound. I want to investigate but I can't. Babies can drown in seconds. Besides, it's just the cottage. It takes on a life of its own at night, creaking and groaning as the radiators clunk into action and the foxes howl in the garden.

The sounds unsettle me. Matt says I'm too used to living in the city where a constant background hum drowns out all other noise. Perhaps he's right. But this place doesn't feel like home. Dark crevices have formed behind the piles of boxes and looming walnut furniture. We need to declutter and unpack. Then maybe I'll stop jumping at every sound.

I lift Olivia out of the bath. She screams as the cold air hits her and I quickly wrap her in a towel. I hold her close and then take her to the bedroom, putting her on my breast for what I hope will be the final feed before she settles for the night.

Once she's in her cot, with her bunny beside her, I lie on the bed watching her face scrunch up in anger as she gets redder and redder. The books say I should let her cry for a bit, teach her to self-soothe. Just knowing I'm here beside her should be enough to calm her.

Whoever writes the books doesn't have a baby like mine. Every muscle in my body is tense as I lie beside Olivia listening to her scream. I wonder if I'll sleep more than two hours tonight. My limbs feel heavy and I'm so exhausted I can hardly move.

I wish I had someone to talk to. But I have no one. In London, I worked such long hours that most of my friends from school and university fell by the wayside. I made new friends at work, but they were mainly drinking buddies. Transient friendships that didn't stand up to the challenge of our lives moving in different directions when I left journalism. If only I had my mother. Or Miriam. Miriam was my closest friend. The one person who I always made time for, no matter how hectic my job was. We met at secondary school, where we'd spend hours talking about our plans for the future. My ambition was to be a journalist and Miriam wanted to be a detective. We stood by each other until we both got there. When we first started working, we'd go to the pub every Wednesday night and speak on the phone most days, sharing the emotional roller coaster of our new lives in London.

But then Miriam turned against me. I made a mistake and she couldn't forgive me. One day she stopped speaking to me. I tried to explain, but she wouldn't listen. She stopped answering my calls, ignored me in the street. She cut me off entirely, when I needed her the most.

I try to put her out of my mind. I'll make other friends. Maybe Emma and I will become as close as Miriam and I once were.

I don't even have Matt to talk to any more. It feels like the distance between us has grown since we've had Olivia. Today at Richmond Park was the first time in a long time that we really connected. In the last few months we've only spoken about practical things: caring for Olivia, the logistics of moving house, setting up the surgery.

We've both been busy. That's all. We need to start making time for each other, work on our relationship. When Matt gets home, I'll talk to him about it. I know we can build a happy life here. We both just need to put in the effort.

CHAPTER 5

I pull my smart, green nursing shirt over my head and look at myself in the mirror. It's the second top I've put on this morning, the first was surrendered to baby sick. Olivia's cries chase me up the stairs and into the bedroom. Matt is with her. Even though I know I don't need to respond, my shoulders still tense instinctively.

I stand up a bit straighter. I put in stud earrings to protect my earlobes from Olivia's grabbing hands and apply mascara. It's the first time since Olivia's birth that I've bothered. I want to look my best for Sunday lunch at Ruth and Jack's.

My reflection frowns at me, sizing me up and finding me wanting. Now I know my mother-in-law a bit better I worry she will think the same. I don't want to consider what Matt thinks of my post-pregnancy body. I need to get back into shape.

Today is about making an effort, being Matt's wife and Olivia's mother. Pretending to be the perfect family. I take a deep breath and go downstairs. I'm ready for battle.

Matt is in the kitchen, pacing up and down in beige trousers and an ironed shirt. From the window I can see Ruth busying herself with preparing the meal, checking on the roast in the oven, then pulling the cutlery out of the drawer to set the table.

Matt looks at his watch.

'Five to one,' he says.

I nod and pick up Olivia.

Matt has told me that we can't be early and we can't be late. We have to ring the doorbell on the dot of the arrival time.

I swallow as I put my coat and boots on.

We leave our front door, head down the drive, turn left on the lane, and then walk down the tree-lined gravel driveway to their house.

At the door, Matt checks his watch, waits for the minute hand to click over to 1 p.m. and then knocks.

Ruth greets us, beaming. 'Here's my beautiful granddaughter.' She wraps Olivia up in her arms, smothering her in kisses. I stand stiffly, waiting until she is handed back, and I'm given a perfunctory kiss on the cheek.

We're ushered into the kitchen, where Ruth pours me a lemonade and Matt a beer.

Ruth looks beautiful as usual.

'Lovely earrings,' I say. They are aquamarine, an exact match for the tiny flowers that embellish her scarf. I look round the kitchen, but there's no sign of her husband. 'Where's Jack?' I ask.

'In his study again,' Ruth says, sighing. I'm not sure if he avoids Matt and me or if he is trying to minimise the time he spends with his wife.

I remember the warmth I felt when I first met Ruth and Jack. How perfect and beautiful they seemed, in their immaculate house in the country. Now I feel uncertain, not quite sure I'm welcome.

'How can I help?' Matt asks. 'Should I set the table?'

'No, everything's done. You just relax.'

I can feel the tension vibrating from Matt. He seems constantly on guard, ready to bolt out of the door at any moment.

The doorbell rings and I jump.

'Sarah!' we hear Ruth exclaim as she opens the door. 'I'm so glad you could make it.'

I look at Matt quizzically and catch his sigh.

'Who's Sarah?' I whisper. But before he can reply, Sarah is in the kitchen, petite and vibrant, telling me how pleased she is to meet me and how beautiful Olivia is.

She kisses me on the cheek, then turns to Matt hesitantly.

There's an uncertain pause, and then Matt leans in to kiss Sarah's cheek, while she holds out a hand and then withdraws it, before awkwardly accepting his embrace.

'It's good to see you,' she says, her right hand nervously tucking her wavy, auburn hair behind her ear.

'You too,' Matt says stiffly. He's usually so gregarious, but his parents' house has a weight to it that seems to flatten him.

Sarah turns to me and beams. 'It's so lovely to meet your wife and family.'

'Sit up, everybody,' Ruth announces. 'Lunch is ready.'

Ruth has a wooden high chair for Olivia, but she's far too young for it. I suggest I put her on the floor on the rug.

'I can't have my granddaughter on the floor.' Ruth laughs.

'I could go and get the baby seat from the car,' Matt suggests.

'No, don't do that,' Ruth says. 'She should sit with us.'

I hold her close to me over dinner, trying to contain her cries. She claws at my breast to feed, but I discourage her. I fed her just before we left. Her cries block out the conversation and I pick at the roast dinner one-handed with my fork, eating one carrot at a time.

Ruth comes around with the wine. She offers it to Matt and he refuses, glancing over at me. I would love a glass, but Ruth skips right past me like she always does and offers it to Sarah. As I watch Ruth pour the wine, I feel my face flush.

'I'm so pleased you came back, Matt,' Ruth says. 'I knew you would eventually. The village is the perfect place to bring up children.'

Matt doesn't respond. He never talks about his childhood, never shares happy memories or sad ones. Never says anything at all. I wonder if it was as idyllic as I'd thought.

Ruth continues. 'A child couldn't ask for any more growing up here. It's so far from the dangers of the city.' She looks at me. She thinks I kept Matt in London for too long. She doesn't realise he didn't want to come back here, that I had to persuade him. I was the one who wanted to escape the city, not Matt.

'It's lovely here,' I say, through gritted teeth.

I manage to manoeuvre Olivia so she lies across me, her head in the crook of my arm. Now I have enough freedom to move both my hands and cut up some of the Yorkshire pudding and beef into tiny bite-sized chunks. It takes my full concentration just to eat my food.

I let the conversation wash over me. I'm the outsider here. Everyone knows their lines, except for me. Ruth is the perfect host, the caring mother, always laughing and the centre of the conversation. She carries everyone else as they perform to her script. Matt is the good son, returning back home to his mother at last and working hard for his family. Jack is the unflappable, supportive husband, taking her side in any argument. Even Sarah has a role, to recall memories of the village.

And me... I'm not sure what my part is. Before we came here I thought Ruth and I got on well, I imagined I might be her confidante. But now I think my role is simply Matt's wife, or Olivia's mother. I don't feel part of the family; excluded from the inside jokes, the subject of raised eyebrows.

Ruth is reminiscing about Matt's childhood. 'Do you remember how you used to follow Matt around?' she asks Sarah.

Sarah smiles politely. 'It was a long time ago.'

'Not that long ago. You were quite the little pair. Always together.'

I see Matt and Sarah exchange a glance. 'There weren't many children living round here. I had to put up with Matt.'

Matt laughs nervously and Jack's face adjusts into a half-smile.

'How's your new practice going, Matt?' he asks, changing the subject.

'We're opening next week. I've spent this week speaking to potential clients. Farmers mainly. But we're planning on treating domestic animals too.'

'You know Sarah's been looking for a job,' Ruth chips in.

Sarah looks up from her roast potatoes, her face flushed. 'Well yes, just something local. I'm working at the supermarket at the moment, but I'm looking for a receptionist role.'

'You could do so much more than supermarket work, Sarah,' Ruth says. 'You wanted to be a vet too, didn't you? You had a place at Cambridge.'

Sarah stares at the floor, the atmosphere tense. 'Well, you know. Things turn out differently to how you expect.'

I wonder why Sarah never took up her place at university.

'I was lucky,' Matt responds. 'I had the opportunity to leave and study.'

'But you've come back,' I say. 'We've come here to make a life for ourselves.' My voice sounds hesitant, as if I'm no longer certain.

'Sarah could work for you, Matt,' Ruth suggests, ignoring me. 'Surely you need some help with running the surgery?'

'Well, yes,' Matt says, sounding unconvinced. 'But not at the moment, we're still setting up.'

I think about all the hours Matt's been working. He needs all the help he can get.

'Couldn't Sarah help you get the business off the ground?' I ask. 'You've been swamped. You could do with some assistance.'

He frowns. 'Maybe.'

He shoots me a look, but I refuse to be quiet. If he had some help, he'd have more time for Olivia and more time for our marriage.

'Why don't you just give it a try?' I say.

Ruth nods at me, encouragingly. 'You'd have more time for your family, Matt.'

'OK,' he replies, turning to Sarah. 'But it would only be admin, answering the phone, that kind of thing.'

'Don't feel you owe me,' Sarah says, looking embarrassed.

'Sarah, don't be silly,' Ruth says, her jolly tone out of keeping with the muted atmosphere in the room. 'Of course Matt wants you to work with him. He'd be mad not to.'

'I just need to check I can afford your rates first.' Matt laughs and Sarah's face flashes with something that looks like anger. The look disappears as fast as it came.

'Well, if I don't have any better offers, I suppose I'll have to accept.' She laughs, but I can see it's forced.

'Congratulations, Sarah,' Ruth says, raising her glass. 'Let's drink to that.'

I raise my glass of water and notice that Sarah is holding up her wine glass as reluctantly as I am.

'Any more?' Ruth asks, serving spoon hovering over the potatoes. She looks at me pointedly and I realise everyone else has finished their meal.

'No thank you,' I say, and try to eat faster. But it's gone cold and I've lost my appetite.

Sarah reaches out her hands towards Olivia. 'I'll take her,' she says. 'So you can finish.'

I smile gratefully, and look at Matt. It should have been him offering, but he seems distracted, staring into the middle distance.

I eat the cold food on my plate, trying to satisfy the twin demands of speed and appreciation of Ruth's cooking. Ruth frowns at me, but I'm not sure why. There are so many rules in this house that you trip and stumble over them. You never know which you are breaking, but you can't help leaving feeling you've done *something* wrong.

We are evicted at 4 p.m. Ruth wants to get the washing up done before she goes to her tennis club committee meeting. As soon as the door shuts behind us, the argument starts. Ruth doesn't realise we can hear her through the open kitchen window as she launches into a tirade at Jack. He didn't help prepare the lunch, he didn't make enough conversation, he spilt food on the floor.

I want to intervene, to protect Jack from Ruth. I turn to Matt. 'Should we go back?' I ask.

He looks at me in surprise. 'Are you crazy?'

*

I've been baking all morning and the kitchen is a mess, the granite counter covered in a sprinkling of white dust. I smile to myself. This is one of the few things that brings me pleasure. The smell of freshly baked cakes changes the feel of the house. It's warm and inviting rather than oppressive and closed. My daughter watches attentively as I mix and stir and pour. In these moments, just the two of us, everything feels normal and homely. I had imagined life like this when I was a child. A family, a kitchen, togetherness.

I hum to myself. I'll spend the afternoon clearing up, changing the house back to the clinical, clean space my husband likes to live in, but for now I enjoy the mess, the ordinariness of a dirty kitchen.

When the cakes are ready, my daughter and I sit at the table across from each other and dig in. I smile at her and she smiles back, her green eyes a reflection of mine. I can't describe how much I love her. All I want for her is a happy family life with two doting parents. The childhood I missed out on myself.

I hear a key in the door.

No. It can't be him.

No.

I look around the kitchen, alarmed, but he's already in the room. 'What's going on?' he asks.

'I didn't expect you back.'

He surveys the kitchen. 'Clearly.'

He reaches for the cake on my plate, takes it and throws it in the bin. 'You don't want to get fat.'

I shake my head.

Our daughter is watching, her eyes wide.

'Why don't you go to the other room?' I say, desperately. She wants to take the cake with her and, sensing my husband's impatience, I let her. A trail of crumbs marks our path as I carry her wriggling body to the living room. I know I'll be punished for that.

I come back into the kitchen and start clearing up.

'Who are the cakes for?' he asks.

'For us,' I say. 'Of course.'

He knows I'm lying. He never eats cakes or chocolate or sweets. He watches his physique with care. When I bake, I only bake small batches. I hide them at the backs of cupboards and my daughter and I consume everything while he's out of the house. I hide the smell with synthetic air freshener.

Suddenly, his face is in front of mine. 'I know you're lying. Are you seeing someone else?'

I laugh. The idea is absurd. I never leave the house. I'm black and blue with bruises. I've no idea who he thinks would want me.

'Don't laugh at me! Don't you dare laugh at me.'

I freeze, cloth in my hand, the worktop still white with flour. I steady myself, grip the kitchen surface and brace myself for his fists.

CHAPTER 6

'Breathe,' the yoga teacher instructs, as she looks serenely into the middle distance. 'And hold your pose.'

My eyes are heavy and I let them close for a second as I follow the instructions. It's 10 a.m., but it feels like midnight. I only had an hour and a half's sleep last night before Olivia woke up for her morning feed. But I'm glad Emma has dragged us to mother and baby yoga. Both of us needed to get out of the claustrophobic cottage.

When I open my eyes Olivia is quiet, staring up at me quizzically from the mat in front of me as I balance on one leg. She's calmer here, distracted by everything going on around her.

Even this basement room feels lighter and airier than our cluttered, dark cottage. I'm going to start sorting the house out. I can't wait for Ruth to do it.

'Relax, Claire.'

The yoga teacher smiles at me encouragingly. My shoulders have tensed and I try to switch off my thoughts as I pull myself into the next stretch. The other mums in front of me are straight-backed and tranquil, in lines on the mats, with their designer yoga pants and neat ponytails. In front of them the baby girls are dressed in pretty dresses and the boys in trousers and T-shirts. There's an unsightly stain on the front of Olivia's sleep-suit, which I hope no one has noticed. I didn't have time to change her clothes before Emma picked me up. I don't know how the other mothers find the time not only to put their babies in clean clothes, but to also look after themselves; dyeing their hair and doing their make-up. Sometimes I can barely find the time to change out of my dressing gown.

Emma smiles over at me. I really don't know what I'd do without her. I only moved in two weeks ago and we're already firm friends. She's always coming over for a chat and a cup of tea.

I've missed having a best friend to confide in. After Miriam stopped speaking to me, I didn't have anyone who I could call up for a chat when I was feeling down. I had friends from university who I met for dinner or coffee occasionally and some new friends with babies, but no one I could truly confide in.

I sigh. I don't want to think about the way Miriam and I fell out. I still feel guilty. And angry that she wouldn't listen to me, wouldn't let me explain myself. I didn't think she'd let our friendship slide after all those years.

'Squeeze your pelvic floor as you exit the stretch,' the yoga teacher instructs.

Olivia is smiling at Emma's baby, Lizzie, on the mat next to her. I feel a rare glimmer of affection for her, that I want to bottle and keep. This is how I should feel all the time. I'm so grateful for how serene she's been today.

'Breathe,' the teacher repeats. I focus on the point above the teacher's head and maintain the pose.

In the break, Emma and I go to the seats just outside the hall. Olivia starts to whimper. She's due a feed so I adjust my yoga top and bra and manoeuvre her onto my breast. The chairs are hard plastic, without armrests, and this, combined with my tight yoga top, makes it difficult to find a comfortable position. Olivia slips off my breast and starts screaming.

I try to put Olivia back on, but she is wailing at full volume now, and won't calm. I rock her back and forth as I pull my top back over my exposed breast.

Emma puts her hand on my shoulder. 'Do you want me to take her?' she asks, reaching out one arm as she balances Lizzie in the other.

'No, it's OK. Thanks though. I just haven't really got the hang of breastfeeding yet.' I smile apologetically.

Around us, other mums form groups and chat as they feed and rock their babies. I think of the NCT group I attended in Balham. I miss having that network of mums to meet with for coffee and share tips. Emma is the only local mum I've met so far in the village.

'Breastfeeding is so hard,' Emma says sympathetically. 'I gave it up.'

'Good for you,' I reply, smiling. 'There's too much pressure these days.' And even though I believe this, I'm still desperate to master breastfeeding myself. I'm so lacking in every other way as a mother.

'I admire your persistence,' Emma says. 'It wasn't practical for me to continue unfortunately. Sharing custody with Dan meant Lizzie was on the bottle with him, and she got too used to that.'

'I'm sorry, Emma. That sounds really hard.' I reach out and touch her arm, and she looks down at the floor, blinking back tears.

The other mothers start to wander back into the class, and I try once more to put Olivia on my breast. She fidgets, and I feel my stress levels rising.

'You go back in,' I say to Emma. 'I'll stay here.'

'No, I'll stay and help you.'

I smile sheepishly. 'I'm not sure there's much you can do.'

'Why don't I hold Olivia while you prepare yourself and then I'll put her on.'

I smile gratefully. The other mothers have gone now, so I feel comfortable exposing myself more to enable Olivia to feed. I pull back my top and squeeze my nipple between two fingers to make it an easier shape for Olivia to grip. I see Emma watching and I feel the flush rising in my face.

'That's what the health visitor said to do,' I explain quickly. 'To help her to latch.'

Emma laughs. 'I know,' she says. 'I remember. Make your nipple like a sandwich, right?'

I grin, embarrassed. 'Yeah, all of that rubbish.'

'It works though,' Emma says, as she lifts Olivia to my nipple. It feels surprisingly intimate, and I cringe as I feel the back of her hand brush my bare skin.

But then Olivia latches and it's all worth it.

Emma beams at me. 'There you go.'

'Thank you. Thanks so much.'

As I feed Olivia, Emma takes out a bottle for Lizzie and we compare notes on sleepless nights. We both feel like we haven't had a proper night's sleep since the babies were born. You wouldn't know it from looking at Emma though. I don't know how she does it.

We go back into the class and find our mats. The other mothers pull faces at their babies and mimic their expressions and babbles. The love beams out of them. Why can't I feel the same? Perhaps if I watch them and copy what they do, then the feelings will come. It must be like everything else. Just practice.

The yoga teacher claps her hands. 'We're ready to start again.'

I return to the mat with Olivia and hold her in my arms as the teacher goes through the exercises for the babies. I sing along to the nursery rhymes from my own childhood, awkwardly doing the actions. Out of the corner of my eye, I watch the other mothers smiling adoringly at their babies, giggling with them and tickling their tummies. I try to copy. But as I tickle Olivia's belly, I feel no connection at all. A rush of emotion builds in my chest and I worry I might burst into tears in front of everyone. I feel like a complete failure as a mother. I hold myself together long enough to get through the class, but when Emma and I have put the babies in the car seats and we're finally out of the door in the fresh air of the car park, the tears flow freely.

'What's wrong?' Emma asks, putting down Lizzie's car seat.

'I just…' It's so hard to explain how I'm feeling. It's the despair that rises inside me during every silence. The knowledge that I'm getting it wrong as a parent. That I'm not bonding properly. It's the guilt of knowing I'm not good enough.

Emma strokes my arm. 'You can tell me,' she says.

I struggle to say the words though my tears. 'It's just when I see the other mothers with their babies. Well, I suppose it just brings home what I'm missing – or rather what Olivia's missing out on.'

'What do you mean?' Emma hugs me close, and the warmth of her arms around me feels so much better. I shake with sobs.

'I just can't connect with her,' I say. 'I don't deserve her.'

'Oh, Claire, you're a great mum. Think of how you've persisted with breastfeeding. I saw your nipple. It was bleeding. I'd have given up long ago.'

'Thanks,' I say. 'You just make it look easy. Lizzie never cries.'

At that moment, Lizzie decides to whine, as if to disprove my point.

We both laugh.

'She's getting cold,' Emma says. 'We'd better get going.'

'Oh, I'm sorry,' I say. It's my fault we've been standing in the car park talking for so long. My selfishness isn't only affecting Olivia now, it's affecting Lizzie too.

'Don't be silly,' Emma replies. She squeezes my arm. 'You needed to get that out. And you know that any time you want to, you can talk to me. Any time, day or night.'

When I get back from yoga I'm in a better mood. In the corner of the living room there's a pile of framed pictures, ready to be hung up over the peeling, stripy wallpaper. Matt has warned me that Ruth will be unhappy if I put nails in the walls, but I don't care. I need to make this house feel like home. My home. I smile at the thought of this minor rebellion.

Olivia can't grow up in a shrine to her great-grandmother. I imagine painting the whole house, tearing down the oppressive wallpaper, and cutting back the trees that shade the living room. The cottage would be filled with light.

I put my fantasy aside and focus on the task in hand. Hanging one picture.

I select a canvas of a photo I took myself when I was working as a travel journalist in Vietnam. It was ten years ago, but it feels like yesterday. I'd finished my shift and was relaxing with a drink in a bar when I saw the teenage biker meticulously cleaning his motorcycle by the side of the bustling road, his single-minded concentration drawing me to him. I watched him for an hour, as he polished the battered metal frame until the sharp sunlight bounced off it and reflected the mass of movement behind him. When he finally stood, admired his work and got astride the bike, I jumped up from the bar and went over to photograph him.

Matt had the picture blown up onto canvas and gave it to me as a birthday present two years ago. There was never a place for it in our tiny flat in Balham, but it will work perfectly here, between the alcoves in the living room. It'll change the look of the room entirely.

I put Olivia on her playmat and turn on the mobile that hangs over it. I find a tape measure and stretch it out between the two alcoves, marking a dot exactly in the centre. Blocking out the tinny music from Olivia's mobile, I hold the canvas in the space and the motorcyclist's gaze meets mine. He's only fifteen or sixteen but he sits confidently astride the sparkling bike, one boot-clad foot the only contact with the dusty ground. The bright blue sky reflects off his helmet. His eyes meet the camera in an expression of defiance, his mouth and nose obscured by a black mask. In the background people mill around him, buses and bikes clamour by, dust circulates and animals scavenge. Amongst the chaos he has an air of knowing calm and adventure. The world is his and he will do what he wants with it.

The picture fills me with longing. I imagine I'm back in Ho Chi Minh City, filled with excitement about the adventure ahead of me, absorbed by a new city, bursting with life. When I close my eyes I can feel the dust in my hair, smell the petrol, hear the rumble of the busy road. I loved being an international journalist, travelling all over the world, investigating issues like human trafficking and illegal animal trading. I tried to get behind the headlines, talking to the locals and finding the human stories that brought the injustices to life. That was before I settled in London and worked my way up at one of the national newspapers. The city changed me. It sculpted me into a different person. All the sensitivity I'd nurtured when I was working abroad was gone. My job was no longer about helping to showcase hardship. Instead it was about telling the story that would sell the paper, and getting the scoop by any means possible.

I find a hammer and some old nails in the toolbox in the shed. We have our own, but they're in one of the many unpacked boxes. As I hammer the nail into the mark I've made, Olivia starts to cry. I sigh. I'm very nearly finished. I survey my work. The nail is slightly wonky. I straighten it up with the edge of the hammer and then resume. I hang the picture up and step back to consider it. It's perfect there. It gives the room a new energy. It feels more like home already.

Olivia's screams drag my attention away. Suddenly exhaustion overwhelms me. The strain of so many sleepless nights catches up with me. I must rest. But I can't. I have to look after Olivia, to comfort her, to feed her, to be a good mother. I'm not a journalist any more. My job is to look after Olivia. I have to respond to her every whim.

When I took the photo I was free, happy and determined to make my mark on the world. I'm someone else now, a new Claire.

A mother and a wife with a house in the country. I pick Olivia up and stare at the picture as I wipe away a tear. The photo reminds me too much of the world I left behind.

*

I wake up, sit bolt upright and stare round the room. Objects start to make themselves known in the shadows. Pamela's wardrobe. The chest of drawers. The vanity table.

It's OK. I'm in the cottage.

I turn in the bed. I'm alone.

I reach out for my phone: 8 p.m. I must have fallen asleep straight after I'd bathed Olivia and put her to bed. I must get up. Matt should be home soon and I need to make dinner.

I can hear something. Rushing water.

I'm not sure if the noise is real or if I'm still trapped in the echoes of my dream.

I ease out of bed and open the bedroom door. The noise is louder. It's coming from the bathroom.

The door is shut.

For a confused second, I think that Olivia's in there, that I never took her out of the bath. That she's drowned.

I force the door open, afraid of what I'll find.

The bath is full. Water gushes into it from both the taps.

There's no baby in the water.

I swallow and blink rapidly, trying to get the image of Olivia floating dead in the bath out of my head. My heart's still pounding.

For a moment I thought my nightmares had come true.

I stare at the water, cascading into the tub.

I clearly remember taking Olivia out of the bath, draining the water. Why would I have turned the taps on again? The water threatens to flow over the rim of the bath and I reach over and quickly turn the taps off.

I run to Olivia's room, hold my hand above her mouth and feel her breath on my palm. She's OK. I sigh with relief, stroking her soft hair to soothe myself as much as her. She murmurs in her sleep. Warm and alive.

Back in the bathroom, I stare incomprehensively at the full bath, wracking my brains to try and remember.

But I can't. I remember lying down, but not turning on the taps.

It must be Matt. He must be home early.

'Matt?' I whisper, so as not to wake Olivia.

He'll never hear me.

I go downstairs. All the lights are off and the dark crevices of the house are threatening, as if hiding the secrets of the past. I get to the bottom of the stairs and turn the light on in the hallway, chasing away the shadows.

'Matt?'

He isn't home.

I must have left the taps on. It's the only explanation. There's no one else here.

I must have started running the bath and then been so exhausted that I went to the bedroom and fell asleep. How could I be so stupid?

I feel the familiar stab of worry, niggling at me. I'm so absent-minded lately. How can I be a fit mother if I can't even remember to turn the taps off?

CHAPTER 7

The clock on the mantelpiece strikes midday, its insistent chimes echoing around the clutter of the living room. I glance up from my parenting book and see that Olivia is red-faced in her baby chair, tears streaming down her cheeks, taking fast, shaky breaths between her wails.

How long have I ignored her for? I didn't mean to, but somehow I've learnt to tune out her screams, the way you'd tune out the sound of next-door's lawnmower or the traffic on the road outside. Olivia's screams have turned into background noise. The soundtrack of my life.

I unstrap her from the baby seat and pull her into my arms.

'I'm sorry, I'm sorry, I'm sorry,' I say, rocking her back and forth and stroking her hair the way I've seen other mothers do.

I have that feeling again. Goosebumps on my arms. That desire to look behind me. Someone is watching. I can't put my finger on how I know, but every instinct I have is telling me, putting my body on high alert.

I go over to the venetian blinds at the bay window and pull the cords one by one so no one can see in. The living room is dark now and I have to turn the light on. I feel afraid, hiding in my own house.

I hear a sound from the kitchen. Did I imagine it?

I stand stock-still, trying to listen above the noise of Olivia screaming in my arms.

I'm sure I can hear something.

Footsteps.

Someone is in my house.

'Hello?'

The door of the living room opens.

I just about manage to hold back my scream as Ruth appears, smiling.

My pulse is still racing as I force a smile. My fear turns slowly to annoyance. I thought I'd made myself clear I didn't want her letting herself in.

I think about changing the locks. But I know this would be a step too far. This isn't my house.

I close my eyes and take a deep breath. When I open them, Ruth is beside me in the living room. I'm not sure I have the energy to confront her. I haven't slept for more than two hours in a row since Olivia was born.

'Hello, love.' She leans towards me to kiss me on the cheek, and I have to stop myself recoiling. Then she puts her face right up close to Olivia's and coos. I tense. Olivia whimpers.

Ruth frowns at my half-drunk mug of tea on the coffee table, and I realise it has veered slightly off the mat. She picks it up, alongside a plate with the last remnants of my breakfast toast.

'There's no need to clear up,' I say, finding my voice at last, shifting Olivia from one arm to the other and reaching to take them from her hands. I still feel shaky.

'It's no bother,' she says, striding off into the kitchen. I hear the tap running and the washing up being done.

I sink onto the sofa, defeated. But there's only a few moments of respite before she returns.

She sits herself beside me and hands me a fresh cup of tea, pulling a mat across the coffee table so it's right in front of me. I put Olivia back in her chair, hyperaware of the danger of the hot drink.

Ruth looks at the picture of the Vietnamese motorcyclist on the wall and frowns.

'I'm not sure that really goes there,' she says.

'I wanted to brighten up the cottage a bit.'

'I suppose it's an acquired taste. How did you put it up? I hope you didn't just use a picture hook? We'll have to repaint before we sell in that case.'

'Sell?' I can't hide the shock from my voice. It will take Matt and me a while to save up to buy our own place, and Ruth had given the impression we could stay as long as we needed.

'Well yes, we'll have to sell it eventually, of course. You can't expect to live rent-free forever in someone else's house.'

'No, I wasn't expecting that.' Confusion ripples through me. She'd offered. We'd moved away from our friends and the city because she'd made it sound like we'd be able to live here until we saved up a deposit. I feel a bit queasy.

'Where are the china elephants?' she asks.

I've moved them from the mantelpiece. I'm planning to put up photos of Matt and me and Olivia in their place. I want the cottage to feel like a family home. Our home.

'I put them in the cupboard. I didn't want to risk them falling on Olivia.'

She frowns. 'You'd have to be pretty clumsy for that to happen.'

'Do you want them in your house?' I offer.

'Oh no. I don't want the clutter. But you must look after them. They're part of the family.'

I nod. I'm part of the family too, but perhaps not as important as the china elephants.

Olivia starts to grumble. I sip my tea, feeling uncomfortable, and wonder how long my mother-in-law is planning to stay.

'Aren't you going to see to her?' Ruth asks.

I go over and pick Olivia up. 'She's like this all the time,' I say, as I try to comfort her. It sounds like an excuse.

'Matt said you were finding it hard,' Ruth says, and leans in closer. 'It's difficult looking after a little one. Sometimes my two really made me lose my temper.'

What has Matt told her?

I try to hide the anger that bubbles up inside me. It's none of Ruth's business how I'm coping.

'I'm fine.'

'I wanted to come round to see if you'd read the paper.'

'The paper?'

'Yes, the local paper. There's a story in it about a mother who burned her baby.' She pulls the newspaper triumphantly out of her bag.

'Look,' she says, holding it out to me.

The article fills the front page. An accident with a pan of boiling water. A baby scarred for life. I feel the familiar fear rising up inside me. That fear that I will take my eyes off Olivia for one second and something awful will happen.

'They think the mother was negligent,' Ruth says, hammering the message home. She looks round the room disapprovingly at the scattered baby toys and teethers. 'It just shows, you can never be too careful.'

I know she's warning me, telling me I must tidy up or it will be my fault if something awful happens. I feel overwhelmed. I'm so exhausted. Looking after Olivia takes every waking second.

I pass Olivia over to Ruth and bend over, rapidly picking the toys off the floor and placing them in a pile in the corner of the room. There's nowhere else to put them. All the cupboards are full.

Ruth hands Olivia back to me as soon as I sit back down. She returns the paper to her bag and changes the subject. 'It must be hard with Matt out at work all the time,' she says, her eyes suddenly kind.

'A little,' I reply, unsure of her intentions.

'You know he only employed Sarah because he's a kind man.'

'Sarah?'

I remember how insistent Ruth was that Matt offer Sarah a job.

'I thought maybe that's what was bothering you.'

'Why would that bother me?' She must think I'm jealous. Any excuse to believe I'm not coping.

'A lot of people would be bothered by their husband employing his ex-girlfriend. But not you, clearly.' She laughs and reaches out to touch my shoulder. 'I'm lucky to have such a well-adjusted daughter-in-law.'

I feel my shoulders tense as reality hits me. Matt hasn't been home before 9 p.m. since we moved. He's been spending all his time working. With his ex.

He's misled me. He never told me that he and Sarah had history. My stomach knots round itself. I thought I could trust him. Why is he keeping things from me?

Ruth is staring at me intently and I realise she knows I wasn't aware. She wants a reaction. That's the reason she's come to see me.

'Why would it worry me?' I say, trying to sound casual.

'Oh, you're a brave woman,' Ruth laughs. 'Of course, it shouldn't worry you. Matt's such a loyal partner. But I know how easy it is to get paranoid. He's a good-looking man.'

'Matt loves me,' I say, but my voice sounds hesitant.

'I'm so glad you feel like that, dear,' Ruth says. 'I just wanted to check you were all right with it.'

I frown. Why did Ruth invite Sarah round for Sunday lunch with us and then insist she take a job with Matt?

'It doesn't worry me,' I say. 'I'm sure she's a good employee.' But Matt hasn't mentioned her at all. I have no idea what goes on when he goes to work. Is it suspicious that he never talks about her? He spends all day with her. Surely there must be something to report.

Ruth sees right through me. 'Matt's never been good at communication,' she says. 'There are lots of things he probably hasn't mentioned to you.'

I desperately want to ask her what she means, but I'm determined not to rise to the bait.

She scans my face as I try not to react. Then she laughs. 'You know, there are probably things he hasn't even told me. He's always been secretive.'

I get the feeling that she's testing me, seeing how far she can push me. I stay silent as she searches my face, and then she seems to tire of her game.

'Well, I just came round to check you were all right,' she says. She kisses Olivia on the cheek. 'I've got tennis in half an hour so I'd better be off. Unless you need me, of course?'

'I'm fine.'

'I've watered the plant in the kitchen for you. It looked a bit dry.'

'Thank you.'

'And this place could really do with a hoover. It's filthy.'

*

'Mary had a little lamb, little lamb, little lamb.' I sing loudly and tunelessly over Olivia's screams as I grate the cheese on top of the lasagne. I just need to get it in the oven and then I'll give her my undivided attention.

I close the oven door and glance at my watch. Half an hour later than I intended to put it in, but not too bad. Matt will just have to wait a little while for his dinner. He should be back any minute.

My phone beeps.

Sorry. I'll be another hour. Got to wrap up the accounts. Can't wait to see you later.

I sigh. Why can't he just come home? I'm with Olivia all day, every day. I just want him to take her off my hands for an hour.

I wonder if Sarah is working late too.

My stomach knots into a ball of doubt. I've got no way of knowing what he's doing. I just have to trust him. And I do trust him. But why didn't he mention that Sarah was an ex?

I feel a wall of resentment rising inside me, and tears sting my eyes. I try to put Sarah out of my mind. I can't let Ruth's words get to me.

I shouldn't be annoyed with Matt for working late. When Matt and I first met I worked day and night, while Matt was often home, preparing dinner in the evenings. But our roles have reversed. I'm at home all day with Olivia, and Matt is always out working. It feels like his life is continuing, while mine remains stuck in a relentless cycle of nappies and breastfeeding.

I know I'm being unreasonable. I think of all the meals that Matt used to cook that I often thoughtlessly missed because I was still in the office, rushing round to meet deadlines and submit my copy to the editor. He'd always understood. Why can't I?

But I just want him to come home. I thought he would put Olivia to bed, rock her to sleep, then wrap his big arms around me. I've been looking forward to that all day.

I pick up my phone, my finger hovering over Matt's number. I shouldn't ring him. He's under so much pressure already. The practice has to make money, otherwise we'll never be able to buy our own place. And I don't want to be needy and dependent, the wife at home waiting anxiously for the husband to return.

But motherhood has changed me. Here I am with the baby I'd longed for, dependent on Matt coming home to feel human again.

Olivia is still screaming and I pick her up and rock her. I should bath her and put her to bed, but it all seems too much. I want to scream myself. I lift her and carry her up the stairs, holding her under one arm while I turn on the bath taps. I pace up and down the upstairs landing as I rock her back and forth.

By the time I've got Olivia ready for bed, put her down and waited for her screams to silence, I'm exhausted. Matt should be home by now. This time I do text him. I'm angry. I can't help myself. I look at Olivia asleep and think how peaceful she looks, so still, almost like a doll. I think about lying down on the bed next to the cot, getting a bit of sleep, when I remember the lasagne. It's been in the oven too long. It'll be burnt by now.

As I'm turning the temperature down on the oven, I hear Matt's key in the lock. I look at my watch. He's been half an hour longer than he said he would be.

I hear him come through the door and go upstairs to the toilet. He hasn't even said hello.

'Olivia looks peaceful,' he says as he comes into the kitchen. He tries to kiss me on the cheek, but I turn away.

'She's been screaming all day,' I reply. 'And your mother came over unannounced. Let herself in the kitchen door, without even knocking.'

'I'll speak to her.' Matt tries to wrap his arms around me, but I'm too angry to accept his embrace.

'You told her I wasn't coping,' I say accusingly. 'Why did you do that?'

'I didn't say that, Claire. All I said was that it was difficult for you with me working all day. And that it made it harder because the house was full of stuff. I was trying to get her to start clearing out.'

I sigh. He's made it sound like it's only me that wants the house sorted. Because I'm not coping.

'I wish you hadn't asked like that. And anyway, she says she's going to sell it once it's been cleared.'

'She doesn't mean it.'

He always brushes away my concerns.

'Let's just eat,' I say. I turn to the oven and open it. I see the charred cheese on top of the lasagne. I'll have to scrape that off. 'It's been ready ages, it's burnt.'

'Thank you,' Matt says. 'I'm sorry I'm late. I just got caught up with work.'

'Was Sarah there?' I blurt it out without thinking.

'Well, yes she was. She wanted to help out.'

'Right,' I say, putting the lasagne dish on the kitchen surface with a clatter. 'Your mother told me she's your ex.' I hate the way my voice sounds, shaky and on the verge of tears. But I can't hold back.

'Yes. From a long time ago. We were teenagers.' He sighs and leans heavily against the counter.

'Why didn't you mention it?' I scrape the black bits off the top of the lasagne with a sharp knife and cut two helpings for me and Matt. I'm not even sure if I'm hungry any more.

'I didn't think to say anything. It was Mum who wanted me to employ her.'

'So you're at work together all day, late into the night, and I just stay here cooking and looking after our baby, being the perfect little housewife, putting your dinner on the table?'

Even as I say this, I know that it isn't true. The kitchen looks like a bomb has hit it. There are utensils and dirty plates everywhere. The surfaces are spattered with sauce. I am far from the perfect housewife.

Matt sighs. 'Let's not talk about it now. We're both tired.'

'I'm the one that's tired, Matt. I'm the one that gets up three times in the night to feed Olivia, while you sleep.'

'And you're the one who wanted a baby.'

He says it so quietly that I think I must have misheard him.

'What?'

'Nothing. Let's just eat.'

Shock reels through me. 'I was the one who wanted a baby? But you did too!' I want to throw the lasagne at him, to hurt him. Make him understand how hard this is for me.

'I suppose I did. But it was something you just suddenly set your heart on. When we were dating we both said we didn't want to be tied down. We had our jobs, we had enough money, loads of holidays. Don't you remember?'

I know this is true. When Matt and I met, my career was more important to me than anything and I loved the life we built for ourselves.

But over time, my priorities changed.

'When we discussed children, you said you wanted them too.'

'I said that if that would make you happy, then I wanted what you wanted. I... I just wanted you to be happy. You were so sad, Claire, after what happened. And you seemed to think that a child was the answer, that a baby would fix everything.'

There's some truth in what he says, but I don't want to hear it. I don't want to even think about it. I'm angry that he's saying this now, when it's too late.

'Are you saying you didn't want our daughter?' I fight back with the words I know will hurt him.

'You know I'm not saying that. You're being irrational.' His voice is louder now. 'You decided you wanted a child and I went along with it.'

'You went along with it?' Now I'm furious, the pulse in my forehead throbbing so loudly, I can hardly think straight. I remember how hard we tried for a baby. The unexplained infertility. The trips back and forth to the doctors. The baby I lost. The medical investigations to work out what might be wrong with us. I had thought Matt was just as determined as me to make it work.

He sighs. 'You know I didn't mean that. I'm tired. Let's just eat.'

I slam the plate of burnt, tepid lasagne down in front of him. Sauce and cheese splashes up onto his shirt and he glares at me angrily as he rises suddenly from his seat and turns to face me.

'Claire!'

His face is up close to mine and anger radiates from him. For a second, I think he might hit me. I turn and run from the room, tears streaming down my face.

*

They are watching me. The car has been parked opposite our driveway for an hour now, in the only spot with a direct view of our house, through the gap in the trees. In that hour the driver hasn't moved from the front seat. I've checked every ten minutes.

Sometimes I wonder if I'm imagining things, if the car is really empty, the owner visiting one of the other houses. The driver is just a shadow, so still that they're hardly there at all. But then bright sunlight reflects off the screen of their phone and I know they're real, their face turned towards the house, watching. Who are they? They must be able to see me too, looking out.

I can't concentrate with them outside. My body is tense with fear, on edge at what might come next. What do they want?

I can't let anything disrupt our lives here.

I've got used to the way things are, confined to the house. I've learnt to make the best of it, keeping myself occupied. I've learnt to tiptoe around my husband when he's home, navigating my way carefully round his rage. We exist in a strange equilibrium, an unlikely dance of avoidance and togetherness. He is aggressive, I am passive. He is hard, I am soft. Yin and yang, the sun and the moon. It works somehow.

But it's a delicate balance. And now someone is watching, threatening the life we've built. I remember how angry my husband was the other day, when he suggested I was having an affair. Has he sent someone to spy on me?

I shiver, afraid, although there is nothing for him to find out. No affair. No friends. No life.

I don't exist any more. Not in any real sense. I benefit from the trappings of my husband's success: the huge house, my four by four parked in the driveway, my top of the range phone. But I don't own the house. I never drive my expensive car. And I don't have any friends to call. I don't even have social media any more. My husband made me delete my accounts. There's no trace of me. No pictures. Nothing.

CHAPTER 8

Despite my argument with Matt last night, I feel refreshed in the morning. Olivia only woke up once in the night and so I have some energy. After Matt's left for work, I start the clear-out of the house in earnest. I'm sick of tripping over Pamela's things. I don't care what Matt and his mother think. Matt's hardly ever here. I'm the one who has to be in the cottage, all day, every day.

Without a car, I can't remove any larger items so I put them in the garden instead. I tackle the bulky mobility aids first. After an hour, there's a collection of plastic walkers and wooden walking sticks lined up neatly next to the pond.

A part of me wants to throw the equipment into the water and watch it sink beneath the murky surface. But I don't like to go too close to the edge. I'm afraid I'll lose my balance and fall in, become tangled in the darkness beneath, slowly drowning as my baby watches calmly, sitting in her chair, on the other side of the patio doors.

I shiver. I can almost feel the water encircling me, the reeds wrapping round my arms.

I quickly return to the house and look back at the garden. With the walls of the house separating me from the water, I feel safer. I let myself feel a bubble of satisfaction that Ruth will be able to see the equipment from her kitchen window. Up until now she has been insulated from Pamela's mess and clutter, in her huge, neat and tidy house.

I carry Olivia through to the living room, then grab the scissors and pierce the tape of the nearest box. Now the plastic walkers have been moved, there's a little bit more space for unpacking.

The first box contains stationery and notebooks for the study. I pull out the bright orange diary that I wrote in when I was pregnant. I read it back to myself.

> *I've spent the day shopping for baby clothes. I want this so much, I can't believe it's finally happening.*

My words are only from three months ago but it's as if they've been written by a complete stranger. There's page after page of excited scribbles, full of hopes for the baby and for myself. I can feel the anticipation coming off the pages as I count down to my due date. I thought the baby would be a fresh start for me and Matt. A chance to put the past behind us.

No matter how many screaming children I saw in supermarkets and shopping centres, I knew with absolute certainty that motherhood was what I wanted. Friends told me there were ups and downs, but all I saw was the stream of smiling baby pictures on Facebook; proud parents beaming at christenings, neat children in ironed school uniforms ready for their first days of school. Talk of sleepless nights and nappy changes went in one ear and out the other. I wanted a baby so much that I tuned out the negatives. I thought it would fix something inside me. If I had a baby, I wouldn't be so broken.

The diary stopped the day Olivia was born, the many remaining blank pages waiting to record the joy of motherhood. But I haven't been able to continue. The thoughts I have now are too complicated to put down in writing, I can't let them loose on the page.

I planned to share the diary with Olivia when she was older. A gift she could keep forever, detailing her first year in the world. I swallow my guilt. At this rate it'll never be finished. Olivia must never know how I feel about her. I don't even want to acknowledge it myself.

Beneath the diary is a stack of parenting books. During my pregnancy I devoured them, determined to be the perfect mother, to make up for the fact that I wouldn't have my own to guide me. Somewhere I have a folder where I neatly summarised the key points from each book. But no amount of advice could prepare me for the reality of motherhood. And no amount of advice could replicate the natural love I'm supposed to feel for my child. Why can't I feel it? There's something wrong with me, something missing.

I sigh and carry the books upstairs. I shove the diary in the drawer. Maybe one day, when I'm happier, I'll be able to look at it again and complete it for Olivia.

The next box reveals kitchen equipment. Plates and bowls and mugs. I know there's no place for them. Every cupboard and drawer in the kitchen is already full with Matt's grandmother's crockery. There's hardly enough space for our food.

I consider emptying the box and then filling it back up with Pamela's plates and bowls, but the whole thing feels like a waste of energy, so I close it again.

I hear Olivia grumbling upstairs. She must have woken from her nap so I leave the boxes and tend to my daughter.

While I'm breastfeeding, I think about my argument with Matt last night, how dismissive he was when I asked about Sarah. Ever since I've found out that they used to be a couple, I've had that niggling sense of doubt. I wonder why he never told me about her. Unable to resist, I search for Sarah online on my phone. I find her Facebook profile and scroll through the publicly available photos. There's not much there. Just a few of her on a beach and a couple in the countryside. I hover over the 'add friend' button and then decide against it. I can't let my curiosity about her take over.

But she makes me feel uneasy. I don't understand why she's stayed in the village when she had so many prospects. What on earth would possess her?

I abandon Facebook and try typing Sarah's name into Google. She has such a common name and there are too many results from a basic search so I add the name of the village, and then add the county.

The first result is Matt's website. He set up a site for his new surgery before we even moved out to the countryside. He thought he'd get new enquiries, but it only got a few visitors a week. From the data, it looked like it was just the same people coming back to his website again and again. Matt and his mother, we thought. Not new customers. The website hadn't even had any enquiries. I'd forgotten it existed.

Sarah's photo is front and centre of the newsfeed on the site, introducing her as a new member of staff. The only member of staff. She smiles into the camera, looking professional yet countrified, in a neatly ironed blouse and wellington boots, her auburn hair shimmering. She could be a model for one of those country lifestyle magazines. I sigh. There's no point comparing myself to her.

I scroll further down the feed. There's not much else on there. Just the news that the practice is opening, accompanied by a picture of me and Matt, arm in arm. I'm beaming into the camera, heavily pregnant and happy. I wish Matt had asked me before he put the photo up. He knows I worry about privacy. Anyone could see my name on that website and track me down.

I push the thoughts aside. I can tell Matt to take the picture down, but it's unlikely to be a problem anyway. It's already been up a few weeks and clearly no one has been looking at the website. I'm just paranoid. I need to stop thinking like this. I look at the time and realise I must leave. I'm meeting Emma at the park with Olivia.

By the time I've changed Olivia's nappy, put her coat and gloves on, checked the contents of the nappy bag and settled her in the buggy, I'm running fifteen minutes late. I text Emma to apologise and then rush out, pushing the buggy up the hill at speed, working up a sweat. When I arrive at the park I see Emma sitting on the bench alone, staring into the fountain.

'Emma.' I smile at her and she gets up, wrapping me in a hug.
'It's so good to see you,' she says.

'You too. Sorry I'm a bit late.'

'Don't worry about it. I was just enjoying the rare sunshine.'

Despite the cold, the sky is clear and the sun beams down,
warming our bare faces between the hats and scarfs.

'Thanks,' I say, looking around for her buggy. 'Where's your
lovely daughter?'

'Oh, she's with Dan.'

A wave of envy washes over me. While her ex looks after Lizzie,
Emma has some time to herself, without a clinging, needy baby.

'You're free,' I say brightly. 'You can do anything you like.'

I see the expression on Emma's face and wish I could take it
back. She's told me that when she's not with Lizzie she feels bereft,
as if she's without a limb.

'I'm sorry,' I say. 'What time are you picking her up from Dan's?'

'Not for ages, so we have the whole afternoon.' I see her trying
to force a smile and I desperately try to think of a way to cheer
her up. I can see how hard it is for her without Lizzie.

Olivia interrupts us with a scream. It's a welcome distraction and
I take her out of the buggy and hug her close. Her cries continue.

'Is she hungry?' Emma asks.

'I don't think so. I only just fed her.'

'Do you want me to take her?' Emma reaches out her arms for
Olivia and she immediately calms in Emma's embrace.

'You've got the touch,' I say quietly. I feel like such a failure
next to her.

'I always wanted lots of children,' she replies. 'But I might
have to stick with just one.' She blinks back tears and stares into
the fountain.

'Oh, Emma.' I hate to see her like this. She's normally so full
of life. 'You're such a great mother. I really hope you'll get another
chance. You've got so much going for you. You're kind and caring.

And beautiful too. You'll have your pick of men when you're ready to date again.'

She doesn't smile like I expect and I wonder if I've been insensitive. I don't want to dismiss her heartache.

'Maybe,' she says despondently.

I don't know what to say. I'm grateful I've got Matt. He's always been a good husband to me. At least, he used to be. I try not to think about the distance that's grown between us lately. About my bubbling fears over Sarah.

'What's difficult,' Emma says, 'is knowing that I'll never have the life I planned. I imagined it so differently. A family. Happiness. But just one person can take that all away from you in an instant.'

'You don't need Dan,' I say. 'He hasn't taken everything. You still have Lizzie.'

'I know,' she says. 'I wish she was here now.' She looks at me intently and strokes Olivia's hair. Together they look like an advert for motherhood. Jealousy washes over me. Why can't that be me with my daughter?

'You're so lucky to have Matt,' Emma continues. 'You two are perfect together.'

I remember what Matt said last night about not wanting children. I dab the corner of each eye to stop the tears falling.

'My marriage is far from perfect,' I admit. I instantly regret my words. How can I complain about Matt's small flaws when Emma is struggling on her own?

But she turns to me, concerned. 'Is everything OK, Claire?'

'It's nothing. Well, not nothing. I've just got an uneasy feeling.'

'About what?'

'Do you know Sarah?' I ask.

'No,' Emma says, eyebrows raised.

'She's a friend of Matt's. Actually, an ex-girlfriend. Who he's started employing at the surgery.'

'Gosh, I can see why you'd be a bit… concerned.'

'Can you?' I'm so relieved she doesn't think I'm just paranoid. 'I mean it's probably nothing, but…' I continue uncertainly.

'It does seem a bit strange.' Emma confirms my own thoughts.

'I trust him. It's just odd he didn't mention to me that she's an ex. I found out from his mother.'

Emma is quiet, her brow furrowed.

'What do you think?' I ask. It's been so long since I've been able to confide in someone, I'm desperate for her opinion.

'I don't know. Every relationship is different, I suppose.' She glances down at the floor, before she continues hesitantly. 'But the whole thing reminds me a bit of Dan. When he was cheating, he just stopped telling me things. Things that were important.'

I take Olivia back into my arms, and put her in her pushchair.

'I can trust Matt,' I repeat. 'I know I can.' But even I can hear the waver in my voice, as I try to convince myself it's true.

We walk through the park side by side, lost in thought. I spot a grandmother pushing her granddaughter in a pram, talking gently to the child as she strolls down the path. I imagine what the mother might be doing. Working out at the gym. Resting. Shopping. Anything she wants.

I swallow my jealousy.

'Do you ever wish your parents were around to help out?' Emma asks, reading my mind.

'Yeah, I do.' I think of how much my mother would have loved Olivia. The close relationship they could have had. But some things aren't meant to be.

'Me too,' Emma says wistfully. 'My parents died when I was tiny. I never had anyone to guide me.'

'I'm sorry,' I say, feeling bad for her. At least I had a mother growing up.

'It's OK,' she replies. 'I haven't thought about it for years, but now when I see grandparents with their grandchildren I think of my own parents and remember how I felt as a child. How alone and lost. I don't want Lizzie to miss out on that love the way I did.'

'I know exactly what you mean,' I say. 'I just have my mother-in-law. And although she tries to help…'

Emma laughs. Every single time we've met I've complained about Ruth.

'She's difficult,' Emma confirms.

'Yep. She keeps coming into the house unannounced, moving things around. Matt says he'll speak to her but—'

'Sometimes family aren't all they're cracked up to be,' Emma says. 'That's why we have friends.'

I smile and nod, blinking back tears.

'We can be family to each other,' Emma continues, putting her arm around me.

I feel warm inside. It's so nice to have someone around who listens and understands me. Even if my own family aren't here and Matt's family don't seem to like me, I'll still have Emma. I'm so grateful for that.

We walk round the park for hours, just chatting. I start to feel alive again, normal. Claire the person, rather than Claire the mother.

Emma suggests we go and feed the ducks.

I hesitate before I agree. I'm nervous around water, especially with small children. But I know I have to get over it. The future will involve paddling pools and swimming lessons. I can't let my fear rule Olivia's childhood.

We head over to the corner shop on the edge of the park to buy bread.

All around the water's edge children are throwing bread clumsily in the direction of the ducks. Some goes in the water, some falls onto the path.

Emma and I watch.

Olivia is far too young to feed the ducks and I start to wonder why we thought this was a good idea. Two adults standing side by side, throwing bits of sliced bread into a pond.

I can't take my eyes off the children. As I throw my bread absent-mindedly, I count them and assign each one to a parent.

The reeds are tall and thick. It wouldn't take much for a child to fall into the water and become tangled up. I'm not sure if anyone would even be able to see them from the path.

A child on the other side of the pond wanders closer to the water, drawn in by the swimming swans. His mother is casually chatting behind him.

Watch him! I want to scream. *Watch him!*

But I don't and the child returns safely back to his mother to get more bread.

Another child to my right. Walking just a bit too close to the edge.

My heart beats faster. I can feel the heat rising in me. Despite the day's chill, I'm sweating under my winter coat. I feel sick. I can't catch my breath.

I need to get out of here now. I grab the handles of Olivia's buggy and push at it. It doesn't budge. I push harder and the back wheels rise off the ground, moving forward an inch.

The brake. I put my foot under the lock and release it. The wheels free and I speed away from the pond.

'Are you all right, Claire?' Emma shouts after me.

A minute later I have to stop. I bend over, my breathing ragged and fast. I throw up onto the grass.

CHAPTER 9

Emma appears beside me, breathless from running.

'Claire, what happened? Are you all right?' Her eyes crinkle in concern.

'I'm fine.' I stumble over the words, embarrassed.

'You've been sick.' Emma takes the buggy with one hand and uses the other to guide me over to a bench. 'Sit down,' she says. 'Get your breath back.'

I slide onto the bench, still feeling unstable and wobbly. I can't seem to control the panic still flowing through my system.

Emma places Olivia opposite me. She's staring at the bright blue sky above us, unaware of the fear that's taken over my shaking body.

I bend over, put my head between my knees and try to calm down.

Emma strokes my back. 'It's OK, Claire. Take as long as you need.'

When I finally sit up, I stare at the sky and try to take deep breaths. I let my hands rest on the wooden bench, attempting to ground myself.

'How are you feeling?' Emma asks.

'A bit better.' I manage a half-smile. 'I'm so sorry.'

'There's nothing to be sorry for.'

'I just panicked, that's all. Sometimes the water…' I pause as I feel a wave of nausea washing through me. I don't think I can explain how I feel, not even to Emma.

'It's all right,' Emma says. 'There's no need to be sorry.'

'I have them occasionally – the attacks. For a while I really struggled. I'm almost better now.' I smile ruefully. 'At least I thought I was.'

'It must be so scary,' Emma says.

'I'm OK.'

Emma smiles at me and pulls some tissues out of her bag, offering me one. I dab at my eyes and then wipe the sick from around my mouth. I'm so embarrassed. I wish she hadn't seen me like this. I look like I'm not coping.

'Are you sure you're all right?' she asks.

'Yes, I'm fine now. I'm so sorry.'

'Please don't apologise. I was worried about you.' She puts her arms around me, gives my shoulders a rub.

'Don't worry about me,' I say, slowly getting up from the bench. 'Let's get going.'

I look at my watch. If we don't hurry Emma will be late to collect Lizzie from Dan's.

'Are you sure you'll be OK?' Emma asks once more, wrapping me in a hug when we reach the gate.

'Yes,' I say. 'I think I'll have a walk in the village, distract myself a bit.'

'I wish I could come with you, but I really need to pick up Lizzie.'

'It's OK, really. You've got to go.' She's been so kind to me already.

She gives me one last squeeze. 'I'll call you later, OK?'

'Sure.'

I watch her walk away and then I spend an hour or so wandering around the village. I go to the post office and browse the cards. I see a comedy card with a picture of a woman berating a man and an awful pun that only Miriam and I would ever find funny. I remember that Miriam's birthday is next week and for a moment I consider buying it for her. She'd find it hilarious.

I replace it on the shelf with a sense of regret. In the last three years, I've sent Miriam cards on every single one of her birthdays, but I've never had one back. Maybe it's time to stop. She clearly hasn't forgiven me and it's time for me to move on. I have a new life now. Miriam has chosen not to be part of it.

I know as soon as I push the door open to the cottage that someone has been in. The air is still and yet it feels disturbed, as if each molecule has repositioned itself.

'Hello?' I call out.

The silence is so complete that it feels like it's lying in wait for the noise that will disturb it. A clatter. A bang.

But there's nothing.

I carry Olivia through to each room in turn and open the blinds and draw the curtains, letting in the light. There's no one here.

Upstairs, I sit on my bed and place Olivia on my breast. I rest my head against the pillows. If I can just rest while she feeds, then maybe I'll feel a little better.

I look around the bedroom. Our toiletries and books and electronics cover every surface. There's so much clutter that it feels like the room is closing in on me. The wooden cupboards and the dressing table are overflowing with Pamela's things. Our clothes are relegated to a cheap soft cupboard, which sags in the middle under their weight. Pamela is still at the core of this cottage and our life is just a superficial layer on top.

I frown. Something is wrong. I look round the room again. Matt's things are everywhere. His deodorant, his aftershave, a vet periodical and paperwork. My books are there too. But my personal items are gone. My hairbrush. My deodorant. The watch I've stopped wearing because it scratches the back of Olivia's head when I'm breastfeeding. They were on the bedside table this morning. I know they were.

My whole body tenses and Olivia pulls away from my breast and starts to whine.

Someone has been in my bedroom.

I get down off the bed and look back at it. It's neatly made, the duvet folded down a bit. The pillows are fluffed, except for the indent where my head rested a few seconds ago. I didn't have time to make the bed before I went out to meet Emma. I was rushing around, feeding Olivia, finding the spare nappies. And besides, I never fluff pillows.

Someone's been here. In my room.

Ruth?

I shiver, imagining Ruth in this room, judging the mess, judging me. I have no privacy. My life isn't my own any more.

By the time Matt comes in, I've put Olivia to bed and I've just started dinner. It's already past nine o'clock, much later than we used to eat. But I'm determined to cook. I want to have accomplished something today aside from changing nappies. And I want us to sit down at the table together, eat homemade food and talk to each other for once. We never spend any time just the two of us any more.

Matt comes into the kitchen and gives me a kiss on the cheek as I cut up the chicken. He washes his hands and starts on the vegetables.

I pour oil into the wok and turn on the heat.

'Your mother's been round today,' I say, unable to hold it in.

'Sorry?'

'It's got to stop, Matt.'

'When?'

'While I was out. She let herself in and went through our things in the bedroom.'

'Why would she do that?' Matt looks puzzled.

I finish cutting up the chicken and chuck it into the pan, followed by the vegetables.

'I don't know. She'd moved my hairbrush, my deodorant and my watch. You've got to talk to her. I thought you had already? Why won't she listen?' I glare at Matt. He always tiptoes around his mother. He doesn't seem to be able to stick up for himself with her.

'Are you sure you didn't move them yourself?' Matt asks, doubtfully.

'Of course I'm sure.'

But then I pause and reconsider. I'd found the hairbrush and the deodorant wedged between the bed and the table. The watch was on the floor. It's possible I'd knocked them off and they fell there. But that doesn't explain the neatly aligned duvet and the fluffed pillows.

'The bed was made too.'

'You didn't do it before you left?'

I hate the doubtful expression on his face. 'No, I was in a rush. I think I would remember. You need to speak to your mother. This has got to stop.' But as I say the words, they sound wrong. Could I have forgotten?

We pick at our food. Neither of us seems hungry.

'I'm worried about you, Claire,' Matt says eventually.

I can't look at him. I think that if I meet his eyes, he might be able to see through me, to see I'm not coping.

I want to hide away, but at the same time I have a desire to let him take me in his arms and fix everything. I'm so torn.

'I'm not getting any sleep,' I admit. I think of how he lies there each night fast asleep, while I breastfeed Olivia. He's even bought earplugs so he's not disturbed when she cries.

'I don't think you're well.'

'I'm fine,' I lie. 'It's just the sleep, honestly. Maybe if you got up and helped in the night, I'd be less tired.'

'This reminds me of before.'

'Before what?'

'When you were ill before. You said some crazy things back then too.'

I pick up my plate and scrape most of my dinner into the bin. I don't want to have this conversation. I thought we'd moved on from the past. I don't know why Matt's brought it up.

'I'm going to bed.'

'We need to talk,' Matt says. 'You can't blame my mother for everything.'

I walk away from his voice, up the stairs.

I hear his chair scrape back and within moments he's on the stairs behind me.

'Claire!' He raises his voice. 'Don't walk away from me.'

I reach the top of the stairs and he grabs my shoulder. I shake him off.

'Not now, Matt.'

I go into the bathroom, lock the door behind me, and sit down on the lid of the toilet, my head in my hands. I just need some time on my own. Without anyone watching or judging.

Matt pounds on the door.

'Claire! Claire!'

Olivia wakes and starts screaming.

'Claire! Open the door. I just want to help you.'

'You've woken her up now,' I shout through the door. 'It took ages to get her to sleep.'

'Open the door, Claire!'

'No. You can deal with her. You woke her up.'

My baby's screams get louder.

There's a thud and then the bathroom door bursts open. The loose screw in the bolt bounces across the bathroom floor.

Suddenly Matt is in the room.

I stare up at him from the toilet.

'Claire. You can't behave like this. You need to see a doctor. You need help.'

'What about you? What about your mother? She can't do this. She can't keep coming in, moving things around, making me think I'm going crazy.'

I stop, realising what I've just said. I'm not going crazy, am I? This isn't like last time. Suddenly I'm filled with self-doubt.

Matt stares at me. 'Maybe something *is* wrong with you, Claire. Maybe you're not well.'

I burst into tears.

'I can't do this again, Claire. The practice is taking every ounce of my energy. I need to make it work otherwise we'll be financially ruined. I can't be around 24/7 to look after you too. It's not like last time you were ill. We both have responsibilities now.'

I know he's right. I need to pull myself together. Put Olivia first.

'I'm sorry,' I say. 'I'm sorry.'

He paces up and down the tiny bathroom as Olivia's screams increase to a volume that seems impossible. I hold my hands against my ears, trying to block them out. I can't deal with her right now.

'Go and see your daughter.' I can only just get the words out through tears.

He grits his teeth, and reluctantly goes towards the bedroom, leaving me sitting in the bathroom on my own, shaking with sobs.

*

Is fear a feeling or a way of being?

The car has been parked outside my house for two weeks now. Every day for two weeks. I don't know how they sit out there in the heat, without the engine on for air conditioning, the hot sun glaring through the car windows. They hardly take a break. These days I keep the curtains shut, twitching them open in the dead of night, when I think they might be gone. But even after dark, they wait.

There are shadier places to park. But that spot has the best view of my house. Two huge conifers mark the entrance, and there's a high hedge between them. You can only see the house if you park opposite the gap. My husband chose this place for its privacy, but the reality is the trees block the light all year round, casting the house in shadow.

When we go to bed, I check the street once more. Still there. I get changed into my pyjamas and lie beside my husband. I feel the tension all the way through my body. He snores peacefully but I can't relax, not when I know there's someone still out there, patiently waiting. But for what? I resist the temptation to go to the window and peer out once more.

Instead I lie completely still, on my back. I've learnt to sleep this way. If I move in the bed, some unknown part of my body protests, a forgotten bruise.

I sleep fitfully and then wake with a jolt. Something's wrong.

I hear a sound. It's very faint but I'm sure of it. Footsteps.

I go to the window. The car is there but it's empty.

Where are they?

Are they in our garden? Or already in the house?

What do they want from us?

I shiver with fear.

I should wake my husband. But I can't. He'll be furious at being disturbed.

I stand stock-still, listening for noise. There's nothing but the rustle of the wind through the trees.

I need to check on my daughter. Just in case.

She's sleeping peacefully.

I lean over to kiss her cheek. I want to hold her close to me, take comfort in her small, warm body. I resist the urge, not wanting to wake her.

'Everything's going to be all right,' I whisper, to reassure myself more than her.

I go to the window and look out at the car. I see movement on the path that leads from our house to the road. Light, fluid footsteps, carefully avoiding the sensors of our security lights.

I let out the breath I didn't realise I'd been holding.

I watch the figure get in the car and I blink as the headlights flicker on, illuminating the shadowy street. The engine starts and I stay at the window until the car has pulled away and disappeared around the corner, out of sight.

CHAPTER 10

Olivia watches me as I go through the bathroom cupboard, pulling out toiletries and putting them on the tiled floor. Old face creams. Hardened tubes of medicinal toothpastes. Lavender scented bath and shower gels. Bottles and bottles of talcum powder. Make-up remover. Toothpicks. Old, dried nail varnishes.

Since my argument with Matt, I haven't been able to calm down. I didn't sleep at all last night. I tossed and turned, going over and over our argument again and again. I don't want to think about what he said to me. I'm sure he's wrong. I'm not ill. It's not like last time.

I've told myself that if I just sort out the house Matt and I will be happier. I'll tackle it myself, one room at a time.

I won't throw away anything that might have meaning for Ruth. I know from clearing out my own mother's house that that would be unforgivable. I don't think there'll be anything sentimental in the bathroom, but I'm still careful as I go through the cupboard. I know how unexpected items can bring back memories. People say you can always look at photos, but images are static. Scents, sounds and sensations bring everything back, clearer than any picture. Just the smell of my mother's perfume on a stranger's coat used to bring her back in full Technicolor.

They discontinued my mother's scent five years ago. I wish I'd kept just one bottle of her perfume. I hadn't liked the way the smell of it would jar me back into my grief, but those moments, sprinkled unexpectedly amongst the everyday, gave me another path to my memories. As time goes by, it feels like the roads to those memories are closing off, the paths overgrown and inaccessible.

There are some things I'll never throw away. My mother's red, dangly, fake feather earrings. She wore the same ones every day. Cheap ones from the supermarket. I'll always remember the feel of her earring brushing my face as she hugged me. Sometimes, when I'm feeling lost, I take them out and hold the fake feathers against my cheek, remembering her. If someone else had been sorting through her house, they would have thrown them out. A ball of anxiety forms in my stomach. Like most of my things, my mother's earrings are in a box somewhere, waiting to be unpacked.

At the bottom of the cupboard there are boxes and boxes of unopened tights. I feel moisture at the corner of my eye as a tear forms and drops down onto my cheek. I wish my mother was still alive. I wipe the tear away and think of Pamela, and that expectation we all have that our lives will continue indefinitely. Pamela would have anticipated walks that she never took, chatting to friends she never saw again. I hardly knew her, but as I pull out the boxes of unopened tights and put them into bin bags for the charity shop, I feel like she's with me, watching.

Olivia stares at me as tears run down my cheeks. I thought babies were supposed to sense your emotions and respond, but Olivia just watches as my face goes blotchy and my eyes redden. I stand and grab the toilet paper. I blow my nose aggressively, letting the noise fill the silent room.

Looking in the mirror, I wipe my eyes. Sometimes I don't recognise myself any more. I wanted to change, to be someone different. I needed to leave the woman I'd become behind in London. The city had hardened me. All I cared about was my career, getting the front-page scoop. But it got out of hand.

I've tried so hard to change. But who I am now? My eyes search my face for meaning, but there's none. I'm lost.

I look down at Olivia and see she's fallen asleep. My sobs had no impact on her. I wonder if she's learnt to block out my despair. I wonder if she'll grow into an emotionless child, out of tune with the world around her. Perhaps she takes after me. These days I always feel out of sync. Misaligned.

Going back to the cupboard, my vision blurs through tears. I speed up the sorting process, grabbing handfuls of toiletries and shoving them in the bin bag. I no longer go through each item in turn. I no longer let myself feel that stab of disappointment that Pamela never got to use these things.

Soon I have four full bin bags. Three are just rubbish, but one is suitable for the charity shop.

I carefully lift each bag over Olivia's head. I'll wait until Thursday, when the bins are taken, before I put them out. I don't want Ruth to think that I've thrown out any of her mother's things. Although she might see the bags in the hallway if she lets herself in. I take them to the study and shove them in there, on top of a pile of our boxes.

I go back into the bathroom and look at the cupboard. The bottom three shelves are completely empty. I smile. I'm making progress.

As I'm surveying my work, Olivia wakes and I realise she was due a feed two hours ago. I frown, frustrated with myself. What kind of mother forgets that?

After Olivia is fed and changed, and has spat up milk over my shoulder, I shove the bin bag of toiletries in the bottom of the buggy, strap Olivia in and make my way to the charity shop in the village.

There's a woman in front of the till, a collection of overflowing bags of donations at her feet. She picks them up two at a time and hands them over the counter to the volunteer. As she picks up the final bags, one bursts open and baby clothes spill out over the desk and drop to the floor.

'Sorry, sorry,' she says, gathering them up with her hands.

I reach down to pick a baby grow up off the floor. It's tiny, with delicate embroidered blue hearts dotted over white cotton. It would just about fit Olivia.

'It's beautiful,' I say. 'Must be hard to part with it.'

The woman turns and her face reddens.

'Sarah?'

She looks up and I see the tears in her eyes.

We both stare down at the baby grow.

'I didn't realise…' I start, unsure how to finish the sentence. 'Are you all right?'

'I'm fine,' she says, wiping her eyes. She quickly gathers up the baby clothes and shoves them back in the bag, hurrying away before the volunteer has the chance to thank her.

My eyes follow Sarah and it takes a moment for me to realise I'm next in line. 'Do you accept unopened toiletries?' I ask.

The volunteer looks at me over her glasses, eyeing the black bin bag doubtfully. 'Let me have a look.'

She peers into the bag and rummages through the items. 'Yes, we'll take these.'

'Thanks,' I reply, smiling with relief. At least one bin bag of stuff is out of the house.

I leave quickly, keen to speak to Sarah. She's already a little way down the road when I catch her up.

'Are you sure you're OK?'

'Yeah, fine,' she says. Her eyes are red and puffy.

I want to know what's wrong and who the baby clothes belonged to, but I hesitate, not wanting to upset her further.

The moment expands. Sarah seems stuck, as if she wants to say something, but can't form the words.

'Do you want to get some lunch?' I ask. A part of me is concerned and wants to check she really is all right. But another part of me wants to get to know her, to reassure myself about her and Matt working together.

She half smiles, and I can see she's holding back tears. I know what it feels like to be desperately holding things together and I want to reach out and comfort her.

'OK,' she replies. 'It would be nice to get to know you better. I know Matt so well.' I feel my shoulders tense at the reminder of how close she is to my husband.

We walk together to the garden centre just outside the village. The path is narrow, so I go ahead with the buggy. I can feel Sarah's eyes on my back, as she walks a pace behind and the wind rustles through the trees.

The garden centre café is crowded for a weekday, and I manoeuvre Olivia round the different food stations, sliding my brown tray along the ledge. Cutlery clinks and there's an irregular ring from cash registers opening and closing. Sarah offers to take my bag, which gives me a free hand to reach over and grab a sandwich from the shelf. An elderly lady taps her walking stick against the buggy to tell me to move it out of the way of the drinks section.

We take the only remaining seats, in the coldest part of the conservatory-style extension, and place our trays on the tiny table. Sarah takes her napkin and clears the crumbs.

Olivia whines, and I rock her from side to side, holding her higher than usual so she doesn't bang her head on the plastic table.

'So you've been having a clear-out?' I ask.

'Yeah,' Sarah says. She meets my eyes. 'It's been a bit emotional actually. I've been getting rid of things I should have parted with years ago.'

I want to ask Sarah about the baby clothes. I wonder if she has a much older child. She's never mentioned any children before, but then again I hardly know her.

'I've been getting rid of Pamela's old toiletries,' I say. 'So I can create a space for me and Matt to actually live in.'

Sarah smiles. 'Ruth can be difficult.'

'I suppose you've known her a long time?'

'Since I was a child. She's always had a knack for getting her own way.'

'Any advice for me?' I ask, hopefully.

Sarah looks at her coffee. 'If you want me to be completely honest, my only advice is not to trust her. I mean, she can be lovely when she wants to be. And she always puts her family first. That's a good thing. It's just that when you're not part of the family…'

'Matt and I are married,' I say. I want to sound confident in the security of our relationship, but I hear my voice waver.

'Maybe it will be different for you then.' She smiles reassuringly.

'Ruth seems to like you now,' I reply, trying to disguise my jealousy.

'Now I'm not a threat to her,' Sarah says. 'When we were going out, I never knew where I stood. I thought of Ruth and Jack as family. I was wrong. They were quick to cast me out when I didn't fall into line.'

'I thought you and Ruth were friends.'

'Anyone in this village with any sense gets on with Ruth. We play tennis occasionally, that's all.'

I feel uneasy. Everything Sarah's said makes sense. Ruth is friendly one minute and cruel the next. She's right – I can't trust her.

'How are things at the surgery?' I ask, changing the subject.

'You know, fine. I'm glad I had the day off today though. Made me get on with things I'd put off for far too long.'

Olivia's whines get louder and she scrunches up her face ready to scream.

'Poor thing,' Sarah says. 'She's fed up. Can I hold her? I'm good with babies.'

I hand her over hesitantly, but Olivia calms down as soon as Sarah holds her in her arms.

'You're a natural,' I say, seeing how content Olivia looks.

'Thanks,' she replies, as she pulls faces at Olivia. 'I could always babysit for you if you ever fancied a night off. I like looking after babies.'

I nod. Matt and I do need some time together, just the two of us. But can I trust her?

'Thanks,' I say. 'That's really kind of you.'

'Well, any time, just let me know.'

'Are you a mother yourself?' I ask, unable to hold back my curiosity any longer.

'Oh no,' she says. She smiles a little sadly. 'My time didn't come.'

'There's still time.'

'Maybe. I had a miscarriage years ago. I haven't found the right person to try again with since.'

'I'm so sorry,' I say, reaching out and touching her hand. I know exactly how she feels. 'I had a miscarriage too. Before Olivia. I was twenty weeks. I had to give birth to the baby.' A little girl. Olivia's sister. I shiver as I remember the horror of it all and my eyes fill with tears. I can hardly stand to think about it.

Sarah hugs Olivia closer to her, stroking her hair. 'Mine was a late miscarriage too. Fourteen weeks. Brought on by stress.'

'Was that why you had the baby clothes?' I ask gently, wiping the tears from my own eyes with a paper napkin.

She reddens. 'Yeah. I couldn't bring myself to throw them away. Not until now, years later.'

'It's a brave thing to do.' I have my own bundle of clothes for a baby that no longer exists, wrapped up in tissue paper in a box somewhere in the cottage.

'It was a long time ago. It feels like it's time to give away the clothes, time to move on.'

'Yes,' I say, thinking of all the things that I can't move on from, the nightmares that still haunt me from events three years ago.

Sarah contemplates her coffee. 'I hope you don't mind me saying but with you and Matt coming back… somehow it's made it easier to put the past behind me, to move on. I see you with Olivia. You're a proper family.'

I swallow a lump in my throat. 'It's not always easy.'

'Well it's good to see Matt happy again. It sets me free somehow. I can see he's moved on, and it means I can too.'

'We are happy,' I say. If I repeat it often enough, perhaps it will become true.

'And he finally got his baby.'

'His baby?' I look up at her, confused.

She meets my eyes.

'I'm sorry,' she says, awkwardly. 'I thought… I suppose I thought you realised.'

'Realised what?' But I already know what she's going to say before the words come out of her mouth.

'The baby I miscarried was Matt's.'

CHAPTER 11

Matt's not home until late in the evening, his eyes red-rimmed with exhaustion.

'Busy day?' I ask, handing him a glass of water.

'Yeah. Lots of admin. Sarah had the day off and the phone kept ringing.'

'I saw Sarah today,' I reply. 'We went for lunch.'

'Oh?' he says as he collapses down into a kitchen chair. He looks like he might fall asleep where he's sitting.

'She told me a few things, you know, about the past.'

I see Matt's body tense and he straightens up in the chair. I wait for him to speak, wondering if he knows what I'm about to say.

I continue. 'She said that a long time ago, she was pregnant with your baby. And she miscarried it.'

'Yeah,' he says softly, as if he hopes I won't hear his answer.

'Why didn't you mention it?'

'It's in the past, Claire.'

'But it's a big thing. When I miscarried our daughter…' Sobs choke me and I have to pause for a moment. I can hardly bear to remember. 'When I had my own miscarriage, you comforted me. You never mentioned you'd been through it before.'

'It didn't seem like the right time. You were so lost in your grief.'

'Our fertility problems could have been something to do with you. But you must have known that was unlikely as Sarah had been pregnant too. Why didn't you say anything?' I remember how desperately I'd wanted a baby, how I'd thought it would fix everything. We'd had so many tests to work out what was wrong.

'Claire, the doctors couldn't explain the problems. No one ever really thought it was a problem with me.'

I hear the implication of his words. That it was a problem with *me*. My high levels of stress. My anxiety. I wonder if he was secretly relieved each time the pregnancy test was negative.

'I just wish you'd told me. It's such a big thing. How could you keep it from me?'

When we go to bed, Matt falls asleep instantly, as if he hasn't got a care in the world. But my anger grows as I lie awake, listening to the house creak and the wind groan. Why has he hidden so many things from me?

His phone vibrates, but he doesn't stir. Usually I'd leave it, but this time, I reach over. The display says he's got a text from Sarah, but I can't see the contents. I tell myself that it could be about work, perhaps she's sick or going to be late in tomorrow. But it's 11 p.m. Why would she be texting him this late?

I look at Matt's sleeping body beside me and feel more alone than ever.

*

The sun's shining and the people in the pub gardens swill their pints as they gaze at the river. Olivia is older, about two. Her blonde hair has grown out long and wavy and she has the same determined jawline as Matt. She holds a stick and prods it into the shallow water, trying to lift up a pebble from just below the surface. She gazes adoringly at her father as he crouches beside her.

The sun beats on the back of my neck and I smile. Matt lifts Olivia up so that her feet dangle over the surface of the water and it tickles her toes. She laughs and I laugh with her.

Then Matt starts to wade into the water, going deeper into the centre of the river. My laughter catches in my throat.

Matt's jeans are soaked, turning a deep, dark blue. I can't see his face. The only noise is the rush of the river. An empty plastic water bottle flows past, faster than I'd expect. The current's strong.

I watch as Matt holds Olivia above the water and then suddenly submerges her. I'm frozen in place on the riverbank as her face disappears below the water. Matt holds her down. I want to run to her but I can't move. I want to scream but I can't open my mouth to breathe. Seconds pass. Then minutes.

Matt pulls Olivia's limp body from the water and holds it in his arms, staring down at her face as if he can't understand what's happened.

I wake.

My scream catches in the back of my throat as I bolt up in bed. My breathing is fast, and my heart beats faster. I'm drenched in sweat. I see shadows in the room, flitting across the curtains.

I turn on the light. There's no one there.

It was just a dream. Beside me, Matt stirs in his sleep and rolls over, pulling the cover over him. I creep under beside him, wrapping my arms around his warm back. It offers no comfort.

I lie still, my body tense, despite Matt's warmth. The dreams are back. I used to have them every night in London. I thought they would stop when we moved but it seems I'll never escape them. Why do they haunt me? Why can't I let go of the past?

I hear a creak.

A pipe. Or someone on the stairs.

I listen intently. Outside, the wind blows through the trees. A car roars down the main road. Another creak. A footstep?

Matt snores gently.

I know I'm imagining things, but I won't be able to sleep until I've checked.

I ease myself out of bed and pad softly over to the door. I stand stock-still, listening. There are no sounds. Just my imagination. It would be amusing if I didn't still feel the ball of fear inside me, solid and hard in the centre of my stomach.

I wonder if I should take something from the bedroom. A weapon. If I really think there's an intruder, isn't that what I'd do?

I glance at Matt's still body. I can't wake him just because of my paranoia. He'll only start going on about me being unwell again.

I go to Olivia's room. Her nightlight illuminates her, sleeping soundly, one arm above her head. I can see her chest rising and falling gently with each breath.

I catch a movement out of the corner of my eye.

It's just a car's headlights casting the shadow of a tree onto the bedroom curtains.

Olivia stirs and I leave, not wanting to wake her.

In our bedroom, Matt sleeps on undisturbed and I feel a flicker of resentment.

Something still doesn't feel right.

I turn the light on in the hallway. It's too bright for four in the morning and I blink myself into a fuller state of consciousness. I make my way downstairs and check the front door. It's double locked. We never use the bolt, but now I reach down and slide it across the bottom of the door.

I go through the kitchen to the back door and try the handle. The door doesn't budge. It only has a simple key lock. I peer out into the darkness. I wonder if we should add a bolt, so it can only be opened from the inside.

I stare out at the garden. If there's someone staring back then they can see right into the house. There's no blind to cover the glass of the back door. I'll order one in the morning.

Suddenly I see a reflection move in the glass. They are behind me. I scream as I turn, bracing myself for attack.

Matt.

It's only Matt.

'Why are all the lights on?' he asks, rubbing his eyes.

'I thought I heard someone in the house.' I look at my bare feet, feel the cold tiles beneath them. I realise how ridiculous the whole thing sounds. I have come down alone in my nightdress to confront an intruder.

'What? Why?'

'I... I...' I don't want to tell him about the dream. Especially when he already thinks I'm going mad.

'I'm sorry,' I say finally. 'I just thought I heard something, that's all. It's nothing.'

He grips the kitchen counter and I can see he's frustrated. His bloodshot eyes tell me how much he needs to rest. He's been working too many hours. It's taking its toll.

Finally, he reaches out and puts his arms around me. I can tell he is going through the motions, calming me down, so he can get back to bed.

'There's no one here, Claire.'

Even in his embrace, my body's tense and I can't relax. But I know he's right. All the doors were locked. There's no sign of a break-in. No one's in the house.

'Are you having the dreams again?'

He can read me so easily.

I look up at him and nod, ashamed. I feel like a disturbed child with a calming parent. Our relationship shouldn't be like this.

'They just mean you're stressed,' he says.

Matt means to reassure me, but I can still feel the adrenalin flooding through me. I know I'm stressed. I thought I'd left my fears behind in London, but I haven't. Out here there's even more to deal with. The never-ending dusty clutter that fills the house, my interfering mother-in-law, Matt spending so much time at work. With Sarah.

The thoughts ricochet around my head. But to say them out loud would be ungrateful. I was the one who insisted we move. I was the one that wanted all this.

Matt's arms around me should comfort me, but something still doesn't feel right. I wish I could calm down, but I can't seem to relax.

I pull away from Matt's embrace. I should be grateful that he loves me, both at my best and at my worst. Even when I messed up, he was there to help me pick up the pieces. I know I can rely on him.

Matt goes to the kitchen sink and pours two glasses of water. He hands one to me and I take a sip.

'I think you should go to see a doctor again,' he says.

I don't want to see a doctor. I don't want to have to explain how I feel. I don't want to admit that I'm falling apart.

'It was only a dream, Matt. Let's go back to bed.'

'Claire, please. Just think about it. I'm sure a professional could help.'

'All right, I'll think about it.'

I follow him out of the kitchen and up the stairs, checking the back door and then the front door as I pass. They're still locked.

As we go back into the bedroom, Olivia's screams pierce the night.

Matt looks over at me and sighs. 'She's awake now,' he says accusingly.

'Don't worry. I'll go.'

'Thanks. I need to get some sleep so I'm OK for work tomorrow.' He settles himself into bed under the covers, puts in his earplugs and turns away from me. I sigh as I hear his breathing deepen.

I go into Olivia's room. Her face is wet with tears and I lift her out of the cot and hold her close to my chest. She squirms in my arms and I sit down with her in the rocking chair. I hum a lullaby, to calm myself as much as Olivia. I do the only thing that will quieten her and put her on my breast. She struggles against me before she latches and then settles.

I move back and forth in the rocking chair, but the positioning of the wooden armrests makes it difficult to get comfortable while holding Olivia. My arms start to ache and I keep humming. The tune helps me ground myself, place myself in the real world. Escape the dream. That's all it was, I tell myself. A dream.

But in the deathly silence of the night, reality and dreams seem to merge. It's hard to know what's real. Olivia's nightlight chases away the shadows and I'm grateful. There's no one here but me and Olivia. I checked the whole house. No intruder.

But still I feel the goosebumps on my arms, the sense that something's not quite right. It must be all in my head. I need a proper night's sleep. Then things would be clearer.

Olivia eyes eventually fall shut. I lay her back down gently in her cot, next to her toy bunny.

When I get into bed, Matt's snoring softly. I stare at the ceiling. The adrenalin hasn't left my body and my heart's still racing. I try to relax, but I can't. Something's still bothering me. Then I realise.

The nightlight in Olivia's bedroom. I always switch it off once she's asleep. But when I went into her room the nightlight was on.

I wasn't imagining things.

Someone was in our home.

*

When I wake up in the morning I'm overcome by a sense of dread. It's my birthday, and I feel sick with uncertainty. I like days that are mundane and predictable. Days when I know what my husband is likely to do, how he's likely to respond. But my birthday is not one of those days. I have no idea how he'll behave.

It's still early and the rest of the house is sleeping. I creep out of the bedroom and into the bathroom. I should wash before my daughter wakes and the day bursts into action, but I don't want the sound of the shower to wake my husband. Instead I think about what I might wear. I flick through my clothes in the wardrobe in the spare bedroom, considering them in turn. They are from another life. Designer dresses from when my husband used to take me out for meals, smart suits for work.

I don't know if I should make an effort to look nice today. I'm only going to be in the house with my daughter, just like any other day. But I can imagine my husband berating me if I choose casual clothes. And I can also imagine him getting angry if I do dress up, repeating his accusation of an affair. I don't know which is the greater risk.

I go to the curtains and peer out. The sun beams through the window. The car isn't there today. At least I have that to be grateful for. Who is it that's watching me and what do they want?

I wish I could go out today. Just for once. I imagine myself in a floaty summer dress, the sun's rays warming my skin, my arms slowly browning. Perhaps I will take my daughter into the garden later, staying close to the house to avoid the prying eyes of the neighbours.

I go back to the wardrobe and pick out a dress. It's light and airy and not too showy. I'll have to wear a cardigan over it when I go in the garden, just in case the neighbours spot the blue-green bruise that covers my entire upper arm.

Later, when my husband is at work, the post comes, letters landing with a thud on the mat. But there aren't any cards, only bank statements. I let myself cry, just a little bit, remembering how alone I am. I cut myself off completely from family when I met my husband. My father was abusive and my husband whisked me away from him, rescuing me. My saviour. Without my husband, I'm not sure I'd have ever escaped. But it wasn't long before I found out that he was no different from my father.

I'm anxious about my husband's return home, not sure whether he has any plans for my birthday. But an hour earlier than usual, I hear his key in the lock. My body tenses at the sound and I rush downstairs.

'For you.' He presents flowers and chocolates and kisses me on the lips.

'Thanks,' I splutter, surprised. 'But you don't like chocolates.' I'm confused.

'But you do,' he says. 'They're all for you. A special treat.'

'Oh,' I say. I feel the tears forming at the corners of my eyes. I'm so relieved he's being nice to me.

'Are you going to go and get ready then?'

'Get ready?' I feel a ball of anxiety knotting in my stomach. Is he taking me out? The thought makes me queasy. It's been so long since I was out in the world that the idea of crowds of people talking and laughing seems oppressive and frightening.

'Yes, put your nicest clothes on.'

I go upstairs and dress with trepidation. Designer dress. The diamond teardrop earrings he bought me for our fifth wedding anniversary and the matching necklace. Make-up, layers of it, until my bruises are covered and I look human again. But I feel afraid. I really don't want to leave the house.

When I go downstairs, my husband offers me a glass of red wine and I take it, my hands shaking. He has put our daughter to bed. Everything is so out of the ordinary that I'm terrified about what will happen next. We are off script, in an unknown land.

I hear noises from the kitchen, pots and pans banging.

My husband smiles at me. 'That's the chef,' he says. 'I've hired a professional chef to cook for us.'

I smile, glad we are staying in, and even gladder that a third person is here as a witness. My husband always behaves impeccably in front of other people.

The dinner is delicious and at some point I relax and we laugh and joke together. It's like old times. I force down a feeling of sadness that this situation is so rare, that our relationship isn't always like this. I focus on the moment, focus on enjoying myself.

After dinner, he takes me in his arms and kisses me, his tongue delving into my mouth, his hands casting over my body roughly.

Upstairs, he throws me onto the bed. I feel a flush of fear and arousal as pushes my skirt up and then unbuckles his belt.

'Happy birthday,' he says.

After it's over, I listen as he goes to the bathroom, brushes his teeth and goes downstairs.

I wrap the duvet around myself, still dressed apart from my knickers.

I feel the wet tears on my face, the flood of despair. I don't know why I'm crying. He still wants me. He still loves me. Doesn't he?

Hugging the pillow to me, I let my tears spread across it.

I don't know why I feel like this. He's been kind to me today. I should be grateful. Shouldn't I?

CHAPTER 12

When I wake up, Matt isn't in bed. I roll over groggily and check my phone. It's already 7 a.m. Confused, I go into Olivia's room and see Matt sitting with her, cooing at her. She smiles up at him and I feel a tinge of jealousy.

'How are you feeling?' Matt asks.

I've been tossing and turning all night, totally convinced someone had been in the house. But now it seems so unlikely. It could only have been me that left Olivia's nightlight on.

'Bit tired,' I reply. 'Thanks for letting me sleep in.'

'I think you needed it.'

'Yeah, I think I did.'

'Are you going to go to the doctor today?'

'I'm not sure I need to. I was just being paranoid last night.'

He looks at me intently. 'But there's more going on than that, isn't there? You haven't been yourself since Olivia was born.'

'I suppose not.' He's right. Something's wrong with me. I'm so forgetful, so paranoid.

'Will you ring the doctor?'

I agree and Matt stands over me when the phone lines open at eight. I'm pleased to get an appointment for the morning, as I've arranged to see Emma in the afternoon.

Matt strokes my back. 'It will be OK,' he says. 'Just tell them the truth.'

'I'm not sure how to.'

'Is it that bad?' he asks, concerned. 'I'm worried about you, Claire. It reminds me of last time you were ill.'

I'm worried too. I don't want to ever get to the state I was in last time, when it seemed like there was no way out.

'It's different this time,' I say. 'I'm not as bad.' I sigh. I wonder if I can confide in him.

He's looking at me so intently. 'What is it then?'

I take a deep breath. 'It's Olivia. I feel like I haven't bonded with her. That I don't love her the way I should.'

The words sound even worse out loud. They are words that no mother should ever say. I notice Olivia watching me and I turn away from them both, ashamed.

Matt wraps his arms around me and hugs me tight. 'It will be OK, Claire. You're a good mother. Just talk it through with the doctor. I'm sure they'll be able to help.'

Two hours later, I sit on a sofa at the GP's surgery, which operates from a converted house on the edge of the village. My hands shake as I thumb through an old copy of a celebrity magazine looking at wedding pictures of a minor royal I've never heard of. I don't know what I'm going to say when I go through the door and see the doctor. I look at Olivia, smiling up at me from her buggy, and feel the familiar guilt rising inside me. She deserves so much more.

I worry that the doctor will see my history of depression in my notes and judge me when I tell them how down I feel. What if they think I'm an unfit mother and take my daughter away from me?

I had wanted Olivia so much, but I didn't let myself get excited the way I did the first time I got pregnant. We'd been so organised back then. We named the baby Martha Rose as soon as we found out she was a girl and bought drawers of baby clothes. I imagined bringing her home from the hospital in the blue and white striped dress that was neatly folded in the drawer waiting for her arrival.

When we finally got pregnant again, two years after my miscarriage, I refused to name the baby until she was born – a living, breathing being. When I went past twenty weeks I started making promises to my unborn baby, as she kicked me from the inside and sat on my bladder. I would be the best mother. I would love her no matter what. I would never get angry or raise my voice. All the baby had to do was come out alive and I'd be forever grateful.

I had broken all of my promises in the first two months.

The buzzer rings insistently and it's my turn. I swallow back tears as I push the buggy into the consultation room.

The doctor smiles at me. 'She's very happy,' she says, looking at Olivia.

My heart sinks. How can I possibly explain how I feel towards her?

'What can I do for you?' the doctor asks as I take a seat.

'I... I...' I start to speak but the words won't form. And then I'm sobbing. 'I've been feeling a bit down,' I mumble.

She leans closer. 'How long have you been feeling like this?'

'Since she was born.'

'OK,' she says. 'I'm just going to run through a few questions with you about how you're feeling and then we'll decide on the best course of action.'

I swallow back tears as I answer her checklist of questions about my mood, anxiety and sleep.

'Sometimes I look at her and I don't feel anything at all,' I whisper, overwhelmed by guilt. 'And other times I wonder if I hate her.'

The doctor scribbles in her pad. I wonder if she'll ask for more detail. I think of all the other things that are going on: the feeling that someone's watching me, the forgetfulness, the dream last night.

I see her looking at my notes on her computer and I hold my breath. I don't know if she'll see the record of what I tried to do to myself three years ago. I don't know if she knows.

She turns to me and smiles. I smile back, relieved. She can't have seen anything in my notes.

'It sounds like you've got postnatal depression,' she explains. 'It's very common.'

'OK,' I say. The word depression echoes in my brain. I don't want it to get worse. I don't want to feel the way I did last time, like there was no way out.

'I'll refer you for cognitive behaviour therapy,' she says. 'That will help you change your patterns of thinking and control how you feel.'

'How long's the wait?'

'I can't say at the moment, but usually it's not too long. Around two to three months.'

Tears start to well up. I need help now, not in three months.

She stops typing into her computer and turns to me.

'In the meantime, you need to start looking after yourself. Do you have family to support you?'

'Yes,' I say. 'My husband's parents live nearby.'

I see her eyebrows raise and she takes a second look at her computer screen. My surname will have told her just whose daughter-in-law I am. She probably knows Ruth. Everyone does. There's nowhere to hide in this village.

'OK,' she says, as she searches around in her desk drawer and pulls out two leaflets. 'Don't be afraid to ask for help from friends and family. And it's important to eat well and exercise.' She hands me the first leaflet, with a picture of a smiling woman jogging through a park on the front.

'Thanks,' I reply, feeling crushed. Exercise isn't going to be enough. It took so much effort to tell her how I felt, but I won't get professional help for ages. I'll have to struggle on with Olivia, on my own.

'In the meantime, here are the numbers for some mental health helplines. Just in case you need them.'

I take the leaflet from her but I know I'll throw it straight in the bin. I don't want to ring a helpline. I just can't. I swallow back tears as I wheel the buggy out of the room. Three months sounds like a lifetime to wait. I don't know how I'm going to get through each day.

When I arrive at Emma's flat later that day, I'm still shaken by the appointment. I settle down on the sofa with Olivia, while Emma makes tea and Lizzie wriggles on her playmat. I look around the neat and tidy living room and feel a twinge of jealousy. There's never any clutter at Emma's flat. No baby things lying around on the floor. No boxes. Just clean, neat lines, white walls and tasteful framed prints.

Emma brings me my tea and I let it warm my hands before I take a sip.

'I'm looking forward to this,' she says brightly.

I nod. Today Emma's helping me with an annual ritual: preparing gift packs for the local children's home. It's something my mother and I used to do together every year. I've continued the tradition since she died. But this year I nearly didn't bother. The date crept up on me unexpectedly and I hadn't done any preparations, and I didn't have any connections with the children's homes local to here.

When I mentioned it to Emma, she wouldn't let me just give up. She rang round children's homes, found one that was nearby and willing to accept the gifts, and then took me shopping for the small toys and toiletries we needed for the bags. Today we're wrapping the toys and baking fairy cakes to add to the packs.

We start with the baking, placing Olivia and Lizzie on a rug on the floor so they can watch us. Olivia's eyes follow my every move intently, while Lizzie stares at the ceiling light, fascinated. As I mix the ingredients together with my hands, I think about all the years that have passed since my mother died. For a long time afterwards Miriam would help me put the gift packs together and then we'd reminisce about my mother over a drink at the local pub, where Mum and I used to celebrate her birthday each year. For the last few years I've prepared the gift packs alone. It feels better with Emma by my side today.

'Are you all right?' Emma asks. 'You've been a bit quiet.'

'I'm OK,' I say. It's an obvious lie. A tsunami of emotion rises up inside me. Tears well up as I think of my mother and the doctor's appointment earlier.

'What's wrong?' Emma asks, putting her arm around me. I let the wooden spoon fall with a clatter into the mixing bowl.

'I went to the doctor this morning. She diagnosed me with postnatal depression.'

'I'm so sorry, Claire. That must be awful.'

'It… I'm just finding it hard,' I say. 'I wish I was like you.'

'What do you mean?'

'You and Lizzie. It seems to come so naturally. Being a mother is such a struggle for me.'

Emma puts her hand gently on my shoulder, and I shudder with sobs. 'It's OK,' she says, comforting me as I wipe away my tears with the back of my hand.

'Sometimes I don't think I even love her. I… I don't have it in me.'

I glance up at Emma, waiting for her to judge me.

But she says nothing and just holds me, letting me cry on her shoulders. 'You know you can talk to me anytime?'

I nod.

'We should arrange something to cheer you up,' Emma says. 'There's a new boutique wine shop opened in Oxford. We could try the wine tasting there one day.'

'Maybe,' I say, noncommittally. When I'm feeling down, alcohol is the thing I want most in the world, but what I need least. If I start drinking when I feel like this, I'm not sure if I'll be able to stop.

'You need a night out.' Emma smiles.

I imagine myself in a club, dancing and carefree. It seems like a distant dream. I'll never have that life again.

'I can't,' I say. 'Matt works all hours and I'd never get a babysitter. Besides, Matt and I never go out together any more ourselves. He spends more time with Sarah than with me.'

'His ex?'

'They work late together a lot. They're very close.' I remember the text Sarah sent Matt late at night the other day.

'I could babysit,' Emma says. 'Give you two the chance to reconnect.'

'Thanks,' I say, feeling grateful. 'We need that.'

I hope a night out together will be enough. But in my heart I know our relationship needs a lot more work. We moved out here to bring us closer together, but each day the distance between us seems to grow. I'm terrified that one day the gap will be too big to ever bridge again.

CHAPTER 13

My eyes flick open and I look at my phone: 6.30 a.m. I lie still and listen to the sounds of the house creaking. I can't hear any noise from Olivia's room. She's normally awake by this time. I roll over and try and get comfortable under the duvet. I'm exhausted. I turn the pillow over and rest my cheek against the cold cotton. I can feel the minutes ticking away until Olivia wakes up. But I can't get back to sleep. My body clock has been reset by my daughter.

Matt murmurs in his sleep, and I watch as he slowly wakes. He sees me and rolls towards me, his arm wrapping around me and cupping my breast. I sigh. Last night we finally had the time to talk properly. As well as opening up about my postnatal depression diagnosis, we talked about getting the intimacy back in our relationship. It's something we both want.

But not right now. Right now I just want to sleep. I roll away from Matt. If I can get just half an hour's rest, then I'll feel so much better.

Matt ignores my signals, snuggling close to me, his fingers stroking the nape of my neck. I feel my body awakening, but I don't want it to. I want to drift back into the soft cocoon of sleep.

'Not now, Matt,' I murmur.

He moves away from me, turns the other way and I hear his grumble of frustration.

'I thought this was what you wanted,' he whispers.

'It is, just not now.'

'Then when?'

'Later,' I mumble, trying to switch my brain back off, to let myself drift away.

Then Olivia groans and every muscle in my body tenses.

Stay asleep. Please stay asleep.

Another groan. Followed by a full-blown scream.

I put the pillow over my head.

At least it's Saturday. Matt can do some of the childcare.

'Can you pick her up?' I ask.

He moves closer to me again, his arm encircling my body, wanting me to respond.

'I can't do it while she's screaming,' I mumble.

'She'll calm down.'

'Can you pick her up, Matt?'

I feel the bed shift and hear his footsteps on the carpet as he heads into Olivia's room.

He picks her up without speaking and brings her back into the bedroom.

I reach for her drowsily, placing her on my breast.

Matt slips back into bed beside me.

'What shall we do today?' I ask. It's the first day we've had together as a family in such a long time. I wonder if Matt will help me catch up on the housework. Maybe we could do a bit more of the unpacking and then go out for lunch. It would be nice to get out of the house.

'Mum wants us to go to the Winter Fair with her.'

I turn my head towards him. 'You did say no, didn't you?'

He sighs. 'It will be nice, Claire. She only wants to get to know you a bit better.'

'But I haven't seen you all week.' Even as I hear myself speak I know it sounds selfish. But I had hoped Matt and I could talk some more today. About his past. About Sarah. About our relationship. All the unanswered questions that keep me up at night. We can't do that with Ruth there.

'Try and be nice to her,' Matt says. He leans over and kisses my cheek, before getting out of bed and going to the bathroom.

As I hear him turn on the shower, I lie as still as I can. With my eyes closed, I listen to the rush of the water, as Olivia feeds from me vigorously.

This is my life. A wonderful husband. A beautiful baby daughter. A cottage in the country. I should be happy. What's wrong with me?

The fair is at the garden centre where Sarah and I had lunch the other day. Ruth insists Matt drives and Jack sits in the front while Ruth and I squeeze into the back next to Olivia's car seat. Throughout the journey, Ruth chats to Olivia as if she's an adult, telling her all about the other women at the tennis club; who's having an affair, who's had a breakdown. Matt stares straight ahead at the road, oblivious.

The garden centre café is covered in garish multicoloured lights and as we approach, a man in a high-vis jacket directs us towards parking in a field. In the time it takes to park and get Olivia and the buggy from the car, we could have easily walked. I pull my hood up over my head against the wind and walk through the muddy field a little ahead of Matt, Ruth and Jack, enjoying imagining, just for a moment, that I am completely alone.

Inside the entrance, curry and pizza food stalls sit uncomfortably beside the local craft displays where men and women in eighteenth-century clothing demonstrate everything from blacksmithing to basket making.

I watch as a man puts an iron rod in a fire to heat it and then attacks it with a hammer to bend it into shape. I'm glad Olivia is safe in the buggy, unable to reach out and burn herself. I don't know how parents with older children cope. They must have to be constantly vigilant to keep their children from harm.

Jack wanders off to look at the farmers' market and Ruth falls into step beside me. 'We haven't seen much of you lately,' she says. 'It's good we're getting some time together today. It's nice to have you so close.'

I look at her, surprised.

'It's what I wanted,' I say. 'Family nearby.' I leave the rest of my thoughts unsaid. That it hasn't worked out as planned. That I regret moving.

'I saw my mother's walkers by the pond the other day.'

I look at her guiltily. The mobility aids had sat by the pond for five days in full view of Ruth's house, before Matt had taken them away.

'I just wanted them out of the house. They were getting in the way.'

'I'm sure they were.' She laughs. 'I bet you were tempted to throw them into the pond. They'd disappear then. It's very deep.'

'No, of course not,' I say. But she's reminded me of another thing I need to worry about, another hazard for Olivia. 'We'll need to drain the pond,' I continue, 'if Olivia's going to play outside in the summer.'

'Yes. It's very dangerous otherwise. Jack and I can help you dig it out. And I must clear out the house soon,' she says, unprompted. 'I just want to do it properly. Make sure I'm not throwing away anything sentimental.'

'Thank you,' I say, swallowing my guilt about the things I took to the charity shop the other day.

I smile at Matt as he catches us up. 'Your mother's going to help us drain the pond. And start clearing out the house.'

'That's great,' he says. 'Have you seen what's over there?'

He points to a fairground ride, rows of chairs hanging from the rotating top of the carousel. Loud nineties music bursts out from its speakers, asserting its presence. They've put it at the edge of the field, far away from the farmers' market stalls selling expensive cheeses, artisan bread and sausages. It's the kind of ride where you feel like you're flying. I remember going on something similar when I was a teenager, the sense of being on top of the world, adrenalin coursing through me, butterflies in my stomach. This one's probably older than me. It's rickety and doesn't seem to be attracting many customers. A man sits smoking next to the booth which announces it's £3 a ride.

Matt turns to me and grins. 'Do you want a go?' he asks. For a moment, I want to say yes. I want to be free again, childlike, just focusing on the sensation of the wind through my hair, my feet dangling below me. I look down at the buggy.

'No,' I say. 'I can look after Olivia.'

And he's off without a backward glance, over to the ride. His boyish impulsivity was something I fell in love with. I smile. I'm glad he's enjoying himself for once. He's seemed so down lately, worrying about the practice.

Ruth turns to me and laughs. 'He never changes.'

I watch as he hands over his money to the operative.

'One of us will always have to look after Olivia,' I say. 'It will be a long time before we do that kind of thing together.'

'Oh. Did you want a go too?' Ruth says. 'I can stay with the buggy.'

That's not what I'd meant, not really, but I grab my chance at freedom.

'Are you sure?' I reply. 'Thanks.'

I run after Matt, paying my money and pushing myself up into the swing beside him.

'You're joining me?' he asks with a grin.

'Yep,' I say, laughing and looking around. As an adult I notice things I'd have never paid attention to as a teenager. The rusty cogs in the rotating wheel on top of the ride, the way the swings sway in the slightest wind, the fact that the guy who comes to lower the bars across us is no more than eighteen. My heart thumps loudly in my chest.

The ride starts to turn, slowly at first and then faster. I try not to think about the fact that it has only been assembled today. I look back towards the ground, seeking out Ruth and Olivia. I can't see them at first. The chairs gather speed and it's hard to pick them out in the blur.

We start to rise high in the sky as the ride goes faster and faster. I feel the breeze in my hair. Matt laughs. I spot Ruth's purple coat in the crowd. But I can't see Olivia, my eyes searching desperately for her. Then I see something. A pram zigzagging across the field, away from me and into the distance. A grey and blue pram. *My pram*. Being wheeled away by a woman in a long, dark coat.

I feel sick as the ride spins and I try to turn my head to follow the pram.

'Olivia!' I scream. 'Olivia!'

But no one can hear me. The wind is too loud. Beside me, Matt hasn't turned his head.

'Matt!' I crane my neck, but the g-force works against me and it's a struggle to keep looking at him. 'Matt!' I wave my arm, reaching out to hit him, gripping the metal chain with my other hand.

I make contact with his elbow and he turns.

'What?' I see him mouth the words, but I can't hear the sound.

We're going even faster now, the wind blowing into us. As I turn to Matt, my swing loses its straight trajectory and veers from side to side.

'Olivia!' I shout.

I try to point, but we're moving so fast that I can't identify the woman with the pram any more. She's merged into the blur of the crowd.

'Olivia?' Matt mouths.

'We need to stop the ride!'

'What?'

But there's no button to press. Nothing I can do. My heart beats faster and faster.

Right at this moment, my daughter is being taken away from me. Right now. I'm blinded by panic.

'Stop the ride!' I shout.

No response. No one can hear me.

'Stop the ride!'

It's slowing of its own accord now, the beat of the music slowing with it, and I can see Ruth in the crowd again, looking at her phone, oblivious to the absence of the buggy beside her.

'What's wrong?' Matt shouts and now I can hear him.

'Olivia. I left her with your mum. But now the buggy's gone.'

The ride's still spinning, but I'm close enough to the ground to release the bar across my chair and jump down. I fall, banging my knee on the metal floor.

Matt jumps down beside me. I run, pushing aside spinning chairs. I get to the small gate and run down the steps, dizzy and unsure of my footing. I rush over to Ruth.

'Where's Olivia?' I ask, breathless.

She looks up from her phone. 'Good ride?'

'Where's Olivia, Mum?' Matt says, catching up.

'Oh, Sarah took her. She needed a nappy change.'

I burst into tears. She's safe.

'Mum,' Matt says. 'You need to tell us before you hand her over to someone else. Claire was worried.'

'I could hardly tell you, could I?' Ruth looks perplexed, her eyes flicking back to her phone. 'You were on the ride.'

'She's OK then?' I ask, struggling to get the words out through the wall of relief.

'Of course she's OK.'

I see Sarah coming towards us with the buggy. I break into a run towards my baby.

Sarah's smile turns into a frown when she sees my face.

'What's wrong?'

But I already have my arms in the buggy, desperately undoing the buckle and pulling my daughter out into my arms.

'Olivia,' I whisper into her hair. 'Olivia.'

*

I never thought I'd ring a helpline, but I don't know what else to do. My birthday was a one-off event, a taste of how family life could be if things were different.

Now everything's returned to normal. I'm trapped inside the four walls of this house, trying to entertain my daughter all day, every day. Trying to convince myself I'm OK. I know I shouldn't feel this way. I'm lucky. I have a successful husband, a big house, a beautiful daughter.

A leaflet for a helpline for mothers dropped through my door a few days ago. Since then I've been reading and rereading it, turning it over in my hands until the edges are worn. I just want someone to talk to.

My daughter is asleep upstairs. This is my chance. I type the number into my phone and then stare at the digits.

I swallow and then, without letting myself think, I click the call button.

The phone rings and rings before it connects.

'Hello?' The voice on the other end sounds harassed, as if I might have interrupted something.

'Hi,' I say. 'Umm… have I got the right number? Is this the helpline for mothers?'

'Yes,' she says, her voice softer now. 'How can I help you?'

'I don't know really.' I laugh. 'I'm not the kind of person who rings helplines. I normally have it all together…' This whole thing's a mistake. I shouldn't have rung. I consider hanging up, but something makes me hold on.

'What kind of person rings helplines?'

'I don't know. Lonely people.'

'Are you lonely?'

I swallow. 'Perhaps a bit. I don't go out that much.'

I run my hands over the bruises on my arms, pressing each in turn and flinching at the pain.

'You don't go out?'

'No, I… I don't like to.'

'Why not?'

Can I tell her? I'd be too ashamed to tell a friend. And besides, I have no friends to tell any more.

'I have a lot of bruises. And I don't like to go out in public.'

It sounds so pathetic, so impossibly vain.

'How did you get the bruises?'

'My husband… he has a difficult job. He gets stressed…'

'Are you saying he hits you?'

I feel uncertain now, as if I might be making a huge mistake, to reveal the part of our marriage that's just between me and my husband. The part I'm ashamed of. But I desperately need to talk to someone.

'Is this conversation confidential?' I ask.

'Of course.'

'Yes, he hits me.' I say it so quietly I think she might not hear. But she does. 'I'm so sorry,' she says.

My stomach knots and I instantly regret saying anything. I'm not a victim. I don't need her pity. Calling the helpline was a mistake. I need to get off the phone before I tell her anything else.

'Gosh,' I say, trying to smile, so my voice sounds more upbeat. 'I didn't realise the time. I really have to go. My daughter will be waking up from her nap.'

'Sure,' the woman says, but I don't think she really believes me.

'I never got to ask your advice on activities to do with my daughter in the house,' I say, trying to convince her that I called for a practical reason. But my voice cracks as I speak. We both know that's not what I really called about.

'Well, you can call back anytime. We're open twenty-four hours a day. Seven days a week.'

CHAPTER 14

When Emma arrives at our door, I wrap my arms around her in a bear hug. I'm so grateful she's offered to babysit.

She steps over the threshold into our house and I take her coat and hang it on the rack.

'I know I'm a bit early,' Emma says, 'but I didn't know what to do with myself at home without Lizzie. Dan's looking after her. So I thought I'd come and help you get ready.'

I take her through to the living room where Olivia lies on her playmat. She starts to whine and Emma leans over her. 'Hello, Olivia,' she says. 'Hello, hello, hello.' She tickles her feet and Olivia manages a smile.

I escape to the kitchen to make tea, snatching a precious break away from my daughter. When I take Emma her tea, she holds out a wrapped gift towards me. 'I have a present for you,' she announces, smiling.

'Oh,' I say, embarrassed. 'There's really no need.' She's the one doing us the favour.

'Well, it's really more for Olivia than you. I couldn't resist spoiling her.' Emma watches intently as I tear open the wrapping paper.

Inside is a picture. It's a drawing of children playing on a bridge over a river, dropping sticks into the water.

'I found it in a charity shop,' she says.

'Oh.' Just like that I'm back in my nightmare from the other night. The river. Matt holding Olivia below the surface of the water. I feel the fear rise up inside me and try to swallow it back down. It was only a dream.

Emma sees my expression.

'Don't you like it?' she asks, her voice filled with concern.

'I do. It was just unexpected. Thank you.' I give her a hug and hold her for a couple of seconds, allowing myself a moment to calm my nerves.

'Let's go and hang it up,' she says. 'It'll cover the wallpaper I know you hate. Make Olivia's room into a proper nursery.'

'Don't worry, I can do it later.'

'No, let's do it now. We'll never get round to it otherwise.'

At her insistence, we go upstairs and I try to push the memory of the dream out of my mind.

In Olivia's room there's a hook above the cot. Emma hangs the picture, while Olivia wriggles in my arms. Emma stands back to appreciate it.

'There!' she says. 'It really works in the space.'

I stare at it.

I hate it. I want to tear it straight down.

Tears start to well up as we leave the room.

I can take it down later, I tell myself. I can't say anything to Emma now. I can't be ungrateful.

Emma is already onto the next thing. 'What are you going to wear?' she asks.

'I don't know.' I haven't had time to think about it. Olivia has been restless all day and I've been counting down the hours until tonight.

'Let me help you,' Emma says.

She heads towards our bedroom and for a moment I hesitate. I don't want her in my personal space. I haven't cleared away the nappy bags from earlier and the washing basket is overflowing.

I follow her with Olivia. I'm being silly. Emma knows me. She's my friend and she has her own baby. She won't care if the bedroom is messy. She knows what it's like trying to keep on top of everything.

I strap Olivia in her chair in the bedroom, but she immediately starts crying. I draw the curtains and sit on top of the tangle of duvet on the unmade bed to breastfeed her. Emma steps over Olivia's rattle on the floor and goes over to the temporary fabric cupboard that's sagging under the weight of our clothes. She thumbs through my dresses.

'This one's nice,' she says, holding up a blue and white striped dress that I last wore to a spring wedding five years ago.

'Definitely doesn't fit,' I say. I've kept it in the cupboard hopefully, thinking that one day maybe I'd squeeze back into it. I indicate my stomach. 'I guess it takes a while to shift the baby weight.' I say it lightly, but I feel horribly self-conscious. I've been meaning to do some more exercise, like the doctor suggested.

Emma holds it up in front of the mirror. Even in her jeans and fitted T-shirt, she's beautiful. I can't help comparing her body to mine. Her flat stomach doesn't overhang her jeans and her breasts are pert and small. I try to control my jealousy. If you saw Emma in the street you'd find it hard to believe she'd recently had a baby.

'Can I try it on?' Emma asks.

'Oh yeah. Sure.' I feel a stab of annoyance. I know Emma will look better in the dress than I ever looked in it, even when I was much thinner.

Emma wriggles out of her jeans. I can see the scar of a caesarean etched across her belly.

Not so perfect after all.

I immediately feel guilty.

Emma pulls her top over her head and slips the dress on. It fits perfectly, clinging in all the right places. Her straight blonde hair hangs neatly down the back.

Self-consciously, I run my fingers through my own messy hair. I want to straighten it before I go out.

I notice Emma's perfectly manicured nails. 'How do you look after Lizzie without breaking a nail?' I ask.

Emma laughs as she twirls round in front of the mirror, looking at her reflection over her shoulder. 'Practice,' she says.

'You make childcare look easy.'

'Thanks,' she replies with a smile.

I take Olivia off my breast and she whines. Emma picks her up and spins her around, the skirt of my dress swirling with her.

I go over to the cupboard and pick out a blue-grey pinafore. It isn't as sexy as the other dress, but it's flattering. I've worn it since I've given birth and it disguises my stomach.

I pull it over my head and look in the mirror. I must be nearly twice the size of Emma.

'You look awesome,' Emma says, and I try and smile. 'Matt's going to be blown away. Now let's do your hair and make-up.'

Emma puts Olivia back in the baby seat. Then she starts straightening my unruly hair while I apply my mascara. It feels nice to be pampered for once.

When we hear Matt's key in the lock, we're concentrating so hard that we both jump and the mascara wand jabs my eye.

'Ow!' My eyes start to water and I blink rapidly.

'Don't worry, I'll redo it,' Emma says. 'There's plenty of time.'

Matt comes into the bedroom and puts down his rucksack. He nods at Emma.

'Hi,' he says. 'I'm Matt.'

'Emma,' she replies, holding out her hand with a smile.

'That's Claire's dress,' he says. His eyes dart over Emma's body before he corrects himself and looks at her face.

He turns to me briefly. 'You look beautiful,' he says, as if he hasn't noticed the mascara down my face.

'Thanks,' I reply, feeling invisible as his eyes return to Emma.

*

Forty-five minutes later, Matt and I wander up Oxford high street, navigating the pavement easily without a buggy to manoeuvre. I feel so free. Matt puts his hand gently on the small of my back and I feel a tug of affection for him. We haven't had an evening out since we moved and I want to make the most of it.

We find the small Italian restaurant that Ruth recommended. It has a handful of intimate, candlelit tables. I look at Matt. We desperately need these moments together.

The waiter pulls out a chair for me and I sit, tugging the skirt of my dress down. The extra weight on my stomach has made it ride up, but Matt doesn't seem to notice. He's already studying the set menu intently.

I'm handed the wine list by the waiter and I scan it quickly. Would it really hurt to have a drink tonight? Just the one. To celebrate our time together.

'We could get a bottle,' I whisper to Matt, as if it's the naughtiest thing in the world.

Matt shakes his head.

'You know that's a bad idea, Claire.'

My heart sinks. Matt's never liked me drinking. He prefers a life of colas at pubs, water at weddings. He thinks the alcohol makes me out of control. But I'm not like that any more. And sometimes, I just want a drink. I need to unwind after the stress of the day. But it's not worth an argument, so I drop it.

He reaches across the table for my hand. 'Let's just enjoy tonight,' he says. 'Enjoy being alive and having each other.'

The evening flies by in a haze of conversation. We've hardly spoken since Olivia was born. Not properly. We've talked about nappy changes and feeding schedules and what baby equipment we need to buy. We've discussed moving house and unpacking and fixing the toilet that isn't flushing properly. But we've hardly spoken about ourselves. Tonight is different. I feel connected again. Part of a partnership.

'Are you settling back into the village OK?' I ask, remembering Matt saying that it was difficult returning to his childhood home.

He smiles. 'I'm getting there,' he says. 'But I feel like an impostor sometimes. Like I'm just playing a role. Vet. Family man. People have known me too long here. I feel like they can see right through me.'

I nod. 'I feel like an impostor as a mother sometimes, too.'

'You're a good mum, Claire,' he says, reaching for my hand.

'It doesn't feel that way,' I reply, turning my face away from him to try and hide the tears that are forming.

'You have postnatal depression. It's an illness. It doesn't mean you're a bad mum. Is there anything I can do to help?' He reminds me of the old Matt now, the one who's kind and caring and looks out for me. Not the stressed man he's become since we moved.

'I need to see you more. Now Sarah's working for you, can you get away from the office earlier? Can you help more with Olivia?'

'I can try,' Matt says. 'But we really haven't got enough business yet, enough customers. We're haemorrhaging money.' He sweeps his curly, dark hair out of his eyes.

I feel guilty. It was me that was so set on moving out of London and starting afresh.

'We don't have to stay here, you know. We could move back.' I say the unthinkable. I know in my heart I can't return to London. I want to keep that part of my life in the past, put it behind me.

'No,' he says. 'We should try and make it work. I want the practice to be a viable business. I want us to have the family life we moved for.'

'Me too,' I say.

Our main course arrives, and Matt attacks his lamb steak with his knife.

'It will be much better once your mother's cleared out the house. And we've drained the pond.' Ruth and Jack are coming round to help us with the pond tomorrow.

'Yes, I'm glad you persuaded Mum to sort the house.'

I nod. I wish Matt was better at sticking up for himself with her, rather than leaving things to me.

We start to talk about the future and the mood lifts. Between us, we conjure up a different life. A life where Matt's surgery becomes profitable and he hires enough staff to work four days a week and spend more time with Olivia and me. A life filled with laughter, with lots of family time. In our fantasy I find freelance work as a journalist and diligently write articles after Olivia's gone to bed. Ruth clears the cottage and helps with babysitting and eventually we have enough money to put down a deposit on a house of our own.

'I think we can do this,' Matt says, smiling.

'Me too.' I'm relieved we're on the same page again, sharing our dreams and aspirations, imagining our lives together.

Matt leans across the table and takes my hand in his. I want to reach out and touch him properly. It feels like we've found each other again after being lost in the wilderness. We've been two individuals leading separate lives in the same house, with a screaming, unreasonable baby between us.

I want us to be a couple again.

The waitress brings the dessert and Matt moves his hand out of the way, so she can put the piece of chocolate cake in the middle of the table between us. I take the fork, cut off a corner and put it into Matt's waiting mouth. He laughs and crumbs sprinkle across the table. I laugh too.

Matt rubs his leg against mine under the table. I raise my eyebrows at him, and a slow smile plays out on his face.

'I want to take you home,' he whispers, his eyes playful.

'I want that too.' I feel a restless excitement as he squeezes my hand.

'Do you want to get a hotel room?' he asks.

'We can't afford it,' I reply. But I know that if we don't take this opportunity we'll never get another one. Olivia breastfeeds every two hours at night and the curtains in our bedroom don't quite close. I'm convinced my mother-in-law can see in.

Besides, I want Matt now. If we wait, go home, speak to Emma, settle Olivia, the moment will be lost.

A cheap hotel seems worth it to get our marriage on track. Space completely to ourselves, without having to worry that Olivia will wake up.

Matt settles the bill quickly, leaving a big tip.

He's grinning from ear to ear as we stroll down the high street hand in hand. I feel all the anticipation of a first date or a one-night stand. The world has a sense of unreality to it, an excitement. I feel so alive. I need Matt. Now.

Matt knows a B&B around the corner, and he takes my hand and leads me down the street. We walk quickly, half running, drunk with desire.

Suddenly I think of Olivia and I have to stop to check my phone. There are no messages from Emma. She must be fine.

As I put my phone away, Matt pushes me lightly into a doorway and puts his mouth over mine. His kiss is deep and eager, and I shiver with excitement. I feel young again as Matt presses his body into mine. It's been so long. Too long. Matt's weight pushes my body against the glass panel of the shop door and I worry the alarm will go off. I feel his hot breath on my neck as his hand moves down my dress and brushes my bare skin.

'I want you,' he whispers.

'Not here.' I'm breathless as his mouth moves lower, his kisses moving down my neck. I look over his head to the map on my phone.

'The B&B's only five minutes away,' I mumble into his hair.

I push him lightly and we move back into the street. A man glances sideways at us and I run my hand through my tangled hair and blush.

Matt reaches for my hand.

'I can see the B&B sign,' I say, and we speed towards it. The entrance is a small blue door, with a tiny sign on the doorbell. Matt prods the doorbell confidently. There's no speaker phone, and no immediate answer. Matt's mouth is back over mine, as we hear footsteps on the stairs.

The door swings open.

'Do you have a room for tonight?' Matt asks, breathless.

'A hundred and fifty,' the woman says, looking us up and down. It sounds too much and for a moment I question the whole idea.

'We'll take it,' Matt says.

'Follow me.'

The check-in is painfully slow and we listen to the details of the breakfast that costs an extra fifteen pounds and a description of the local area. Matt catches my eye and grins. Neither of us wants to admit we live locally.

Eventually we're left to our own devices. We follow the threadbare carpet, down an unlit corridor to room seven. I open the door with trepidation. The handle is sticky.

We turn on the light, but the bulb is so weak it does little more than cast shadows. I can just about make out the brown and green 1970s zig-zag pattern of the carpet. In this light it's impossible to tell whether the room has been cleaned. But right now, I couldn't care less.

Matt interrupts my thoughts, wrapping his arms around me and pushing me back onto the bed. I relax.

As Matt positions himself on top of me, I reach one last time into my handbag and check my phone. No calls from Emma. Olivia is fine.

Matt's body sinks into mine and I wrap my arms around him. We kiss and I roll him over so I'm on top of him. I'm eager to discover him again. Everything feels new and exciting, as if we've only just met.

I unbutton his shirt slowly, my fingers lingering on the small patch of hair on his chest. His torso lifts, muscles defined as he shrugs out of his shirt. He doesn't have time to go to the gym any more, but his body remains ripped from his physical work. I run my hands through his hair and then back down over his chest. He cups my breasts, then lifts my dress over my head.

I wish I'd dressed for sex, but I hadn't. When I got ready, I automatically put my dress on over my nursing bra. My breasts are trapped inside, but it's only a second before Matt releases them and my nipple is in his mouth. I pull away, the sensitivity too much.

He kisses my neck and I stretch myself out, welcoming his lips and his hands, as they delve lower. As I fiddle urgently with the buckle of his belt, I realise I've needed this. I wonder if this connection can fill the desperate emptiness inside me, if this is all it will take to fix me.

Matt sits up and pulls off his trousers and boxers. I pull down my off-white cotton knickers. I climb back on top of him and he's inside me in one swift motion.

I see the reflection of my phone flashing on the ceiling, but I ignore it. I'm lost in the moment, the feel of Matt inside me, my skin against his. At last. I savour it, closing my eyes and losing myself in his rhythm.

We've waited too long for this and when it comes it's fleeting, intense. My orgasm draws me in and then lets me loose. Too soon.

His quickly follows.

I allow myself a few minutes in his arms, our naked bodies sharing warmth. I want to linger here forever, but I picture Emma waiting for us patiently, sitting straight-backed on our sofa, and I pick up my phone to check the time.

There's a missed call from Emma. I remember the flash of the phone against the ceiling, my brain fuzzy with desire, my choice to ignore it.

Panic consumes me.

There's only one reason Emma would have called.

Olivia.

Sounds and images flash through my head. Olivia screaming. Olivia's limbs broken and bent. Olivia burned. Olivia drowned. The clunk of Olivia hitting her head as she falls out of her cot. The smell of bleach at the hospital. A tiny body surrounded by nurses.

I pull away from Matt's arm, a deadweight around me. I jab at the call button on my phone.

It rings. And rings.

Listening to it ringing, I collect my knickers, bra and dress from their scattered locations across the room. I imagine us racing to the hospital. I give Matt a hard push to get him out of the bed.

Voicemail.

I press the call button again, as I wriggle into my underwear.

'What's wrong?' Matt asks from the bed.

I shush him even though the only sound at the other end of the phone is the incessant ringing until it goes to voicemail once more.

Why isn't she answering? Maybe they aren't allowed phones in the hospital. Maybe Emma doesn't want to answer because she can't bear to tell me bad news, to tell me my daughter's dead.

Maybe I should be sitting down to make this call.

'Hello, Claire?'

She's picked up. I can't speak. I'm terrified of what she might say.

But the background is quiet. There are no hospital sounds. No sirens.

'Claire? Is everything all right?'

I force the words out. 'Where's Olivia?' I ask.

'She's upstairs,' Emma says, 'in her cot.'

The relief is so intense that I sink back onto the bed. I let out the breath I was holding.

'Oh,' I say. 'Oh.'

'How's your evening been?' she asks.

'Good,' I say, glancing at Matt, who is staring at me, bemused. 'It's been good.'

Matt starts stroking my arm and I push his hand away.

'Don't rush back,' Emma says. 'Everything's fine here.'

'You rang me?' I ask, my voice shaking. The adrenalin has not yet dissipated.

'Oh, yeah, I did. Just to tell you she went to bed OK and not to worry. Be out as long as you like.'

'I think we'll come back now,' I say. I can't lose the uneasy feeling, can't slow my heartbeat. I need to get back to my daughter.

'No rush.'

I hang up the phone and turn to Matt.

He wraps his arms around me, kisses my neck.

'Everything OK?'

'Yeah,' I say. But I can't get the images of Olivia in hospital out of my head.

'One more time?' he asks, his eyes lowering to my breasts.

'No, let's get back.'

'Come on, Claire. We've paid for the room.'

'I can't. I need to check on Olivia.'

'Seriously?' He thumps the pillow in frustration.

Somewhere down the corridor, I can hear the rhythmic creaking of bed springs. I dress and wash my hands.

Matt turns on the shower but I switch it off again, handing him his boxers.

He turns it back on.

'Claire. Just let me shower!'

I stand and watch him, tapping my foot impatiently as the soap suds cascade over his muscled chest.

There's the beep of a text message from the bedroom and I rush back in to check my phone.

But it's not mine. It's Matt's. Another text message from Sarah. His phone is locked so yet again I can't see what it says. I swallow, feeling slightly sick. Why is she texting him on Friday night?

Matt appears behind me, the threadbare towel wrapped around his waist and I quickly drop the phone back onto the bed.

'We need to get back,' I say. 'Hurry up and get dressed,' I hand him his clothes one item at a time, wishing he'd speed up.

I still can't lose the sense of panic I feel. The sense that something awful is about to happen to Olivia. That something's going to tear my family apart.

There's not enough time.

I have to get home.

I need to make sure my daughter is safe.

CHAPTER 15

My hands tingle in the bitterly cold air. The grass is hard with frost, but Ruth has arrived with Jack and Sarah in tow, determined to fulfil her promise to dig out our pond. In wellington boots, she issues instructions to Jack and Matt, telling them how to get leverage as they dig out underneath the frozen reeds. Emma is here too, pulling on gardening gloves, ready to help.

Sarah has the shears in her hands and is cutting back the plants that grow round the edges to make it easier for the others. She looks like an advert for the fresh country air, her auburn hair barely contained by a neat ponytail, her freckles still present even though the summer is long gone. She has a silk scarf wrapped tightly around her neck; yellow and orange and entirely inappropriate for outdoor work. I think of the text messages she's been sending Matt late at night and wonder what they're about. I bet Ruth would have preferred Matt to marry her. Homely, comforting and seemingly with no desire to move from the place where she grew up. She's the ideal match.

I park Olivia's buggy by the back door. She's wrapped up warm in her winter snow suit, hat and mittens. She stares out at the pond, fascinated by everything going on around her.

I can feel my wellington boots chafing the back of my ankles as I bend over my baby. Ruth has found them for me in the shed and they are slightly too small, digging into me.

'She's beautiful.' Sarah is beside me, cooing into the buggy.

'Thanks.'

Olivia manages a smile for her before she twists her head round, trying to get comfortable.

Sarah puts her hand on my arm. 'I'm so sorry about the fair,' she says. 'I didn't realise you'd notice Olivia was gone while you were on the ride. I thought I was being helpful, changing her nappy.'

What does she mean, she didn't think I'd notice? I wonder for a moment if she was testing me, seeing if I'd miss my own daughter. I dismiss the thought. It's just paranoia.

Instead I smile at her. 'It's OK,' I say. 'Next time, just ask me first.'

'Of course,' Sarah says. 'Honestly, I'm sorry.'

Ruth interrupts us with a shout. 'Bring Olivia over here.' She points to the path leading to the pond. 'She can watch the action.'

I hesitate for a second and then remind myself that I can't let my fear of water define my life. Olivia will be fine. She'll be right next to Ruth.

I wheel the buggy over, making sure it's not too close to the pond's edge. As I park it next to Ruth, in a shady spot on the concrete path, it feels like a relief to hand responsibility for Olivia over to someone else.

Ruth looks down at Olivia and waves at her, before turning back to issue instructions to Matt, who is now calf deep in the pond, tugging at the reeds. An image enters my head, uninvited. A tiny arm tangled in the reeds. I push the thought away.

'I expect we'll all want a cup of tea soon,' Ruth says to me and I gladly retreat to the kitchen, away from the pond. I'll be pleased when it's empty, and I no longer see the light reflecting on the water when I look out into the garden, taunting me.

I turn on the kettle and get out the mugs. For a moment I observe the scene outside. A harmonious family, working together. It feels good, like a warm embrace. Maybe I can learn to like Ruth, or if not, then at least understand her. They are the only family I have, after all, and I'm lucky to have them around. I watch

Ruth bend over the buggy to talk to Olivia. She clearly loves her granddaughter. I can't ask for more than that. I just wish I could love Olivia the same way.

Someone squeezes my shoulder and I jump.

'I didn't mean to scare you,' Emma says, joining me at the sink. 'I scraped my hand on a thorn. I just need to clean it up.'

'I'm sure there are some plasters somewhere.' I go to the cupboard that's still full of Matt's grandmother's medication and root around. There are some plasters at the back and I take one and hand it to Emma.

'Are you all right?' she asks.

'Just about coping,' I say, forcing a smile.

Her eyes crinkle in concern. 'You don't have to carry everything on your own, Claire. You can talk to me anytime.'

'Thanks, I know you're there for me. But I think I'm used to it now – I've felt this way since she was born.'

I remember when Olivia was first handed to me. I'd expected to feel the overwhelming love everyone had told me about, that I was looking forward to so much. But she was a bloodstained, scrunched-up bundle of flesh. She screamed and screamed, a high-pitched mewling, like a strangled cat. Skin to skin, that's what they'd said, and I held her close against me. Two bodies together. I waited to feel something, willing myself to feel anything. But my first feeling towards my baby was resentment. My second feeling was crushing guilt.

'Things will work out the way they should,' Emma says, putting her arm gently around me. 'I promise. It may not seem like it now. But there's karma in the world. Everything corrects itself in the end.'

'You'd better get back out.' I'm ashamed of my tears and I suddenly want to be on my own. I can't bear the thought of her judging me. 'They'll be wondering where you are.'

I run upstairs to the bathroom and dab at my eyes with loo roll. When I look in the mirror they are still red-rimmed and I stay a little longer, sitting on the closed toilet. I want to stay here forever, but eventually I get up, take a deep breath and leave the bathroom.

I go into my bedroom to apply some make-up over my blotchy face.

I stop stock-still. Someone's there.

'Sarah?'

She's by the window. In her hand is a photo of me and Matt that she's picked up from the dressing table. We're on our honeymoon in Borneo. I'm smiling ear to ear with my arm around Matt. There's an orang-utan just about in shot behind us, if you look closely. I got the photos printed a few days ago and put them out to remind myself what Matt and I have together.

'What are you doing?' The way she was staring at our photos so intently makes me feel uneasy. She's in my personal space, touching my property, scrutinising the photos of my honeymoon. With my husband.

She puts the frame down clumsily and it falls face down. She quickly rights it.

'Oh, I'm sorry.' She seems flustered. 'I was waiting for the bathroom and I wandered in.'

I frown. I'm sure the bedroom door was closed. Why did she think she could just come in?

'The bathroom's free now,' I tell her, abruptly.

She leaves and I go over to the dressing table, rearranging the photos so they align. I hate the thought of someone moving my things around, touching what's not theirs. It reminds me of my hairbrush falling between the bed and the table the other day. I'm certain Ruth moved it when she was nosing around – no one seems to respect anyone's privacy around here.

I apply my make-up quickly and hurry back to the kitchen, still feeling annoyed with Sarah. I pour the hot water over the teabags and position the cups on a tray.

Ruth, Jack and Emma have started to move the rocks that line the edge of the pond, but they stop for a tea break. Matt is talking to Sarah, their heads bowed together. He tips his head back and laughs. I bristle. He hardly ever laughs with me any more.

I force a smile as I hand them their mugs, before giving the remaining cup to Jack.

Emma comes straight over. 'Are you OK?'

'Fine, thank you,' I lie.

She follows my gaze to Matt and Sarah.

'They get on well,' she says quietly.

'Well, you know they have shared history.' I think about how much time they are spending with each other, much more time than Matt spends with me. Then I think of Sarah in my bedroom. And the late-night texts she's been sending. What does she want with my husband?

Emma frowns and we watch Sarah and Matt go over to Olivia's buggy and coo at her. Olivia's tiny hand grabs at Sarah's bright patterned scarf and Sarah laughs as she pulls it away.

'She's broody. She wants a baby,' Emma says, matter-of-factly.

'But she doesn't have a partner.' I laugh, but as I watch Sarah fussing over Olivia I wonder if there's something in it. She had said she hadn't found the right man since she miscarried Matt's baby. What if she's not over him?

'I'd watch her,' Emma advises.

'Matt and I are fine.' It sounds more defensive than I intend.

'It's not Matt you have to worry about. It's women who are manipulative, not men. They betray your trust. I've learnt that the hard way.'

'They're just friends,' I insist.

'Well, just be careful. Anyone can see she wants what you have. Your perfect daughter. Your perfect husband.'

'No one's life is perfect,' I say as I watch Sarah slap Matt on the shoulder and giggle girlishly at a joke he's made.

*

After a few minutes, I collect the mugs and take them back to the kitchen. The others stand chatting round the buggy, obscuring Olivia from my view.

'I'll come out and help as soon as I've washed up,' I say. The truth is I long to be on my own, away from everyone. I'm finding it difficult being by the pond. It brings back too many memories. Memories I'd rather forget.

I turn on the taps to fill the sink, when I notice a movement out of the corner of my eye.

The buggy. Olivia's buggy.

It's rolling down the path, towards the pond.

I shout out, but no one turns. They can't hear me through the kitchen window.

I run to the door, push it open and run down the path.

'The buggy! The buggy!'

They turn to me, away from Olivia, and I watch as the buggy reaches the pond and the front wheel tips into the water. The whole thing teeters on the edge for a terrifying second before the back wheels follow. Within moments, it submerges.

*

'Hi.'

'Hi.'

I'm glad it's her on the other end of the phone, the calm, familiar voice. I call the helpline so often that I feel like I know her now. I've lost all pretence of ringing about parenting activities. I ring because I need to talk. I ring because she listens.

'What's been going on in the last few days?' she asks softly.

'I think… I think that I can't live with him any more, his behaviour. I think I've lost my sense of what's normal.'

'What's he done?'

'Nothing unusual. Well, not for him.'

I'm sitting on the bed. There's a bloodstain on the corner of the pillowcase and I run my hand over the hardened surface. I'll have to wash the sheets this afternoon, before he gets home.

'What's he done?'

'Well, nothing. We had sex last night. I suppose that's good. Sex is important in a marriage, isn't it?'

'But?'

'But I guess I didn't really want to. It was more him than me. I said no initially, but I eventually gave in.'

'You gave in?'

'Yeah, I had to. He's a passionate guy.'

'You know that's wrong, don't you?' Her voice remains soft, but I can hear the accusation in it. She thinks I'm weak, that I can't stand up to him.

'I don't think it's wrong.' I twist the corner of the pillow slip in my hand, tying it into a knot. 'I… well I must have wanted it, mustn't I? Because I had sex with him. I guess he persuaded me.'

I feel the bubble of confusion rising up in me. I'm exposed. I can see the lies I'm telling myself and I don't want to face them.

'Does he have any history of this?'

'What do you mean?'

'Well. I guess, in my experience, men who treat women like that have often done it before, to others.'

'In your experience?' Has she gone through this too?

'Lots of women are harassed, assaulted, injured.'

'Lots?'

'By men like your husband.'

'Have you been?' I ask hesitantly. 'Have you been treated like this?'

'Not in the way that you have,' she says. 'But no woman is immune. Not in the world we live in.'

'Thanks,' I say. 'That makes me feel better.' I wish I was with her now, by her side, having coffee instead of talking over the phone. We speak so often she feels like a friend, not a volunteer on a helpline.

'That's OK,' she replies. 'That's what I'm here for.'

'Are you married?' I ask. Even though we talk all the time, I know so little about her. I want to check she understands what it's like to be married, the give and take that's required and the sacrifices you have to make.

'Yes.'

'Do you ever feel, like being married, you have to give up a part of yourself?'

'Sometimes, yes.'

'I feel that too,' I say. 'And when he treats me badly, I wonder... I wonder if I deserve it.'

'Why would you think that?'

'Because I knew him before. I'd heard rumours. And I still chose to marry him.'

CHAPTER 16

Matt reaches the pond first. He tugs at the buggy, but it sticks. Olivia is submerged, drowning. I'm in the water within seconds, my hands feeling for the straps that hold Olivia under, as Sarah joins Matt, grabbing the buggy's handle and pulling as hard as she can.

My hands find the straps over Olivia's waterlogged clothes and I struggle to undo them. The buckles are filled with silt. It's not working. I reach down into the murky water and find the front wheel. I lift it with all my strength and eventually it releases. Matt and Sarah fall back onto the path, the buggy with Olivia inside following them and tipping over.

Silence. There should be screams but there's silence.

Terror rips through me.

I hear a disconnected voice and realise Ruth is on the phone to the ambulance service. 'Come now,' she says, her voice a whisper. 'Please.'

Matt has released Olivia from the straps. The waterlogged hood of her winter coat covers her mouth. I pull it off her face. She can't breathe. How long has she been unable to breathe?

Matt holds her as he runs his fingers round her mouth, pulling out small bits of pond weed. He turns her upside down, hits her back and a spurt of water shoots out. He lies her on the grass and starts mouth to mouth.

I crouch beside her and hold her tiny hand. She feels so fragile. This can't be happening. Not again. Her hand is muddy and cold. I kiss it over and over, tasting the algae from the pond on my lips.

She's freezing. Her winter clothes stick to her.

'Go inside,' I shout at Emma. 'Get her warm clothes. And towels. They're upstairs in the bathroom cupboard.'

I don't know if Emma heard the last bit. She's already gone, closely followed by Sarah.

'The ambulance will be here any minute,' Ruth says over and over again, as she paces the garden.

Olivia finally screams and I hug her close to me, overcome with relief. Her wet clothes soak through my jeans and I start to strip her as Emma appears with a dry outfit.

Paramedics are in the garden, kneeling over her before we have the chance to put the clothes on. They wrap her in blankets, check her and then take her to the ambulance. Matt and I get in and I sit strapped to the seat, hugging Olivia. I realise that we haven't got her clothes with us.

Emma shouts into the ambulance.

'I'll follow in the car.'

'Bring some nappies,' I call back. 'And the clothes.'

Olivia whimpers in my arms and I hold her closer, hugging her tightly to my chest.

'Keep her warm,' the paramedic says.

Her tiny face gazes up at me, meeting my eyes. Guilt rips through me.

'I'm sorry, I'm sorry, I'm sorry,' I whisper. How can I have taken my eyes off her, even for a moment?

I feel the vomit rise in my throat. I can't do this. I can't watch her every second. I'm not good enough. I don't deserve a child.

The inside of the ambulance is full of noise, the sirens and Olivia's cries echoing around us. I never thought I'd be so grateful to hear her scream.

We arrive at the hospital and we're taken through the double doors to A&E. It's like a warm welcome to hell. All the seats are full, and people sit on the small coffee tables between the chairs, on the floor, anywhere. A drunk man lies sprawled across the floor and an elderly couple on the seats next to him stare stoically ahead. A young woman holds her boyfriend's head in her arms, while a group of men laugh uproariously by the vending machines, one of them bleeding from the head.

The paramedics take us straight past the chaos, through the doors at the end of the waiting room, to the relative calm of the paediatric ward. We're shown to a bed, where we're left waiting to see a nurse. Despite the harsh lighting and noise of A&E, Olivia has fallen asleep in my arms. I shift positions and gently place my hand on her to check she's still breathing. The relief is overwhelming as I feel her little chest rising and falling.

Emma appears, her face flushed as if she's been running, a plastic bag of clothes and nappies in her hands.

I smile at her gratefully, thankful that she's here.

'How is she?' Emma asks.

'We don't know. We're waiting for the nurse.'

'She looks so peaceful, fast asleep,' she says, stroking her head.

'What happened?' I direct the question at Matt and Emma. 'I was watching from the kitchen window… It all seemed to happen so suddenly. One minute the buggy was still, the next minute it was rolling.'

'I don't think the brake was on,' Emma says. 'There must have been a gust of wind. Or someone knocked it, and because the brake was off it just rolled.'

'What?' Matt turns to me, his voice a roar. 'You left the brake off?'

He looks at me incredulously.

'I…' I think back, remembering Ruth asking me to bring the buggy nearer to the pond. I remember feeling uneasy about bringing Olivia closer to the water. I was distracted, caught up in my fear of the water. Had I set the brake?

I can't remember. But it must have been me who forgot. I was the one who moved the buggy.

'I'm sorry,' I say, my face flushing.

'She could have died.' Matt puts his head between his hands, unable to look at me.

'I'm sorry,' I repeat, his words sinking in. This is all my fault. I could have killed her. I'll never forgive myself.

Emma puts an arm on my shoulder. 'It could happen to anyone,' she says.

Emma reaches down and strokes Olivia's face, and I hold my daughter closer. She's so precious, so small. I don't want anyone to touch her.

'How could you have forgotten the brake?' Matt studies my face for answers, but I have none.

'I don't know,' I whisper.

'Claire, this can't go on. You're so absent-minded… it's putting our daughter in danger. We can't ignore it any more.'

'Go easy on her,' Emma says. Her voice has an authoritative edge, and I'm grateful to her for stepping in.

She turns to me. 'Don't blame yourself, Claire. We all forget things.'

'But… she could have drowned,' I reply, unable to process what's happened. I shiver and try to block the memories from my mind. I can't bear to think about it.

'She's safe and sound now,' Emma continues. 'That's all that matters.'

Matt paces back and forth in the small cubicle.

'That's not all that matters,' he says. 'It could happen again. If you keep imagining things, getting confused, forgetting stuff… it could happen again.'

A nurse appears at the curtain and I redden. What if she overheard? What if she thinks I'm an unfit mother? Will they take my daughter away?

I stand, presenting a sleeping Olivia to her.

Matt turns to Emma.

'You can go,' he says, bluntly. I see the hurt expression on Emma's face, as she shakes her head.

'I was there when it happened. I can help explain.'

'I want her here,' I say softly, needing her support. I need someone here who's not angry with me, who doesn't blame me.

The nurse turns to me and Emma.

'Which of you is Mum? Can you remove the blanket and lie her down?'

Emma has automatically moved forward to help, but then she catches herself and steps back.

'I'm Mum,' I say.

As I take the blanket off Olivia and lie her down, she wakes and starts screaming.

The nurse looks down her throat, listens to her heart and chest and checks her temperature and oxygen levels. As she examines her, she asks what happened and we explain how Olivia fell into the pond.

'I think she'll be fine,' she says. 'Anything else you're worried about?'

I shake my head, relief flooding through me.

'She swallowed a lot of water. Is she OK?' asks Matt.

'She seems fine. But the doctor will need to check her over,' she explains, going to the sink and washing her hands. 'Just wait here and the doctor will be with you when she's finished with her other patients.'

I dress Olivia, and Emma sits down on one of the two plastic seats in the corner of the room. Matt chooses to stay next to me, stroking Olivia's soft baby hair.

He puts his arm round me and I feel grateful for his touch.

'Are you all right?' he asks.

'Yeah,' I reply, although I still feel shaky. 'I just can't believe what's happened. I feel awful.' Tears prick my eyes.

He nods, and we both stare at our daughter. 'We need to do something, Claire, you're not well.'

'I'll go back to the doctor,' I say.

Matt nods. 'Be assertive this time. Insist you need help.'

'I will.'

Matt seems calmer now. He looks down at Olivia.

'She's so beautiful, isn't she?'

When I look at her, for once I can see what other people see. Her features are delicate and her lively eyes twinkle. She's beautiful. I feel an unfamiliar surge of love for her and I want to hold onto it forever. But somehow I know I can't. A voice deep inside tells me that I don't deserve her.

It's 9 p.m. before the doctor comes in. Both Matt and I have told Emma she can go multiple times, but she wanted to stay. She's such a good friend to me. She insisted that Dan keep Lizzie a bit longer today, so she could be with us at the hospital.

The doctor looks frazzled, her eyes bloodshot, her hair falling out of her messy bun. But she greets us with a warm smile. 'I'm Dr Rajah. Which of you are the parents?'

'We are,' I say, pointing at Matt.

The doctor turns to Emma. 'And you are?'

'A family friend.'

'Right. Great. I know it's getting late, so I'll take a quick look at…' She consults her notes for a moment and then continues. '… I'll take a quick look at Olivia and then hopefully you should be able to go on your way.'

I put Olivia back on the bed and undress her as the doctor instructs. She examines her and asks me to explain again what happened. I go through the story and she listens patiently, occasionally asking for clarification.

She turns to me. 'Good news. Her general health seems fine. And I can't see any ill-effects of what's happened. It must have been quite a shock to you.'

'It was,' I say. 'Thanks so much for looking at her.'

'No problem. There's just one more thing.'

She turns to Matt and Emma. 'Would you two step outside while I speak to Claire for a minute? There's a vending machine in the adults' A&E. I imagine you'll need some refreshment.'

Matt looks at me uncertainly. 'Is that OK with you?'

I nod and look at the doctor nervously. My heart beats faster. Does she want to talk to me about my postnatal depression? Or my previous mental health problems? What if she thinks I can't look after Olivia? What if she's right?

The doctor holds the door open for Matt and Emma. 'There's space in the waiting room for you to sit,' she says smiling.

Olivia squirms and the doctor holds open her legs. I see two bruises, one on each inner thigh. There are the size of five pence pieces, a shade of dark purple.

'Have you noticed these before?'

I frown. The bruises would have been right in front of me every time I changed Olivia's nappy. I should have spotted them. But I can't recall seeing them. I often change the nappy on autopilot, in a daze.

'I don't think so,' I mumble.

'OK. Do you know how they might have got there?'

'No. Umm… I don't know. She must have bumped herself.' I feel sick. Have I hurt Olivia by mistake?

The doctor looks directly at me and sighs. 'Claire, babies do bump themselves. They hit their heads, they roll off beds, they bump into things. But babies this age very rarely get bruises in this kind of position unless someone else has caused them.'

I swallow. 'Do you think I could have hurt her when I was changing her nappy?' My voice is small. I feel like I'm confessing to some awful sin.

'Possibly. But I doubt it. You'd really have to be quite rough with her to cause that.'

'Maybe I'm not gentle enough?'

'Claire. You need to think about whether anyone else could be hurting Olivia. Your husband perhaps? Is he happy to be a father?'

I recall our conversation the other day. He said he'd gone along with my desire to have a baby, that he hadn't wanted her as much as I had. But that doesn't mean he'd hurt Olivia. He loves her. I push the doubts back down.

'He's like anyone,' I say. 'He has good days and bad days.'

'OK,' the doctor says. 'I'm going to refer you to social services. It's nothing to worry about but they'll visit in the next few days. In the meantime, I suggest you keep an eye on things and if at all possible, supervise anyone who's looking after your child.'

CHAPTER 17

Social services are unexpectedly efficient and arrive the next day. I put on an act for their benefit, pretending to be a competent, loving mother. I'm shocked when they believe me. They look at the bruises on Olivia and tell me to watch out for more. But then they leave. They leave her with me. For some reason they trust me. They're not going to take her away.

I tell myself that everything's going to be all right.

But now it's 9 p.m. and Matt's still at work. It's been such a long day and I'm exhausted. I'm still on my own, Olivia's still screaming and I've done everything I can possibly think of to calm her. I've fed her until my nipples ache, I've changed her nappy, I've rubbed her back and burped her, I've hugged her, I've held her, I've whispered to her, I've sung to her, I've rocked her. But nothing works.

I started to think she must be getting sick of my voice, so I played her nursery rhymes on my phone. When that didn't work I tried white noise. And now I've resorted to bringing her downstairs to watch television with me. Maybe the flickering light of the television will stimulate her to the point of exhaustion.

On days like this all I want is a glass of wine. I can imagine the tang of a cold glass of Sauvignon as it rests on my tongue before hitting the back of my throat. But Matt won't allow alcohol in the house. He says if it's in the house then we won't be able to control ourselves. That once we start drinking we won't be able to stop. When he says 'we', I know he really means me.

Olivia keeps screaming and I turn the volume up on the television. I'm trying to watch a new crime drama that I've been meaning to watch for ages. I watch a man attack a woman on the screen, his hands crushing her throat. I turn Olivia's face away from the image.

I look at my daughter in my arms. She's beautifully fragile. But so angry at the world. Angry at me. Her little lungs must have almost run out of breath from screaming. The back of her throat must be red raw.

Then Olivia seems to tire, pausing for a second, her eyes staring towards the ceiling. In the silence, I hear a noise. A very faint high pitched sound that I've been hearing on and off for the last few nights. I think it's coming from the loft.

I'll have to look into it when Matt's around. There's no way I'm going up there on my own.

There could be mice up there. Or worse. Rats.

Olivia's screams restart and drown out everything else.

If there was something in the house, or someone, I wouldn't even know.

I shiver. On the television, the man has taken the woman's body into the woods and is meticulously cutting her into tiny pieces with a chainsaw.

I don't want to be here on my own any more. I have to get out of the house. I get up from the sofa and turn the TV and light off. The pure darkness alarms me and I quickly turn the light back on.

It's so cold this winter, and the threat of snow has been on the horizon for a couple of days, but I can't stay inside. I pile Olivia into her snowsuit and then into the buggy and leave the cottage, waiting until the final moment to turn the lights out once more.

Olivia's screams lessen as the cold air hits her. I know I should have put her hat on but we won't be out long. There's nowhere to go in the village at night. I'll just walk her long enough to get her to sleep and then return home.

The bulb in the porch has gone and so our driveway is pitch black. I can just about make out the bramble bushes that line the entrance to the cottage. From this position, standing on my doorstep with the cottage looming above me, I can't see any other signs of human life. But that doesn't mean there's no one there. Anyone could be watching.

I had forgotten how different the countryside feels at night. In London there was always light. The streetlights. Car lights. Light streaming from people's windows. But here it's different. The dark is all embracing. The stars above watch, but they're so far away they don't feel part of my world.

When you lose the ability to see, every other sensation is accentuated. The crunch of the gravel under the wheels of the buggy. The cold air circling my fingers as they grip the ridged plastic of the buggy's handle. That unique country smell. Fresh air, they call it. But there's more to it than that. Manure and hay and grass.

The lane that leads to our cottage seems longer at night. When I reach the end I look left and right as if I expect to see a car. But the road beyond is empty. It seems narrower than it did, constrained by the tall trees on each side. The footpath starts just ten metres or so from the end of the lane and usually I don't give a second thought to the short walk on the road. But now I realise that no car would be able to see me if they came around the corner. And I don't have my phone with me to light the way.

I wonder if I should go back to get it, but when I turn back towards the cottage, my stomach knots. I don't want to go back in. I wish Matt would hurry up and come home.

I take the few steps to the edge of the footpath and stand there with Olivia in the buggy. She's quiet now, as if even she realises that something is not quite right, as if even she is aware that her screams might draw attention to us.

A car comes from nowhere and its headlights illuminate us.

Matt? Is it Matt?

It speeds by.

I keep walking towards the village. It's deserted at this time of night. I pass the post office and make out my reflection in the glass. I pass the quaint thatched houses, their front windows looking directly out onto the pavement, thick curtains tightly closed for privacy. I see the amber glow from a pub window. A place with people and noise. Away from the silence of the night. Welcoming.

The car parked outside has a shade over the back window to protect a baby from the sunshine. It has a smiling cat motif, the same as the one we've got. I look closer. It's our car. Matt's car.

At first I feel relief. I've found him. He can take me home and look after me. He can tell me the noises in the house are in my head and hold me in his arms until I fall asleep.

But why's his car here? His practice is a few miles away. Isn't he meant to be working?

I peer through the window of the pub. It's almost empty, except for a couple sitting in a corner, a glass of red wine and a pint in front of them, talking animatedly.

Matt. And Sarah.

Before I can think, I've rammed open the door and pushed the buggy inside.

Matt doesn't even look up.

But the man drying glasses behind the bar does.

'No children after eight p.m. I'm afraid, love.'

'Oh,' I say. 'I'm sorry… I… I just need to speak to my husband.'

'You'll need to leave. He'll have to come to speak to you outside. We can't have the little one in here.'

He indicates Olivia, who's now sound asleep and looking angelic.

I see Sarah glance over and then whisper to Matt.

He stands and comes over.

'Claire,' he says. 'I… I was just having a quick after-work drink with Sarah. We had things to talk about… About the practice… I hope you don't mind.'

Of course I mind. I'm alone in that house and I need you.

But I can't say that.

'When will you be home?' I ask.

'I'll be back after I've finished my pint, it won't be long.'

'Can't you come now?'

'I need to speak to Sarah about something. I'm sorry, Claire. But I'll be back in half an hour. I promise.'

He gives me a peck on the cheek and then turns and walks back to his table.

'Matt?' I call after him. 'Can you be quicker?'

He doesn't answer and I feel my fists clench in anger.

'You'll need to go now, miss,' the barman says, coming out from behind the bar.

I look at him, considering shouting across the pub at Matt, telling him to come home. But I don't want to make a scene. I don't want anyone else in this village to think I'm crazy.

I smile tightly at the barman.

'I'm going,' I say.

I open the door and step back out into the darkness.

*

My daughter is napping and I settle down on my bed and ring the helpline. I need to talk things through with someone. I feel like I'm finally starting to figure things out.

She seems tense today, as if she wants to rush our conversation.

'Did I interrupt something?' I ask.

'No,' she says. 'Of course not.'

'Sometimes I wonder why you listen to me.'

'It's my job.'

'Oh.' I wanted more than that. 'Do you enjoy it?' I know I'm looking for validation, but I need to know our conversations mean something to her. They mean so much to me.

'Yes. Well, not all the time. But I enjoy speaking to you.'

My face flushes. I'm so glad she feels the same way.

'Do you think—?' I'm embarrassed to finish the sentence. 'Do you think in real life; do you think we might be friends?'

She laughs lightly. 'Yes,' she says. 'Definitely. I feel like I know you.'

I grin. 'I feel like I know you too.'

'Why do you stay with him?' she asks. 'When he hits you?'

'Because he's good to me. Because he puts a roof over my head. Because he looks after me and works hard and loves me.'

'But he hurts you.'

'I deserve it.'

'You don't deserve it.'

'I'm not good enough. I used to have a good job, in the city. But I don't do anything any more. I'm no one. Just a mother. The only thing I have that means anything to me is my daughter. And she needs a father. I can't take her away from him. I can't.'

CHAPTER 18

I lie wide awake in bed, straining my ears to listen to the faint beeps from the loft. I can only hear them when the house is completely silent, when Matt and Olivia are asleep and when the creaking and grunting of the central heating has calmed.

I can't sleep. Matt lies comatose beside me, breathing peacefully. The image of him and Sarah deep in conversation at the pub has been circling round in my head all night. They looked so cosy together, like a couple. I'm sure there's more to their relationship than I know. He prioritises her over me. He left me alone with our baby to go for a drink with her. He let me walk home on my own while he stayed with her. I'm sure he could see my distress, and yet he chose her over me. I felt like such a fool.

I should have spoken to him about it when he got in, but I couldn't shake off the fear of being in the cottage on my own, and the relief that he was home overshadowed any other emotion. I was exhausted. I didn't want an argument. I just wanted to rest my head on the pillow and let sleep take over.

But sleep hasn't come. I look at Matt lying peacefully beside me and I'm jealous. How can he sleep so soundly?

Olivia screams.

I get out of bed noisily, grumbling. I want Matt to wake up, to share the work of looking after our daughter. But he doesn't even stir.

When I go to Olivia's room, she's still half asleep, trapped in a nightmare. Her eyes flick rapidly from side to side below her eyelids and she screams again. I can see her chest rising and falling, her breathing fast. I put my hand to her forehead. It's hot and clammy.

I shouldn't have taken her out in the cold. I should have put a hat on her. I go downstairs, find the medicine and then go back to Olivia's room. I lift my baby out of the cot to administer it through the syringe, into her mouth. She screams louder and pulls her head away. The syrupy mixture spills down her sleepsuit, a sugary mess.

I check her nappy. It's full. I place her on the nappy mat, undo it and retch. I try to swallow my frustration as anger bubbles up inside me. Matt should be dealing with this too.

Olivia tries to roll over and I lay one hand on her tummy to stop her. The bruises on her thighs have turned to a pale yellow. Yellow circles like thumbprints. Could I have done that? Held her down too forcefully while changing her nappy? I inspect her for more bruises, looking at her legs, then her arms, her stomach, her back. There are none.

I carry her into the bedroom and put her down beside Matt's sleeping body. She screams, almost in his ear, and he stirs ever so slightly and rolls further away. As usual, he has his earplugs in.

I shake him awake.

'Matt!'

'What?' he mumbles. 'What's wrong?'

'Olivia's not well.'

'Give her some Calpol.'

'I have done.'

'Well there's not much more I can do about it.' He turns away.

I put Olivia on my breast and she calms.

'Why were you in the pub with Sarah?' I ask, unable to hold it in. I'm so angry I can't stop myself.

'Do we need to talk about this now? It's the middle of the night.'

'Just tell me why.'

'She was upset.'

'About what?'

'Nothing, Claire. It's nothing to do with you. Just something that happened a long time ago, that's all.'

'The miscarriage?'

'No.'

'Matt. When are we going to talk?' I don't like the sound of my voice. It's pleading and desperate. It doesn't sound like me.

'Look, Claire, we can talk tomorrow.'

'When? You're always busy at work.'

'Why don't you meet me for lunch? I've got a quiet day. Not enough customers, no matter what I do. So meet me for lunch.'

'OK then,' I say. It's a small concession, but it will have to do. We need to talk.

He rolls away from me, letting me know the conversation is over. I let Olivia feed for forty-five minutes, until she falls asleep against me. With my child and my husband fast asleep, I lie awake, unable to drop off, listening to the beeping from the loft.

The next day, I wait in the doctor's surgery, fidgeting on a hard chair. Olivia's still feverish this morning. Since we found the bruises on her thighs, I want to get every little thing checked out.

We're called through and the doctor smiles at me. It's a different doctor from the last time I went to the surgery. I should have booked the same one, then she'd remember me.

I sit down.

'So, what can I do for you?' the doctor asks.

'My daughter's got a fever and a temperature.'

The doctor turns to her computer, pulls up Olivia's notes and then examines her, looking in her eyes and ears and listening to her chest. Olivia giggles and smiles, trying to grab the doctor's pen from the desk.

'She's very lively,' the doctor says.

'Yes, but she's been up all night.' It's a white lie. I want them to take Olivia's health seriously. It's me who's been up all night, worrying about Matt and Sarah. Worrying that I'm going crazy, or worse, that there's really something going on.

'OK,' she says. I can tell by the way she looks at me that she thinks I'm just another nervous first-time mother.

'It just looks like a virus,' she says. 'All she needs is lots of rest and plenty of paracetamol.'

My chest tightens. I've given her so much children's paracetamol that her breath smells sugary sweet.

'Are you sure?' My voice is high, panicked.

The doctor smiles gently. 'Motherhood's hard. I have two kids. It's easy to google things and get scared, but really your daughter is fine. And you're doing just fine too.'

I feel hot all of a sudden, as if I might faint.

Because she's wrong. I'm not doing fine. I'm not.

'Is there anything else?' the doctor asks, looking up from her computer.

I should ask her about the counselling. Matt said I needed to follow that up, to speak to someone. I'm on the waiting list, and I haven't heard anything yet.

But she's standing now, moving over to the door, holding it open for me.

'No,' I say, as I stand. 'Thank you.'

I manage a quick smile, before I push Olivia's buggy out of the door and burst into tears in the waiting room.

It's raining when I leave the doctor's surgery, but I've arranged to meet Matt for lunch. I put my umbrella up, but it's too difficult to hold it over me and manoeuvre the buggy, so I give up, instead shoving it in the shopping basket underneath and pulling my hood over my head.

At the bus stop people grumble as they stand uncomfortably close under the shelter. They're all waiting for the midday bus. If they miss it, there isn't another one for three hours. When the bus arrives it's packed, but I manage to squeeze on. My hands grip the buggy tightly in case Olivia gets knocked by the mass of swaying passengers. I check the brake compulsively. I wrap her blankets a bit tighter around her. It's so cold, she could easily catch a chill.

I get off the bus near Matt's practice and walk the rest of the way in the rain. When I push open the door of the surgery the bell rings loudly and Olivia screams.

'Shush…' I say.

There's no one behind the reception desk, so I take a seat on one of the armchairs and wait. I take Olivia out of the pram and put her on my breast. Matt has done a good job of the decor. It's understated, but warm, with pictures of countryside scenes dotted round the walls. I wonder if Sarah helped him. Certainly, more thought has gone into the decoration of the practice than the decoration of our cottage. This practice is Matt's love, his passion. Our cottage is just where he comes home to sleep.

Sarah breezes through into the reception area, clutching some paperwork.

She jumps when she sees me.

'Oh, hello,' she says. 'How are you?'

'I'm well. And you?' I remember what Matt said about her being her being upset last night.

'Good, thanks,' she replies, clutching the papers closer to her chest. 'We're picking up a few more clients, which is great. I'm sure Matt's told you all about it.'

There's an awkward pause and I can see that she's about to ask about Olivia, but then she sees that I'm breastfeeding and she glances away.

'Make yourself at home,' she says and then reddens, as if she thinks she's said something wrong.

'I won't be here long. I'm just waiting for Matt. We're meeting for lunch.'

'Oh, he just left. The man in the house just up the road came in to see us. A fox attacked his chickens last night. He wanted Matt to take a look. I don't know how long he'll be.'

Disappointment flushes my face. I check my phone and see the message from Matt. He only sent it a few minutes ago.

Been called to an urgent appointment. Sorry. We'll have to do lunch another day. xx

'Where's the farm?' I ask Sarah.

'It's not a farm, just a man retired from the city living the rural dream. He keeps a couple of chickens for eggs. If you turn right, it's a few houses down.'

She opens the door and points out the house to me.

'Thanks,' I say. I remove Olivia from my breast and bundle her back into the pram.

Luckily the rain has stopped. I walk quickly over the bumpy pavement, avoiding the puddles. The grounds of the house stretch out alongside the road, blocked only by a waist-height hedge.

I see Matt in the garden. He stands next to a man in jeans, arms crossed, surveying a chicken pen with one bird lying dead, the other twitching. I can see from here that it's badly injured, its head twisted unnaturally to the side.

I think about shouting hello, but I don't want to interrupt. I can wait.

The man says something I can't hear and Matt laughs, nodding.

He bends over the pen and picks the live chicken up by its legs. It twitches and twists under his grip, its wings flapping feebly. It's half-dead. Matt moves one hand to its head. He pulls it quickly, then twists the neck. The wings flap wildly in a burst of energy. I swallow. It's still alive. But then the bird stills and Matt tosses it back into the pen. He and the man return to the house without a second glance.

I feel a bit queasy. It's not that Matt's done anything wrong, it's just that when I imagine him doing his job I think of him curing sick animals. I try not to think about the times he puts them down.

I wait outside the house for five minutes. I think about knocking and going inside, but I don't know what I'd say. There's no reason I need to see Matt urgently, and besides, he cancelled our lunch.

When it starts to rain again, I decide to leave. It's far too cold to stand outside getting wet, and I'm not even sure I want to see him. I can't stop thinking about last night, seeing him cosying up with Sarah at the pub. Do I even know the man I married any more?

I walk to the bus stop and wait, shivering, for half an hour before the bus finally arrives. I'm windswept and soaking wet and miserable and Olivia is crying as usual. I lift the wheels of Olivia's buggy up into the bus, push it into the allocated space and go to pay the driver. There's another buggy beside me and the woman holding it leans over and smiles at Olivia.

'She's pretty,' she says.

'Thank you.' Politely, I look into her buggy, ready to say the same.

'She's—' But I pause mid-sentence. I recognise the baby. It's Lizzie. She's wearing her distinctive red winter coat. 'She's lovely,' I stammer.

The woman must be Dan's new girlfriend. Emma has told me all about her. How she split her and Dan up. How she slept with him when Emma was pregnant. I know Emma hates the thought of her looking after Lizzie.

I listen to the woman talking to the baby, cooing at her and comforting her.

I feel angry with her on Emma's behalf and I want to say something, to confront her about taking another woman's partner, taking a baby away from its mother. But instead I turn away and watch the raindrops slide down the bus windows. I'm in no mood for a fight.

That evening Matt arrives home early, full of apologies about cancelling lunch. For once he'll be around to put Olivia to bed. For once, we'll be able to have a conversation over dinner. These moments feel precious, fragile threads between us, holding our marriage together. I don't want to talk about Sarah. Not now. I don't want to ruin the only chance we've got to have a conversation.

'I'm so sorry about lunch,' he says again. 'There was an urgent appointment. A new client.'

'It's OK.' I don't tell him I already know. I can't explain why I watched them and then left without saying anything. I'm not quite sure myself.

He doesn't say any more and I don't ask. He's already left the room and gone to the kitchen. I hear him turn on the tap and pour a glass of water.

I breastfeed Olivia while Matt starts heating up our dinner. As I sit on the sofa, I google Sarah on my phone. It's become a habit. I go through pages and pages of results, but nothing comes up other than the website for Matt's practice. I look at her publicly available photos on Facebook, but they're all old. It's not enough. I need to know more. I click on 'add friend.' It seems justified this time. After all, I've met her a few times and she's come to my house. She could think I want to be friends.

I hear the bath taps running upstairs. I carry Olivia to the bathroom and hand her to Matt. I watch as he undresses her. I remember the bruises on her thighs and feel a shiver of doubt wash over me, my anxiety building. I observe him closely. He's gentle enough with her, but something is bothering me. It's like my brain is screaming 'No!' trying to warn me.

I remember my dream. Matt holding Olivia down, submerging her. I remember watching him wring the chicken's neck without a second thought and then discard it like rubbish. I think again of the yellow bruises on her thighs.

Matt hands Olivia to me, and then checks the temperature of the bath water with his hand.

My pulse quickens and I look down at the tiny, naked baby in my arms. She's totally dependent on me. It's my job to keep her alive.

Fear grips me. Every instinct tells me not to hand her back to Matt. I feel too hot, the air in the bathroom seems too thick. I can't think straight.

Deep breaths. I must take deep breaths.

Breathe in, I tell myself.

Matt reaches out his arms and takes her from me.

No. No. No. My scream is silent inside me.

He starts lowering Olivia into the bath.

I see her touch the water.

'No!' I hear a shout.

It's my voice.

I can't let him bath her. I don't know why, but I can't. I just can't.

I snatch Olivia from him and cradle her in my arms.

Matt looks at me in confusion.

'I'll bath her,' I say.

'But—'

'I'll bath her.'

At that moment, I realise that I no longer trust Matt with our daughter.

CHAPTER 19

The snow has finally come. Outside the window, the fields behind our house are a never-ending blanket of pure white. I shiver as I slip into my dressing gown and turn up the radiator. Matt's car is blocked in by a snowdrift and we're trapped in the cold cottage together.

Matt changes Olivia's nappy and then asks where we keep the spare packs.

I look at him. I've been meaning to buy nappies for ages. But the nearest shop that sells them is four miles away. We'd need the car.

'We don't have any?' he asks.

'No,' I say, checking the downstairs cupboard. We've run out.

The only thing to do is walk. I don't want to go alone and I'm not convinced Matt will be able to cope with Olivia's screaming if I leave him on his own, so we agree to set off together. Matt goes over to Ruth's to borrow wellington boots, but I remember mine rubbing when we cleared out the pond, and so I opt for trainers, even though I know the snow will soak through. We dress in layer upon layer of jumpers and jackets, hats and scarfs. We double up Olivia's baby grows and add a jumper and snowsuit, before strapping her to Matt in the baby carrier.

I know it was my anxiety talking last night when I wouldn't let Matt bath Olivia and I've tried to put it to the back of my mind. I look at her now. She's completely calm strapped to Matt. He's her father and he loves her. I can't believe how ridiculous I was being.

I start down the lane to the village, but Matt knows a shortcut and we ease ourselves through a narrow opening, into a field. The landscape around us is more beautiful than any Christmas card, and I drink it in. I reach for Matt's hand. This is what I imagined when I thought about our lives in the countryside. Long, romantic walks through vast, stretching emptiness. Space to ourselves. Space to be us.

I hadn't thought of the cold bite of the winter air that seeps through my clothes and into my bones. I hadn't thought of the isolation and the stretching, endless loneliness.

We're completely alone here. The three of us.

I grip Matt's hand tighter, our fingers interlocking through gloves. I can't tell how he feels underneath. If he's warm or cold. He's staring straight ahead, his expression tight. Does he want to be here with me? Is he just thinking of getting back to his paperwork? Missing the surgery? Missing Sarah?

I think of them in the pub the other night, their faces close, co-conspirators. I know I should bring it up again, ask him why. But we feel so fragile at the moment, so distant, that I feel my words might break us. We are cracked and it will only take one more blow to break us completely. I don't want to do that. Instead I just want to pretend we're the couple I imagined we'd be, walking hand in hand down a country road. A romance story. An album cover.

And besides, if there was something going on between them, what could I do? I no longer have my job or my friends or my life. Everything is tied to Matt and his mother and the cottage. I'm completely dependent on them.

'It's nice to be out in the fresh air,' I say, my words lacking conviction. It's like escaping a cell only to find you're still in a prison. The countryside stretches out before me, roads unwinding, unknown, treacherous. At least in the cottage the unease is contained within four walls. At least there's the illusion of outside, another world, an escape.

Here, amongst the fields, with my loving husband and daughter, reality hits. There is no outside. There is no escape. The endless sky and fields contain me as much as the walls of the house. I'm trapped.

Matt hasn't replied to my comment. He seems as lost in thought as I am. We walk on, hand in hand, but worlds apart.

Who is this man whose hand I'm holding? What secrets is he keeping?

A bramble nicks my jeans and I'm jarred backwards. I turn and remove the thorn, seeing the small patch of blood spreading in the dark denim. I'm glad Olivia is enclosed tightly next to Matt in the sling, away from the brambles. I don't want her legs to be caught, rivulets of blood forming on pale skin and seeping through her fleecy white snowsuit.

The wet snow creeps through the fabric of my trainers and my socks cling to my feet. I look at my phone to see where we are, but there's no GPS connection here. Instead I try to estimate it by the time. We've only been walking fifteen minutes. There's a long way to go.

We must have walked over a mile without speaking, when we stumble upon a farm. It announces itself before we arrive, in a scattering of abandoned machinery, covered in snow. The main house is in a state of disrepair, the stone walls crumbling and letting in the light.

Matt stops suddenly.

I stand beside him and take his hand.

'It's so…' I struggle to put into words the feelings the farm evokes. 'It's so desolate.'

'It belonged to Sarah's parents. They left years ago.'

'Did they live here when you were growing up?'

'Yeah. We spent our childhood playing in these fields. We only had each other. Sarah's parents… well her dad was violent, her mum was timid. The usual story. And you know what my mother's like…'

I remember how Sarah warned me about Ruth. 'Did your mother like her?'

Matt laughs. 'At first she did. When I was younger, she was someone I could play with. It got me out of the house, stopped me messing up her things, I suppose. When we got older and started dating, she was pleased. She thought Sarah was a good influence, studious and kind. But then she turned against her…'

'Why?'

'I suppose she thought Sarah would hold me back. And once she'd decided that, she made her life difficult.'

'How?'

'Just simple stuff really. She always used to give Sarah a lift to school in the car. But when we split up, she stopped. Sarah used to have to walk for an hour each way. My mother didn't care. Other things too… she just wasn't nice to her.'

Matt sniffs and removes his hand from mine, raising it to his face and rubbing at his eyes.

'Matt?'

I see the tears on his cheeks.

'What's wrong?'

'I… can't explain.' His words are an effort through sobs.

I take his other hand, grip it tighter.

In all our time together, I've never seen Matt cry. What could it be? What is it he isn't telling me?

Matt breaks away from me, walks off the path, towards a dilapidated cow shed. The corrugated iron roof sags under the weight of the snow and hangs loose at the corner.

I follow. 'Are you all right?' I ask. I reach out and touch his shoulder. He turns away from me and leans into the wall, his face resting against his folded arms, Olivia hanging between him and the bricks.

I hesitate before I walk over, unsure. It's always been him comforting me. Never the other way around.

'What's wrong?' I whisper. 'Matt, what's wrong?' I feel a rising panic. Matt's always so strong. I don't know what I'd do if he fell apart.

'I should never have come back,' he says and I'm not sure if he means the village, or to this place, this farmhouse.

'It's OK.' I try to soothe him. I desperately want to make things better.

'I just have so many memories, Claire. They haunt me.'

'What happened?'

He sighs and looks away towards the rest of the farm's out-buildings.

'You see that building there?' He points to a large wooden barn, the roof partially caved in.

I nod, holding my breath, unsure what's coming next.

'It happened there. The accident.' Matt stares at the barn, completely lost in his memories.

'What accident?'

'It was Sarah's sister. She fell out of the hayloft. Banged her head.'

'Did she…?' I don't want to say the word.

'No, she didn't die. At least not at first. She was left paralysed. But she did die eventually. Years later. She never recovered from her injuries.'

'That must have been so hard.'

'Yes. You know, I've never been back here. I've been to the farmhouse since, but not to this building. I didn't realise it would still affect me so much.'

He starts to walk slowly towards the barn, as if he's drawn to it.

'I'm so sorry,' I say, falling into step beside him and reaching out to hold onto his arm.

'It affected the whole village. It was that kind of tragedy. Young girl brain-damaged. Never fulfils her potential. Whole community in shock. You know the kind of story. Of course you do. It was the kind of story you were looking for when you worked at the newspaper.'

I wince at the slight, but let it lie. 'I had no idea. You never mentioned it.'

'I moved on. Moved to London. I escaped it all.'

'How did the family cope?'

'They didn't. Sarah's parents never got over it. They left shortly afterwards. Abandoned the farm. Abandoned their livelihood. Sarah was eighteen by then. She stayed and cared for her sister.'

'Sarah was left on her own?'

'Yeah, she cared for her sister until she died. She gave up everything. She wanted to be a vet too, had a place at Cambridge. But she never took it up. She wasn't the same again. She lost her ambition, her drive. She stayed in the village, taking any job going. She seems completely lost now, she's never got over it. It was the anniversary of the death on Thursday.'

'Oh.' Thursday was the day I saw them together in the pub. 'Is that why you were in the pub with her?'

'Yeah. Sarah was upset at work. She didn't want to be alone.'

'Poor Sarah.' I regret being so suspicious of them. All Matt was doing was trying to help. 'It must have been a tough day for her. I just wish you'd told me why you were there.'

'I'm sorry. I didn't think she'd want to talk to you about it. And I could see you were already angry. It didn't feel like the right time.'

We're in the shadow of the building now. 'It's OK, I understand.'

Matt nudges the rotten door open and steps inside, his face still tear-streaked. I follow.

Inside the cold shell, I put my arm around him. He pulls away and kicks a stone on the floor of the barn.

'I just have a lot of regrets. I wish I'd done things differently. I didn't treat Sarah well. I just left her here to pick up the pieces, while I went to university.'

'You couldn't let an accident change the course of your life.' But my words don't ring true, even to me. Doesn't that happen all the time? Something tragic happens and the ground beneath you shifts. Your life is never the same again.

'I promised myself I'd never return here,' Matt says. 'I thought I'd escaped.'

'I'm sorry I brought you back,' I reply. And I mean it. I'm sorry we ever came here.

*

'Another one,' my husband says angrily, slamming his fist into the table. 'Another stupid girl.'

I don't need to ask him what he's talking about. I can guess. Someone else has accused him of sexually assaulting them. The same rumours have circled him for years. When we first met, I was always so certain he was innocent. He was attractive and charismatic and he had girls throwing themselves at him. He could have had anyone he wanted. I thought his accusers were making it up. But now I'm not so sure.

I know better than to say anything. Besides, I don't want to hear about it. Don't want to picture what he might have done to those girls. I think of how the volunteer at the helpline told me that our sex life wasn't right, how it wasn't consensual if I gave into it out of fear.

I dish up his food, placing each piece of broccoli carefully beside the lamb.

He starts digging in before I've laid out my own plate. I can see he's furious.

'Who do they think they are?' he says. 'They're just after my money. Think they can accuse me and then take me for all I have. But they can't! They won't win.'

I listen to him rant as I pick at my food. I don't want him to take this out on me.

Later, when we're getting ready for bed, he comes into the bathroom while I'm brushing my teeth. I watch in the mirror as he reaches for the moisturiser he puts on before he sleeps. As he rubs it into his face, he looks so benign, so innocent. He's calmer now, more relaxed.

In the mirror I see an image of married bliss, a comfortable couple, getting ready for bed side by side.

The words slip out of my mouth, unbidden.

'You didn't do it?' I say tentatively. It's the first time I've asked. Up to now, I've just blindly believed. But I need to hear him say it. 'You didn't do it, did you?'

I hold my breath.

He turns to me, rage in his eyes. 'Of course not. You know me. You're my wife. How can you think that of me?'

'I'm sorry,' I say, and mean it. He isn't that type of man. He may have a temper, but he's a loving father, a family man.

I deserve what comes next. I shouldn't have questioned him.

He pulls back his right arm and I brace myself for the impact. But instead, he turns and punches the mirror. And then he punches again and again and again, until the crack at the centre bursts outwards towards the edges of the glass, and blood from his knuckles runs down our reflections.

CHAPTER 20

I open the door with a forced smile and Ruth comes bustling in, bundles of old plastic bags and bin bags in her hands. She's here, ready to start clearing her mother's things. I can't believe I've finally got through to her.

She marches in and pecks Olivia on the cheek. Olivia moans. Ruth frowns. 'Why's she grumbling? Don't tell me you've been turning her against me?'

'No,' I say, laughing nervously. 'She's just tired. No sleep last night. She kept waking up.' I smile, hoping she will take my cue and realise how exhausted I am too, and maybe offer to watch Olivia for a bit. But she ignores me as I shift Olivia's weight in my arms.

Ruth looks uncertainly at the specks of dirt in the hallway and then takes off her shoes reluctantly. I sigh. I only hoovered two days ago, but the house seems to breed dirt.

'Thanks so much for coming round,' I say. 'It will be great to have a bit more space for our things.' I know it will be a long process but at least she's willing to start.

'It's fine,' she replies. 'It needs doing. I'll never sell the house with all this clutter in.'

I bite my tongue. I know she's simply keeping me in my place, making it clear that I can't outstay my welcome. Matt has told me she has no plans to sell the house until we've saved up for a place of our own. She's just asserting her authority.

'Do you want a cup of tea?' I ask.

'Yes, please. I thought I'd start upstairs.'

I feel my stomach start to knot. There are still bin bags of Pamela's toiletries piled high in the study. I hope she doesn't see them. I never told her I'd cleared out the bathroom and thrown some of Pamela's things away. Surely she can't be angry about me throwing away old make-up and tights?

Ruth is halfway up the stairs and I abandon thoughts of the tea and follow her.

She's already in our bedroom, opening up the cupboards. It makes me feel uncomfortable, even though I know that this is one of the most useful areas she can clear out.

'Do you need any help?' I ask.

She turns to me and I see the tears in her eyes as she touches the material of one of Pamela's coats.

'Just that tea, please,' she says and I scoot out of the room with Olivia.

I pace around the kitchen anxiously as I wait for the kettle to boil. I can hear Ruth moving about upstairs.

When I leave the room to take the tea up, Olivia starts to cry. She needs another nappy change.

Upstairs, Ruth is now taking the clothes out of the cupboard one by one and shoving them unceremoniously in the bin bag.

I hand her the tea.

'Thanks,' she says, putting it down on the mantelpiece above the old fireplace.

Olivia wails downstairs.

'I'd better go. I'll be back up soon.'

After I've changed the nappy, I tidy up the living room and kitchen, afraid of Ruth's judgement. Then I carry Olivia upstairs to see how Ruth's getting on. She's still going through the cupboards. I put Olivia in her bouncy chair in the bedroom and start to tidy some of my things on the bedside table. I long to start moving the clothes from our flimsy temporary cupboards into the gaps appearing on the rails that Ruth is clearing, but it seems rude to start while she's still here.

I remember the way Ruth looked at the hall floor when she came in and I decide to get the hoover out and clean the bedroom. That way I can keep an eye on Ruth and show her I'm looking after her house.

Olivia watches me plug the vacuum cleaner in and Ruth turns as she hears the click of the plug being turned on at the socket.

'It needs a clean in here,' I say, to justify my presence.

She nods distractedly, one of Pamela's dresses in her hands.

The whir of the vacuum alarms Olivia and at first she screams. Then she gets used to it and watches me curiously. I feel calmer as I clean, all my worries of the last few weeks fading away. I'd been so concerned about Matt's relationship with Sarah, but seeing the farmhouse the other day and hearing from Matt how hard Sarah's life has been has made me see things differently. They are bonded by grief from the loss of Sarah's sister. Matt's only been trying to help her out of a sense of loyalty. It's me he married, not her.

And now even Ruth's being nice, clearing out the house. I have a feeling everything will work out after all. Matt and I will be able to start our lives here properly, make the cottage our own. I remember all the ideas I had about village life before I moved here. I longed for close family nearby, Olivia playing outside in the fresh country air in a house of our own. All that's starting to feel possible again.

As I clean round Olivia's baby seat, I start to hum to myself. Olivia reaches out ineffectively to grab the cord. I lean down to pull it away from her and catch sight of a flash of orange behind the bed. I can't think what it could be.

I peer closer. It looks like material. Orange is such an unusual colour, a colour I never wear. I pause and reach down, find an end and pull at it.

It's a silk scarf.

I examine the pattern. Yellow squares dot the orange material.

'That's nice,' Ruth says, from the other side of the room.

'Yes,' I reply.

I wrack my brain for where I've seen it before. I know I've seen it somewhere.

Sarah. She was wearing it when we cleared out the pond.

Sarah has been in my room.

In my bed.

With my husband.

My world comes crashing down around me.

CHAPTER 21

I stare at the scarf in my hands. My mind whirs with possibilities, trying to find an alternative explanation. An explanation that doesn't involve my husband cheating on me.

Perhaps Sarah dropped it when she was in the house on the day we cleared out the pond. Perhaps it got dirty at work and Matt offered to take it home and wash it for her. Perhaps it's not Sarah's at all. Perhaps Pamela had a similar one. Perhaps it's a local design that everyone has round here.

Without thinking I lift the scarf to my nose and sniff it. Sarah's perfume.

A strangled cry escapes me and I drop it.

I look up and realise that both Olivia and Ruth are watching me. I wonder if Ruth knows the significance of what's just happened. Sarah must have been here with Matt, in my bed. But when?

I feel sick as it dawns on me. It must have been the day I found my hairbrush wedged down the side of the bed. I thought it had been Ruth who'd been in our bedroom. It must have been Sarah. With Matt.

Everything fits together. All the time they spend together at work. Their cosy drink at the pub.

'What's wrong?' Ruth asks. If she does know the scarf belongs to Sarah then she's very good at hiding it.

For a moment, I feel illogically embarrassed. I don't want Ruth to know I've been humiliated, to know what's been going on behind my back.

'Nothing,' I reply, trying to stop my face flushing. 'Just something else for the charity shop.' I stuff the scarf into one of Ruth's bin bags. 'Can you watch Olivia for a moment?' I say quickly, and leave the room before my tears start rolling.

Back downstairs I can't sit still. I pace up and down, not sure what to do with myself.

This can't be happening to me. It just can't be.

Matt wouldn't do that to me. He wouldn't.

But then I think about how secretive he's been lately. All the things he hasn't told me. All the late nights. I'm not confident about anything I thought I knew about him.

When I mentioned that someone had been in our bedroom to Matt, he'd tried to convince me I'd imagined it. But he must have been there himself, with Sarah. Sarah must have swept my personal things off the bedside table, wanting to remove the traces of me from our bedroom while she slept with my husband, taking my place. I wonder if she meant to put them back, or if she'd left them hidden deliberately. Has Matt told her about all the things I've been forgetting? Did she plan it, so I'd think I was going mad?

I think of all the ways I've felt uncomfortable in my own house. Has Sarah been watching me, waiting for the perfect moment to steal Matt from me? I remember her in my room, touching my photos. Had she dropped the scarf then? No, she can't have. She was wearing it later that day. Olivia was grabbing at it, just before she fell into the pond.

My thoughts are spiralling out of control. I'm not sure if this is really happening or it's just the paranoia talking. Matt wouldn't cheat on me, would he? I'm going round in circles, not thinking straight.

'Hello?' Ruth is at the living room door, holding Olivia. I've no idea how long she's been standing there. Or how long I've been downstairs.

I wipe my red-rimmed eyes with the back of my hand.

'Claire…' She pauses mid-sentence, seeing my tears. 'Are you all right?'

'Yes,' I say. I can't tell her what Matt's done to me. I can't face it myself. I manage a half-smile. 'It's just emotional, that's all, seeing you clear out your mother's things.' The excuse seems feeble and I know Ruth sees right through it.

She pauses for a moment, as if carefully considering what to say next. 'Do you want me to take Olivia for a bit? Give you a break?'

I'm too shattered to worry that she thinks I can't cope. I need some time alone, to work out what I'm going to do.

'Yes, please. That would be great.'

'OK, well I'll bring her back in a couple of hours. You get some rest. It looks like you need it.'

The door shuts behind Ruth and the house is eerily silent. I don't know what to do now. I should confront Matt. Chuck him out. But what if it's all in my head? What if the scarf doesn't belong to Sarah at all and there's a reasonable explanation?

I wish I could talk to my mother about this. She would have calmed me down, made me think rationally. For a second I wonder if I could call Miriam. We supported each other through so many difficult break-ups. I know she'd understand.

I'm getting ahead of myself. Why am I even thinking about breaking up?

But I need to talk to someone. I pick up my phone and ring Emma. She'll understand, after everything she went through with Dan.

I pace the room as her mobile rings. Maybe I'm wrong about this whole thing. Maybe it's all a silly misunderstanding and Matt and I will laugh about it this evening.

Or maybe not.

I look at the unopened boxes that surround me. I should have unpacked them. But how soon will I be packing them back up again? If Matt and I split up, will Ruth and Jack even let me stay in the house? I don't mean anything to Ruth without her precious son.

Emma finally picks up and I jump.

'Claire? Is everything all right?'

'I'm so sorry. I didn't know who to call.'

'Don't be silly. What's wrong?'

'It's Matt. I think he's been cheating.' When I say the words out loud, the weight of what's happening sinks in. I start sobbing down the phone.

'Are you at home?'

'Yes,' I manage to splutter.

'Stay where you are. I'm coming over.'

By the time Emma arrives I have once again convinced myself that there must be some kind of reasonable explanation.

When I open the door she throws her arms around me and presents me with a box of chocolates and some flowers.

'I'm so sorry,' she says. 'I thought we could share these.' She hands me the chocolates. 'And the flowers will brighten up the house. They smell nice too. I always like the scent of lilies. This type anyway. They really cheer me up.'

'You know you shouldn't have,' I say, as she walks through the doorway. I suddenly feel embarrassed. What if I've made a fuss about nothing?

She looks at me, concerned. 'You're not allergic, are you?'

'No, it's not that. It's just such a kind gesture, that's all. Thank you.'

I take the lilies from her, run water into the sink and then cut off the bottom of the stalks. We have our own vase somewhere in a box waiting to be unpacked, but I settle for one of Pamela's and arrange the flowers.

'The room looks brighter already,' Emma says. 'Now, can I make you a cup of tea?'

I think I might prefer some neat whisky right now, but I know that's not an option, so I nod. Emma pulls out some mugs as I switch on the kettle. She's at the house so often that she doesn't need to ask where anything is any more.

Emma pours the tea and carries it through to the living room.

'So,' she says, taking a sip. 'What happened?'

I explain how I found the scarf.

'Maybe there's another explanation,' I say, looking at her hopefully. I want her to say it can't be true, that I'm missing something obvious.

But instead she sighs. 'I need to tell you something, Claire. I should have told you weeks ago.'

'What?' I ask, my heart sinking.

'I was browsing the shops in Oxford the other day and I saw Matt with Sarah. He was buying a bracelet. At first I thought it was for you and that maybe he was asking Sarah to help him choose. She was trying on the different bracelets, you see, and I thought that it was just to see how they looked on someone. I didn't believe...'

'He was buying it for her?' I say incredulously. Matt knows we're trying to save every penny we can so we can move out of Pamela's house.

'I didn't want to believe that at the time. But it looked that way. He handed the package over to her at the end. I'm sorry, Claire. I really should have told you.'

'Why didn't you?' I think of all the suspicions I've had about Matt and Sarah. If only she'd told me, that would have confirmed it.

'I suppose I wanted to believe the best of him. When I saw him hand the bracelet to Sarah, I told myself it was probably a gift for her hard work. But I didn't really believe that, if I'm honest with myself. I'm so sorry, I should have told you. I just didn't want to split you up. I wanted Olivia to have her father around. Everything that me and Lizzie don't have.'

'It's not your fault,' I say, bursting into tears.

Emma puts her hand on my arm. 'What a horrible thing to do, leaving the scarf there like that.'

'I guess she must have wanted me to find out. So she could take Matt from me. You know, I don't think she ever met anyone else after Matt left the village years ago. She wanted him back.'

The reality of my situation hits me once more. A wave of anger takes me over and I can hardly breathe. How could he? How could he sleep with her? In the bed where I breastfeed our child.

'I want to punish him,' I say.

'Don't let him come back,' Emma says. 'Don't ever let him come back. You deserve so much better.'

Emma finds a bin bag and I start stuffing Matt's clothes into it. Polo shirts, trousers, underwear. I crumple each item into a ball before shoving it into the bag. When it's full, Emma and I put the bag on the porch in the rain.

I feel better already.

Emma gives me a hug. 'Well done,' she says. 'You're so brave. I wish I'd done that with Dan the first time I discovered he was cheating.'

I manage a small smile, not feeling brave at all.

'Where's Olivia?' Emma asks.

'She's with Ruth,' I reply. 'I'd better go and get her.' I don't want Ruth using Olivia as some kind of bargaining chip when she finds out I've chucked Matt out.

Emma and I walk over to Ruth's, and she gratefully hands Olivia back to me.

'Are you feeling better?' she asks.

'Yes, thanks,' I say, glancing at Emma, before we make our excuses and hurry out the door.

When we get back, Emma helps me craft a text message to Matt.

I know what you did. Don't bother coming home tonight. Your stuff's outside.

'Why do you think he cheated on me?' I ask.

'I have no idea. Why does anyone cheat on anyone? There are so many amazing women out there who've been treated like this.'

'I thought we were good together,' I say. 'Me and Matt. We've been struggling a bit since Olivia's been born, but I still thought we were good together.'

I want to ask her if she could see the cracks in our relationship. If it was obvious to everyone but me.

'I thought you were good together too,' Emma replies and I'm relieved. 'But you had your doubts about Sarah, didn't you?'

'Maybe a bit. I can't bear the thought of him with someone else. If he leaves tonight he might go to her.'

I check my phone, desperately wanting to see a reassuring text from Matt. A text that explains how I'm mistaken. That everything's going to be all right.

But there's nothing. My face flushes and my body tenses as I fill with rage. He clearly doesn't think it's important to check his phone. What if something had happened to Olivia?

I want to scream at him. Ask him why he cheated, why I wasn't enough for him. If he doesn't love me any more.

My phone beeps and I jump.

What are you talking about?

No apology. I reply:

You know what I'm talking about.

My phone beeps again.

We can talk about this tonight.

Tears prick at the corners of my eyes before they cascade down my face. He hasn't even tried to call. He should be rushing home from work early to try and fix things. But he's not. Instead he's staying with Sarah at the surgery.

My resolve hardens.

Like I said, your stuff's outside.

I show the texts to Emma.

'Don't worry,' she says reassuringly. 'I'll stay with you until he comes back. You won't have to deal with him alone.'

I'm relieved, afraid that if I see Matt, I might crumble. If he apologises, I'll fall into his arms and forgive him. I don't want that.

When I hear Matt's key in the lock, I freeze. He tries it several times, pushing on the door before he shouts through the letter box.

'Claire?'

I come to the door. 'I've bolted the door,' I say.

'What? Why?'

'Your stuff's outside.'

Emma comes up beside me and touches my arm.

I hear Matt pick up the bin bag and rifle through it.

'Claire? What's going on?'

'You know what's going on. You're sleeping with Sarah.'

I realise I'm shouting. It is so quiet round here that my voice echoes.

'That's crazy. What are you talking about?'

'Just leave.'

'Claire. I'm tired. I just want some rest. Let me in and we can talk.'

'We're not talking about this, Matt. If you wanted to talk to me about our relationship, then you should have done it before you slept with her.'

He is quiet for a moment.

Emma takes my arm and we go back into the kitchen.

For the next twenty minutes Matt bangs on the door, shouting my name again and again. Finally he gives up and leaves. In the silence, all I can hear is the screeching of the foxes.

*

She picks up the phone after two rings and I'm relieved to hear her voice. I'm always scared that someone else will pick up when I ring the helpline. I only want to speak to her.

'Hi,' I say. 'It's me.'

There's a moment's hesitation and I worry I've been presumptuous, that she won't recognise me. She must take dozens of calls a day. I'm just one of many to her, but she is my only lifeline.

'Hi. How are you?' I can hear the smile in her voice and I smile too, reassured.

'I wasn't sure you'd know who it was,' I confess, with a nervous laugh.

'Of course I do. I'm always glad when you call.'

My heart lifts. It's something a friend would say.

'How are you?' I ask. I'm curious about her, about her life outside our conversations.

'I'm good,' she says. 'You know, busy.'

'You work long hours on the helpline.'

'Yeah,' she says. 'We're a bit short-staffed at the moment, so I'm on a lot of shifts.'

'It must be hard work.'

'Sometimes it's tiring.' She sighs. 'But that's not what you called to talk about. How are things going?' I'm disappointed she's changed the subject, that she doesn't want to tell me about herself.

But there's a reason I've called today. There's something that's been playing on my mind. She said that men like my husband were always the same, that they often have a history of abusive behaviour.

'It's my husband,' I say. 'Someone's accused him of sexual assault.' I hear her intake of breath.

'What have they said?'

'I'm not sure exactly. He's been vague about the details.'

'Do you believe them?'

I breathe in deeply, it's hard to form the words. I feel like I'm betraying my husband, betraying my marriage vows. But I've thought about this again and again. I can't get the images out of my mind.

'Yes,' I say. 'I believe them.'

CHAPTER 22

Olivia's screaming. I roll over in bed drowsily and check my phone. Three in the morning. Time for her feed. I reach over towards Matt's side of the bed into the empty space. I'm on my own now. Just me and Olivia.

I pad over to Olivia's room and lift her out of her cot, pulling my nightdress down and holding her to my breast. My arm aches under her weight. Using my other hand, I check my phone. The screen is lit up with messages. Fourteen missed calls from Matt from last night. Two voicemails. I ignored them yesterday, unable to face them.

I listen now. The sound of Matt's voice makes me well up. He says I should call him, that he loves me, that he doesn't know what he's done but he's sorry. His voice breaks as he rings off.

Without letting myself think, I call him back. I know it's the middle of the night, but I need to hear his voice, need to know someone's at the other end of the phone.

He picks up after two rings. 'Claire? Are you all right?'

'Yeah.' I haven't thought about what to say. I just want him to wrap his strong arms around me and tell me everything's going to be OK. But I know I have to be brave. He cheated on me. It's over.

'Claire,' he says softly. 'What happened last night?' I hate that gentle voice he's using. He's trying to calm me down, as if I'm a child.

'I found Sarah's scarf. Under our bed.'

He pauses before he answers. 'Are you sure it was Sarah's?'

'Yes,' I say. 'I'm sure.' For a second, a doubt crosses my mind. I only saw Sarah wearing the scarf on one occasion, when she came round to clear the pond. But I dispel the thought. I know what I found.

'And you're sure it was under the bed?'

'Yes, of course.' I feel disappointed anger rising inside me. I'd hoped for an apology. Instead he's questioning everything I say.

He sighs. 'I don't know why it would be there, Claire. I'm sorry, but I don't.'

'What about the bracelet?'

'What bracelet?'

'The one you bought Sarah.'

'Honestly, I don't know what you're talking about.'

He thinks he can lie his way out of this. I wonder if he's with Sarah now, if they're both laughing at me.

'Where are you?' I ask.

'I'm at Mum's.'

'Oh.' I try to keep the relief from my voice.

'Claire – is there anything I can do to make this better? You've been unwell. I just want to be with you to help you.'

I hate him then, turning this on me, making me think I'm going crazy. I know that's not what's happening.

'Forget it. I'm fine on my own.'

I hang up the phone, sighing with frustration, as Olivia continues to suckle.

I wish he'd just apologised. At least that would be a start. But he thinks he can just deny everything.

I try to distract myself by browsing the internet, but as usual I find myself looking at Sarah's Facebook profile. She still hasn't accepted my friend request. Now I know why.

Her old photos are still the same, but this time I see them differently. There are a couple with another girl, who must be her sister. I didn't realise they were the same person at first. In one photo Sarah and her sister smile at the camera arm in arm, young and vibrant and ready to take on the world. In the second picture they are still smiling, but the sister has aged, and is wheelchair-bound, the left side of her face lopsided with paralysis. I remember how upset Matt was when he told me Sarah's story and I feel an unexpected flicker of sympathy for her. The photo must have been taken between the accident and her sister's death.

As I look at the photograph, something bothers me. My instincts are telling me that there's something not quite right about Matt's explanation of the accident.

I take Sarah's sister's name from Facebook and google it along with the word 'accident'. Eventually, after pages and pages of irrelevant results, I find a newspaper article.

September 1998. '*Tragic accident for local family.*'

I read the article three times.

The accident happened late at night. Sarah's sister fell from the hayloft in the barn and cracked her head on the concrete floor. The article has a timeline of events and an annotated diagram. Despite this, it isn't quite clear exactly what happened at the moment she fell. But it's clear that Matt hasn't told me the whole story. There were only two witnesses to the accident. Him and Sarah. Both were interviewed by the police.

Why would he keep that from me? What other secrets does he share with Sarah?

I go through Matt's Facebook profile and look through the posts from the last few months, and then go back years and years, to see if there's something there about him and Sarah. Something I've missed. There's nothing. No hint of a relationship with her. But it wouldn't be on his public profile. I need to look at his private messages. I log out of my account and type in the password he used to use for everything. It doesn't work. He must have changed it. He must be hiding something.

At least he's not with her now. He's with Ruth. I bet she's furious with me for chucking out her beloved son. I'm sure she won't let me stay in the house for long without Matt. But where can I go? I should have thought this through before I packed his bags. I should have had a plan.

I think of my life back in London, how much I miss it. Or at least I miss parts of it. I could move back. I wonder if the newspaper would take me on again. A mix of emotions rise inside me. I remember the excitement I felt when I first entered the buzzing newsroom. The thrill of chasing down the story. That was at the beginning. By the end I hated the newspaper and I hated who I'd become. Could I really go back?

But I'm stronger now, I tell myself. I wouldn't get sucked into that cut-throat, competitive world, doing everything I could, no matter what, to get the story. I wouldn't get caught up in the testosterone of the newsroom, I wouldn't let my article come before the people.

I take a deep breath and compose an email to the editor. I have nothing to lose. He's new and he probably won't even know who I am. I introduce myself, tell about him my track record, let him know the prizes I won and ask if there are any vacancies. I hesitate for a moment after I reread the email, wondering if he ever heard the rumours about why I left at the height of my career. I hope not. I swallow my doubts and then click send before I can change my mind.

The glow from my phone lights up Olivia's face. I look down and see she's fallen asleep on my breast. I lift her gently back into the cot, lay her next to her toy bunny, and go back to bed. It's cold without Matt's body beside me. Sleep threatens to submerge me, but I keep starting awake, picturing Matt with Sarah.

In the quiet, I can hear the faint beeping from the loft. I wish it would stop. When daylight comes, I'll have to go up there and check out the noise.

I stare at the wall, watching the flickering shadow of a moth fluttering around the bedside light that I can't bring myself to switch off. What if there's someone up there? What if I'm not alone in the house?

At eight, after a couple of hours of fitful sleep, I get dressed and take Olivia out to the supermarket. I swing into the mother and baby space, narrowly avoiding a collision with a shopping trolley, carelessly abandoned in the middle of the car park. Olivia wakes as soon as the car stops, my ten minutes of respite over. When I open her door, a cold blast of air hits her and she starts to cry. A mother with a toddler in tow looks at me curiously and I wonder if she's judging me.

Olivia's hat has fallen off in her car seat and I replace it awkwardly on her head. She pulls it off again. Holding it in one hand and Olivia in the other I lock the car and go into the supermarket. I find a trolley with a baby seat, but Olivia seems too small for it. I steer it slowly to stop her banging her head as she slides from side to side.

Olivia's eyes light up as she looks at the multitude of products on the shelves. I throw things into the trolley beside her. Lamb chops for dinner. Vegetables. Fruit.

An old lady comes over and starts cooing at Olivia, leaning over the trolley and pushing her face close. My baby smiles angelically and I tense. She never smiles that way at me.

'She's lovely,' the woman says. 'What a good baby.'

I nod politely. She has no idea. Olivia reserves all her love and affection for others. Never for me. I must try harder. I walk round the supermarket pretending to be a good mother, bending over and talking to Olivia in that high voice I've heard other mums use. It's easier here in public, where there's an audience. Easier for me to play my part.

I spot a grandmother shopping with her daughter and granddaughter. The grandmother pushes the trolley as she offers well-intentioned advice on childcare to her daughter, who pushes the buggy beside her. The daughter bats the advice away, irritated. I listen to them as they bicker over what they'll have for dinner.

When they move away, I can still hear the rise and fall of their voices.

I long for the relationship they have, missing my mother. I'd do anything to be with her right now. If my mother was here, what would she say? I can hardly picture her any more, let alone hear her voice. Would she tell me everything would be OK? Would she help me?

I find myself at the end of the supermarket I avoid. The alcohol aisle. I feel my trolley turning, see the glimmer of thousands of glass bottles lined up. I stop at the Chilean reds, remembering a vineyard tour I did back when I went travelling after university. I pick them up one by one, reading the labels and feeling the cold glass against my skin. I can almost taste the tanginess running over my tongue and down the back of my throat. It reminds me of balmy summer evenings when I sipped a cold glass of wine after a long day's work.

But I'm not that person any more. I can't be that person again.

I put the bottles back.

Further down are the New Zealand Sauvignons. I find Matt's favourite and hold it for a moment. There's no point buying it and I put the bottle back reluctantly. I tell myself it would be silly to drink on my own, as much as I want to. I go to the till. Olivia starts to whine. The queue's too long and I fidget as the man in front painstakingly fills his plastic bags. I can still imagine the taste of the Sauvignon on my tongue, see the wheat yellow colour of the wine in the glass, feel the rim of the glass on my lips.

It's my turn. The till assistant swipes through my purchases and I pack as fast as I can, returning the bags to the trolley.

She tells me the total, and I pause.

'Hang on a minute,' I say. 'I've forgotten something.'

I dash back to the wine aisle and grab the nearest bottle.

I pull up in front of the cottage and sit for a moment in the car. I don't want to go inside. I want to drive far away, away from my life and away from my family. I want to forget everything that's happened.

A knock on the car window jars me back to reality.

Matt.

I close my eyes for a second before I open the door.

'Why aren't you at the practice?'

'I couldn't go to work. Not with all this going on. We need to sort this out. I'm worried about you.'

I sigh. He's always been a good actor. I wish he'd just admit what he did.

'Claire.' He reaches for my arm and I pull it away sharply. 'Do you really believe I'd sleep with Sarah? Why would I risk losing you? Risk losing our family?'

I feel uncertain now, as if I might have imagined the whole thing.

I see Ruth appear from the side path. I don't want her here.

She goes round the back of the car and opens Olivia's door. She gives her a quick kiss on the cheek and tells her how beautiful she is and then comes to the front of the car.

'What are you doing out here?' she asks Matt.

'You know what I'm doing. I needed to speak to Claire.'

'I wouldn't waste your breath. Look at what she's done to you. Evicting you from your own home for no reason at all.'

'You're not helping, Mum.'

Ruth turns to me, her voice venomous. 'Who do you think you are, coming here, living in my mother's house and treating my son this way? After all we've done for you, you throw him out with only a bin bag of his things?'

I look down at the gravel. 'He's cheating on me.'

Ruth glances at Matt. 'Is he? Well good for him, in that case. He's carried you long enough. Looked after you. Protected you. You can't expect someone to love you when you behave the way you do. He's told me about you, you know. That you're paranoid. That you've been forgetting things. No one would put up with that forever.'

I swallow, afraid. How much of my history has Matt told his mother?

'Mum, please—'

Matt grabs her arm, tries to pull her away.

'And another thing. Don't think you can just live in this house forever, rent-free. The house was for my son to live in while he set up his new business. Not you.'

'What about your granddaughter?' I say. 'Don't you care what happens to her?'

'Don't worry, nothing will happen to Olivia. In fact, she'll end up better off. There's no chance you'll get custody with all your problems.'

I stare at her, shocked.

'Matt, come on,' she orders. 'We've got company this evening.'

Matt turns to me. 'We'll talk later. On our own.'

I watch as they walk back down the path together. How have I ended up in this position? This was meant to be a fresh start, but Ruth wants to take my daughter away from me and make me homeless.

I go round the back of the car to Olivia. She's happily patting at the toy that hangs above her car seat. I go to undo her buckle.

It's already undone.

I stare at the loose straps in horror.

Did I forget to fasten her in? Have I driven all the way back from the supermarket without my daughter strapped in the car? If there'd been an accident, I could have killed her. Just like when I left the brake off the buggy by the pond. Maybe Ruth is right, maybe Matt would get custody. If I can't even be trusted to strap my daughter into her car seat, then maybe I don't deserve her.

CHAPTER 23

In the afternoon, I don't know what to do with myself. I stare around the house, looking at the boxes surrounding me. It feels pointless to unpack them now.

I wish I could talk to Miriam. I just want to pick up the phone and call her, confide in her the way I always did in the past. I still have her number in my phone. So much time has passed, maybe she'll have forgiven me by now. It's worth a try. I have nothing to lose.

I painstakingly compose a text message.

> *Hi. It's Claire. It's been too long. I'd love to catch up. I hope we can put the past behind us.*

I'm about to delete the last bit and redraft it, when Olivia cries for her feed.

I read the message again. She's never going to reply anyway. I click send.

While I'm feeding Olivia, Emma messages me to see how I am and suggests a trip to Oxford to take my mind off things. Dan has Lizzie and she's at a loose end.

She comes round to collect me half an hour later and soon we're in the city centre, wandering round the shops.

'I've organised a surprise for you,' Emma tells me. 'To cheer you up.'

I grin. 'Really?'

'Yep. It's just round the corner.'

She leads me to a side street and I see the small wine shop she's mentioned to me before. My heart sinks. I really shouldn't buy more wine. Not when I'm feeling so down.

'Maybe not today.'

'Come on, Claire. I've organised a tasting session for you. My treat. You have to try it. Everyone raves about this place.'

'I'm not sure…'

But Emma is already inside the shop.

I follow her in reluctantly, wheeling the buggy in behind her. It takes up all the floor space in the tiny shop. I hope no one sees me and judges me.

The man behind the small desk at the back welcomes us with a smile and I tell myself that a tasting can't do any harm. It will only be tiny portions.

'Beautiful baby,' he says, looking down at sleeping Olivia.

I smile proudly. It's so rare for her to be quiet. I should make the most of this opportunity.

The man talks us through the history of the shop, the grapes and the wine-making process, as I relax, breathing in the smell of the alcohol and imagining the taste of it on my tongue.

Finally, he takes two plastic cups and pours us each a small glass of the dry white. I swirl it round my mouth, savouring the tang on my tongue. I hold it there for a moment, letting the flavour overwhelm my senses. I wonder if I'm supposed to spit it out, but that's not been mentioned so I swallow and then take another sip.

We try another wine and then a third and a fourth. I'm starting to feel a bit giddy. It's so long since I've drunk alcohol, that I'm not used to the rush I get when it starts to flow through me. But it feels good. Emma keeps asking questions about the grapes and the fermenting process as the proprietor pours increasingly large portions.

I smile at Emma and she giggles at me and clinks her plastic cup with mine.

'Having fun?' she asks.

'Yes.' I laugh. I am having fun. For once I feel relaxed and free.

After the wine tasting, Emma suggests we sober up with a coffee. We need to give it a bit of time before Emma can drive us back home.

In the coffee shop, Emma leans across the table and asks me how I'm feeling.

'OK, I suppose,' I say. 'I miss Matt. And he's still denying sleeping with Sarah. I'm starting to wonder if he's telling the truth.'

'They all deny it at first,' Emma replies. 'That's exactly what Dan did.'

I stare into my coffee.

'And Ruth is getting involved too, which isn't helping. I think she might evict me from the house.'

'Oh no. That's awful.' Emma gives me a sympathetic glance. 'You and Olivia could always come and stay with me if you need to.'

'Really?'

'Of course. My pleasure.'

I sigh with relief. It feels good to have a choice, even though I've no intention of leaving the cottage without a fight.

'Thanks.' I sigh, reaching across the table to touch Emma's hand. 'You don't know what that means to me.'

'It's no problem. Lizzie and I would love your company.'

Emma looks out at the street beyond the coffee shop. 'What do you fancy doing now? We've got the rest of the afternoon.'

'I should be getting back.' I've perked up from the caffeine, but underneath I'm exhausted.

'Really?' she says, disappointed.

Then I think of the oppressive cottage and imagine an afternoon of feeds and dirty nappies, and change my mind. 'What were you thinking?' I ask.

'How about we go to one of the churches? They're beautiful.'
I smile. 'Sure.'

There's a church a short walk down the road, and we wander inside. Emma seems thrilled that the church spire is open today. 'Do you want to climb up it?' she asks excitedly.

I look up at the tower. The views must be spectacular. 'Why not?'

'Great,' Emma says, and before I can think twice, she's paid our entrance fees to the man behind the trestle table at the bottom of the steps. I look doubtfully at Olivia in her buggy. Can I carry her up?

'Don't worry,' Emma says. 'She'll be fine in the sling.'

Emma's right. I take Olivia out of the buggy and strap her to me.

The steps are uneven and I have to concentrate on the climb. After a while, I start to feel dizzy from the spiralling staircase. It goes on and on and it feels like Olivia is getting heavier and heavier strapped to my front. Her weight pulls me off balance, each step harder than the next. The air in the spire is thick with dust, the handrail's rusty, and I'm starting to feel claustrophobic.

Olivia lets out a small whimper.

'Not far to go now,' Emma shouts down from above me. 'I can see the top.'

'OK,' I say, as I force my legs to keep climbing.

Olivia starts to cry and it echoes around the narrow stairwell. The loud group of tourists on the stairs below pause their conversation, and I'm embarrassed. 'Don't worry, Olivia,' I say over and over, as I push on towards the top.

This whole thing is starting to feel like a really bad idea. What if I slip and fall and Olivia's skull cracks on the stone steps? That's the kind of accident you read about in the tabloids. The kind where the mother is always blamed. I wish I hadn't had a drink. My giddiness is fading, but the light-headedness remains, and I'm not sure if I feel unsteady because of the drink or because I'm carrying Olivia.

Finally I see a glimpse of blue sky and I'm at the top of the spire. The wind hits me and knocks me off balance as I step out onto the narrow walkway.

'Are you OK?' Emma asks, her hand on my shoulder to steady me.

'Just a bit dizzy.'

The wind whips round Olivia, and I look out over the view. It's beautiful. The dreaming spires of Oxford dot the compact city below us, and beyond there are miles of rolling fields.

'Come on,' Emma says, and I realise that I've hardly moved away from the steps.

I go to the edge. The stone wall is only up to waist height and a thin, netted barrier has been put up to stop people throwing things over the edge.

Suddenly I feel sick. If I was knocked or fell, Olivia and I would go straight over. The net wouldn't break our fall.

The rustle of pigeons in the tower next to me startles me. The world starts to spin. I step back suddenly and knock into a tourist taking a photo.

'Sorry,' I mumble.

I can't look down. Images are cascading through my head, flooding me with memories. I'm back on the roof of the car park, standing on the edge of the concrete barrier. Alone. The world is tiny and undefined below me. A blur of people and cars and movement. I can no longer be a part of it. My heart pounds in my chest, my hands are clammy. I'm ready to jump. Ready to end everything.

'Claire! Claire – are you all right?' Emma asks.

She catches me as I faint, reaching out for Olivia and blocking her fall. The motion forces my head backwards and I feel it hit the cold, ancient stone.

When I come round a couple of tourists are looking at me quizzically, while others continue to take photos, oblivious.

Olivia is screaming in Emma's arms while she rocks her. My first instinct is that I want my daughter back. I want her in my arms, not Emma's. She's been removed from the sling, she's not secure. I imagine someone knocking her out of Emma's arms, her flying over the barrier and down to the streets below.

Emma crouches down beside me, still holding Olivia.

'Just stay there for a moment, don't move.'

'Olivia,' I say.

'Don't worry, I've got her. She's OK. I caught her.'

I reach out for my daughter.

'It's all right,' Emma says. 'Everything's going to be all right.'

*

I go into the bedroom and sit down on the bed beside my sleeping husband. It's 3 a.m. and I watch as he breathes deeply and peacefully, his chest rising and falling.

The scene doesn't feel real. How can he rest after what he's done?

I've been in his study. The key was easy to find, hidden at the back of the drawer in his bedside table. He can't have expected me to look for it. The study has always been out of bounds. I'd never dared to go in.

I've been searching for evidence. About the girls. About the accusations. The helpline volunteer asked me questions that I couldn't answer and I'd realised I'd buried my head in the sand.

I needed to know the truth.

I know everything now. The accusations go back years. Sexual assault. Rape. He's been paying them off so nothing goes to trial. There are dozens of them. Young girls mainly. Working for him. Wanting a step up on the ladder.

Some of them have sent him letters, begging him to apologise, to admit what he did and give them closure. Their despair seeps out of the paper. They sound broken. By him. He did that to them.

All I want to do is talk to someone about it.

But it's 3 a.m.

The helpline is open twenty-four hours a day, but there's no way she'll be on shift at this time. She always seems to be on the daytime shift.

My finger hovers over the call button. I could ring anyway. On the off-chance she's there. Or I could speak to someone else.

But she knows my history. She understands me. She's helped me make sense of things.

I only want to talk to her.

I lie awake and wait until the morning, wondering what time her shift starts. Seven o'clock? Eight? The minutes pass slowly.

At 7.01 my husband and daughter are still asleep. I know there's a high chance she won't be on shift even now, but I go into the spare room and press call anyway. I need to talk to her.

The phone rings and rings, and I stare out the window at the trees blowing in the wind, praying she'll be the one who picks up.

'Hello?' I hear the voice as I'm just about to give up. I shake with relief. It's her.

'Hi,' I say. 'It's me.'

I don't hear the footsteps behind me.

I'm not aware of his presence until he grabs my phone from my hand and throws it across the room.

I hear the thud as it lands.

I can still hear the voice on the other end of the line, fainter now. 'Hello?'

'Who are you on the phone to?'

He grabs me by the shoulder and shakes so hard, my bones rattle. 'Who?' he shouts in my face.

'Nobody,' I reply.

'I knew you had another man.'

'I don't. I really don't.'

His rage rains down on me until the world goes black.

CHAPTER 24

I get off the train at Paddington and join the mass of people streaming towards the entrance to the Tube. I'm on my way to meet the editor of my old newspaper. I was pleasantly surprised that he got back to me so quickly and wanted to see me when I'd been out of the job market for so long. I haven't been employed as a journalist since I quit three years ago.

I try to quiet my doubts and focus. I'm stronger than I was back then. I stand tall, no longer hunched over a buggy, and I listen to the click-clack of my heels on the concourse. I think I'm ready now. The newspaper feels like it might be an opportunity rather than somewhere I need to escape. I feel a stab of anxiety in my stomach as I wonder if I'm really up for returning to that ruthless world, or if I'm just kidding myself. I feel like I'm recovering a part of myself that's been in hibernation for a long time.

When I reach the darkness of the Tube, I push myself onto the carriage, squashing myself between the door and the heaving mass of bodies. In the crush, I feel like I could belong. Ambition burns in the air. Suits and newspapers and headphones. I want to be part of this again.

I change to the Central Line and then I'm spat out at Bank, the tide of commuters forcing me off the train and onto the platform. I flow with the crowd, following the river of legs above me as they climb the stairs. Outside, it's cold and fresh, and the air feels thin after the thickness of the Tube. It's raining, and the people on the pavement are sheltered by a canopy of umbrellas. I open my black umbrella and join them, lifting it up and down constantly to avoid bumping it into the others.

The streets hum with people, pushing and shoving their way through, shouting into mobile phones and jumping into taxis. A suited man walks beside me, but not with me, plugged into the rhythm of his headphones. Buses meander down the road, a slipstream in the middle of the sea of pedestrians.

The atmosphere's so unlike the countryside, with its emptiness and fields and quiet. Here the world is vivid and alive. Colours are brighter. Noises are louder. I've missed it all.

As I approach the revolving doors of my office, I have a sudden flash of fear. I stop on the pavement. Stare through the glass. I'm not sure I can do this.

I ignore the feelings that rise inside me. Surely it's time to move on. Surely I can forget what happened here. What I did.

I take a deep breath and let the revolving doors carry me into the entrance hall. I go over to reception and speak to the false lashes and designer eyebrows behind the desk. Neat white blouse, low-cut enough to catch a glimmer of flesh, but formal enough to look discreet. Anyone could tell that this building is occupied by male dominated industries: investment bankers, insurance brokers and the newspaper.

'I'm here for a meeting,' I say.

She sighs and looks me up and down, as if even engaging with me is too much effort.

'Name?'

'Claire Hughes.'

'Not your name,' she huffs. 'The name of the person you're meeting.'

'Adrian. Adrian Lister.'

She raises her eyebrows but picks up the phone. 'I'll ring him to confirm and get you a visitor's pass.' She indicates a seat in reception and I go and sit down.

I check my phone and see there's nothing from Emma. It's so kind of her to babysit. She's said she'll take Olivia to the park with Lizzie. I didn't want to ask Matt to look after her, or for him to know I was looking for a job in London.

Half an hour later, I'm collected from reception by Adrian's PA. Nerves hit me as I we travel up in the glass lift. Being back in the offices brings back an overwhelming feeling of guilt. I remember coming into this building three years ago, heart thumping, my front page scoop on my laptop in my bag. It was the biggest mistake of my life. After that, everything changed.

When we reach the news floor, Adrian, the editor, comes out of his glass-fronted office and holds out his hand. He's broader than the pictures I've seen, and rounder. His face is graced with the rosacea of a serious alcohol problem. He shakes my hand firmly.

'Claire, a pleasure to meet you. I hear you were one of our best journalists, back in the day.'

'Great to meet you too. I've followed your career.'

'Well, come through. Let's talk in my office.'

He puts his hand on my back to guide me into his office and it stays there a little longer than necessary. He sits on a comfy chair and indicates the low sofa in front of him. I sit down, but it's hard to get comfortable. The angle makes it almost impossible to cross my legs.

'So, what have you been doing the last three years?'

'Has it really been that long?' I laugh. I'd hoped he wouldn't bring that up. He must have heard why I left the newspaper, how I couldn't take the pressure any more, how I broke down.

I look at my feet, my confidence seeping out of me, into the carpet. 'Copywriting, mainly.'

'OK,' says Adrian, dragging out the sound, waiting for an explanation. When I don't provide one he continues. 'Human interest stories. That's your speciality, isn't it?'

'Yes.' I reach into my satchel and pull out my notebook. 'I have some ideas for new features.'

I run him through them and he listens attentively. I feel a surge of pride. He respects me. I'm no longer just a mother, but a professional once again.

When the meeting finishes, we both stand and he leans in and gives me a light peck on the cheek, as his arm reaches round my shoulder.

'We could use someone like you,' he says. 'I'll be in contact.'

As I travel down in the lift I feel relieved, as if a weight has been lifted. I'd been so nervous about coming back, so worried that people in the office would be whispering about the reason I left three years ago.

Walking back to the station, I pass one of my old haunts, the Rose and Crown pub. I push open the door and enter the dimly lit front room. It's still early and the pub feels surprisingly soulless without its usual crowd of city workers and journalists.

I'll just have one drink here to celebrate how well the meeting went, and then I'll go home. I sit down and relax at a table in the corner, savouring my wine and remembering all the good nights I had in this pub, unwinding with work colleagues: celebrations of finally nailing a story, welcoming new people to the team, leaving parties. There was always an excuse to come here, it was like a second home. I miss the sense of camaraderie, the feeling of belonging. I could have that again if I came back.

As I sit sipping my wine, I smile out at the bustling city. Suddenly, everything seems possible. Everyone in the office has forgotten about my mistake and moved on. It's time for me to move on too.

CHAPTER 25

I spend the next morning cleaning the house, vacuuming every dark corner, dusting every crevice. I've cleared all the surfaces of Pamela's things. The cottage smells of oaky furniture polish and I feel hopeful again.

The meeting with Adrian yesterday alleviated some of my fears about returning to work. A part of me hopes that Matt and I still have a future, but if I have to move, at least it might be possible to start my own life again. I loved journalism once. I think I could love it again.

Everything seems to be coming together. I think I finally might be able to put the past behind me. Then maybe my nightmares will stop. Things are even looking up with Miriam. She replied to my text. I was so shocked I had to read it four times in case I'd misunderstood. But I hadn't. We're meeting this afternoon in Oxford. It's halfway between the two of us.

The white noise of the vacuum has lulled Olivia to sleep. In the silence, I can hear the distant beeping from the loft.

I take Olivia upstairs, and strap her into the chair on the landing. There's a ladder in the spare room and I put it against the wall, next to the loft hatch, climb up and push the hatch open. A cloud of dust drifts down from the darkness above.

The sound is louder now, an insistent, regular tone. I climb higher and feel around for a light switch. Unable to find one, I go back down the ladder and set my phone to torch mode. I feel slightly sick climbing the ladder, afraid of what I might find in the darkness above.

There's a cord switch dangling from one of the rafters, but when I pull it nothing happens. The bulb probably went years ago.

The beeping is coming from the back of the loft, under the eaves. I shine my torch around and realise that it's not properly boarded. Boxes are balanced precariously along the beams.

I creep along, watching where I tread, stooping under the rafters. The noise is coming from an open box, full of random electrical wires. I see something flashing and pull it out. A smoke alarm. The battery must be almost dead. Then I recognise it. It used to be in Olivia's bedroom.

Someone's removed it and put it in the loft.

I swallow. Why would anyone do that? The smoke alarm's here to protect us. I imagine a fire ripping through the clutter in the old cottage, flames curling up the wallpaper. Without a smoke alarm, we wouldn't have a chance.

I feel sick. I thought I was going mad, but now I can see I was right to be worried. Someone wants to hurt me. To hurt us. Olivia and I are in danger.

Olivia's on the landing. On her own.

I need to get back down from the loft. I need to protect my child.

I make my way carefully along the beam, my body shaking, my phone in one hand, the alarm in the other.

Who would have taken the smoke alarm from Olivia's room and put it up here?

Clunk.

I jump at the sound.

Is there someone in the house?

Has someone come for Olivia?

As I hurry to the loft opening, I feel my foot slip underneath me. I reach out into empty space. The alarm flies out of my hand.

I am falling.

*

I land with a crash next to the loft hatch. Another inch or two and I would have tumbled out and down the stairs. Olivia would have been left all alone.

I peer down onto the landing, fearing that Olivia's chair will be empty, that someone will have taken her.

But she's fine, contentedly swiping the toy above her chair.

I'm still holding my phone. The smoke alarm has landed a couple of feet away from me in the unboarded part of the loft. Awkwardly, I manoeuvre myself onto my stomach, so my weight remains on the beam, and reach out for it. My fingers grip its yellowing plastic and I pull it towards me.

When I place my foot on the ladder, my ankle complains. I pull the loft hatch shut and climb back down slowly, wincing with each step.

I wash the dust off my hands and then pick Olivia up, holding her close. My heart pounds in my chest.

I hear a snapping sound and freeze.

What was that?

I peer down the stairs, anxiously, hugging Olivia tightly.

There's a white piece of paper in the hallway.

It was just the letter box. Someone's delivered something. Most likely junk mail. An advert for a cleaner or a local babysitter.

I take a deep breath and try to centre myself. I can't calm down.

Beep.

I jump at the smoke alarm's sudden interruption.

The thought of a fire makes me shiver. I must replace the battery and put the smoke alarm back in Olivia's room where it can protect us. The cottage doesn't feel safe.

I go downstairs to look for a screwdriver.

On my way past the door I pick up the piece of paper.

It's a single sheet, folded in half. I open it.

It's not an advert for a cleaning service. It's a message.

Printed neatly across the middle of the paper is a single line: *You don't deserve Olivia.*

*

When I wake, the sunlight beats into my pounding head through the open curtains. My memory comes back slowly as I try to move my limbs. I remember my husband's fists pummelling into me again and again until my world went black. He was angry with me because he thought I was on the phone to a lover. But I'd been on the phone to the helpline.

My daughter screams from the other room, demanding my attention. I go to her room and lift her up, holding her tight. She's all I have in the world.

I glance at the clock. An hour has passed since I called the helpline. My husband must have left for work.

Once I've calmed my daughter down, I find my phone where it fell when he knocked it out of my hand. The screen is smashed, but otherwise it seems to work.

I have five missed calls. All from the helpline.

I panic. She must have heard my husband knock me out. What if she called the police?

Surely she wouldn't do that. She must know it would only make it worse.

My heart pounds as I call her back.

She doesn't bother with a greeting. 'I'm so glad you called. I was worried about you.'

'You shouldn't worry. I'm used to it.' I try to laugh lightly but it sounds close to a sob. The movement of my chest triggers a sharp pain in my ribs. I struggle to breathe.

'I am worried. About you. About your safety. What are you going to do?'

Tears prick the corners of my eyes. Someone cares about me. She must be the only one.

'I don't know what to do. I went through his study yesterday. There are dozens of girls accusing him of things, going back years.'

'What kind of things?'

'*The worst kind.*' *The word is hard to get out. But it needs saying.* '*Rape.*'

I hear her intake of breath.

He's paid them off.' *I continue.* '*All of them. He must have done it.*'

'*You've seen all this?*' *she asks.* '*You have all the evidence?*'

'*Yes.*'

'*You have to leave him.*' *Her direct words shock me.*

'*But I love him.*'

'*What about your daughter?*'

I can hear the sounds of my daughter playing downstairs, the tinny music of her toy bear circling round on repeat.

I don't know what's best for her any more. I've told myself I'm giving her the childhood I never had, two loving parents, a home.

'*He loves her. He'd never hurt her.*'

'*How do you know that?*'

The tears are running down my cheeks now.

'*I just know,*' *I say, but I'm not so sure of my own words any more. I didn't marry the man I thought I did. I don't know my husband at all.*

Maybe she's right. Maybe I need to get my daughter away from him.

'*Do you have anywhere to go? Family? Friends?*'

'*No.*' *I realise how stark my situation is. I have no friends left. I don't even have a bank account in my own name. He has completely cut me off.*

'*Anyone you could stay with? Someone you could confide in?*'

I don't know what to say. She's the only one I can talk to about this. The only person I trust. I have to be honest. I need her help.

'*I don't have anyone.*'

She pauses for a second. '*You could stay with me. If you're desperate. You could come and stay with me.*'

CHAPTER 26

I read the single typed sentence again and again, until the letters start to blur into each other.

You don't deserve Olivia.

I start to feel faint and I sit down on the stairs, staring at the stark black type, my baby in my arms.

You don't deserve Olivia.

Whoever wrote the note can see right through me. I know I'm not a good mother. I know I don't deserve her. The words echo in my head.

You don't deserve Olivia.

I hug my daughter closer to me, tears of regret welling up. I must do better. But I'm so scared, scared I'm just not good enough.

Someone knows I don't deserve my daughter. Someone hid the smoke alarm so that if there's a fire then Olivia and I wouldn't stand a chance. What do they want from me? And what will they do next? They must be in my house, creeping around when I'm not there.

Ruth. It must be Ruth. She's trying to convince me I'm going mad, so Matt gets custody of Olivia. She said the other day that

I'd never get custody with all my issues, and now she's making sure it's true.

I must get away from her. I can't stay in the cottage. I don't feel safe here.

Picking up my phone from beside me on the staircase, I call Emma. She'd said that Olivia and I could move in with her for a while.

At first, I didn't want to take her up on it. I didn't want Ruth to force me out of the house.

But now things have changed.

My heart is still pounding and I can't catch my breath, as I listen to the phone ringing and ringing. I wish she'd pick up. I want to leave as soon as possible. Tonight if I can. I don't think I'll be able to sleep another night in this house.

'It will be OK,' I whisper to Olivia. 'We'll move in with Emma and Lizzie. We'll be safe there.'

The phone clicks onto answerphone.

I hang up and immediately redial. I think about what I'll need to take with me. Clothes. Toiletries. Nappies. Wipes. How long would I be staying with Emma? A week? Two? Longer?

If I get offered a job at the newspaper, then I can move back to London eventually, but it will take me a while to find a place to live. And going to London would be admitting it really is over between me and Matt. I know I still love him, I still feel the longing in my chest when I think of him. But there's no way we can get back together after what he's done.

Whatever happens with the job, I'll have to be in the village a little while longer. I imagine living with Emma in her flat. It will be warm and cosy, not cold and draughty like the cottage. We can cook dinner together, and Olivia and Lizzie can play together. I won't be lonely. I'll be safe there. Able to relax.

Emma still hasn't picked up her phone. I leave a breathless message on her voicemail, explaining that I need to take her up on her offer, asking if I can move in tonight. My voice breaks as I say the words. I hate asking for help, but I know I need it. Besides, Emma will understand.

I feel better once I've left the message. I have a plan to get out of here.

*

Miriam has suggested we meet in an art gallery café in central Oxford. I'm the first to arrive. It's half term and I push the buggy around a group of screaming children running back and forth between the tables, knocking over menus. Their harassed mothers sip coffees as they watch, occasionally making half-hearted attempts to tell them off.

'You've got all this to look forward to,' one of them says to me, glancing at Olivia in the buggy. 'You're at the easy stage now.' My heart sinks. I can't bear the thought that this could get harder.

I find a table in the corner at the back and check my phone. I'm still half expecting to see a cancellation text. After all these years and everything that happened between us, I can't believe Miriam wants to meet up.

I see her come in the double doors to the café. I feel sick with nerves, and for a moment I consider bolting from the café before she sees me.

She's the same as ever. Small and petite and projecting that air of being completely in control. She's had a third child since I last saw her, but she doesn't look any older. The same neat brown bob, the same slim build.

I swallow again. I'm not sure if I can face her after all.

I see her scanning the room and I manage to lift my hand in a little wave. I smile uncertainly. Her eyes meet mine and she half-smiles back. I wonder what she sees when she sees me. Rounder at the waist. Scruffy jeans. No make-up. I'm a world away from the woman she used to know.

She reaches the table and I stand. I'm about to reach out and hug her, but I sense she won't respond. Instead she turns to Oliva. 'She's beautiful,' she says.

'Thanks. How are your children? You've got three now, haven't you?'

She nods. 'They're fine. They're at school and nursery.'

'Oh,' I reply, taken aback by how abrupt she is. I used to be close to her two older boys, babysitting for her and dropping round presents. I don't know what to say. I blink back disappointment. A part of me imagined we'd instantly connect again as soon as we saw each other.

'Coffee?' Miriam asks, glancing behind her at the snaking queue to the counter. 'Or wine?' She seems eager to get away from me again.

'Coffee please,' I reply, quickly. One glass of wine will lead to another, just like the old days. I can't let that happen. I'm driving Olivia back.

I sit back down, tapping my fingers against the table anxiously.

When she returns with the coffees and sits down, we look at each other for a moment, unsure what to say.

'It's been a long time,' I venture.

She contemplates her coffee. 'Let's not talk about the past now. I've missed you, Claire.'

'I've missed you too.' Everything that's unsaid hangs between us.

We catch up and I give Miriam a rose-tinted version of the last three years of my life. The cottage in the country, close family nearby, my precious daughter. I don't mention the breakdown I had around the time our friendship ended, or the fact I've split up with Matt, or my postnatal depression.

'What's been happening in your life?' I ask Miriam.

I'm surprised to see tears pricking her eyes. 'I'm getting divorced,' she says.

Instinctively I reach across the table and touch her arm. 'I'm so sorry.'

'When you texted I'd just signed the papers. And I remembered the old days, how close we were. You were the only person I wanted to talk to.'

And then the tension between us eases and we're talking like old times. Miriam tells me about her husband's affair with a younger woman and I find myself telling her all about Matt and Sarah. And my mother-in law. It's a relief to have someone to confide in. When I look at my watch, two hours have passed in a flash.

'Do you fancy getting something to eat?' I ask.

We each choose an overpriced cake and Miriam suggests a glass of wine once more.

It takes all my willpower to say no. 'I stopped drinking,' I explain, and although it's technically true, I feel guilty. I did stop, but recently I've started again.

'Good for you,' Miriam says.

I bite into my stale cake, while she tells me more of the intricacies of her divorce. Custody. Finances. I might have to go through all of that with Matt. I'm not sure how I'll cope.

She seems to feel better when she's got it all off her chest, and I wonder if I trust her enough to tell her about the smoke alarm in the loft and the note through the door. She might just think I'm going mad. But I need to confide in someone, and I'm running out of people I can trust.

When I finish explaining, I see the concern in Miriam's eyes.

'This is serious,' she says. 'Someone's threatening you. You should tell the police.'

'I don't think they'll believe me.'

'Why not?'

I try to explain. Sometimes I'm not sure if I even believe myself. My brain is in such a fog with the sleepless nights and endless childcare, that facts and fiction seem to merge and I'm not sure what's in my head and what's real.

'Matt never believed me about anything,' I say. 'Even when we first moved and his mother was coming into the house and moving my things around.'

'Why wouldn't he believe you?' She seems genuinely confused and I realise she never knew what happened after our friendship ended. How I'd fallen apart.

I look down at the table, embarrassed. 'Well, because I went a bit off the rails before. Three years ago. After everything that happened.' I know I'm minimising, but I can't bear to tell her the whole truth about my breakdown.

'I didn't realise…' she says, surprised.

'I tried to contact you.'

'I didn't want to speak to you. I couldn't forgive you.'

'I know. It's OK. The things that happened… they're the reason why I went off the rails. And I still feel awful about it.' I flush, the familiar shame rising through my body to my face. 'I'm so sorry.' But I know those words can never be enough. Not after what I did.

We stay at the café another hour, but the conversation is stilted and we can't get the connection back. We're both aware of the huge crack that underpins our whole relationship. The atmosphere has turned and everything about our friendship is starting to feel fragile once more.

'I need to go in a minute,' Miriam says. 'Got to pick the kids up.'

I nod. I was hoping that this meeting would be the renewal of our friendship, a fresh start, but now it feels more like the end, a permanent goodbye. And yet neither of us seem to really want to leave, to abandon the hope of the rekindling the friendship we once had.

'Have you got somewhere to go?' Miriam asks. 'If the worst comes to the worst and you and Olivia have to move out, to get away from your mother-in-law, do you have someone to take you in?'

I remember years ago, when Miriam slept on my sofa for a month after splitting up with an ex.

I nod. 'Yes, I've got a friend I can move in with. She's local.' I glance at my phone. Emma still hasn't called me back.

'I'm glad,' Miriam says, reaching over to touch my hand. 'Take care of yourself.'

'You too,' I say, feeling the door of our friendship starting to close on me.

'If you ever need anything, then you can always call,' she says.

I don't think she really means it and I think I might cry. I don't want things to end this way.

'There is something actually,' I say. 'That you could help with.'

I tell her about Sarah's sister's accident, how both Matt and Sarah were there when it happened and how I can't shake off the feeling that they're hiding something about it from me.

'Do you think it's suspicious?' I ask.

'I don't know, Claire,' she says. 'But it's in the past, isn't it? There are lots of things in the past we'd rather put behind us.' She looks at me pointedly.

'You couldn't have a look into it, could you? See if there's a police file? I mean, I know it's historic but…'

Miriam rises suddenly from the table and I see she's lost patience. I've made things worse.

Her eyes flash with anger. 'I can't do that for you, Claire. How can you ask me that, after everything that happened last time?'

When I get home I feel deflated. I try to pull myself out of it, packing a few toiletries in a bag to get ready to move in with Emma. She still hasn't called me back but I might as well be prepared. Olivia is still napping in her car seat in the hallway and I should make the most of the chance to get my things ready. I tell myself everything will be OK once I get to Emma's. Once I've put a bit of distance between me and Ruth, I'll feel so much better. I'll be able to think straight.

My phone buzzes and I rush over to pick it up. Emma.

'Hi,' I say. 'Did you get my message?'

She's quiet for a moment before she replies. 'Yeah I did.'

'I've started packing my bag and I should be all ready to come over soon. Would that be OK? If I came over tonight?'

'Claire – listen – I'm really sorry but I don't think it's going to work.'

I'm shocked into silence.

'When I offered I didn't think it through. We've got building work starting soon. It was arranged by the landlord. It starts in a few days' time. New kitchen. New bathroom. Nothing will be in use. I'm thinking of moving out myself for a few days. I'm sorry, I just didn't think when I said you could stay.'

I feel rising panic as I stare around the cottage I'm so desperate to leave. 'It's OK,' I say, but I'm close to tears.

'Honestly, Claire. I'm so sorry. Is there anything I can do? Lizzie and I could come round if you like? Tomorrow or even tonight?'

'Umm…' I don't want to sound needy, but the truth is I do need someone. I need someone on my side, someone to look out for me. 'I'll be OK,' I say. 'I'm hoping to move out soon anyway. If I get an offer from the newspaper in London, I'll move back there.'

'Yes,' Emma replies. 'And you really shouldn't let Ruth force you out of your home like this. You've every right to stay put.'

'Sure,' I say, although I don't know if I can bear to sleep in the house another night. I know I'll lie awake, thoughts racing.

'Listen, I know what will help you relax. I'll come round tomorrow and give you a massage. I did a course in Thailand years ago, and I'd love to practise. It will really help. How does that sound?'

'Great,' I say. 'That sounds great.'

'OK. I'll be round tomorrow at ten.'

'See you then.'

She hangs up the phone and I slump down onto the sofa, disappointed. I look at my half-packed holdall and feel the tears start to well up.

I go to the kitchen and pour myself a glass of wine. Just one can't hurt. I take the bottle into the living room and collapse back onto the sofa.

This isn't Emma's fault. It's Ruth's. I haven't been able to stop thinking about the note all the way home. Pulling it out of my bag, I turn it over in my hands.

You don't deserve Olivia.

I feel light-headed, like the words aren't real. I take a gulp of my wine.

I think about what Miriam said. This is serious. I could take this to the police if I wanted to. Ruth needs to understand that she can't do this to me.

Since we moved here, she's been working on breaking me down. Coming into the house. Taking forever to clear out her mother's things. Making constant snide digs. And now she's talking about Matt getting custody of Olivia. She's trying to threaten me. She wants me gone.

I need to sort this out.

I fetch Olivia's chair and carry it through to the kitchen. I put it by the door, and strap her in. It will be in full view from the back door of Ruth and Jack's house.

Slipping my shoes on, I open the kitchen door before I can change my mind. The cold air hits me as I rush down the path, tripping on the uneven paving slabs. I feel giddy and sick. I see the empty pond and remember the flash of fear as the buggy careered over the edge. My baby dragged out of the water, choking on pondweed, before Matt pulled it from her mouth and she came screaming back to life.

By the time I reach Ruth's back door, I'm both shivering from the cold and flushed from running, adrenalin coursing through my veins.

I bang on the glass pane of the back door, so hard I can feel my knuckles bruising.

Ruth opens it a crack and I barge past her into the kitchen. She glowers at the trail of mud that follows me.

'Matt,' Ruth yells. 'Matt! Your wife's here.'

'It's you I came to see, actually. Why did you put that note through my door?'

She stares at me blankly as she removes her washing up gloves. 'You don't seem yourself, Claire.'

'I just want to know why you wrote that note. What's the point?'

'I don't know what you're talking about.'

'I think you do.'

'You realise that I really don't need to talk to you any more, now you're separated from my son.' Her voice is calm, as if she's a reasonable human being.

'You think you can get rid of me that easily? You can send me a threatening note, and I'll be gone?'

'It's my house. And I haven't sent you any notes. In fact, I think I've treated you very well, inviting you into my family and my home.'

I wave the piece of paper at her. 'You don't recognise this then?'

She looks blank and it crosses my mind that I might be wrong. I redden, suddenly unsure of myself. I shouldn't have come.

Matt appears behind her. 'Claire. Are you OK?'

'I'm fine. It's your mother that's not OK. She's wants me out of your lives, she's pushing me out.'

'I'm sure it's not like that.' Matt places a hand on my shoulder and I shrug it off.

'Matt's right,' Ruth says. 'You're not yourself, Claire. Are you sure you don't want to go back to the cottage and lie down?' Her voice is sickly sweet.

'Mum,' Matt warns.

Ruth looks at Matt. 'I don't know why we're all tiptoeing around her,' she says.

Matt shakes his head. 'Not now, Mum.'

'Do you really think it's safe her looking after your child?'

'She's our child, not his child,' I spit out.

'Where's your child now?' She steps towards me, her face uncomfortably close to mine.

I gasp and turn back towards the cottage. I can see Olivia through the kitchen door. I only meant to leave her for a minute. I haven't even looked back to check on her. What kind of mother am I?

I rush out of the kitchen and hurry back down the path. But Ruth hasn't finished her tirade yet.

'You're drunk, Claire,' she shouts after me. 'I can smell the alcohol on your breath. You're not fit to look after Olivia. You're an alcoholic.'

CHAPTER 27

My head pounds. It feels like someone is drilling into it. It takes me a moment to wake up and realise that the banging isn't coming from inside my head, but from outside. I reach for my phone on the bedside table. Eight a.m.

I put my pillow over my head and hope the noise will go away. Images from yesterday start to flash through my mind. Ruth's angry face. Matt's baffled look. Ruth's words echo in my mind. I feel so ashamed. She's right. I do have an alcohol problem. I shouldn't have been drinking in the afternoon while I was looking after Olivia. I've been trying so hard to stop myself giving into the temptation but the note was the final straw. I'm starting to feel like I need alcohol. The taste of it on my tongue. One drink. And then more.

I'd had a whole bottle of wine before I went over to confront her. I'd told myself it would help me sleep easier in the house at night. And after our argument, I'd come home and polished off a second bottle.

I'm turning into the person I was in the past, I realise with horror.

Matt rescued me back then. He helped me recover. He took all the alcohol from the house, threw it away, didn't let me drink again. But I don't have him this time around.

The banging outside continues, and inevitably Olivia wakes, her screams adding to the noise.

Putting one foot tentatively on the floor, then the other, I ease out of bed. My body shakes.

I go to the bathroom and splash water on my face, then go to Olivia's room and lift her out of the cot. Holding her to me, I pull back the curtain, blinking at the aggressive daylight.

Outside, a workman surveys the result of his labour. He's put up a 'For Sale' sign in front of the cottage.

The doorbell rings before I'm up and dressed. Olivia and I have been lying in bed upstairs. I've drunk pints of water to try and disperse my hangover, but it's not enough. I need to rest.

I make my way slowly down the stairs, one step at a time, my whole body aching. I see Matt's silhouette in the window. I don't want to face him, but it's too late – he's already seen me.

'Claire—' he shouts through the door.

I open it reluctantly.

He takes in my dressing gown and unbrushed hair, and I look at the floor, embarrassed.

'Can I come in?'

I have no energy to object and I lead him through to the living room.

He offers to make the tea and brings through the mugs.

I sip it gratefully while he holds Olivia.

'I'm worried about you, Claire,' he says finally.

'I'm sorry about last night. I was out of control. It's just – your mother – she sent me a note.'

'What note?'

'It said – it said I don't deserve Olivia.' I'm embarrassed, because looking at me right now, Matt might think that's true.

'You're a good mother, Claire.'

I feel like crying. It's just what I need to hear right now. If only he hadn't cheated on me with Sarah. Then we could still be together. We could fix this.

'Do you think we could give it another go?' he asks. It's like he's read my mind.

'You cheated on me, Matt.'

'I didn't. I don't know how to convince you, but I didn't.'

I sigh. More lies. How can we move forward from this?

'You have to tell me the truth, Matt.'

'The truth?' he asks. 'I don't think you want to hear it. Because the truth is that none of this is about me. It's about you. It's about you believing all sorts of things that are in your imagination. You think everyone's out to get you. My mother. Sarah. Me. When the truth is that we only want to help you.'

I don't know what he's trying to do to me, yet slowly but surely Matt and his mother are making me fall apart.

'Please, Claire,' he says. 'Let's give it another go.'

'No. Sorry.'

He straightens then, and I see his demeanour harden.

'OK then. If that's the way you want it. But I need access to Olivia. I need to see my daughter.'

'I can't let her spend time with your mother. I just don't trust her.' I think about the smoke alarm. Another thing Matt will think I'm imagining.

'You can't dictate that, Claire. Listen, if we're not together, then Mum wants to take you to court, to win custody. She'll use everything she knows about you against you. I need to see my daughter regularly. You can't withhold that.'

A shiver runs down my spine. Does Ruth really want to take Olivia away from me entirely?

'OK,' I say. 'We'll sort something out. But don't leave Olivia alone with your mother.'

Matt sighs. 'That's ridiculous.'

I shake my head. I'm only trying to protect my daughter. 'It's a condition of you seeing her,' I say.

Matt sighs. 'Look, you're being completely unreasonable. My mother loves Olivia. But if it's my turn to look after her, then I can make sure I'm always there with her, if that puts your mind at rest.'

I nod. 'OK.'

He reaches out and strokes my hair and I recoil at the unexpected tenderness. 'Wouldn't it be easier if I just moved back in?' he asks.

For a moment, I want to say yes, to forget about him and Sarah. But I can't. I'm stronger than that. I shake my head. 'Look, you need to go. Emma's coming round soon.'

Matt stands. 'Well if you need anything, you know where I am.' He kisses me lightly on the cheek before he goes out the door.

Emma gives me a huge hug when she arrives at my door with Lizzie. 'How are you?' she asks, cocking her head in concern.

'I've been better.'

'I'm so sorry about the flat,' she says. 'I completely forgot about the building work.'

'It's OK. I'm sure I'll find somewhere else.'

Emma touches my shoulder as she shifts Lizzie in her arms. 'You shouldn't be looking for somewhere else. You have every right to live here with Olivia. You should stay.'

I nod. I know in theory she's right, but in reality I'm not sure if I can stand to stay in the cottage much longer. I don't feel safe.

'Look, you need to relax,' Emma says. 'Are you ready for your massage?'

'Sure,' I reply, as Emma places Lizzie alongside Olivia on the playmat. I eye Olivia doubtfully. I don't think she'll be quiet for very long.

Emma follows my gaze. 'Leave the babies to me – I'll entertain them. And I'll make you a cup of tea. It's time to focus on you.'

Once I've finished my drink, I double check the blinds are fully closed and then undress, folding my clothes and putting them neatly on the chair. Olivia watches me curiously, while Lizzie stares at the ceiling.

Emma lays a towel across the sofa and I lie face down, inhaling the comforting smell of washing powder.

She puts some soothing music on her phone, turns off the main light and switches on the desk light in the corner. I shiver and Emma places another towel over my back.

I hear the squelch of the massage oil as she squirts it onto her hands and rubs them together to warm it up.

'Just try and relax,' Emma says, pulling the towel down to expose my bare skin. I start as her hands touch my back. They feel cold at first, but as she pushes her hands into my muscles, I stop noticing.

I close my eyes. I can't stop thinking about Matt. I still love him. But he didn't stick up for me when I confronted Ruth about the note. His loyalties are with her, not me. We can't be together. I won't take him back after his affair. My jaw sets in resolve.

'You need to stop tensing up,' Emma says. 'Otherwise it's going to hurt.'

'OK,' I reply.

'OK?' she asks, and I can hear the smile in her voice.

'Yes.'

Her hands come down hard into the muscles. She kneads my flesh, pushing deep into my skin and putting her body weight behind the movement.

The pain takes my breath away and I can only focus on not crying out.

'Is that too hard?'

Emma continues without me answering. I close my eyes. The pain starts to feel good, as if she is pushing the impurities out of me, pushing the thoughts out of my mind.

'It's good,' I say, releasing my breath just enough to get the words out.

'Great. Not everyone likes Thai massage. It's supposed to hurt a bit. You have to take out the knots in the muscles. And that's going to be painful, especially if you're as tense as you are. But when it's done you feel like you're walking on air.'

'OK,' I say as she presses harder into me. Her slim frame hides a strength I didn't know she had. If she held me down, I wouldn't be able to get up.

Olivia whines and she sets Lizzie off, who starts crying. Emma's hands leave my skin. I listen to her go over to the babies, pick them up and soothe them. After a couple of minutes they both calm and I'm overwhelmed by jealousy. Why don't I have that effect on my daughter? Emma returns and her knuckles work their way into the gaps underneath my shoulder blades. I wince.

'You've tensed up again.'

'Sorry.' I grit my teeth, scrunching up my eyes. Emma repeats the motion again and again, until I'm not sure I can bear it. I bite the inside of my cheek until I draw blood, the sharp metallic taste distracting me from the pain.

Emma's hands move to my neck. They wrap around me like a python and I suddenly feel vulnerable. I wonder if she could kill me if she were to squeeze in the right place for the right period of time.

'It's OK,' Emma says, sensing my discomfort. 'You just need to relax.'

I feel the soft cushion against my cheek, breathe in the lavender fabric conditioner. The tinny music from Emma's phone is starting to irritate me.

I've had Thai massages before, but they've never been this hard. I feel sick with the pain. I wonder if it's because I'm more stressed, more tense. Emma says nothing as her hands stretch out the tendons in my neck. She pushes up hard into the bones at the base of my skull. Stars dance in front of my eyes. It's too much.

I should say something.

I feel my breathing quicken. It's OK, I tell myself. It's OK.

I'm about to speak when her hands lift from my skin. I hear her squirting the oil on to her palm, and dread the feel of her hands back on my neck.

But instead she goes to the other end of the sofa and starts running her hands up and down my legs. The movement is smoother, more relaxing. She presses hard, but it isn't as painful.

'You have more tension in your neck and shoulders than your legs,' Emma remarks casually. 'It's a sign of emotional stress.'

'Right,' I say, into the sofa cushion.

'But I've got a lot of the stress out of the muscles now. So you should feel much better.'

'Thanks,' I reply, relieved that the painful part is over.

I relax as Emma continues to work on my legs. I take deep breaths and try to empty the thoughts from my mind, focusing on the sensation. I hear a swishing noise, and I'm suddenly aware of my naked skin pressed against the towel.

I lift my head to look up. Emma gently pushes it back down.

'Don't worry, I just adjusted the blind.'

'The blind?'

'I couldn't see properly. Don't worry. No one can see in.'

When the massage finishes, I sit up, the towel wrapped over my breasts.

'Was that good?' Emma asks. 'I bet you're much calmer.'

She brings me a glass of water and I sip it gratefully. I feel exhausted.

'Thanks so much,' I say.

'It's no problem at all. That's what friends are for.'

When I'm rehydrated I get up to make Emma a cup of tea. It takes all my strength to resist offering her a glass of wine. I need to start controlling myself. For Olivia's sake.

'I'm sorry that moving in with me didn't work out,' she says again. 'Perhaps after the building work has finished…'

'It's OK, I understand.' Despite the how painful it was, the massage has made me feel better.

'How did your interview in London go?' Emma asks. 'Do you think they'll offer you a job?'

I smile. 'I hope so.'

Emma smiles at me encouragingly. 'You'll have a route out of here, soon enough. Back off to start your exciting London life again.'

I nod. But I can't ignore my mixed feelings about returning to London, particularly returning to the newspaper.

'I want to move out as soon as I can,' I say. I tell Emma about my run-in with Ruth yesterday, how she thinks I'm not a fit mother, how she even put that in a note and sent it through the door.

'That's shocking,' Emma says. 'I saw the "For Sale" board she's put up outside. You mustn't let her push you out. You have every right to live here. Can you avoid her?'

'Matt needs to see Olivia, so I'll have to see her sometimes.' I sigh. The whole thing seems overwhelming. No matter how far away I move, Ruth will always be Olivia's grandmother.

'If Matt wants to look after Olivia more, then why don't you do it on your terms?'

'What do you mean?'

'Well,' Emma says, putting her arm through mine. 'We should have a girl's night out. A big one.'

I haven't had a night out for so long. I imagine dancing in a club, forgetting all my worries. 'Let's do it.'

'We can go to London,' Emma says. 'Make a proper night of it.'

I smile. I need to forget my responsibilities and enjoy myself for once. Maybe if I just have some time off from the relentless childcare then I'll feel better about everything.

'When?'

'I could do Thursday,' Emma says. 'If Matt wants to see more of Olivia, then he can have his chance. He can look after her the whole evening.'

She grins deviously and I smile back. Matt has never had to look after Olivia on his own for more than an hour or so. Now he'll be able to see just how hard it is.

And I get to have a night out. Finally, I have something to look forward to.

*

I look at my suitcase, mine and my daughter's clothes neatly folded inside, along with a small selection of my daughter's toys. I wanted to let her choose what she wanted to take. But I couldn't. She can't know we're leaving, in case she somehow lets slip to my husband. We have to leave so much of our lives behind in this house; not just her toys, but the lives we've built for ourselves here: the carefully chosen furniture, the state-of-the-art kitchen, our family pictures.

I'm so grateful to have a friend to move in with. Even if we've only ever spoken on the phone, I know she must care about me. You'd only offer up your home to a friend.

I've explained everything to her. Everything my husband did to those girls. There's only one option. She's right. I have to leave.

I've prepared to move in two days' time, when my husband's away at a conference. I've bought an expensive candle for my new friend as a thank you for letting us move in with her. I borrowed my husband's credit card to buy it. It's only a small risk. He's unlikely to notice until he sees his credit card statement at the end of the month and I'll be long gone by then.

I just need to get her address and then I'm ready. I won't write it down. I'll memorise it. That way my husband will have no chance of finding it.

When I ring the helpline, she picks up on the first ring and I'm glad it's her on the other end. I tell her I'm packed and ready to leave.

'Well done,' she says. 'You're doing the right thing.'

'Thank you. I can see you're right now. I can't live with him any more.' I feel overwhelmed with gratitude towards her. She is rescuing me.

'*That's OK. It's a brave decision to make.*'

'*We'll come to your place on Tuesday,*' I say. '*What's your address?*'

There's a silence on other end of the line, and my heart beats faster. I hold my breath.

Finally she speaks. '*I think a women's shelter is the best place for you. They have policies and procedures to keep you safe and the resources to help get you back on your feet. I've looked them up for you. There's one about five miles away.*'

The words are worse than a physical blow.

'*What about your place?*' My voice shakes.

'*I'm sorry but it just won't work. I was silly to suggest it. You need proper care and protection.*'

'*We'll be no bother, I promise.*'

'*What if your husband comes after you? I can't protect you from him.*'

'*But I can't go to a shelter.*'

'*Why not?*'

I'd wanted to stay with a friend, somewhere I was welcome and felt safe. Why can't she understand that?

'*I'll be out of place. I won't know anyone.*'

'*Where else can you go?*'

'*I don't know.*' I don't want to change things now, not when I've got everything planned. '*We wouldn't need to stay with you for long. Just for a few days, then we could find somewhere else.*'

'*It's against the rules. I'm sorry.*' She sounds frustrated. But it's my life that's about to be turned upside down. Not hers.

I don't know what I'm going to do.

'*Look, you have to leave him,*' she insists. '*You have to go to the shelter.*'

I reach up and touch my face. My eye smarts from where he hit me this morning. I don't have a choice any more. I need to leave.

'*Promise me you'll go.*' She seems genuinely worried for my safety and for a moment I soften towards her. Perhaps it really is against the rules for me to stay with her. Perhaps she does care.

'OK.'

'When?'

I sigh, resigned. I've run out of options.
'I'll leave on Tuesday, as planned.'

CHAPTER 28

When I wake, I'm surprised to see I've slept for four solid hours. I'd been so sure that I wouldn't be able to sleep in the cottage any more, but exhaustion must have overwhelmed me. The day stretches endlessly ahead of me. I've no idea what to do with myself and Olivia. For once, she's still asleep. I browse through baby groups on my phone. The nearest ones are in Oxford, half an hour away. It doesn't seem worth it.

I wish I wasn't alone. If only I'd been able to stay with Emma. It's moments like this that I long for Matt beside me.

I check my phone and see I've got a new email.

From the editor of the paper.

I think of the conversation Emma and I had yesterday. She's right. There is a way out of the mess I'm in. If I could start over again in London, escape the village, I'm sure I'd be happier.

I hold my breath as the email loads.

It's short and to the point and it takes me a moment before I realise that it's not what I'm expecting and the smile slips from my face. The two polite lines of text tell me there are no vacancies at the moment, but he'll keep me in mind and wishes me luck.

I sigh with disappointment. First Emma and now this. Yet another door has closed, another escape route blocked.

I'm not moving to London any time soon. I'll need to find somewhere else to live.

Olivia wakes and her cries pull me out of my racing thoughts. As I lift her out of her cot, I hear a key in the door. I freeze, looking down at my unwashed pyjamas in alarm. I'm in no state for visitors.

'Hello?' I call out tentatively.

I hear voices downstairs. A man and a woman. I'm sure the woman is Ruth.

I put Olivia back down in the cot, quickly brush my hair and run downstairs to the sound of Olivia's screams.

Ruth is muttering under her breath as she moves my washing up from last night away from the sink and into the corner. A suited man sits at the kitchen table, fiddling with an expensive camera.

She glances at me. 'That's the tenant,' she says to the man.

He holds out his hand to shake mine. 'Ryan,' he says. 'Estate agent.'

'Hi,' I say, feeling exposed and vulnerable in my dressing gown.

I glare at Ruth. 'What's going on?'

'Ryan's just here to take a few photos for the listing and then we'll be out of your way.'

Anger rises in me and I flush. They have no right to come into my house early in the morning and take photos without asking.

'Could you come back another time? It's not convenient.'

Ryan's voice is as smooth as silk. 'It will only take half an hour.' He turns away from me, towards Ruth. 'We can get some really good photos of this place. It's rustic. Lots of original features. I already have a few buyers on my list who I know will be interested.'

Olivia's cries from upstairs are getting louder, more urgent.

'This isn't a good time,' I say.

Ruth turns to me. 'Do you want me to go and get your daughter?' she says pointedly, glancing at the ceiling, Olivia's screams echoing from above.

'I'll go,' I say quickly. There's no way she's going near my daughter. Not after the note and the smoke alarm.

As I go up the stairs, I can hear snippets of Ruth's conversation with the estate agent. 'Volatile,' she says. 'I'll be glad to be rid of her.'

I resist the desire to go back down and have it out with her. I pick up Olivia and start her morning feed. Thinking of the mess downstairs, I feel embarrassed that it will be displayed online in the photos on the estate agent's listing, for all to see.

When I come back downstairs, Ryan is in my living room, taking pictures. All my photos from the mantelpiece have been taken down, and my picture of the Vietnamese motorcyclist has been put out of sight of the camera.

'Where are my photos?' I whisper to Ruth angrily.

'In the sideboard in the dining room. They needed to be moved out the way for Ryan.'

'Why didn't you let me know he was coming round?'

She turns and looks me right in the eye. 'If you won't respect my things, then I won't respect yours.'

'I've always respected your house.'

'Have you? Then why did I find bin bags of my mother's things in the study when I was clearing out the wardrobes?' She turns to me, her eyes bitter.

'I – I – it was only opened toiletries, old tights. That kind of thing. Rubbish.'

'Rubbish?' She raises an eyebrow. 'So my mother's belongings are rubbish?'

'No – that's not what I meant. I just wanted a bit of space for my things.' But my mind is racing. She found her mother's things the same day I found the scarf. Could she have planted it as revenge? That would mean Matt hadn't cheated on me. That he'd been telling the truth all along.

When Ruth is gone, I start to put the house back in order. I put the picture of the motorcyclist back up and go over to the wooden sideboard to find my photos. The drawers are overfull, jammed shut and I struggle to get them open. I see my framed photos have been shoved in carelessly, on top of a pile of other family photographs belonging to Pamela. Curious, I pull out a few. Mostly they are of people I don't recognise in black and white. Weddings. Birthdays. Grinning faces, long dead.

Then I see a familiar face, smiling out from the bottom of the pile in colour. Matt. I pull it out. He's with Sarah, at a circular table, arms around each other, smiling happily. A bride stands behind them, her hands resting on the back of their chairs, beaming into the camera. Matt's sister.

They're at Matt's sister's wedding.

I gasp.

The wedding took place just before Matt and I got together. I remember, because when I first met his sister, she showed us the photos from her honeymoon. Were Matt and Sarah a couple when his sister got married?

He told me they'd split up when they were teenagers, but that can't be true. He was with her just before we got together. Why would he lie? Had he two-timed her with me?

That would explain why Sarah has always been hovering around Matt since we moved here. They clearly have unfinished business. The job at the surgery. Befriending Ruth. Was it all to get closer to him?

And eventually it worked. He cheated on me with her.

I swallow. I can hardly believe that just a few hours ago, I was starting to believe Matt, to think there might be another explanation, that Ruth might have planted the scarf.

I feel sick. Nothing is going my way and there's no escape. Matt cheated on me and Ruth wants me out of the house. I can't move in with Emma and there's no job in London. I'm trapped.

I need to get out of the cottage. I can't think straight.

I grab Olivia's coat from the hook and push her arms through the sleeves. It's too small and I can't do up the zip. I find a jumper a few sizes too big for her and put it on over the coat. Olivia squirms as I strap her in the buggy and leave the house, locking the chaos inside.

Outside, the air is fresh, and grey clouds are threatening to burst. My trainers pound on the wet pavement, as I speed through the streets, hoping to miss the rain. In my rush I've forgotten my umbrella.

The threatened rain comes and I tilt my face up to the sky, letting the drops bounce over my skin and run down my cheeks like tears. Olivia's pram is getting wet, and the footmuff is already soaking. I pull the canopy over her so she's partially covered. I hope the rain doesn't seep through into her clothes.

I'm rubbish at this. Rubbish at looking after Olivia. Rubbish at life.

I keep walking, as fast as I can. I feel the urgent need to escape. To run away to anywhere but here. Outside the confines of the countryside. Outside the confines of my family.

I walk and walk and walk. Faster. Faster. Pensioners mill around in the village centre, ignoring me as I weave in and out between them with the buggy. I'm invisible.

When I reach the outskirts of the village, I go down tree-lined streets, rows and rows of identical semis with tarmacked driveways. I peer through the windows at the lives inside. A woman ironing. A child playing. A television flickering. Glimpses of domesticity. Lives that radiate warmth through the double-glazed windows.

This is not my life. This is not me.

I need a drink.

The welcoming amber glow of a pub window casts light into the heavy air.

The sign swings in the wind.

I realise I'm starving. I never got round to having breakfast. These days I keep forgetting. I haven't been on the scales lately but I can feel my clothes getting looser. My jeans hang off me and my belt is on the tightest setting. A while back I would have been pleased with this development, but now it worries me. It's not healthy. I'm tired all the time. I need the energy from food, but I can't seem to remember to eat, or when I do remember, I'm just not hungry. I grab the occasional sandwich here and there, some ready meals from the supermarket, but I have no interest in cooking. Without Matt I can't seem to maintain any sense of time or routine. The days roll endlessly into each other. Just me and Olivia. Battling through, waiting for the time to pass to when she's old enough to leave home and I can have my life back.

I go into the pub. There must be an office nearby because inside there are tables of suited men and high-heeled women. I'm an anomaly in my joggers and trainers, and yet again I'm invisible. They're immersed in their chatter, their deals and their sales targets, their banter and their ambition. I'm an aside, a woman alone in a pub with a buggy and a baby.

I park the buggy at a table by the window. Olivia's sleeping, so I leave her there, and squeeze past an overflowing table of office workers to get to the bar.

'What will it be, love?'

'A glass of white wine. Sauvignon please.' I love the way the word sounds on my tongue. It's like I'm trained to say it. Years and years of the same order. The after-work release of a glass of Sauvignon. The dinners in a restaurant with a bottle or two. So many good memories. How could I have ever stopped? I need this. All along I've needed this.

'It's a bottle for a tenner on Wednesdays. Do you want to upgrade? A large glass is six pounds anyway, so it's not much extra.'

'OK,' I say, strumming my fingers on the bar agitatedly.

I watch as the barman goes to the fridge and pulls out a bottle. I could stop him. I could call him back and ask for just a glass. He places the bottle in front of me and unscrews the cap.

'How many glasses?'

He's assumed I have company. Of course he has. It's Wednesday lunchtime and I'm ordering a bottle of wine.

'Two,' I say quickly. I wonder if he's humouring me, if he's seen me coming into the pub on my own with Olivia.

'My friend will be arriving shortly. We're meeting for lunch.' I've overdone it. Over-explained. He wasn't even asking. But now he looks over to the buggy and I see a slight rise of his eyebrows. He knows. I need a drink so badly, I don't even care.

I tap my card to pay and then take the bottle in one hand and the glasses in the other.

'Thanks,' I say cheerfully, as if it's just another day.

He's already at the other end of the bar, washing glasses.

I make my way back to the table, telling myself I'll only have one glass and then take the rest of the bottle back home. I can have a glass or two this evening to wind down.

I sigh with anticipation as I pour the wine slowly, watching it tumble into the glass, and listening to the glug glug sound of the glass filling. I swirl it round and breathe in deeply through my nose like a seasoned wine taster, forgetting for a moment I'm just in the local pub. I let the wine sit on my tongue for a moment, feeling the sharp tang of cheap alcohol. I swallow, feeling better already.

I look at the people around me. The office workers on the table beside me are already drunk. The conversation has risen to a crescendo of laughter that seems to surround me and Olivia on our lonely island table.

But I feel more at home in the pub than in the cottage.

I think of Sarah, how pleased she must be now she's finally got what she wanted. I wonder if Matt will eventually move in with her. I wonder why he hasn't already. Surely he'd prefer to move in with his mistress than his domineering mother? Perhaps she lives too far away.

I don't want to think about Matt and Sarah, I just want to enjoy the sensation of the cold wine gliding down my throat. But my curiosity gets the better of me, and I pick up my phone and load up my subscription to a site that tracks the electoral roll. I find Sarah easily. She lives on her own in a flat in the village. One of the new builds that Ruth says ruin the look of the place.

I look up the address on Google Maps and then on Street View. It's just an ordinary flat. Going back into the address listing, it tells me who's lived there in the last twenty years. Sarah's been there ages, mostly on her own.

But not the whole time.

Seven years ago, the year Matt met me, Matt was registered at the address too.

Matt was living with her when we first met. He lied to me.

CHAPTER 29

When the doorbell goes late the next afternoon, I know it's Matt. He's looking after Olivia while Emma and I have our night out. It's an arrangement that works for both of us. Matt gets the access to his daughter and I get a night off.

I'm not sure what I'll say to him. Now I know he's been lying to me from the very beginning of our relationship, the trust between us has completely gone. He should have told me about Sarah right from the start.

I open the door hesitantly. Outside, the weather is bleak. The rain pours down behind Matt, a sheet of grey, accentuating his shadow across my doorway. The water droplets in his hair reflect the light. His deep brown eyes bore into mine and, despite myself, I can't help but feel the familiar surge of affection. But I push the feeling down, remembering the photo of him and Sarah at the wedding.

'Come in,' I say.

He nods, and steps into the cottage.

He reaches over to hug me awkwardly, and as we embrace I breathe in the scent of his wet leather jacket, his aftershave. His face is close to mine, his breath hot on my cheek. I want to bury my face in his neck, to forget everything. But I can't.

'I brought some toys.' He holds up the carrier bag in his hand.

'You shouldn't have.'

I should offer him a drink, but I don't. He knows where the coffee is. I leave him with Olivia while I go to get ready.

Upstairs, I strip and critique my body in the mirror. It's far from perfect: I've lost weight and yet my stomach still protrudes over the top of my knickers. My breasts sag. I run my hands over the white stretch marks that curve over my stomach and thighs.

I reach into the cupboard, take out a dress and pull it on over my head. It looks dowdy, mumsy. Too long. Too floral. I take it off and take out another one. Shorter, silvery. It looks good. I look good. I smile at myself in the mirror and then pout, projecting a confidence that belongs to someone else. I do my make-up quickly and go back down the stairs to the living room.

Matt looks me up and down.

'You look beautiful,' he says.

'Matt, don't.'

'Claire—'

'You know where everything is,' I say. I point to the pile of sheets I've placed on floor by the TV. 'The sheets for the sofa bed are over there.'

'Can't I just sleep in our bed?'

'No, you can't. I'm sleeping there when I'm back. There's food in the fridge or you can order takeaway. Bottle of wine in the fridge.'

'Mum was right. You're drinking again?'

'It's none of your business.'

'It is my business. You're my wife. I'm worried about you.'

I feel a flush of shame. He can see through me, see that I'm struggling.

He reaches out to touch my shoulder. 'It's OK. It must be hard for you on your own. Listen, I could move back in here for a bit. It doesn't have to be forever. Just for a little while. To help you out with Olivia and get you back on your feet.'

A part of me desperately wants to say yes. After all, I still love him. But I can't ignore all the lies he's told me.

'No, Matt.'

My words sit heavy in the air between us.

'I've got to go and meet Emma,' I say.

'Claire, you'll be careful, won't you? With alcohol?'

'Of course.' I'll just have one or two drinks. I won't go overboard.

He reaches out, embracing me. 'You promise?'

'Yes.' For a moment, I let myself lean into his strong chest. I feel tears welling up in my eyes. I long to stay in his arms forever. To pretend everything's OK.

But I can't.

I pull away.

I get a taxi over to Emma's. She's waiting for me outside her flat, shivering in a short skirt and thin coat, umbrella held up against the rain. As she scoots into the car, I notice how her necklace and earrings perfectly match her shoes and bag.

'You look gorgeous,' I say.

'You too. I love the dress.'

I touch the shiny material of my dress and realise it's risen up, small creases forming over my stomach. I tug at it self-consciously, pulling it down.

We jump out of the taxi at the station and buy our tickets from the machine. We chat as we cross the bridge to the platform. The train pulls in as we're on our way down the stairs.

'Come on,' Emma says. It will be ages till the next one.' She takes the steps two at a time, her heels click-clacking as she runs, her bag bouncing up and down on her shoulder. I stumble behind her, trying to keep pace, my ankle still not quite recovered from when I fell in the loft.

Emma gets to the bottom of the steps as the train doors start beeping, about to shut. She slips inside, holding her skinny arm between the doors so they stay open for me. They almost close on her, but she pushes them further apart so there is a small gap that I can squeeze through. We both laugh, breathless, ignoring the other passengers and their feigned indifference.

We weave through the carriage to two seats together at the other end and sink down into them. The bright lights overhead highlight the imperfections on the faces around us. Shadowed eyes, concealed spots, smeared mascara, dandruff. There are two groups on the train tonight. Tired commuters with headphones and sunken eyes. And the twenty-somethings on their way into London for the evening, make-up still fresh, eyes not yet glazed.

Emma pulls a vodka bottle out of a Sainsbury's bag, with a smile.

'I thought we could pre-load.'

I raise my eyebrows.

'Seriously?' I laugh but there's nothing I want more than to take the alcohol from her and feel the burn in my throat.

'Drinks in the pub are expensive. And I want to have a big night… don't you? I need to let my hair down.'

'I do too.' I try not to think about the promise I made Matt earlier.

'Yeah, you do. After everything that's happened.'

Emma opens the bottle and takes a swig. The suited man across from us looks up from his newspaper.

'Pass it here then.' I grasp the cold bottle between my hands, lift the neck to my mouth and take a gulp. The spirit stings as I swallow, but it feels great.

'We're free,' Emma says. 'Is Matt staying the night?'

'Yes. On the sofa bed.'

'So both of us have zero parental responsibility. Tonight we're not mothers. We're people.'

I smile. Emma is right. Without Olivia I can be myself.

She takes another swig and passes it to me.

'Cheers to that,' I say, as I lift the bottle.

*

The music pulses through my body; I can feel the vibrations in my bones. My heart beats faster as I let the beat overcome me. I close my eyes and absorb the sound, lifting one hand high in the air, the other clasping my beer. I throw my head back, feeling my hair sway from side to side against my neck.

Emma dances opposite me, weaving in and out, towards me then away again. I know this song. It's one of my favourites. I shout out the chorus to Emma and she sings it back.

I'm on air. Free. Free of Matt and all his lies. Free of my screaming baby. I'm not a mum tonight. I'm myself. The woman I want to be. I grab Emma's hand and swing her round, feeling elated. My arm knocks into someone. Cold skin. Before I know it I knock into someone else. I feel my heels slip on the floor and I stumble to the left and laugh. My wrist is wet. I must have spilt my drink. I laugh again. I am drunk. I am free.

I'm going to feel rubbish in the morning, but I don't care. This evening, this moment, belongs to me. Dizzy and sweaty and out of control.

I look at my watch. The hands are blurry and I try to focus. It's dark in here and I pull it closer to my face, holding it up to the strobe lights. It's half past eleven. I should really text Matt and let him know I'll be home later than planned. There aren't many trains after midnight, but there is a bus. I unzip my bag and ferret around for my phone. I feel the cold plastic. There it is. I hold it close to my face to enter the passcode. It doesn't work. Fat fingers. I try again, stabbing at the digits. Still doesn't work. I try one more time before I give up, chucking my phone back into my bag. Why do I even care about Matt? He wasn't thinking about me when he was cosying up with Sarah.

I look up and realise I'm on my own. Where's Emma? A tap on my shoulder and I turn my head. My vision blurs, the strobe lights dance crazily and I think I might lose my balance. Emma!

Emma's lips move, but all I can hear is the beat of the music. My head hurts with the effort of trying to lip read.

Emma leans in closer, and shouts in my ear, spittle landing on my cheek. 'Do you want another drink?'

I still have a beer bottle in my hand. I tip it up and hold it to my mouth. The last few drops slip down my throat.

'Yes!' I shout back.

She turns and heads away from me as the DJ changes the song.

The first few beats trigger a memory of university. It was my all-time favourite song when I was eighteen. I shout out the lyrics to whoever is around me. I feel arms wrap around my waist from behind and a man grinding against me. I turn my head slightly to see his face. His beard grazes my neck, as he leans down as if to kiss me. I turn my head around and move to the music, then wriggle free and away from him.

The room is spinning. Or am I spinning? Maybe both. I giggle. Who cares?

Another man appears and starts dancing opposite me, copying my movements. They are caving in on me. I'm vulnerable. Drunk. His face is a blur. Two of him. Then three. I need to slow down.

I need the toilet. I'm going to be sick.

Where are the toilets? I stumble across the dance floor, unable to keep my footing in my heels. No one moves to let me pass and I knock into people and push others aside. The bodies are getting closer and closer together, crammed into the space, moving as one in time to the music. I keep going, as the crowd gets denser. The dance floor goes on forever. I thought the toilets were this way, but now I'm not so sure. I bump into something hard and reach out to touch my head where I banged it. I've walked into my own reflection in the mirror that runs the length of the wall. I stare at myself. My eyes are bloodshot and I lift my hand to my smudged mascara. The reflection follows. It's really me. I look a mess. My pretty silver dress has a long wet patch working its way from my stomach down my leg. Behind me the dance floor convulses.

I need to find the toilets. I look round and see the neon sign on the other side of the room. I start heading back the way I came. Where does the dance floor end? The DJ plays a bigger beat and the clubbers become a mass of moving limbs, bouncing into each other as they move left, right, up, down. Gaps between bodies open and then close again. I need to get out. To get to the toilet. People spin around in all directions. Sweaty limbs brush against me and the heat and the noise is too much. I walk as straight as I can, stumbling as I bounce off one body after another.

I push harder. I need to get out. I knock into someone and pause to watch his beer bottle lift out of his hand and tumble down, beer fountaining over his trousers and white trainers. His angry face glares, his lips move aggressively. I can't hear him above the music. I look away. Where's the exit? The music's so loud. Where am I going anyway? Don't I like this song? Should I dance?

The toilet. I need the toilet.

I keep going, not sure if I'm going the right way, or just walking round in circles. Students in jeans and T-shirts swig from beer bottles as they watch two girls kiss. Haven't I seen them before? Yes. This is the wrong way. I turn and head the other way. I barge through the centre of a hen party, dancing haphazardly around their bags. The hen has a sash round her, and horns. Her dress is stained. Her mother dances beside her swigging from a bottle of Prosecco. My foot catches something. A bag strap.

I'm flying through the air. And then landing. A soft body breaks my fall and hands claw at me before the girl falls over into the person next to her and clubbers fall like dominoes. I laugh from my viewpoint on the floor.

Sudden pain. My foot. My bad ankle is twisted at an improbable angle. It should hurt more than it does. I laugh to myself. I'm lucky.

A girl is limping towards me. She's shouting, but there's no way anyone could hear her above the music. It's the bridesmaid from the hen party. She retrieves her handbag from the floor beside me and glares, her face close to mine.

'Bitch,' she spits in my face.

There's too much going on. Too many people. Too much noise. Too much everything.

I try to stand up but my legs crumple beneath me. I put my hand on the sticky floor and push myself up. I wobble and nearly go over again. Why did I wear these heels?

Emma appears beside me with a bottle of wine.

'Are you all right?' she asks.

'Yeah, I'm fine,' I say, swaying.

'Drink up, it will make you feel better.'

She hands me the bottle and the weight of it makes me stumble off balance. Wine spills over my arm and dress. I lift my arm to my mouth and lick off the alcohol. Emma holds my elbow to steady me, takes the bottle from me and swigs it, wine dripping into her cleavage. I reach out my hand to take it back. Emma puts the neck of the bottle to my lips and tips it up. The alcohol cascades into my mouth faster than I can swallow, and spills over my dress. I laugh, not caring.

*

I haven't gone. I couldn't in the end. The shelter wasn't the right place for us.

I'm still planning to leave. But I want to take time to find the right place to go to. I'm thinking of a B&B in Scotland, far away from my life here. It will just take me a bit of time to arrange.

I phone the helpline. I want to say goodbye. I want to tell her that my daughter and I are going to be OK. I've got it all figured out. And I want to thank her.

'Hello?' I can hear the surprise in her voice. I guess she thought that once we'd left I wouldn't need to ring.

'It's me.'

'Are you at the shelter?'

'No. I—'

'Why not? You need to leave. It's not safe.' I hear the alarm in her voice and remember that she does care about me.

'I'm fine. Don't worry. I'm still going to leave. I just need a bit of time to find somewhere. Not a shelter. Somewhere a bit nicer.'

'You can't do that. You need to leave now.'

'Honestly, we'll be fine.'

'Listen to me. You need to leave this evening. You're not safe any more. Not now you've been through his study. Not now you know what he's done. If he finds out, you'll be in trouble. And who knows what he'll do to you then.'

I feel a familiar fear rise in me. What if she's right? What if he really hurts me? What if he hurts my daughter?

'I haven't found somewhere to go yet.' The excuse sounds feeble. I was supposed to leave two days ago. I'd promised her.

'You have to go to the shelter. Tonight. If you want to go to a B&B after, I'm sure they'll help you. But you need to get yourself and your daughter out of that house as soon as possible.'

Perhaps she's right. It can't be that bad at the shelter. I must protect my daughter. 'OK,' I say. 'I'll leave tonight.'

I hear her sigh of relief. 'Do you promise?'

'Yes.'

'OK. Well leave as soon as you can. Before your husband gets home. Don't stay a moment longer.'

'I will do.'

'You're doing the right thing.'

'Thank you,' I say. 'Without you, I don't think I could do this.' I feel an overwhelming surge of gratitude towards her. She's helped me escape.

I hear a gulp on the other end of the line and I realise I've upset her.

'Can I still call you if I need to?' I ask. I don't want to lose our friendship. I've come to rely on her. She means so much to me now.

'You can always ring,' she says. 'Any time.'

CHAPTER 30

My cheek is cold. I shiver, reaching out to pull the covers over me, but my hand meets colder air. I adjust my position, turning my head.

I moan. Everything hurts. Every limb.

My cheek feels like it's rubbing against sandpaper. I wince as I try to move my head. It feels bruised and heavy.

I should open my eyes, but I don't want to. I can feel the light beating on the backs of my eyelids and I don't want to face it. It must be morning. Why is the light so bright? Where's Olivia?

It's cold. So cold. I just want to go back to sleep.

I try to turn over again and my elbow hits something hard.

I open my eyes slowly.

I'm outside, lying on stone steps. I must still be dreaming. Maybe if I let myself doze off, then I'll wake up again back in my own bed.

I lie still. Cold stone against my cheek. My limbs hugging myself, in the foetal position, my muscles stiff. I touch my cheek. Wetness. Blood? Tears? Have I been crying?

I can smell sour milk. My breasts are heavy. I've leaked over my dress and the step and now the two are stuck together. I pull at the edges of my dress gently until it comes away, taking some of the dust with it.

What's happened? Where am I?

Painfully, I ease myself into a sitting position. My ankle throbs and I can see it's swollen. I'm in a huge stone doorway. In front of me a short driveway leads to a road. I shiver. I'm not wearing my coat. I look around and see it behind me, wedged against the wall. I must have used it as a pillow.

My vision is fuzzy. The daylight is too bright.

I stand, leaning on the stone wall for support. I'm so thirsty. My knees buckle. I press my hands against the wall to pull myself back up and straighten my dress. It has a long dark stain running down the front. When I run my hands over the back, they come off covered in dirt. What's happened to me?

My coat is filthy, but I shake it and shrug it on. It's freezing cold. I need a bath. I need to get home.

Where am I? Where's Olivia?

I stumble down the steps, turn around and look behind me. A church. I've slept in a church doorway.

I was out with Emma. I was enjoying myself. I cringe as I remember the feel of the alcohol cascading down my throat. Then what?

Nothing. Darkness.

I blacked out. Just like the old days.

I'm a mother now. I can't behave like this.

I don't want to think about it now. I just need to get home to Olivia and Matt.

My handbag is back at the top of the steps, in the corner of the church doorway. I wince as I put weight on my ankle to climb the steps. Then I reach down and undo my shoes. It's freezing but it's easier to walk in my tights than in heels with my bad ankle.

I unzip my handbag. Purse, phone, door keys, make-up. Everything's here.

I check inside my purse. All my bankcards are there, plus a twenty pound note. I haven't been mugged. I've done this to myself.

I look at my watch. The face is scratched from sleeping on the steps. The hands say eight o'clock. That can't be right.

I pull my phone out of my bag. Dead.

I have no idea where I am.

I walk unsteadily down the driveway, shoes in my hand, bag over my shoulder. I run my other hand over my hair. It's one enormous tangle. My tights are torn.

I should call a taxi but I have no phone battery left.

I get to the road and look both ways. Houses seem to go on for miles. I choose left and start walking. My feet tear through my tights and collect dirt and tiny stones from the pavement. I can hardly feel my toes, they're so numb.

I have to get home. I pass a man and ask him for directions to the nearest station or bus stop. I'm too ashamed to ask him where I am.

He looks me up and down before he reluctantly tells me to turn right at the end of the road.

I see the red and blue sign of the underground in the distance. I'm still in London. I haven't even made it back to Oxford.

Suited commuters are streaming into the station, confirmation that it's morning. I've been apart from Olivia for a whole night. My breasts ache, full of milk. I feel horribly guilty.

I peer at the sign on the station. Leyton. East London.

I go inside the cab office next to the station.

'How much to Paddington?' I ask. I can't face the Tube during rush hour. But I can get the train from Paddington. It should be quieter going out of London.

'Sixty,' the woman behind the desk says. 'And it will be an hour's wait. All our drivers are out.'

I can't wait. I need to get home now. I'll have to take the Tube.

In the cramped carriage, a woman in a trouser suit eyes my ripped tights and short dress warily. An older woman to my right shuffles away from me, placing her hand over the top of her handbag. A young man sniffs and then coughs. The alcohol is sweating out of me. A wave of shame washes over me.

I think of Olivia. I think of how angry Matt will be. How I've proved his mother right. How I've let myself down. I feel the tears welling up and I let them tumble down my face.

I cling to the handrail as the train lurches out of the platform. If I was freezing before, now I feel hot and sweaty and sick. Each jerk brings a fresh wave of nausea. I want to get off, rest for a bit, but I know I need to get home to Olivia. I feel vomit rise in my throat and I swallow it back down. I look at the red line snaking across the Tube map above me. I try to count the stops, but the mental effort exhausts me and makes me feel more sick. I close my eyes and try not to think. Instead I focus on the patches of light floating around on the backs of my eyelids. They are all sorts of colours. Red, yellow, blue.

Focus. Focus on the blackness of your eyelids. Focus on trying not to vomit. Focus on staying upright. Focus on not collapsing. Focus on not crying.

It doesn't work and I can't stop the tears running steadily down my face. I wipe my eyes with the back of my hand. A long steak of mascara comes off onto my hand. Around it there's a pale patch of skin, where the tears have rubbed off the dirt. My tongue feels like sandpaper. My nose is clogged. I sniff loudly. I don't have a tissue. Commuters tut around me, shuffling and rearranging newspapers.

I hear movement in the carriage around me as people reposition themselves nearer the doors. Then I feel a rush of air as the carriage doors open. I don't move or open my eyes. I let people push past me to get off the train, then let others push past me to get on. The doors beep and then whoosh closed. One stop down. Many, many more to go.

CHAPTER 31

I can hear Olivia screaming on the other side of the door as I fumble around in my bag for my key. I know I had it at the church, but I can't seem to find it. I tip my handbag upside down and the contents spill onto the doorstep and into the flowerbed. Oyster card, coins, wallet. House keys. There they are.

I put the key in the lock as Matt opens the door.

'Claire.'

I expect him to be furious, but he wraps his arms around me, holding me close. 'Where have you been?' he asks, his voice concerned.

I collapse into his embrace, leaning against him for support.

'I don't know,' I say, tears running down my cheeks.

'You don't know? Are you OK?'

His hands run through my hair. It's dusty, tangled, dirty.

'I need to see Olivia. She's crying.'

'She's OK, don't worry.'

I hear a strangled sob, and it takes a moment before I realise it's from me. I drop my shoes onto the floor and push past Matt into the living room.

Olivia is on her playmat and I lean over and sweep her into my arms. I feel dizzy, but I hold her close and smother her with kisses. Slowly her screams quieten before stopping altogether.

'Be careful, Claire,' Matt says. He prises Olivia gently from my arms. 'Why don't you sit down and hold her?'

I want to protest, but I'm exhausted. I sink down into the sofa.

Matt sits beside me and holds Olivia up to me.

'Do you want a cup of tea?'

'Yes please.'

I take Olivia and she starts rooting for my breast. My instinct to feed her takes over. I pull up my dress and hold my nipple to her and she sucks eagerly. I am grubby even under my clothes. My stomach has a grey, sooty line across it. What's happened to me?

Matt comes in with the tea.

'Are you sure you should do that?' he asks.

'Why?' My brain is foggy.

'I can smell the drink on you, Claire.'

I look at Olivia and feel a sudden, unfamiliar surge of affection. I never want to let go.

'Let me take her for a bit,' Matt says. 'Drink your tea, then have a shower. It will make you feel better.'

I reluctantly let him lift Olivia out of my arms and then I pick up my tea. The thought of a shower exhausts me. I just want to sleep. I feel my eyes start to close.

'Are you OK?' Matt asks from far away. 'You're spilling your drink.' I feel his hand wrap around mine and take the tea away.

When I wake up, I'm still on the sofa, still in my dress, covered in a blanket. I can hear Matt on the phone in the kitchen. It takes a while to remember what happened. Emma. Drinking. Dancing. Church steps.

Matt comes in. 'You're awake.'

'Looks like it.' I manage a half smile. I feel like death.

'What happened?' Matt asks, his voice steeped in concern.

'I don't know.'

'You don't know?'

'No. I woke up in London… I can't explain it. I suppose I must have had too much to drink. I'm sorry.'

I feel the flush of shame. There have been other nights like this. Big, black abysses of memory. I remember what my counsellor told me. You're never a recovered alcoholic. The addiction will always be there. It's always inside you, waiting to get out. Last night I stupidly gave into it.

'Where in London? Were you... were you with someone?'

'No,' I say quickly. 'It wasn't that.' I can't bring myself to tell him I slept in a church doorway.

Matt strokes my hair, and then pulls his hand away, holding a dried leaf between his fingers.

'How did this get here?'

'I don't know.'

'I was so worried, Claire.'

I swallow back tears. I can't lean on Matt. We're not together any more.

'You can go, if you like,' I say. But I don't want him to go. I want to be here with him.

'I think you need me. Besides, I've cancelled all my appointments for today.'

'You had work. I'm so sorry.'

'It's OK, Claire. You're more important. You're my wife.'

Why is he being so nice to me? I don't deserve this.

'Was that who you were on the phone to just now? Clients?'

'No, I was on the phone to the police, letting them know you were safe.'

'The police? Why?'

'You were missing. I was worried.'

'I'm so sorry,' I say, ashamed.

'I called the police five times. I'd spoken to Emma and she didn't know where you were. We were both so worried.'

'You didn't need to call the police.'

'I couldn't get them to look for you anyway. You hadn't been missing long enough.'

'Oh.'

'They said you were probably out drinking.'

'I'm so sorry.'

'I was scared, Claire. It reminded me of the last time you went missing. You know what happened. I'd never been more scared in my life than when they found you.'

I don't want to think about who I was back then. I was found at the top of the multi-storey car park, staring over the edge, ready to jump.

'I wouldn't do that. Not any more.' But I wonder if I would. What am I capable of?

'I had to tell them about it.'

'Did you?' I don't want the police to know that. I wonder if it will get back to social services. If they'll add it to their growing file of evidence that I'm a bad mother.

'It was the only way I could get them to listen. They didn't take it seriously until I told them. Then they were concerned. And Claire... I was worried too. I thought you might have...'

'I wouldn't,' I say.

'But you have been depressed. I just thought...'

'I'm fine.' The lie tastes bitter on my tongue.

'But you're not fine, Claire. You're not at all fine.'

He leans towards me.

'Your cheek is scratched.'

He reaches out to touch it and runs his fingers gently over the graze. He looks into my eyes.

'I can help you.'

I want his help. I want it so much. But I can't admit it. 'I don't need help,' I say, averting my eyes.

'At least let me clean that graze. And help you get the dirt out of your hair.'

'I'm so tired,' I say, my vision blurring again.

'Let's clean you up and put you to bed.'

I'm so exhausted that I give in.

*

I'm leaving this morning. With my daughter.

I couldn't face leaving last night. I wanted one more night in my house, in my own bed, before I entered the chaos of a shelter.

I have everything ready. My packed suitcase is by the door. I've tidied the house, mopped the kitchen floor. Even after everything he's done, I don't feel I can leave my husband alone in an untidy house. He can't stand it when anything is out of place.

Now is the time. He's left for the office and won't be back until the evening. I go to the cupboard and pull out my suitcase and put it by the door. I look round the house one last time. I'll miss it. The quiet street with the big houses that I'd always longed to live in. I'd thought this was the life I wanted. I'd thought that this was my happy ever after. When my husband whisked me off my feet and helped me escape my controlling family, I'd finally felt safe. The house was a new beginning. My own little family.

But now it's time to go.

When I go into my daughter's room, she's sitting quietly on the floor, thumbing through a book. I sit down beside her and stroke her hair.

This room is everything I didn't have as a child. A bookshelf full to bursting with books. Bright yellow walls, with a flowered border. A toy box with every kind of toy. I wonder if she'll miss it. I wonder if she'll even remember.

My daughter senses something before I do. She freezes, her fingers suddenly still on the page of the book.

Footsteps.

The light changes in the room. A shadow across the door.

My husband. Holding my suitcase.

He puts it down on the floor beside me and takes every item out one by one, holding each up in turn and examining it, before dropping it back to the floor.

'About a week's worth here,' he says, conversationally, as if it doesn't matter at all.

My eyes meet my daughter's and I don't know whether to hug her close or tell her to run away. Run as fast as she can.

She gets the message, jumping up and leaving the room.

His face is in front of me. Right up close to mine. His breath is ragged and angry.

'Where did you think you were going?'

CHAPTER 32

I lie in the bath, staring at the blue-black bruises that litter my arms and legs. I run my hands over them and wince. I let my head sink under the water, my hair fanning out around me. I want to wash myself clean of everything I've done. I want to scrub away my addiction to alcohol, I want to scrub away my postnatal depression, I want to scrub away myself. But no matter how many times I wash, I can't seem to get clean. The graze on my cheek seems to produce more dirt with each minute that passes, small bits of grit easing themselves out of the wound. My hair is no longer caked in dust from the church steps, but despite repeated washing it still feels thick and tacky. The dirt is coming from the inside, from my very core, seeping out of me into the world.

Matt's downstairs, going through the kitchen cupboards and removing all the alcohol. I listen to the bottles clink as he gathers them, hear him opening the door and throwing them into the recycling bin. This is the second time in our lives he's had to do this for me. To protect me from myself.

I pull myself out of the bath. My limbs feel heavy and I wrap the towel around me. I hear Matt shut the front door and start playing with Olivia, chatting to her. I dress and go downstairs to find him reading her a story. She stares up at him, adoringly. She never looks at me like that. When she looks at me I only see need in her eyes; for milk, for a cuddle, for a nappy change. I lean against the wall and let Matt's voice wash over me. If only I could ignore everything else and just concentrate on the love Matt feels for Olivia, and the pleasure of my little family.

Matt insists that he gets Olivia ready for bed. I listen to him run her bath, give her her milk and settle her in the cot, as I lie on the sofa.

I put my phone on to charge beside me. When it loads up, it starts to beep incessantly, updating me on another voicemail or text from the early hours of this morning. Matt and Emma had tried to call me over and over. I can't bear to listen to the messages now. I feel so ashamed of my behaviour. I put the phone on silent and rest my head back against the sofa cushions.

Matt comes back down, sits beside me and starts stroking my hair. He puts on a film, but neither of us can concentrate.

'Claire,' Matt says gently. 'Is now a good time to talk about what's been going on?'

I sigh, feeling too fragile for this conversation. I just want a few more moments with the comfort of his hand on my hair, pretending all of this never happened.

'I don't want to talk about it.' I turn the volume up on the film I'm not watching.

'I just want to understand what's bothering you.'

I can't face this on my own any more. I lean into Matt's warm torso and let everything out. I tell him how there are still noises in the night, that in the day my possessions move around. I tell him that I thought it was just me at first, just my anxiety, a symptom of my postnatal depression. But then I received the note saying I didn't deserve our daughter.

'Now I know it's not all in my head. And that's worse.'

'The note you thought my mother sent?'

'Yes,' I say, looking uncertainly into his eyes, unsure he'll ever believe me. 'She did send it.'

Matt pales. 'She wouldn't do something like that. I know she wouldn't. It's probably someone just messing around, kids even.'

'It's more than that, Matt. The other day I found the smoke alarm from Olivia's bedroom in the loft. Someone had taken it out of her room and put it there. Your mother has a key. Who else would do that?'

Matt looks alarmed. 'I don't know… I really don't know. Are you saying you think my mother's trying to hurt you?'

'Sometimes I think she's trying to hurt me, sometimes I think she's just trying to scare me.'

'She can be difficult sometimes, but I really don't think—'

'And when you think about the other things that have happened lately… Olivia falling into the pond—'

'That was an accident, Claire. You can't possibly be accusing my mother of that.'

My thoughts jumble. He's right. That doesn't make sense. Ruth might want to scare or even hurt me, but she would never deliberately harm Olivia.

'What about the bruises on her legs?' I ask.

Matt frowns. 'I—' but he stops, unsure of himself. 'Perhaps one of us handled her a bit too roughly? There haven't been any more bruises, have there?'

'No,' I say. 'But I don't feel safe here.'

I can see Matt thinking intently, deliberating over whether to finally believe me, or dismiss me as an exhausted woman with depression and an over-active imagination.

'I can move back in. Protect you…'

As much as I desperately want him to move back in, I can tell he's still not convinced. He thinks I need protecting from myself, not someone else. And he lied to me about Sarah.

'I don't know, Matt.'

'Why not?'

I sigh. 'I don't know who to trust any more. And that includes you.'

'I'm your husband.'

I laugh bitterly. 'That doesn't make you innocent. What about you and Sarah?'

'Claire, I've told you. There's nothing going on.'

'I can't just take your word for that. You haven't offered me any explanation. When it comes to Sarah all you do is lie.' The weight of my words hits me as I realise the truth of them. I know I shouldn't take him back.

'I'm not having an affair with Sarah. I've told you so many times. Why won't you believe me?'

'Because of all the other lies.'

'What lies?'

'About your past. I know you and Sarah were in a relationship just before we got together. I found a photo of the two of you at your sister's wedding. I know you were living together back then.'

'Oh,' he says. A flicker of emotion crosses his face. Guilt? 'I can explain.'

'Go on, then.'

'About a year before we met, Sarah contacted me out of the blue. Her sister had died of a brain haemorrhage. They thought it was a result of her accident years before. Sarah wanted me to come back for the funeral.'

I soften slightly. 'And you came back?'

'Of course I did. I had to. I felt so guilty about the way I'd treated her and it was such a long time since I'd seen her. I'd tried to put her out of my mind, I'd run away to university and left her alone to care for her sister.' Tears well up in Matt's eyes.

'What happened?'

'She told me she wanted to get back together. I was overwhelmed by coming back. I knew I shouldn't have left her the way I did. I thought I owed it to her to try again. It sounds awful, but without her sister to care for, I thought we might have a chance.'

'But it didn't work out?'

'No. Too much time had passed. We were different people. Older. She seemed, I don't know, more subdued. She wasn't the ambitious, fun teenager I remembered. It didn't last long. Then I left again, suddenly and without warning. I behaved badly, I know. She was upset, but I knew it wouldn't last. I came back to London. And then I met you.'

'When you were still with her?'

'No, but she found it hard to let go.'

'Did you sleep with her when you were with me?'

'No, I didn't. I didn't get in contact with her again. I ignored her calls and messages. And I moved on. To you. I'd never met anyone like you before. I forgot all about her.'

'I see.' I feel a flicker of pity for Sarah. Matt treated her appallingly. But the feeling of relief is stronger. All those years ago, he chose me, not her.

'I didn't speak to her again until Mum invited her to lunch. It stirred up a lot inside me. Guilt mainly.'

'And now?' I hardly dare ask the question. I'm not sure I want to hear the answer, but I need to know. 'Be honest, Matt. Have you slept with her since we moved here?'

'No. I promise.' He squeezes my hand.

'You hardly ever spent time with me. You were always with her.'

'You're right. I'm sorry. I did spend too much time with her. At work. And after work sometimes. I should have been at home with you. I see that now.'

'It felt like you weren't thinking of me at all.'

'I didn't mean to hurt you. I got so caught up in everything. It's been so long since I've seen Sarah and there was so much in the past that we'd never talked about. I wanted to put things right. But that was all we did. Talk. We were trying to come to terms with how things had turned out. She's a nice person, Claire. And I wanted to make things up to her. But I didn't sleep with her. You've got to believe me.'

I look at him. He's completely straight-faced. His eyes stare at me, hopeful.

'OK,' I say, trying to digest everything he's said. My mind's spinning.

There's one other thing.

'How did Sarah's scarf get under our bed?'

'I've been thinking and thinking about this,' he says, 'but I have no idea how that scarf got there.'

His deep brown eyes stare at me intently. I believe him.

Someone left the scarf there, but it wasn't Matt. I'm sure he's telling the truth.

CHAPTER 33

Before dinner, I make myself listen to the messages on my phone. Most are from last night, but Emma has also been trying to get through to me today. I know I should call her back, but I really can't face her. I'm so embarrassed. I start to compose a text to tell her I'm fine but hung-over, when my phone starts vibrating in my hand.

Miriam. Why on earth would she be calling? I haven't heard from her since we met in Oxford. I don't want to speak to her now. There's too much going on in my head.

An alert comes through to say she's left a voicemail. When I listen to it she says she's just returning my call and to ring her back.

I feel sick. I have no memory of phoning her.

I swallow and check my call records. There it is. At 3 a.m. I called Miriam. During the hours I can't remember. I've no idea why I rang her or what I said.

I was so drunk that perhaps I clicked call by mistake and cancelled it immediately. I go back into the record to check.

That can't be right. It says I was on the phone for five minutes to her. At 3 a.m.

I feel sick.

My phone buzzes in my hand. Miriam again. I swipe across to cancel the call. I can't face talking to her now.

For once, Matt and I sit down to a peaceful dinner, Olivia sleeping soundly upstairs.

'Are you feeling better?' he asks.

'A little.' I still feel grubby and I have a headache, and I can't stop worrying about what happened last night. But I'm glad Matt and I have finally managed to talk without Ruth interfering.

'It will be OK,' he says.

'I hope so.' I can't stop thinking about the scarf.

'What's the matter?'

'I'm just thinking about the scarf. Who do you think put it there?'

He frowns. 'I don't know.'

'It could easily be your mother. She was in the bedroom that day, clearing out Pamela's clothes.'

Matt frowns. 'I don't know…'

'Or Sarah? She could have planted it because she wanted you back.' It seems unlikely, even to me. I'm convinced it's Ruth.

'Sarah wouldn't do something like that.'

'Well someone put the scarf under the bed. And someone sent the note. Someone close to us.'

Matt hesitates for a second. 'Emma?' he says. 'She's the only other person who comes to the house.'

I laugh. 'She's my closest friend. Why on earth would she do it?'

'I've no idea.' He sighs. 'Maybe you were right the first time,' he says sadly. 'Maybe I've been wrong about Mum. Perhaps she's been trying to set me and Sarah up. She always invites Sarah to the house, pushing us together. She knows Sarah will never leave the village, she wouldn't drag me away to London, away from her.'

'Ruth could have planted the scarf to split us up, then sent the note to force me out of the house and get me out of your life.'

'I don't know. Perhaps I can believe the scarf. But the note – it just seems a step too far, even for her. But if you like, I can ask her about it, help us get to the bottom of who sent it.'

I raise my eyebrows. It's hard to imagine him confronting Ruth.

'Look, Claire. Why don't you let me move back in? I can look after you. We can work out what's going on together.'

I hesitate, but only for a moment. I want to be with Matt and be a family again. After all, he hasn't cheated on me. If Matt was here I wouldn't be so afraid. And then I wouldn't need to drink to get to sleep.

'We can give it a go,' I say.

Matt beams at me. 'I can go over to Mum's and get my stuff now.'

'Matt.' I stop him. 'It will only be for a little while. I can't live here long term. I want to move.'

'I just want us to be together,' he says. 'Whatever it takes. We don't have to stay here, in this house.'

I feel a weight lifting as Matt reaches out and touches my arm.

'I hate it here,' I admit.

Matt grips my hand. 'I just want us to be a family again. We can move wherever you want. Out of this house. Out of this village if you like. Even back to London. I could commute to the surgery each day. I don't mind. I just want you and Olivia to be happy.'

I nod, overwhelmed with relief. 'I love you, Matt.'

He takes my hand in his, his touch sending a shiver through my body.

Reaching out, he strokes the graze on my cheek. 'I love you too, Claire.'

I cling to him. I look up and meet his eyes, and he runs his hand through my hair. His lips meet mine and I open my mouth to his kiss, letting myself go, completely absorbed by him. I feel his hands running over my body and suddenly I want him. We strip each other's clothes off quickly and soon he's pushing inside me urgently. My nails dig into his back and I grip him as if I'll never let him go.

It's over too soon, and instead of feeling relaxed, I feel unsettled. I wonder if I've forgiven Matt too quickly. I worry that something's still not right between us.

My phone rings. It's Emma. Again. I've been too embarrassed to answer her calls, ashamed of going missing.

I force myself to answer the phone, and go into the living room, away from Matt.

'Claire! I'm so glad I got hold of you… I was worried about you.'

'I'm sorry,' I say.

'And Matt was really panicking. He thought you were missing. But don't worry, I didn't tell him anything.'

My chest tightens. 'Tell him anything about what?'

'About the guy. Graham, was it?'

I don't know whether to choose yes or no as the answer. 'Right.'

'You don't remember, do you? Gosh, Claire, you were so far gone.'

My heart sinks. 'Did I leave the club with him?'

I remember dancing with men, their bodies close to mine on the crowded dance floor. I wrack my brains to try and recall more, but my memory is a black hole.

'Yep. I just left you guys to it. But when Matt kept calling I had to cover for you. I said I didn't know where you were. That's why I've been trying to get hold of you. I wanted to check we were telling the same story. And to check you were all right, of course. And to hear all about Graham.'

My mind flashes back to the church doorstep. My dress was hiked up when I woke. Did I have sex? I can feel the bile rising in my throat.

'There's nothing to say,' I tell her.

My mind's racing. Would we have used a condom? I don't remember seeing one lying around on the church steps. It's only about eighteen hours since I might have slept with him. There's still time to get the morning-after pill.

'Look, Emma, I have to go. Matt's here.'

'OK. Well let's have a playdate soon. And don't worry, I won't let anything slip to Matt.'

I hang up the phone, run to the toilet and throw up.

*

My vision is blurry, and I don't have time to move before I see his fist coming towards me and feel it making contact with my cheekbone. I hear the crunch of the impact, feel my cheek splitting in two.

A second punch lands across my left ear and I fall backwards against my daughter's bookshelf. Punch after punch after punch, until the pain of each impact is indistinguishable from the last. My body is not my own any more. Just a mass of sensation.

He doesn't care. I've told him I'm leaving him and he is making sure I can't. It doesn't matter to him if I live or die.

I can only see out of one eye now. I focus on the doorway. If I can slide across the floor somehow, then perhaps I could crawl out of the door and reach the phone.

He's kicking me now. I raise my hands to cover my head and he kicks it harder. Stars dance in front of my eyes.

I shouldn't move. If he thinks I'm unconscious maybe he'll stop. Or maybe he won't stop until I'm dead.

There's movement in the doorway. For a blissful second I think it's the police coming to rescue me. But it's my daughter, eyeing the scene silently, thumb in her mouth, clutching the soft toy koala that her father brought her back from a business trip. She meets my eyes but says nothing.

I feel a bitter guilt, as I choke on the blood that fills my mouth.

She's not shocked. I thought I'd protected her, I thought I was giving her a better life than the one I had. But I've failed her.

My good eye meets hers. I try to speak, to get out the words.

'Run,' I garble through blood and tears. It's less than a whisper.

A harder kick to my face. He will not stop me. He will not stop me warning her.

'Run,' I repeat, and I feel the blood running down my chin.

But she stays still.

The beating stops.

There is something wrong with my hearing. The world is foggy.

I see his shadow walk across the room. I see him take her hand. I try to scream out to stop him, but I can't.

CHAPTER 34

The house is quiet. Matt has drifted off on the sofa, and Olivia is still asleep in bed. While I have the chance, I grab the car keys and drive to a pharmacy two villages away. I can't risk anyone seeing me at the local store. I leave Matt a note to say we've run out of baby wipes and I've gone to get some.

There's a queue and I tap my foot impatiently as people hand in prescriptions and the pharmacist goes to search for them out the back. I wish I wasn't here, wish I wasn't doing this. But I have to. Just in case.

When it's my turn I ask for the morning-after pill, but they won't give it to me until they've questioned me about my sex life. I tell them we used a condom but it broke. I tell them I'm with a long-term partner. And yes, we usually use condoms. She asks me about breastfeeding and warns me that I might have a small drop off in milk supply. I nod. There are others standing around waiting and I keep my voice down. Finally, the pharmacist hands over the packet and I leave. When I get home Matt is still asleep on the sofa. I go to the kitchen and take the pill with water, shame overwhelming me.

In the morning, I tell Matt I need some time to myself and I'm going shopping in Oxford. It's the weekend and he's happy to look after Olivia. I take the car and drive to the STI clinic at the hospital.

The waiting room is crowded with people. I glance round furtively, worried I'll be recognised, or that someone will notice me and see the turmoil in my head. I'm overwhelmed with guilt about what I've done. But no one is looking at me. Everyone is engrossed in their mobile phones.

I'll just get through these checks, they'll confirm I'm all right and then I can get back on with my life. And I won't drink again. I can't drink again.

The one thing that's certain is that I woke up on the steps. I didn't get there on my own. The church is nowhere near the club. Someone must have gone with me, taken me there.

I wonder if Emma knows more than she's letting on. She must have known how drunk I was when I went home with him. She let me go. Why would she do that? And then she let Matt worry. Did she really think I was just having a good time?

I could ask her for more details, but she won't be able to tell me if I slept with him. She won't know. And I'll never know either. I just need to move on. Matt and I are happy now. We can move away from everyone in the village and get on with our lives. Put everything behind us.

Eventually I'm called into the nurse's room, and I tell more lies about my sex life to get the tests. Just one partner. Fancied a check-up. Condom broke. Luckily, the tests are quick.

When I get back home, I go upstairs. I don't want to be around Matt or Olivia. I'm too ashamed. I sit on the bed for a moment, listening to the sounds of Matt playing with our baby downstairs. This is it. The life I want. I must make sure Matt never finds out what happened. I should get the test results back in one week. Then my mind will rest.

I dread to think if the test results are positive. They'll want to trace all my partners. I'll have passed on the infection. I'll have to tell him then. I won't have a choice.

My phone rings and I see it's Miriam. I'm about to reject the call when it occurs to me that she might know what happened in London. If I called her in the middle of the night and spoke to her, then I might have told her where I was, what I was doing. I feel sick. She might tell me something awful.

But I have to know. I swipe to answer the call, holding my breath.

'Hi,' I say.

'Claire?'

'I'm sorry I called you in the middle of the night.'

'Oh, don't worry, I had my phone off.'

'Oh,' I say, disappointed. She's not going to be able to tell me anything.

'You left a message.'

'Oh…'

'You don't remember, do you?' Her voice is sad rather than accusing.

'No,' I admit.

'You just said you were worried because you thought Matt's ex-girlfriend was trying to take Olivia off you.' I sigh. Is that all?

'I'm sorry I called you about that. I don't know what I was thinking.' How had I managed to get myself so worked up about Sarah, that I thought it was a good idea to call Miriam at 3 a.m.?

'You seemed really agitated. Quite upset. You asked me to look up the police records. About the accident on the farm.'

'I'm sorry, Miriam. I shouldn't have asked you that. You already told me you couldn't do it.'

'It's OK,' she says. 'I did look in the end. I was curious. I wasn't going to tell you if I didn't find anything.'

'Oh,' I reply, realisation dawning. 'You did find something?'

'There's a huge file on the records, Claire.'

'And?' I hold my breath, afraid of what she might be about to tell me.

'Are you at home?'

'Yes,' I say.

'Is Matt with you?'

'Miriam, what is it?'

'It's not good news, Claire. It's like you thought. The police suspected Sarah of pushing Felicity.'

'She did it, didn't she?'

This changes everything. Matt said she'd felt guilty. It must have been because she pushed her sister. And if she'd do that to her sister, then what else is she capable of? Is she the one who's been tormenting me?

'There's evidence, though it's not conclusive. But there's more. Something I need to tell you.'

'What?' I ask, my heart hammering.

'Sarah wasn't the only suspect. The police also investigated Matt.'

'What?' I gasp.

'It gets worse, Claire. He confessed to pushing her.'

I collapse down onto the bed. Surely Matt couldn't have pushed her?

'Did he go to jail?'

'No. He withdrew his confession a few weeks later. The police were pretty convinced he'd done it. There just wasn't enough evidence.'

CHAPTER 35

I feel like running. Running away. I have so much adrenalin in me, so much anxiety, that I'm struggling to control it.

I've told Matt to go back to his mother's. But I haven't told him why. I need time to digest what Miriam said. According to her, Matt confessed to pushing Sarah's sister out of the hayloft, leading to her eventual death. I can't get my head round it.

No one in this village is who they appear to be. Not Matt. Not Ruth. Not Sarah. I've lived under the same roof as Matt for the last six years. I've married him, had his child, and yet the whole time I've never truly known him.

I want a drink so badly, I feel sick.

Matt's always been here to stop me drinking, to manage me, to ground me.

I've always resented him for it. But now, without him, I'm not sure if I can control myself.

I can almost taste the tang of the wine on my tongue, feel it gliding down my throat.

Without Matt, the only way I really know how to cope is with alcohol.

I need oblivion.

I remember Matt putting the bottles in the recycling bin. Had he remembered to empty them all first?

I leave Olivia on the playmat, go out to the bin and rifle through, pulling out the bottles one by one, not caring about the noise. They're all empty. I dread to think what this might look like, but I'm so desperate, I hardly care.

Ruth passes by the bottom of the drive.

'Sorting out the rubbish?' she asks.

I redden. 'Yes,' I say. And then, 'Just looking for something. I think I threw out a bank statement.'

'Below all the wine bottles, was it?'

'It must be near the bottom of the bin.'

'Olivia OK?'

'Yes. I should get back inside and see to her.'

'Yes, you should.' Judgement radiates off her, as she walks away past the cottage and down the side path to her house.

I go back inside, but I can't focus.

I call Emma and within half an hour we're in the garden centre café having lunch, a bottle of cold white wine on the table between us. She reassures me that I've made the right decision in chucking Matt out again, although I don't go into my reasons. I still can't process the fact that Matt confessed to committing a violent crime, so I let Emma assume it's still about him cheating. We chat about the babies and Emma tells me all the advantages of single life. When she mentions Graham, I brush it off, unable to admit that I blacked out and found myself alone on the church steps. She reassures me there'll be other men and we soon polish off a second bottle of wine.

I feel so much better after lunch. Merry and light. As I walk down the streets pushing the buggy, I feel alive again. I can cope without Matt. I can do this on my own.

But then I remember that he'll want custody and I shiver. Can I really let someone who's committed a violent crime look after my daughter? I'm going to have to fight for custody, and fight hard.

My first priority has to be my daughter. But then Olivia starts screaming and I think of the afternoon ahead of me breastfeeding and nappy changing, and reality comes crashing down. I won't be able to cope. When I stop at the tiny local supermarket to pick up nappies, I see the wine is on offer and grab a few more bottles, telling myself I'm stocking up for the week. By the time I finally wheel the buggy back through the door, Olivia has increased the volume to maximum.

'Shut up,' I mutter under my breath. 'Just shut up.'

Inside, I pause for a moment to sit on the stairs and catch my breath.

'Hello?' a voice calls out. From inside the house.

There's someone in my living room.

I put my shopping down and the bottles of wine clink together. I gather a screaming Olivia into my arms, take a deep breath and step into the room.

There's a woman there. She has a severe grey bob and penetrating green eyes.

She gets up from my sofa and holds out her hand. 'Catherine Clarke. I work in child welfare. Your mother-in-law let me in.'

I look round the living room at the scattered mess of toys, bottles and spare nappies.

'I would have tidied if I'd known you were coming.'

'We prefer to see people as they live normally.'

'Do you want a drink?' I ask, with feigned politeness.

'No thank you.'

Olivia continues to scream and I rock her back and forth.

'You can feed her if you like. I don't mind.'

I nod, but I feel vulnerable and exposed. I don't want to breastfeed in front of this woman. This woman who has let herself into my house and is here solely to judge me.

Olivia keeps crying and I keep rocking her.

'I'll get to the point. I've been alerted about your drinking. There are concerns you're not well enough to look after your child.' She's looks at my red-faced, crying daughter pointedly.

'I'm fine,' I say, wondering who has betrayed me. Ruth? Surely not Matt?

'How many units do you drink a week?'

'Oh, not much. Just the occasional glass of wine.'

I wonder if she can smell the alcohol on my breath, hear the slight slur in my voice. I concentrate hard, trying to focus. I sit up straighter. I think nervously of the three bottles of wine in the bag in the hallway.

'And is it true you used to be an alcoholic?'

'Yes. I had treatment for it three years ago. I hardly drink these days.'

'And how are you coping with looking after Olivia? You've had postnatal depression?'

She's well briefed. The social worker who came round before had only been concerned about Olivia's bruises. She seemed keen to see the best in me. This woman is different.

'Yes, that's right. I was feeling a bit down when she was first born, but I'm fine now.' I think of how desperately I need help, but the only people who ever ask me how I am will use my answer to take my daughter away.

'Do you mind if I look around the house? See how you're coping?'

'Sure,' I say, wondering what she can possibly be looking for. I think again of the bottles in the hallway. That's not evidence of anything, surely? It's not unusual to have wine in the house.

'Who called you?' I ask.

'I'm afraid I can't tell you that.'

It has to be Ruth or Matt. I know what this is about. As soon as I asked Matt to leave again, Ruth was back on her mission to win custody of Olivia for him. And when she saw me rifling through the recycling bin this morning, she saw her opportunity to discredit me. She wants to prove I'm not capable of looking after my daughter. If the social workers decide that Olivia should stay with Matt and Ruth, I'll have to stay in the village too. I'll be trapped.

'Was it my mother-in-law?'

'I can't tell you,' she says as she goes into the kitchen. 'Mind if I?' Her hand is on the handle of the kitchen cupboard.

'Go ahead,' I reply, and she opens each of the cupboards in turn. There's nothing to find there.

I fidget, shifting Olivia's weight in my arms.

'I know my mother-in-law called you,' I say, speaking slowly so I don't slur my words. 'She's vindictive. She wants me out of her life.'

'Really?' Catherine raises her eyebrows and pulls a chair over to a high cupboard, climbing onto it to peer at the contents of the top shelf.

'Yes. She sent me a note, saying I didn't deserve my daughter. And she moved a smoke alarm…' I'm rambling now, my words fast and uncensored.

The woman climbs down from the chair. 'I was told you were paranoid,' she says, touching my shoulder gently. 'A symptom of your depression, perhaps?'

'No, I—' How can I convince her?

'It's OK to admit you're struggling,' she continues. 'To admit you need help.' Suddenly her sharp eyes seem kinder and for a second I wonder if I could trust her. But I stop myself from confiding in her. That would play straight into Ruth's hands.

'I'm fine,' I insist once more. I need to make sure Catherine doesn't hand Olivia straight over to Matt and Ruth. I think of what I learnt yesterday, how Matt pushed Sarah's sister out of the hayloft.

'My husband's a violent man,' I say.

'Does he hit you?'

'No.'

'So what do you mean?'

'He was responsible for someone's death. He pushed someone and they cracked their skull. He confessed to the police.'

'You mean Felicity Duncan?'

'Yes,' I say, shocked. How does she know about that?

'You shouldn't be bringing that up after all this time. That was a very difficult period for everyone.'

'How do you know?'

'I've lived in the area for years. Your husband comes from a good family.'

I laugh. 'You know Ruth?' Things are starting to become clearer. Catherine knows Ruth. Ruth has organised her visit to scare me. I'm not sure she's even a social worker.

'You're looking in the wrong place if you're trying to blame her,' Catherine continues, losing all pretence of being an impartial official. 'You need to look closer to home.'

'Who are you?' I ask, angrily. 'Has Ruth sent you? Are you a friend of hers?'

'I worked with children in schools for years before I retired,' she says. 'Safeguarding their well-being. I can tell when things aren't right at home. I can tell when the mother isn't fit.' Her eyes narrow as she looks me up and down.

'Get out,' I say.

She picks up her bag. 'I've seen enough here anyway. I may not be able to take your child away from you, but I can let the authorities know what kind of mother you are. And I've worked in childcare long enough to know that you won't get custody of your daughter.'

*

I wake to the sound of the key in the lock.

I must have lost consciousness. Everything hurts. Every cell of my body.

The carpet is sticky with my blood. I don't know where I end and the floor begins.

Where's my daughter? Did she escape?

She must have got away, I tell myself. She must have.

Footsteps on the stairs. Just one set. A man's regular clunk, one stair at a time. No accompanying lighter footsteps of a little girl.

She must have got away.

I need to find her.

I try to move but I can't. My body is broken. I fight to move my arm just a little, to reach out into the empty air.

The darkness is coming again. I fight it.

I must stay awake. I must find her.

I feel the world closing in.

As I fade away, I hear the distant sound of sirens, getting louder as they approach.

CHAPTER 36

I lie on the sofa, trying to get some rest. I feel exhausted from the last few days. And yet I have to up my game, be a better mother. I can't let them take my daughter away from me. Olivia lies beside me on her back, playing lethargically with my hair as the TV flickers in the background. My top sticks to me. It needs washing. It's still stained with Olivia's sick from two or three days ago. I should have done the washing, but instead I've lain in bed most of the morning.

I put an arm round Olivia's small body and close my eyes. I wish I could just sleep and forget everything, but I can't let myself drop off with my baby next to me.

I'm so glad she isn't crawling yet. The living room is a maze of hazards. Phone cables that might electrocute her, coins that might choke her, hair gel that she might swallow. Anything could happen, at any time. One moment of inattention is all it takes. A glance at my phone while Olivia picks up a coin and swallows it. Leaving her in the bath to drown while I answer the door. I flinch, remembering my dream of Matt drowning her, remembering her buggy slipping under the water in the pond.

I don't know how people manage as parents. But they seem to. They bring up happy, healthy children. They live fulfilled lives. But not me. I can't do it.

I can't even keep up with the housework. The bedsheets haven't been washed since well before Matt moved out the first time, and in the kitchen the washing up overflows the counter and spreads over the cooker and beyond.

The familiar smell of a dirty nappy wafts towards me. When did I last change Olivia? Surely since she got up? Perhaps not. I reach into the bag for the nappies. Only two left. I change it on autopilot. I know I should be talking to Olivia, laughing with her, tickling her tummy, but I can't summon the energy. I have nothing to say to the squirming mass of chubby limbs in front of me. I'm completely disconnected from her. It's like she's not my child.

Ruth will be here in a minute to collect her. I really don't want her and Matt looking after Olivia, but I had to agree to it. After she sent her friend round yesterday pretending to be from social services I have no doubt she's serious about getting custody of Olivia for Matt. I'm sure she's informing the real social workers of every mistake I make. I can't deny Matt access to his daughter.

I need to smarten up before she comes but I hardly have the energy. I need to find some painkillers. I feel awful. I stumble to the kitchen and go through Pamela's cupboard of pills, pull out some ibuprofen and take a couple with some cold water. There are enough pills to knock me out completely if I wanted. I contemplate the idea for the moment. Handing over Olivia to Ruth and then knocking back some pills and sleeping for the afternoon. But I know I have to pull myself out of this, make myself better. Otherwise I'll lose my daughter.

When the doorbell rings and Ruth is at the other side, I manage feigned politeness. We both know she sent Catherine round yesterday to warn me. I can't make any missteps now. I can't say the wrong thing. So I hand my daughter over to the woman I hate most in the world and tell her to have a good time.

When they've gone, I go into the kitchen to make myself a cup of tea, resisting the lure of the wine I bought yesterday. I've managed not to touch it so far. I can see into Ruth and Jack's house from here. I see Olivia being passed back and forth between Matt and Ruth, cooed over and loved.

I want to turn away, go and catch up on some sleep, but somehow I can't. I know that Matt confessed to pushing Sarah's sister now. And I know just how nasty Ruth can be. I feel compelled to watch Olivia with them. I'm her mother. It's up to me to keep her safe.

They leave the kitchen and I can't see anything any more. I go upstairs to the bedroom and lie down, trying to let my exhaustion take over and sleep. But I can't. All my senses are heightened, alert to any risk.

Ten minutes later, I hear the whir of a car engine and then the sound of wheels on the gravel.

I rush to Olivia's room and look down onto our driveway. Our car is gone. They must have taken Olivia out.

I pace up and down the room, unable to sit still. Where would they have taken her?

I text Matt to ask. As I watch my phone, waiting for a reply, I start to panic. What if they've taken her away for good? They could have moved her out of the village, away from me, to a place I'll never find her.

My phone beeps. Matt says they've gone out in the village and that I shouldn't worry.

But the text doesn't quell my fears. I hate to think of my daughter with them. I still don't know where they've taken her.

I grab my keys and leave the house in my dirty clothes, walking quickly into the village. I look for them on the streets, but there's no sign. I rush around, checking the post office and the charity shop and then the pub and the garden centre. Nothing. My heart races. I'm sure something is wrong. Where have they taken her?

And then something occurs to me. Sarah. Perhaps they've taken her to see Sarah.

It takes me ten minutes to get to her flat. I see Matt's car outside and at first I'm relieved.

But then I wonder what they're doing there. My daughter is with two people who were suspects in the investigation into Sarah's sister's death. What's going on? Why are they all meeting? Are they trying to cover something up? Or was I right about their affair all along?

I creep over to the block of flats. Sarah's in flat 2, which must be on the ground floor. I peer into the windows of the flat on the left-hand side and gasp. They're there. All of them. Ruth. Jack. Matt and Sarah. Sitting on the living room sofas, deep in conversation.

Matt is holding my daughter. He says something and everyone laughs.

Then he gets up and leaves the room, passing Olivia to Sarah. Sarah smiles at my baby, pushing her face close to hers and stroking her hair. I feel a surge of jealousy and fear. I don't want that woman holding my daughter. I don't want her touching her. My hand clenches into a fist.

They look like the perfect, happy family.

Suddenly, everything makes sense. Sarah wants my child. And my husband. She's worming her way into my family, taking my place.

I think of all the odd things that have happened since we moved. Olivia falling into the pond. The bruises on her legs. The note. The smoke alarm. Were these all ways of discrediting me, of getting to my daughter? I remember what Sarah said about miscarrying, how she hadn't found someone who she wanted to have a child with since. She wanted to steal my family all along. What if none of what's been happening has been down to Ruth? What if it's been Sarah?

I must do something. I must get Olivia away from her.

In the living room, Ruth suddenly turns and looks directly at me. Her eyes meet mine and I recoil. She says something to Sarah and Sarah turns to stare at me, my daughter in her arms. There's a moment where they all confer, and then I see Ruth get up.

I rise from my position at the window and go to the door of the block. It opens.

Ruth.

'What are you doing here?'

'I'd like my daughter back,' I say.

'It's Matt's turn for access. And we're having a nice time.' She looks at me pityingly. 'You need to go.'

I barge past her, into the hallway and then into Sarah's flat and her living room.

'Claire?' Matt says as I enter.

I look at the expectant faces and realise I haven't planned what to say.

'I want my daughter back. Why have you brought her here? You said you weren't cheating on me. Was it all lies?'

'Claire – we've had this conversation before. I'm not cheating on you. You were the one who told me to leave.'

Olivia whines and Sarah strokes her back to comfort her.

She needs to get her hands off my daughter. I go towards her to take my baby back.

Matt exchanges a look with his mother and gets up, placing a hand on my shoulder.

'You need to go, Claire.'

I shrug out of his grip.

I point at Sarah. 'She's trying to take you,' I say. 'She wants my family. She wants my life. She wants my baby. But she's not having her.'

'Claire, you need to calm down.'

Matt's hand is back on my shoulder, leading me out of the living room, but I slip away from him.

'Admit it. You're trying to take them from me.'

Sarah stares at me blankly. Her indifference angers me.

'No one knows what you're talking about, Claire.' Ruth speaks slowly and gently, as if talking to someone who's not well.

Jumbled thoughts flash through my head. Matt and Sarah working together. The noises in the house at night. Olivia falling into the pond. Sarah's sister's fall.

'She's dangerous,' I say, turning to Sarah. 'You can't be with Olivia. Not with your past. You can't be trusted.' I struggle for the next words. 'Not after what happened to your sister—'

Sarah's sudden tears shock me into silence. Her body wracks with sobs and Matt and Ruth spring into action. Matt takes Olivia from her and puts a comforting hand on her shoulder, while Ruth brings her a glass of water.

Olivia screams and I go to take her from Matt, but Ruth blocks my path.

'You're leaving,' she says, pushing me towards the door.

'Not without Olivia.' I escape Ruth's grasp and rush over to Matt, snatching my daughter out of his arms.

That night I can't sleep. I relive the day again and again. Matt has sent me a series of angry texts, saying I should never have gone round to Sarah's, that I shouldn't have upset her. I read them over and over, thinking how only a few days ago I wanted to get back together with him. Now there's no one I can trust.

It's not until after midnight that I give in to the temptation and go downstairs and open a bottle of wine. I need it to help me sleep. If I don't sleep I'll be too exhausted to look after Olivia properly tomorrow. I don't mean to polish off the bottle, but I can't stop myself. When I've finished the last dregs, I put my head in my hands and sob.

I'm losing control.

*

I wake up covered in sweat. I feel sick. I can taste the sourness of stale alcohol on my tongue. I roll over in bed and my head pounds.

Switching the light on, I look round the room. I'm at home. I'm OK.

The baby monitor is flashing, the blue lights reflecting off the white ceiling. Something must have set it off.

I stare at it, but it makes no sound.

Olivia must have woken up and gone back to sleep. I turn the pillow over and try to get comfy. I'm in a cold sweat and I feel shaky. I need more sleep before the alcohol wears off and I feel stable enough to pick my daughter up. It will be even longer before the wine leaves my milk and I can breastfeed her.

Outside, the foxes scream and screech, dividing and conquering our back garden. Maybe they set off the baby monitor.

'Rock-a-bye baby on the tree top.'

I freeze.

The voice sings softly through the monitor.

'When the wind blows the cradle will rock.'

Am I still asleep?

'When the bough breaks the cradle will fall.'

The voice is ghostly, almost a whisper.

The lights of the baby monitor flicker and then go off. The air is still. Even the foxes are silent.

I stumble out of bed, knocking my bedside light onto the floor with a crash.

I race down the corridor to Olivia's room.

She's lying in the cot, next to her toy bunny, fast asleep. The room is still. I watch my daughter's chest moving up and down.

I release my breath.

Then I notice the rocking chair, where I sit to breastfeed Olivia when she wakes in the night. It's moving.

There's no breeze in the room. No reason for the chair to be rocking back and forth.

I turn to the baby monitor beside the cot. It's been turned off.

It was on a few minutes ago. In my bedroom the blue lights had been flashing. I heard the voice singing softly through it. Didn't I?

Someone has turned it off in the last few minutes. Someone has been here, in my baby's room. I have to stifle my scream.

I gather Olivia up in my arms.

We are not alone. There's someone in the house with us. I hear the stair creak and I jump. Olivia starts to cry.

I daren't go downstairs. I don't want to confront whoever's down there. I'm too woozy, too confused.

All that matters is that Olivia's safe and that I'm with her. I take her into my room and hold her in the bed with me. We breathe as one, as I lie awake, my ears pricked up, terrified of who might be lurking in the dark shadows of the house.

*

They come in noisily. Trampling boots and loud ringtones.

They don't know I'm here, until they enter my daughter's bedroom and I'm pointed out.

'Is she dead?'

Their hands are on my neck, feeling for my pulse.

'No. She's alive.'

'God, I didn't even realise that was a woman.' A younger voice, high pitched.

'Ambulance on its way.'

I want to ask them about my daughter, but the words come out slurred and incomprehensible.

'Don't try to speak, love. Just rest. The ambulance will be here soon.'

But I need to speak. I need to tell them to find my daughter.

CHAPTER 37

The feeling from last night hasn't left me. I'm convinced there was someone in the house. I know I heard them singing softly through the baby monitor. I'm sure of it. The voice had sounded half-familiar, but I still can't think why, or who it might have been. Would it have been Ruth? Or Sarah? In the cold light of day, the details that replay in my mind are hazy and dream-like. But as much as I'd like to believe it was a dream, I'm certain there was someone in the cottage.

I can't stay here a moment longer. I must get out. If I have to keep walking and walking forever, I don't care. I just need to escape. I pile Olivia into her buggy in her sleep-suit and coat and leave the cottage, letting the door slam behind me. I need to get away. From Matt. From Ruth. From Sarah. From a cottage that's a shrine to a dead woman. My head is full as I walk down the street. I push the pram as fast as I can, twisting it this way and that to avoid the dawdling shoppers on the pavement.

I wonder when Emma's kitchen will be finished, when I might be able to move in with her. Or if I could find work and move far away, back to London. But neither of these are short-term options. I think about asking Miriam to take me in. Just for a few days, until we get ourselves settled. But our relationship is still rocky. Despite the help she's given me recently, I don't think our friendship stretches that far.

I need to get out for my own sanity. This morning I found myself going through Pamela's cupboard of pills. There are more than enough to kill me. I hate myself for it, but I'm starting to feel the way I felt before, when I ended up standing on the edge of a multi-storey car park in London, intending to take my own life.

Olivia starts screaming from her buggy. She'll want feeding again and I'll need to find a place to do it. A café maybe. I could stop and get a coffee, rest for a while. But I don't want to. I don't want to be alone with the stillness, alone with my thoughts. I need to keep walking, to keep moving.

'Look right, look left, look right again.' I repeat the mantra my own mother taught me, as I go to cross the side road. I wish she was beside me now. I need her more than ever.

Concentrate, I think. Concentrate. My mind is so crowded that I can hardly see in front of me. A car I didn't see zooms past.

'Look right, look left, look right again.' I repeat the process, focusing on the road, making myself look for cars before I step out.

When I get to the other side Olivia's screams are the only sound in an otherwise peaceful countryside scene. Breathe. A bus careers down the main road at speed. I grip the pram tighter as images flash through my head. The bus hitting the pram and skidding. The pram concertinaing in on itself, Olivia inside, her small body trapped within the frame and the frame trapped under the huge wheel, as the bus continues to travel further down the road before it comes to a stop.

I need to go back to the doctor. I need help. I need the counselling now. Or antidepressants. Something. Otherwise, I am spinning out of control, speeding towards the end.

I wonder if I should ring someone. But who do I have? Emma has already told me she's busy today and there's no one else. No husband. No mother. No family. I want someone to tell me everything will be all right. That I'll be all right. I consider ringing one of the helplines on the leaflet the doctor gave me. Just to have someone to talk to, someone to listen. But I can't bring myself to. I can't. I can't trust anyone. I have to look after myself.

We get to the park and Olivia is still screaming. I try and block it out and focus on the morning sunlight shining through the branches of the trees, the fresh, crisp air. Another mother smiles at me sympathetically as she pushes her own screaming toddler in his buggy. I keep my head bowed and find a bench to sit on. I adjust my top and put Olivia to my breast.

I have a water bottle filled with vodka in my bag. I know I shouldn't, but I only have it just in case. For emergencies. But now it's calling me. I take it out and have a few sips. The thrill of the burn on the back of my throat hits me and I'm content for half a second, before I'm taken over by shame and regret. I take another few sips. At least if anyone sees me, it doesn't look as if I'm drinking.

Olivia pulls away from my breast, and spits up. I put her over my shoulder and burp her, before I remember that I should have put a muslin cloth over my coat to protect it. I take her off my shoulder and crane my neck to see the back of my coat. A white splatter of baby sick runs down the green fabric. Holding Olivia in one arm, I root around in my bag until I find the baby wipes. I twist my arm round and dab at the shoulder of my coat.

As an afterthought I wipe round Olivia's mouth.

I don't know what to do with myself. There are no playgroups on today. Not that I've been to any before anyway. I spend all my time with Emma, the only friend I've got around here.

With Olivia back in the buggy, I walk to clear my head, but I'm foggy and confused from lack of sleep. I must start looking for jobs. I need to get away from Matt and Ruth and Sarah. Any work will do. Freelance work for the papers would be a good start. If I have to share custody with Matt, then I might have time to do it from home. And then I can save enough money to return to London.

After four circuits of the park, Olivia is asleep. There is nowhere to go but home.

*

Olivia doesn't wake as I lift the buggy carefully over the threshold and into the cottage, putting it down gently.

Silence.

I shut the door and hold my breath as the latch clicks.

Olivia shifts slightly in the buggy, but remains asleep.

I go into the living room to look for my laptop. I should email more editors to ask about freelance work.

The clock on the mantelpiece strikes three. It always makes me jump. I must take the battery out.

Then there's another noise. The stairs creaking.

My imagination.

But no. It's not. Someone is coming down the stairs.

Slowly.

Creak.

Pause.

Another creak.

They are placing one foot down at a time, carefully, deliberately.

I can hear my own breathing and I still it, holding my breath.

They must know I'm here. They'll have heard me come in.

Now the footsteps have stopped.

They're at the bottom of the stairs.

I look desperately round the room for something to grab, but there are only Olivia's toys, scattered. Pamela's walking sticks are long gone.

Seconds pass.

The silence is so loud that I can hear my own watch, ticking half a beat behind the clock on the mantelpiece.

And then there's a knock on the living room door.

'Claire?'

I remain still. This feels like a test, a game.

The door swings open.

And there's Emma, smiling uncertainly.

'Emma!' I say. Confusion quickly follows the relief. 'What are you doing here?'

She pauses, looking uncomfortable.

'I don't know how to tell you this, Claire.'

'Tell me what?'

'Let's sit down,' Emma indicates my sofa as if this is her house. I sit, and she perches down beside me, and turns to me.

'I've been worried about you.'

'Oh,' I say. The vodka clouds my brain and I find it hard to digest her words. A part of me is relieved, glad someone cares. If only there was a way out of how I'm feeling.

'Matt told me about your problems with alcohol. I wish I'd known. I could have helped you.' She puts her arm round me.

Matt. Again. He's trying to control me and now he's got to my best friend, shared my secrets.

'I'm OK.'

'We're both worried about Olivia.'

'I didn't realise you were friends with Matt.'

'I'm not. But ever since you disappeared on the night out in London, we've both been concerned. And when Matt told me you were an alcoholic, I didn't want to believe it. But when I thought about it, it made sense. You were off your head at the club.'

'We were letting our hair down.'

Emma looks at me sympathetically. 'I think you need help, Claire. With your postnatal depression and everything else going on, you're not coping.'

'You don't need to worry,' I say. But my words are empty. I'm not even sure I can look after Olivia any more.

'I think I do.'

'What are you doing in my house? Did Matt send you?'

'Well, yeah. He wanted to see if you were OK. You wouldn't let him in. He asked me to check how you were coping, to see if you'd stocked up on alcohol again after he left. He lent me his key.' I stare at her, disbelieving. I feel totally betrayed. I wish I could take the vodka out of my bag and knock it back to numb my pain, but I know I can't. That would only prove Matt right.

'You shouldn't trust Matt,' I say.

'I know he cheated on you, but he's doing this in your best interest.'

'It's worse than cheating.'

'What?'

I haven't told Emma the reason I chucked Matt out for the second time. But I need to tell her now.

'Matt confessed to a murder,' I say.

'What?' She looks bemused.

'He pushed Sarah's sister. She fell from a hayloft. And eventually died.'

'I didn't know Sarah had a sister… And why hasn't he been arrested?' Confusion etches Emma's face.

'It was years ago. Before we met. But the case was never solved. And he was the main suspect.'

'Claire…' Emma strokes my arm. I have a bad feeling that she doesn't believe me.

'It's the truth,' I say urgently. 'It's why we're not together any more.'

'Claire, I hate to say this, and I know it's going to hurt you, but I'm only saying it because I care.'

'What?'

'I think you're confused. Matt told me you were paranoid, that you thought you were being watched in the cottage, that you had vivid nightmares. And sometimes when we're that confused and down, then we imagine things, or forget things. We think things are true that aren't true. Especially when we've been drinking.'

'I'm telling the truth!' I don't know how to convince her, how to make her believe me.

There's no one left on my side. My closest friend has betrayed me.

She touches my arm. 'I'm sorry it's come to this. But you need help, Claire.'

She's right – I do need help. I want it so badly. I'm not coping but I can't confide in Emma. She'll just tell Matt. And Matt and Ruth will tell social services. Then I'll be left all alone, Olivia torn away from me.

'I'm OK,' I insist. When my tears start to fall, she puts her arms round me and holds me, then goes to make me a cup of tea.

She places a mug down in front of me and we sit in silence, sipping our drinks.

Then she looks at her watch.

'Matt will be here in a minute,' she says.

'I don't want to see him.' But my words come out in a whisper. I've lost my energy. I've lost myself.

'We all want to help you,' Emma says. 'Just speak to him.'

*

I'm aware of the sounds first. The beeping of a machine. Idle chatter.

For a moment I wonder if I'm asleep, dreaming of somewhere other than the confines of my house.

Then the panic overwhelms me, taking over every ounce of my being. Something awful has happened.

Where is my daughter?

A staccato of images I can't make sense of: A packed case. A key in a lock. Footsteps. My daughter standing in the doorway, her eyes meeting mine.

Where is she?

I open my eyes, see the blue curtain, the row of beds. I'm in hospital. The fear takes my breath away.

Where is my daughter?

CHAPTER 38

Consciousness rises in me as if I'm struggling out of a deep, black hole. I can smell sour milk, antiseptic and sweat. My sweat. I'm exhausted. I ease open my eyes and look around, expecting to see Olivia.

It hurts to turn my head.

Olivia's not here.

Where am I?

My eyes pound, pain radiating from the sockets, as if they might burst. The fluorescent strip light above me shines brightly. A blue curtain surrounds my bed. The bed itself is propped up at an angle, with metal bars to stop me rolling out.

Realisation hits me. I'm in hospital.

I must have been in an accident.

I move each limb in turn, checking for injuries, and then reach down under the sheets and run my hands over my body. No pain. No bandages.

What's happened to me? I feel a flash of fear. What if something's happened to Olivia?

'Hello?' I call out tentatively. There's no response.

I jump down from the bed, wincing in anticipation as my feet hit the ground. But there's no pain in my body. Only my head pounds.

There's a small metal set of drawers next to my bed and I open each one in turn, searching for my phone. They're all empty.

I draw back the curtain. Eyes from the bed opposite meet mine and I jump.

I find my voice. 'Where's my daughter?' I ask them. 'Where is she?'

But they just stare.

I scan the room for medical staff. No one.

I push open the double doors and step out of the ward. Rows of doors on each side of a corridor. Another ward. And another one. I go the other way. I find a nurses' station.

I lean over the desk and interrupt the bleary-eyed man as he picks up the phone.

'Excuse me – do you know where my daughter is?'

The man looks me up and down and sighs. He puts his hand over the mouthpiece of the phone.

'Your daughter?'

'Yes, Olivia Hughes. Did she come in with me?'

'Which ward are you on?'

'I don't know.'

'Your name?'

'Claire. Claire Hughes.'

He drags his mouse lethargically across the mouse mat.

'And your daughter's name?'

'Olivia. Olivia Hughes.' I repeat the name quickly. He clicks the mouse a few times and his eyes scan from side to side.

'I can't see any record of her here. Sorry.'

'She's a baby,' I say. 'She's just a baby.'

'Claire?' A nurse appears beside me and places her hand on my shoulder. 'We've been looking for you. You weren't in your bed.'

'Where's my daughter?'

'Your daughter? I don't know.' She takes my arm to lead me away. I try to shrug her off, but she grips me tightly and escorts me to my bed. I see my name in marker on the whiteboard above it.

'What happened to me?'

'The doctor will be round later to talk to you.'

'You won't tell me what happened?'

She puts a hand on my shoulder and repeats herself calmly. 'Don't worry. I'll tell the doctor you're awake and she'll be round later. She'll answer your questions. You just sit here and relax.'

She points to an easy chair beside the bed.

'Did my daughter come in with me?' I ask.

'No, she didn't.'

The nurse refuses to say any more and guides me down into the chair before she leaves. 'Stay here until the doctor comes.'

I spot my handbag underneath the bed. I pull it out, open it up and find the comforting plastic of my phone. I'm desperate to know what's happened to Olivia.

I dial Matt's number.

The phone rings and rings. Fear grips my heart. Olivia must be OK. She has to be. Where is she?

Matt finally picks up.

'Claire.' He sounds exhausted.

'Have you got Olivia?' I ask, my voice cracking.

'Yes. She's here. She's—'

'Is she hurt?'

'No, she's fine. Claire, you don't need to worry about any-thing. OK?'

'I'm coming back,' I say. 'I want to see her.'

'You don't need to. Mum and I have got it under control. Take as long as you need to rest.'

I don't want Matt and Ruth looking after my daughter. I don't trust either of them. I need to get home.

'I don't need to rest. I'm fine.'

'Have you seen the doctor yet?'

'No. I—'

'You should see her before you leave. And honestly, we've got it all covered here.'

'Matt – what happened? Was I in an accident?'

'You should speak to the doctor.'

I need to get home. I can't leave Olivia with Matt and Ruth.

'I have to go, Matt.' I need to try and find a way to get out of here. Back to Olivia.

'OK,' he says. 'Have you got the suitcase I left?'

'What suitcase?'

'It's under your bed.'

I look and see a battered blue suitcase deep under the end of the bed.

I hang up.

I will leave. I'll go home. No one can stop me.

I look around for my shoes but can't find them. Then I pull the suitcase out. There are several changes of clothes, but no shoes. Toiletries. Books. My stomach twists. Why do I have so much stuff? Matt's packed for at least a week. It must be because he wants me to stay in the hospital. He wants me out of the way.

At the bottom of the case is a framed photo of Olivia, taken from the mantelpiece in the living room at the cottage. I stare at her tiny face and feel a surge of longing to be with her. I must get home.

I don't want her alone with Matt and Ruth.

I phone Emma.

She picks up on the second ring.

'Hi, Claire.' She sounds surprised. 'I didn't expect you to call. Are you all right?'

'I've been in an accident. I'm coming home, but Matt and Ruth have Olivia. Can you go round and stay with them until I get back? I don't trust them with her.'

'Claire,' she says, her voice filled with concern. 'What do you remember?'

'I don't know,' I reply, feeling the panic rising. 'I've been in some kind of accident.'

302   RUTH HEALD

'Look. Don't worry about anything. Just get some rest. I can go over to your house, check how things are going. I can even stay overnight if that helps?'

'What about Lizzie?'

'She's with Dan.'

'I really need to come home. Matt's dangerous. He hurt Sarah's sister. I can't have him looking after Olivia.'

'Look, I think you need to stay in hospital. Have you seen the doctor?'

'Why is everyone asking me if I've seen the doctor?'

'Do you know why you're there, Claire?'

'No,' I admit.

'You took an overdose. Yesterday afternoon Matt found you on the floor of the cottage.'

*

The police officer comes to see me. She's neat and tidy with a badge that says her name is 'Miriam' and a freshly ironed uniform. Her hands shake as she pulls the curtain around my hospital bed.

'Do you want to go to a private room?' she asks, her voice so soft it's almost as if she doesn't want to be heard.

I know what she's going to say. I just need her to say it, to put me out of my misery.

'She's dead, isn't she?'

'We don't need to have this conversation here. We can go somewhere more private.'

I can't wait. 'Just tell me what happened.'

In the seconds of silence that follow I send a thousand prayers to a god I'm not sure exists. The hope is painful, fighting against the sense that I already know the answer. That sense of an empty space, deep inside me, where my daughter should be.

She takes my hand and my heart stops. 'I'm afraid your husband and daughter have passed away,' she says. She's calm and polite, but her hand in mine tells me something else; it's sweaty and clammy. 'I'm so sorry.'

For a second I don't believe her, holding on to some desperate fantasy that this is all a mistake. But it's only a moment's reprieve and then the truth hits me like a train, smashing through my very being. My body convulses with sobs.

'What happened?' I fight to get the words out.

'Your daughter – she drowned. In the river.' Tears form in the police officer's eyes. 'Your husband took her there. Afterwards, he hung himself in your attic.'

CHAPTER 39

I can't have tried to kill myself. I must have misheard.

'What?'

'I'm sorry to be the one to tell you, Claire,' Emma says. 'I thought you'd remember. I really think you need to stay where you are. Speak to the doctor, get some rest. And don't worry about anything. I can deal with everything at home.'

I hang up the phone, fear coursing through my veins. Is it really true?

Maybe Emma is right. If I'm so unwell that I don't remember a suicide attempt, then the hospital is the best place for me.

I search for a memory of what happened, but as hard as I try, my brain is just a foggy emptiness. How could I have done this? I have a daughter.

But then I remember how desperate I felt, how out of control. I remember looking at Pamela's pills in the kitchen cupboard. How welcoming they seemed. Did I cave in? Why don't I remember?

All this time I've been protecting Olivia from other people. But the biggest threat was me. I was the one who was going to take her mother away from her. Abandon her. Leave her alone with a family I don't trust.

My breasts are rock hard and leaking. I just want to latch Olivia on and feel her suckle. I want to be close to her. The physical need surprises me. I seem to want Olivia the most when I can't be with her. A part of me, deep inside, must know how to love her.

I need to self-express so I get up, drawing the blue curtain around me. I sit squeezing my breasts under the covers, forcing my milk out with my hands into tissues. This is not how it's supposed to be. It reminds me of all I am and all I am not. I should be with my daughter. I should be being a mother to her. Yet again, I have failed her.

The curtain twitches open and a male nurse draws it back angrily.

'Curtains open in the day, please,' he says. He sees me massaging my breasts before I have the chance to pull the covers up further, looks at me with disgust and sighs. I expect him to say something, but somehow it's worse when he says nothing. As if I'm no longer human.

I try not to make eye contact with the others on the ward as I quickly cover up. I make my way down the corridors to the toilets. In the ladies, I put the lid down and continue to self-express into the toilet paper. My hands and top are sticky, but I don't care any more.

I know I must rest. But I feel disconnected, unsure what to do with myself. I sit in the bed and look through my phone at photos of Olivia. I feel an unfamiliar surge of love for her as I flick through pictures of when she was first born, sitting in her baby chair, her first smile. And a photo of our first day in our new home. A selfie of the three of us, holding one another. I look so hopeful. The perfect family. Little did I know what would follow.

'Hello?' A woman in a white coat stands over me, clipboard in her hand. She's all neat straight lines and ironed uniform.

'Hi.'

'Claire Hughes?'

'Yes.'

She talks me through how I'll be monitored and prescribes me antidepressants. After less than five minutes, she replaces my notes at the foot of my bed and manages a tight smile.

'Any questions?' she asks.

'How long will I be in for?'

'It's hard to say. I want to speak to social services before we discharge you.'

'Social services?' The blood drains from my face. I'll never keep custody of Olivia if they find out what's happened.

'Yes, I want to check with children's services about the care of your daughter. It shouldn't take too long. We need to keep you in for a little while anyway, to monitor you and see how the ketamine has affected your body's function. We don't know what dose you took, so we just like to be sure.'

'Ketamine?' I say, shocked. I wrack my brains for where I've heard of it before. I don't remember seeing it in Pamela's cupboard.

'Yes. It's a party drug.'

'A party drug? But I haven't been—'

'Its primary use is as a general anaesthetic. We use it in medicine sometimes and vets use it on animals. Of course, it's safe then. In appropriate doses. But we think you mixed it with alcohol. Which caused your loss of consciousness.'

My mind is spinning. I know I haven't taken ketamine. Someone must have given it to me. Someone with access to animal anaesthetics.

Matt.

The doctor is still talking, but I'm not listening any more.

The truth is sinking in.

I didn't overdose.

Matt drugged me.

By the time I've realised what's happened the doctor has moved on to her next patient.

I need to get home. Now.

I pull a jumper on over my clothes and root through the suitcase, but still can't find any shoes.

I can't waste any more time so I walk out of the ward in my socks. I desperately want to break into a run, but I don't want to attract attention.

Outside, the corridor is empty. I hold my breath as I pass the nurses' station. They're huddled over a rota, and they don't look up. I see the whiteboard behind them with line after line of patients' names. There's no way they'll know who I am.

When I reach the main corridor, I start to run.

Matt has poisoned me. And now he has my daughter. I need to get to her.

I run past patients, doctors and nurses on their break. No one stops me. I reach the stairs and hurry down to the ground floor.

When I come out at the bottom, I follow signs to the exit. I see the winter coats and wet umbrellas and I realise how inappropriately I'm dressed for the weather.

'Can I help you?' a man asks, glancing quizzically at my shoeless feet.

'No,' I say, barging past him. I don't look back.

Outside, the cold air hits me. I pick up my phone and order a taxi. It will be five minutes.

I ring Emma.

She picks up immediately.

'Hello?'

'Emma, I'm coming home.'

'Why?'

'I didn't take an overdose. Matt's poisoned me. I need to get back.'

'What are you talking about? Are you OK?'

'It's Matt. He's dangerous. He's drugged me. That's why I'm in hospital.'

'Claire, you're not making any sense. You need to stay in the hospital. Get some rest. Please. You have to listen to me.'

'Emma, honestly. Matt isn't who we think he is. I don't know what he's capable of. Are you still at the house?'

'Yeah, I'm here,' she says softly.

'Well, don't let him out of your sight. Olivia can't stay with him. I'm coming back to get her.'

'OK, if you're sure. I'm worried about you though.'

'Just promise me you'll keep an eye on him.'

'I promise. You're coming back now?'

'Yeah. I'm just getting into a taxi.'

'OK. See you in a bit. And Claire?'

'Yeah?'

'Don't panic. I'll look after Olivia.'

In the back of the taxi, I google the effects of ketamine. Hallucinations. Confusion. Agitation. Panic attacks. Memory loss. I thought I was going mad, but the truth is far more terrifying. Matt has been poisoning me. All the time he was telling me I was just paranoid, he must have been slipping drugs into my drinks, watching me slowly unravel.

He could have killed me.

*

I'm completely on my own. I have no one.

I pull out my phone and ring the only person I know who might care. It's 4 p.m. I pray she's on her shift.

I listen to the phone ringing and ringing and ringing. I imagine her in a room somewhere, on the line to another caller. Or maybe she's popped out to get a cup of tea or to go to the toilet.

Eventually the phone cuts to voicemail. Just a standard phone provider's voicemail, with no personalised message for the helpline.

I try again. I need to speak to her. She's the only one who will understand.

My daughter is dead and it's all my fault. I should have left him earlier. I should have been braver.

The phone rings and rings until it goes to voicemail.

I press redial again.

Again and again and again.

Voicemail. Every time.

She's not there.

I have no one.

CHAPTER 40

The taxi grinds to a halt on the outskirts of Oxford and I fiddle impatiently with my phone, checking it over and over for messages. There are no updates from Emma or Matt. I wish I was home already with Olivia, protecting her. I can't help feeling something awful is about to happen.

Outside the car, people go about their day-to-day lives, oblivious to my rising anxiety. Mums with buggies carry bags of supermarket shopping balanced precariously on the handles. Pensioners stop to chat on the pavement. Their unhurried lives irritate me. Don't they know my daughter's in danger?

The car eases forward a few inches. A young man presses the button at the crossing and I feel an irrational sense of rage as the lights change from green to red. I watch the people amble across the road, waving their hands in thanks when they cross after our light has already turned to green.

'Can we go any faster?' I ask the driver.

'There's traffic, love. Can't do anything about that.'

Eventually we start moving and the rows of identical semi-detached houses turn into new blocks of flats by the ring road, followed by miles and miles of brown fields.

A tractor slows our journey and our car peers out to look for a spot to overtake. But the roads are too busy and we crawl along behind it until it pulls in to let us pass.

When the taxi finally pulls up in front of the cottage, I thrust some crumpled notes into the driver's hands, jumping out before he's turned the engine off. My feet hit the gravel and the stones dig through my socks as I run to the front door. My keys are in my hand and yet I fumble with the lock, fingers trembling.

Olivia. I must get to Olivia.

I open the door and dash through the house.

Emma's in the kitchen. Matt stands beside her.

'Claire,' Matt says, his eyebrows raised in surprise. He takes in my rumpled hair, my dirty clothes.

'Where's Olivia?' I ask. 'Where is she?'

Emma glances at Matt and then at me. 'She's upstairs,' she says. 'In her cot.'

I run. I take the stairs two at a time until I reach her.

She's asleep. I put my hand over her chest and feel it rise and fall. I hover my hand a little above her mouth and feel her breath. I'm overwhelmed with relief.

'She's OK,' Emma says from behind me. 'I've been here the whole time.'

'Thank you,' I reply. Emma puts her arms round me, strokes my back.

'I need to get Matt out of this house,' I whisper.

'I can stay out of your way,' Emma says, 'with Olivia.'

'No. I need you. I don't know how dangerous he is. He's been poisoning me, Emma.'

Emma's eyes widen. 'Are you sure? That's awful. How could he?'

The full horror of it hits me once more. 'He could have killed me.'

'Don't worry,' Emma says. 'I'll be here as long as you need me.'

We go downstairs. Matt's in the kitchen, a pint of beer beside him. How can he be so casual? Clearly he didn't expect me to come back.

Anger rises within me. I hate him. I hate him. I hate him. He put me in hospital. He poisoned me. He made me believe I was going mad. He's trying to steal my daughter.

He sips his beer.

My hand sweeps across the counter and pushes the glass onto the floor. It shatters, and the liquid paints the walls.

'Claire!'

I don't care about this cottage any more. I don't care about Ruth or Matt, or Pamela's antique furniture.

'Why did you do it?' I shout.

'Do what, Claire?' He sounds frustrated.

He steps towards me and I recoil.

Then I think about Olivia. I rise up towards him. He won't threaten me. I won't let him. I'm stronger than that.

'Why did you poison me?'

His laughter is sharper than a knife.

'What, Claire? You think I poisoned you now?'

I want to punch his smug, patronising face. He's always been in control. Since we moved here, I've been dancing to his tune.

'You did poison me,' I say. 'I know you did.'

'Claire.' He takes another step towards me. He's right in my face now, so close I can see the tiny scar on his chin from childhood chickenpox.

I hate him.

He puts his hands on my shoulders, holds me in place. I am weaker, he is stronger. I am female, he is male, and the odds are stacked against me.

'Claire, calm down. You need to be in hospital. You're confused. I haven't poisoned you.'

'I'm confused because of you. Because you drugged me.' I spit the words in his face.

His grip on my shoulders tightens and my stomach knots.

I turn my head to look for Emma. She's there, leaning against the kitchen counter, watching.

'Sit down,' Matt says, pushing me into a chair. 'I'm going to call the police, get you back to the hospital. You'll be safer there.'

'No.' I can't go back. I need to get Olivia away from Matt.

He picks his phone up from the side, and I stand and knock it out of his hand. It crashes to the floor. Emma grabs it, meets my eyes and then puts it in her pocket.

'Thanks,' I mouth. She nods.

Matt turns to her. 'Call the police,' he instructs.

Emma glances at me and then back at Matt.

'Maybe you should talk,' she says.

Matt looks me in the eye. 'I don't want you to be unwell, Claire. But you are. You're ill.'

'Stop lying. You know I'm not ill.'

Upstairs, Olivia wakes from her nap with a whine.

I move towards the door.

'Do you think that's a good idea?' Matt asks. I push past him.

Emma holds up a hand. 'Don't worry. I'll go. Shout if you need anything.'

'Thanks,' I say.

'You need help, Claire,' Matt says. 'I can drive you back to the hospital.'

He steps closer to me and I think he might restrain me. I jump away, running across the kitchen to the knife rack. I pull out the nearest one and hold it in front of me.

'Claire? What are you doing? You're crazy.'

'I'm not crazy. For the first time, I'm seeing things clearly. You've got a pattern of behaviour, Matt. You're a violent man. You murdered Sarah's sister and now you've drugged me. You'll hurt anyone that gets in your way.'

Shock is plastered all over his face. 'I didn't hurt Felicity. Who have you been speaking to?'

'Don't lie to me, Matt. You confessed. It's in the police file.' I grip the handle of the knife tighter, my hand trembling.

'You looked at the police file?'

'Miriam saw it. She told me you confessed.'

'I didn't do it, Claire. You have to believe me. I'm sorry I didn't tell you everything before but I couldn't.'

'What do you mean? Who are you protecting?'

But I know there's only one person he'd go to these lengths to protect. 'It was Sarah, wasn't it? Sarah pushed her sister.'

Matt looks at the floor. 'Yes,' he says quietly.

I feel relieved and angry all at the same time. Matt didn't cause Sarah's sister's death. But he was prepared to go to any lengths to protect Sarah. He could have ended up in prison. Our marriage has fallen apart because of the secrets he's kept from me.

'Why? Why did you protect her?'

'It was a mistake, Claire. Felicity was jealous of her sister's success. Sarah was always their parents' favourite. One night, we were up in the hayloft, chatting. Felicity had had a lot to drink, and she turned nasty. She threatened to tell their parents Sarah was pregnant. Sarah thought her parents would make her abort the baby. They argued and then Sarah pushed her sister. Not hard. It would have hardly hurt if she hadn't fallen out of the hayloft. Sarah never got over the guilt.'

'Why did you confess?'

'To protect her. To protect our baby. She couldn't go to prison when she was pregnant.'

'And then she miscarried?'

'Yes. And I withdrew my confession.'

My mind whirrs. If it was Sarah that pushed her sister and not Matt, then Matt hasn't done anything wrong. He's not got a history of violence. This changes everything. I think back to how cosy Sarah looked with my baby the other day at her flat. I think about how she always seems to be with my husband. Sarah works at the surgery. She'd have access to ketamine too.

'Sarah,' I say to Matt. 'Sarah's been poisoning me.'

'No one's been poisoning you Claire. You took an overdose. Of sleeping pills. I've seen them in the house, in the cupboards. I should have moved them, but I didn't realise you were that bad, that depressed.'

'Sleeping pills? It wasn't sleeping pills, Matt. The doctor told me I'd taken ketamine.'

The knife is still in my hand. I hold it by my side, gripping it tightly.

'Ketamine?' The blood has drained from his face, his skin is translucent.

'Yes. Someone gave me ketamine. It must be you or your precious Sarah.'

'Sarah wouldn't do that.'

'Wouldn't she? She pushed her sister. She was there when Olivia fell into the pond. What if she let the brake off the buggy?'

'She wouldn't…' Matt says. I put down the knife as he paces the floor. 'She just wouldn't…'

'Well, only you and her have access to the drugs at the practice.'

'Claire – it can't be her. She's away this weekend. Visiting a friend in Brighton.'

I'm not sure I believe him. Is he still covering for her?

'Then who could have done it? If it's not Sarah, it's you.' I pick the knife back up, terrified I've made a mistake and it's my husband I should be afraid of.

Matt looks at me, his face pale. 'You're sure the doctor said it was ketamine?'

I nod. My hands shake as I point the knife at him.

'It could be anyone,' he says. 'Anyone who's been in the cottage.'

'What do you mean?'

'I made a mistake, Claire. You're supposed to store ketamine in locked cupboards. But when I first set up the practice, I ordered the medical supplies to the house. I was planning to take them straight over to the surgery as soon as the delivery arrived. But I didn't. I was exhausted with the paperwork and I waited a couple of days. You remember the package that came for me when we first arrived? Well, while it was in our house, someone opened it. Some of the supplies were missing.'

I drop my hand, hold the knife by my side. I want to believe him. 'When was this?'

'Not long after we moved in. It was the day we visited your mother's grave, her birthday. I didn't want to tell you. You were preoccupied.'

I remember. When we went to Richmond Park. I'd met Emma the day before. We were just still settling in and everything was chaotic. Matt had misplaced a delivery box.

'Did you find out who took it?'

'No. I couldn't tell anyone, couldn't report it. The rules about storing drugs are very strict. I didn't want to be investigated. But some of the ketamine was stolen from our house. So either it was someone who had a key. Or someone who broke in.'

'Why didn't you tell me?'

'What was there to tell? I didn't know who did it, didn't want to report it. You were already paranoid about my mother coming into the house. I didn't want to worry you. I just put it to the back of my mind, got on with things. But if you've been drugged with ketamine… then I don't know what to think.'

Something surfaces in the back of my mind. 'Matt,' I say, 'were you with me when I went to the hospital?'

'No. Emma told me about it afterwards.'

'So Emma found me?'

'She rang me and told me you'd taken sleeping pills.'

'Sleeping pills?'

'Yes. Pamela's pills. She said she was there when you took them. She said she tried to stop you.'

We both look at each other.

Emma.

I'm running, heart racing as my feet thunder up the stairs. Matt's a pace behind me, his breath on my neck.

I push open the door to Olivia's room. The cot is empty. She's gone.

*

I don't want to go back to the house, but there's nowhere else. I limp from the taxi to my green front door, leaning heavily on my stick. When I turn my key in the lock, the emotions nearly floor me, and I want to sink down onto the concrete step and never get up. But I resist the temptation and shut off the pain, operating on autopilot. The despair lingers, a dull ache in the pit of my stomach.

As I open the door, I push back the memories of my daughter. Instead the memory of the first time I crossed this threshold enters my mind, uninvited. I remember how joyful I was, how certain I was that my life was coming together, that here I would be safe, that here I could start again and create a family home.

Once I'm inside the house, I don't know what to do with myself. Everything is the same and yet my world has stopped revolving. I wander around aimlessly. The house is a cross between a show home and a crime scene. A corner of the kitchen is still shining from where I cleaned a few days ago, but in the hallway patches of dried blood lead a trail through the house and up the staircase. The police have gone, but they've left traces: a discarded cigarette just outside the back door, an empty coffee cup on the window sill in the living room.

Upstairs, I peer through the door of my daughter's room and then shut it quickly. I can't look at her toddler-sized bed, her doll's house, her toys. They'll always be waiting for her.

The hatch to the attic still lies open, the ladder down as if inviting me up. I wonder if the police were stupid enough to leave the rope there, waiting for me, the next victim.

I don't go up there. It would be too neat an ending, too easy for me. I push the ladder up and close the hatch.

Instead I go to bed, lie down in my clothes and swallow the painkillers and sleeping pills the doctor prescribed. I toss and turn before sleep eventually takes me. Even then, it provides scant relief from my living nightmare. In my dreams my daughter is alive. And then the world turns and pivots in on itself. Each dream is different: a fire, an accident, a drowning. But the outcome is always the same. My daughter always dies.

In my dreams I seek revenge. I stab the person responsible again and again and again, until they are unrecognisable, a mess of blood and pulped flesh.

When I wake in my own bed I'm relieved they are just dreams. And then realisation dawns, a brick crushing my heart.

My reality is worse than my nightmares. My daughter's already dead.

I can never punish my husband. He took that opportunity away from me when he killed himself.

I will never get revenge.

CHAPTER 41

'Emma!' I scream. 'Emma!' My voice cracks.

Matt is at Olivia's bedroom window, looking down onto the driveway. I rush over.

'Her car's gone,' he says.

I think I might vomit. Blood rushes to my head as I run down the stairs, slip my shoes on, jump in our car.

Matt is in the doorway.

'Call the police,' I shout to him before I slam the car door shut. 'Show them where she took Olivia. I'm going to Emma's flat.'

In the car, I can hardly focus on the road in front of me. My sweaty hands grip the steering wheel as I swerve round bends, my thoughts racing. I try to make sense of things, but I can't. Why would Emma take Olivia? She has been by my side all this time, my only friend from the beginning. Could she have taken Olivia to protect her from Matt? Is she trying to help me?

But Matt didn't give me the ketamine. And the last person I remember before I passed out is Emma. She was the one who told Matt I'd overdosed. She told him it was sleeping pills. I remember the symptoms of ketamine poisoning I read about in the taxi. Hallucinations. Confusion. Drowsiness. I've had these since we moved. Since I met Emma. I remember what the doctor said about the dangers of mixing alcohol with ketamine. And I think about how I collapsed when Emma and I went up the church spire after our wine tasting. I think of how I blacked out when we went clubbing. I'd thought it was the alcohol, but could she have drugged me?

My mind's spinning out of control. Nothing makes sense. Why would Emma drug me? And why would she take Olivia? She has her own family. She has Lizzie.

I pull up outside her flat and jump out of the car. I have to find my daughter.

There are no lights on but it doesn't mean she's not there. I jam my finger on the buzzer, but no one answers. I jab again and again and again, until someone pokes their head out of an upstairs window and asks me what I want.

'I'm looking for Emma,' I shout up. 'From Flat 2. I need to speak to her. I'm a friend.'

'Well, if you keep buzzing and she doesn't answer, it means she's not in.'

'It's an emergency,' I say, heart racing. 'I need to speak to her.'

'Can't you phone her?'

'She's not answering. Can you let me in?'

'What good will that do if she's not in?'

'I think she might be hurt. She might have hurt herself in the flat,' I say. 'I can't get hold of her.' The lie tumbles out of my mouth easily.

The woman visibly sighs.

'I'll come down,' she says.

She comes down and lets me in, then goes to Emma's door and knocks loudly.

'Emma!' I shout through the door. 'Emma!'

Crouching down, I peer through the letter box. The flat's dark and I can only make out the vague shapes of furniture in the shadows.

'I don't think she's here.' She looks at me doubtfully.

I'm sure she's in there. Waiting me out. Waiting for me to go away.

A baby screams and my heart clenches in my chest.

Olivia!

She's in the flat. I must get to her.

I bang on the door furiously. 'Emma!'

I need to get rid of the woman hovering over my shoulder. 'I'll wait here for her,' I say. 'Don't worry, you can go.' I put on my calmest voice, but inside I'm shaking.

The woman sighs and then retreats back to her flat.

The police will be on their way to our cottage by now. I pull my phone out of my handbag. Matt hasn't called. They can't have arrived yet. I wish they'd hurry.

But I can't wait for them. I need to get to Olivia now. There must be a way of getting into the flat.

I know Emma rents, so I go to the land registry website, pull off the records for the flat and see the name of the owner. I'm still a member of the online address directories from my days as a journalist and I quickly find the number for his landline. He lives locally. He'll have a spare key.

The phone rings and rings.

'Hello?'

'Hi. I'm sorry to bother you. I'm trying to locate your tenant, Emma Burch. It's an emergency.'

'I don't have a tenant called Emma.'

'You don't rent out 2 Overlook Heights?'

'Yes, that's my flat. But it's rented to Stephanie. Stephanie Pickard.'

I collapse against the door.

Stephanie.

Emma is Stephanie.

She's finally come to find me. To get revenge.

Everything makes sense.

Stephanie wants to hurt me, the way I deserve to be hurt.

The past is coming back to claim me.

*

It's days before I leave the house, but eventually I have to. I've run out of food and toilet paper and it's too late to arrange an online delivery for today.

I know it will be good for me to get out, get some fresh air. In the confines of the house, I relive my nightmares, again and again. I have no one to talk to. I've tried to ring the helpline, but the phone goes straight to voicemail, filling me with despair every time. It must have closed down. I'm totally alone.

I walk the long way to the supermarket, down the main road, avoiding the river. I lean heavily on my stick. My face is so disfigured that it's unrecognisable. My nose is broken, my jaw, my cheekbone. No part of me is intact. People look at me and then away again, embarrassed by my injuries. I dig into my handbag, find an old scarf and wrap it round my head.

In the supermarket, I walk around mindlessly, picking up ready meals and putting them back. I'm not hungry. But there's something soothing about watching other people going about their daily lives, picking up pre-prepared meals and turning them over to check the sell by dates, planning what they'll have for dinner.

I have a huge list of things I need, but I don't have the motivation to look for them. I wander up and down each aisle, immersing myself in the bustle. It's slow progress with my stick and I appreciate the delay. I don't want to go home. The supermarket feels like a film set, a comforting recreation of normality.

I go past the newspaper section, pick up a national paper and flick through it.

I freeze when I see my husband's face, staring out at me. The blood rushes to my head and I collapse to the floor.

The crowd closes in on me.

'Are you OK?'

The world is an overwhelming blur of colour and movement. I try to focus.

'Yes,' I say. 'Yes, I'm fine.' It surprises me how easily this reassuring banality slips out as I struggle to my feet.

I take the paper to the till with my shopping, rushing to escape.

Outside I find a bench, take deep breaths and open the paper again. On the inside pages, I see my husband's smiling face. I want rip that smile into shreds.

My daughter's name jumps out at me, in bold print.

I stare at it for a moment, reading and rereading each letter in turn. Lily.

'What drove him to it?' the headline shouts indignantly.

Pictures of my husband litter the article. There are none of me or Lily.

I see other words in bold. Rape accusations. Exposed by this newspaper.

They knew. After years of cover ups, somehow the press had found out.

Did he know they were going to write this? Is that why he killed himself and drowned our daughter?

I scan the article for more details.

There's a self-congratulatory paragraph near the beginning of the text. The newspaper had conducted a long-running investigation and had finally succeeded in exposing him.

I reread the section, trying to make sense of it.

They published the exposé on the day he took Lily.

He must have seen the paper when he got to work. He wouldn't have been able to cope with being found out. He'd have had to act.

And he did. He came home, beat me up and murdered our daughter.

All because of the exposé.

I feel a well of anger bubbling inside me. Why didn't they think before they published the article?

Despite myself, I keep reading.
There are quotes pulled out in italics. All of them of attributed to me.
I don't understand. I haven't said those things to anyone.
Except I did tell someone. I told the woman on the helpline.
Claire.
Then I notice the byline under the article's headline.
'Investigated by Claire Hughes.'
It's her.
I feel sick. It can't be true.
Claire was never my friend. She was never my confidante.
The whole time, she was a journalist.
She was just after a story.

CHAPTER 42

I drop the phone, the landlord still talking on the other end.

I'm shaking as the images come back to me. The river. The reeds. The lifeless child.

Blood drains from my face as I remember the horror of those moments.

It was all my fault.

When I'd started the investigation into Stephanie's husband, I'd never imagined it would end the way it did.

I never imagined that Stephanie's daughter would die.

I just wanted the story. That was all. I wanted my byline on the front page. I wanted the journalism prize.

I ended up getting all those things. But the cost was unimaginable.

If I could send back the prizes, if I could turn back time and change what I did, I would. But I can't.

I'll never be free of that image of the small girl being dragged from the water. It haunts me when I'm awake and it fills my nightmares.

But I deserve all of it. I deserve my fear of water. I deserve my nightmares. I deserved my breakdown. Because I'm not the one who had to pay the true cost. Stephanie paid the ultimate price for my mistakes. She was the one who lost her daughter.

And now she's taken mine. An eye for an eye. A daughter for a daughter. It all makes sense.

I remember Olivia's buggy careering into the pond. Stephanie. She must have wanted me to know how it felt, to see my daughter drowning.

I've been running away so fast and for so long that I had convinced myself the past would never catch me up. But it has. Now I will have to pay for my mistakes too.

Stephanie will see to that.

The baby's sudden screams echo around the corridors of the block of flats.

My baby. Olivia.

I must get inside. Stephanie wants revenge. She wants me to pay the price she paid – my daughter. Fear is a fist around my heart and I can hardly breathe as I shoulder barge the door, repeating it again and again until my upper body aches. It's useless.

I run outside the block of flats and try the kitchen window. I remember Stephanie complaining that it didn't close properly. I can see where the plastic frame doesn't quite meet the edge of the window. There's a small gap and I manage to slip my fingers between the window and the frame. I pull with all my might. It doesn't loosen.

I need something that I can use to wrench open the window. Something strong enough. I root around in my bag, pulling my phone out and angling it into the gap. Then I push the other end of it as hard as I can, to jimmy it open.

The screen of my phone cracks.

Then the catch gives and the window shoots out towards me.

I stagger backwards.

I pull the window out as far as it will go.

There's a blind on the other side. My heart pounds as I wonder if Stephanie is standing there, waiting for me.

Olivia has stopped screaming. What has Stephanie done to her? I feel sick with fear. What if I'm too late?

I put my hands up on the ledge and push myself up. I climb up through the window, sweeping away the blind.

It's dark in the kitchen.

Something digs into my back. The tap on the sink.

I scoot further in and knock into something.

Smash.

The sound shatters the silence.

My eyes are still adjusting to the dark. I see plates from the drying rack in pieces on the tiles below.

I jump down from the sink.

Is Stephanie hiding somewhere? Waiting for me? Where is Olivia?

I creep across the dark shadows of the kitchen.

I can hear my baby's screams again. But they seem quieter now, further away.

I remember the sounds in my own house. The noises at night. The creaks on the stairs. The singing through the baby monitor. I hadn't been imagining it. It was Stephanie all along. She was preparing the ground. Watching me the whole time. Making me think I was going mad. Getting ready to take my daughter.

I go out of the kitchen and into the hallway.

There are three doors. The door to the living room is open, revealing a scene of ordinary life. An empty coffee cup. A book. An open newspaper.

I'm about to try the door to Stephanie's bedroom when I hear a key in the lock. The front door eases open.

*

Today

I pull up in front of my former home. I remember how excited I was when Chris first showed it to me. It was the house of my dreams. Huge and detached, with a garden for our future children to play in. Shielded from the road by big conifer trees, newly whitewashed walls. It was perfect.

I haven't been back since I sold the house to a developer. Today the expansive front lawn is tarmacked over, divided up into spaces, filled with parked cars. Not the Porsche that Chris drove, or my four by four. Older, cheaper cars, parked neatly in the delineated spaces. The conifers have been cut down and you can see the whole house from the road. There's nowhere to hide.

I unstrap Olivia from the car seat and pick her up. At the doorway there's a neat line of buzzers, with printed labels telling me the names of the occupants. Six flats. They must be tiny.

Olivia whines and I turn to her.

'This was our home,' I tell her. 'You, me and Daddy. We used to live here.'

As I stare at the buzzers, fear rises in me. Flashbacks. Flying punches. Blood on kitchen tiles. The crack of bone.

I don't want to go in. But I know I must. I have to face the past.

My heart beats faster as I reach out for the first buzzer and press it. I wait for a moment, but there's no answer. I press the next one and the next. They must be at work. Flat 5 answers and I'm so shocked that I hardly know what to say.

'I used to live here,' I say. 'I wonder if I could come in and see what it looks like these days? I want to show my daughter.'

She pauses as if considering it. 'Sure,' she says. 'Come on up.'

The flat is on the second floor, in what used to be the loft.

She opens the door with a smile, looking down at Olivia. 'Oh, I didn't realise you had a baby with you. I assumed your daughter was older. I'm Joanna, by the way.'

'My husband and I lived here before she was born. Before it was converted into flats.'

'You lived in the whole house? Wow. It must have been huge.'

'Yeah,' I reply. I'm staring round the small living room. Chris and I had talked about getting the loft converted, but we never got around to it. Now I can see what it would have looked like. Without the huge trees in front of the house, the room is light and airy.

'Do you want a drink?' she asks.

'No, thank you.' I'm not sure how much longer I can bear to be in this room, with all its reminders of the family I lost.

I look up at the rafters. They've been painted white like the rest of the flat, giving an illusion of space. I feel sick as I imagine the thud as Chris pushed away the stool he was standing on. In my mind's eye I see his body hanging there, swaying gently back and forth. I wonder if Joanna knows what went on in this house, in this room.

Olivia starts to cry. It's as if she knows.

'This is where we used to live,' I say, and kiss her forehead. She cries harder.

I feel a tug of resentment towards her. Lily was such a good baby. A placid baby. Olivia is different. She's just like her mother.

CHAPTER 43

A man fills the doorway of Stephanie's flat, his features indistinguishable in the dark.

'Stephanie?' he asks, as he flicks the light on. He blinks in surprise when he sees me.

'Who are you?' he asks.

'I – I know Stephanie.'

Before I can say any more, a woman with a baby appears in the doorway behind him. For a second I think it's Olivia and my heart leaps. But then I see her blue eyes and freckles and my heart sinks back down. It's Lizzie.

'Have you seen my baby?' I ask the woman desperately, trying to step around the man, who blocks my path.

'I haven't seen any other babies here,' the woman says. 'And I live next door, so I'd have heard them even if I didn't see them.'

I look at the woman and feel a spark of recognition. I've seen her before. I saw her on the bus that time, with Lizzie. I'd assumed she was Dan's partner.

'Is Stephanie here?' I ask. 'Are you babysitting for her?'

'She's not here. And she babysits for me sometimes. I don't babysit for her. She doesn't have any children.'

'What?' That doesn't make sense. I stare at the baby. 'But Lizzie?'

'Lizzie's mine.'

Shock hits me and I struggle to process what's happening. Lizzie isn't Stephanie's baby. Stephanie's been lying to me from the moment she introduced herself. She doesn't have a child.

'Where's Stephanie?' I ask the woman urgently. 'Where's she taken my daughter?'

The man reaches out and grabs my shoulders. 'You need to calm down,' he says. 'And tell me what you're doing in my flat.'

'Your flat?' My mind is still spinning. 'Oh, we spoke on the phone. You're—'

'I'm the landlord,' he says, his face up close to mine. 'How did you get in?'

The woman with the baby chips in. 'I heard noises. Smashing.'

I don't have time for this conversation. I wrack my brains to work out where Stephanie might be. Could she still be in the flat?

I wriggle free from the landlord's grip and push open the door to Stephanie's bedroom. It's empty.

I try the door to the other room. The room I'd always assumed was Lizzie's.

The door shoots open, revealing a baby's nursery. For a moment I think I must be mistaken. Stephanie does have a baby.

But there's something wrong.

Everything is too neat and tidy, too sparse. There's a cot, but no nappies. There is no changing mat, no baby bottles. No toys. There's no chest of drawers for baby clothes. Just two outfits and Lizzie's red coat, neatly folded on a table.

The motif on the wall. A child's name painted in sunny letters. But it doesn't say Lizzie. It says Lily.

The name of Stephanie's daughter. The daughter who drowned. The child whose death I caused.

In the cot is Olivia's toy bunny.

The realisation slams into me.

Stephanie wants Olivia to replace Lily.

I took Lily from her and she will take Olivia from me.

'I need to go,' I say again, trying to push by the landlord.

'You can't. I'm calling the police.'

Panic rises in me. I have to find my daughter.

'I can explain,' I say, my face flushing. 'Just let me go.' I feel hot tears running down my cheeks.

'You need to stay here until the police come. You broke into my property.'

'I can explain to the police later,' I say. 'Or on the phone. They're already with my husband. Our daughter's missing.'

The landlord glares at me. 'I don't need a sob story,' he says. I see him jabbing 999 into his phone.

I take out my own phone to call Matt. The screen is cracked from jimmying open the window, and for a moment I panic. But luckily it still responds to my touch and I'm relieved to hear it connecting. As it rings and rings, I see the landlord with his mobile phone to his ear, hear him asking for the police.

I wish Matt would hurry up and pick up.

Finally the ringing stops and there is the fuzz of background noise.

'Matt?'

Silence.

I don't wait for him to speak.

'Matt, I'm at Emma's. She's got Olivia. I know she has. And she's not Emma at all. She's Stephanie. You remember Stephanie?'

My speech is garbled and rushed.

There's laughter on the other end of the phone. A woman's laugh.

Stephanie.

I remember back at the cottage: Matt threatening to call the police, me sweeping the phone out of his hand, Stephanie picking it up from the floor. She put it into her pocket. She still has it.

'Stephanie,' I say.

'Claire.' Her voice is icy, with none of the warmth she had for me when she was pretending to be Emma.

'You've got my daughter.'

'Yes.'

'I need her back. Please. I'm so sorry for what happened to your daughter, for what I did. I truly am.' I feel the guilt rising in me and swallow it down. This is all my fault. 'But don't punish Olivia for my mistakes. She's not to blame.'

'You've never deserved her, Claire. You know that as well as I do. You don't even love her.'

I think of all the times I confided in 'Emma' about how down I felt. How I wasn't sure if I loved Olivia. How I wasn't coping. I'd thought she was my friend. That I could trust her.

'Stephanie, please. Where are you?'

'Where do you think I am? I'm back at the place where it all began.'

'The river?'

'Yes, the river.'

Across the room the landlord is pacing back and forth. It's clear the police won't be here for a while.

He turns to me. 'Is that Stephanie on the phone?'

'Who's that?' Stephanie asks.

'Your landlord. He won't let me leave.'

'Hand him your phone. I'll tell him it's a misunderstanding. I want to talk to you properly. Face to face. Come to the river.'

*

Today

It's a short walk from our house to the river. My husband took this walk three years ago with our daughter, before he drowned her. I imagine her, aged four, so pleased that for once in her life her father was giving her some attention.

It was the height of summer, early morning. A beautiful day. I was in my daughter's bedroom, lying next to my packed suitcase, slipping in and out of consciousness.

I like to think she knew nothing of what was to come. She can't have done. I imagine her smiling and laughing as she realised she was going to the river with her daddy. I like to imagine the sun warming her face, her giggling. I want her to have been happy in her last few moments.

There were no witnesses to the drowning. Later, people with good intentions told me that it might have been a mistake, that he might have been playing with her in the river and lost his grip. After she drowned, the guilt made him hang himself. But I know better. He wasn't the type to feel guilt or remorse.

He knew he was ruined when he read the newspaper that exposed him. Everything he had built up over his career would be taken away. And he thought I was the one who'd gone to the press. I was quoted in the article. He left me lying on the kitchen floor with one intention only; to make me hurt more than I knew was possible. He killed our daughter as revenge. He wanted to destroy my life like I had destroyed his. He didn't hang himself because he felt guilty. He did it to protect himself, so he wouldn't have to face the consequences.

Olivia is grizzling as I carry her down the path. She's a difficult child, not at all like Lily.

At the riverbank, I sit down and stare at the water, Olivia in my arms. It's so calm and peaceful, but I know there's a strong current in the middle. I know it can drag you under if you let it. Drown you.

Olivia keeps whining and I think she must be cold. I want to put her on my breast to comfort her, but I can't. I have no milk.

I wish she would be quiet, so I can sit and think about Lily. Her smile, her giggle, her loveable little face and the way her eyes were the exact same shade of blue as mine. I imagine her here now. She'd be seven. She'd love the water, love to feel it splashing over her.

I imagine my life with her now. It would have been so different. Everything would have been perfect. But Claire took that away from us.

Olivia fidgets and wriggles.

I look at her. I want to start again. I want to feel the same love for her I felt for Lily. But when I look at her I feel nothing. Nothing at all.

CHAPTER 44

Whatever Stephanie's said to the landlord, it's worked. He hands back my phone and steps aside, letting me out of the door.

I jump into the car.

I want to speak to Matt, to tell him where I'm going, but there's no way of contacting him. We hadn't bothered to connect a new landline when Pamela's contract ran out.

Instead I just drive. There's no time to waste. It's over an hour's drive from here to the village. I must find Stephanie and get Olivia back.

In the car, I go back over everything in my head. I remember when I first heard the story of Stephanie's husband. Miriam told me in a whisper over drinks that her police force were investigating him for sexual harassment. At the time he had a huge media profile. He'd grown a media empire from nothing and had shares in magazines, TV stations and technology start-ups, as well as running a talent agency.

I feel a flush of shame as I think back. I was a different person back then. I wanted success at all costs. My colleagues would do anything and everything to get a story. They'd trail people for days, camp outside the houses of grieving widows, even hack the phones of murder victims. Morals were thrown out of the window. I had to compete.

I sat outside Stephanie's house for two weeks in my car, waiting for her to come out, so I could question her about her husband. But she stayed inside the whole time. I should have given up then, but I didn't. I was so desperate that one night I went through her bins. I found a letter from her psychiatrist, saying she had missed appointments.

That gave me an idea that I now bitterly regret. No one ever came to the house and Stephanie never left. She must have been going stir crazy in there all day on her own. She needed help. I put together a leaflet advertising a mental health helpline for struggling new mothers and slotted it through the letter box. Stephanie was the only person who had the number and I was the only person at the other end of the line.

I never thought it would work, but a few days later she rang me. I'm ashamed of how pleased I was with myself that I'd fooled her. Over several weeks I gained her trust and eventually she told me everything. The story was even bigger than I thought. He was regularly raping young women who worked for him. His crimes went back years and he'd been paying the women off to keep them quiet. It was the biggest scoop of my career. I knew it would make my name as a journalist.

But I was worried about Stephanie's safety. Her husband was dangerous and I persuaded her to leave him. She promised me she would. I delayed going to my editor with the story until I was sure that she'd be long gone. But she changed her mind when she realised she couldn't stay with me. She didn't want to go to a women's shelter. When I spoke to her later she was still at the house.

The story was on the editor's desk by then. He was going to publish the next day. I couldn't stop the chain of events I'd started. I was terrified of what Stephanie's husband might do to her when he read the article and saw that she had betrayed him, telling a journalist everything. I begged her to leave as soon as she could. I couldn't tell her why, but somehow I managed to convince her to leave that night. I was so relieved when I hung up. I thought everything was fixed, that she'd leave that evening before her husband saw the story.

But she didn't. She waited until the next day. By then it was too late.

I imagine her husband turning up to work in the morning, seeing his face on the front page of the paper. I imagine him seeing the quotes attributed to Stephanie. The accusations. The revelations. He'd have been overcome by rage when he realised the source was his own wife. He'd returned home to find her about to leave with their daughter.

I was in the office early that morning, ready for a busy day following up the story. I was so convinced I'd adverted disaster for Stephanie that I hardly thought of her at all. I was busy celebrating my scoop, accepting the congratulations of colleagues. They were thumping me on the back, cheering me. I was walking on air. I knew great things were just around the corner for me. All my hard work was finally paying off.

I didn't stay long. My editor wanted me to go over to Stephanie's house with a photographer and wait outside to snap a picture of Stephanie's disgraced husband and try to get a quote.

As we neared the house, feelings of guilt started to rise in me. I told myself that Stephanie was OK, safe in the women's shelter I'd recommended. But I couldn't help feeling bad about betraying her. We'd become close over time and I'd grown to like her. I naively thought that in time she'd forgive me, understand that I needed to expose her husband, so that he'd go to prison and be punished for his crimes.

Just as we were approaching her home, we got a call through with a tip-off. There were reports of a body in the river nearby. I wondered for a second if it was connected to Stephanie, if her husband had drowned himself, and I felt a shiver of fear. Even so, I had no idea of the horror to come.

I arrived shortly after the police. I watched helplessly as they pulled the little girl from the water, her body limp and lifeless, her hair fanning in the water as they dragged her to the shore. As soon as I saw her, I knew she was Stephanie's daughter. A scream pierced the air and it was a moment before I realised it was mine, as I sank to the muddy ground.

The paramedic did chest compressions by the riverside and I watched as her body jumped and shuddered with the force, praying her heart would restart, praying she'd live.

But her soul had already left her. She was gone.

I threw up again and again on the grass, until there was nothing coming out but bile, my body convulsing with sobs.

I overheard the chatter of a group of locals standing just outside the police barrier. Half an hour ago, they'd seen the little girl walking beside a man they'd assumed was her father. It was Stephanie's husband. He'd drowned her to punish Stephanie. He wanted to take away the only thing that mattered to her. It was his revenge.

It was all my fault. If I hadn't written the article, Stephanie's daughter would still be alive.

Tears stream down my face and I can hardly see the road in front of me. I feel so ashamed of what I did. Stephanie's right to never forgive me. She's right to punish me.

She's done to me what I did to her. Watching me the way I watched her. Following me, observing me, worming her way into my life. Pretending to be my friend, manipulating me into trusting her.

I welcomed 'Emma' into my life. I didn't recognise her because Stephanie and I had never met, only spoken on the phone. I'd never even seen a photo of her; her husband had controlled her social media so tightly that it had been impossible to find a picture to accompany my article.

I confided in Emma about my relationship with Matt and my struggles with my baby. I trusted her the way she'd once trusted me. She babysat my daughter and took her to the park. She hugged her and tickled her tummy and held her. She looked after her in a way I didn't feel able to.

And from the beginning that was all she wanted. To befriend me and then destroy me, the way I destroyed her.

I need help. I pull over into a lay-by. I'm about to call Matt but then I remember Stephanie has his phone.

Instead I call the only other person who knows the history between me and Stephanie.

Miriam.

Miriam never forgave me for betraying her trust by using her tip-off to target Stephanie. But now I need her.

She picks up immediately. 'Claire?'

'It's Stephanie,' I say breathlessly.

She gasps. 'Stephanie?'

'She's taken Olivia. To punish me. For what I did.'

'Slow down… Where has she taken Olivia?'

'Back to the village,' I say. 'To the river.'

'I'll be there as soon as I can.'

I turn my key in the engine and skid out of the lay-by back onto the road. With my foot pressed down on the accelerator, I recklessly overtake car after car. All that matters is that I get to Olivia in time. I have to save her.

*

Today

I can hear her coming for me. The screeching of brakes. The dulling of the engine. She'll be here in a minute.

I hold Olivia tight.

I never knew it was possible to hate someone as much as I hate Claire. My anger ripples out of me in waves. Every time I used to google her and see her image I would feel like I'd be sick. The smiling Twitter profile. The list of awards. She didn't deserve to be happy. How dare she get away with it?

I was obsessed. I knew where she lived in Balham. Friends on Facebook with lax profile settings meant I'd seen her wedding photos. I know what dress she wore, how happy she looked. I went to the church where she got married, walked up and down the aisle, feeling sick and filled with rage. Imagined it all.

But I kept my distance. Told myself she wasn't worth it.

Until I learnt that she was pregnant. I found out from her husband's website. He'd set it up for his veterinary surgery, and put a picture of him and a heavily pregnant Claire pride of place on the homepage.

She was going to have a child, when she had taken mine away from me.

That was when I knew. I couldn't passively observe any more. She didn't deserve a baby. Not after what she did. She couldn't have what was rightfully mine.

Her husband's surgery was in a village near Oxford. I knew Claire would be moving out of London. It didn't take much detective work to learn that Matt's parents lived near the practice and to engineer a meeting with his mother. She was chairperson of the tennis club and when I enquired about membership and told her I was thinking of moving to the area, she was only too happy to tell me about her high-achieving son, who was shortly due to move in next door to her with his wife and daughter.

It was easy to find a place to rent in the village. I even managed to move in before Claire herself and I could introduce myself to her as a local resident. Thanks to my new neighbour who was so desperate for a babysitter that she'd leave her three-month-old with me, almost a stranger, I was able to pretend I was also a mother. I wanted Claire to trust me as much as I had once trusted her. I wanted her to depend on me.

We'd never met so she didn't know what I looked like and I knew that there had never been any photos of me printed in the press. My husband had kept my online profile so low that no one had been able to find one. But I was sure she'd recognise my voice. I shivered when she spoke to me the first time, clutching her baby in her doorway, her jumper stained with baby sick. Her voice was so familiar. It brought everything back.

But she was so caught up in herself that she didn't seem to register any familiarity. In fact, she seemed lonely, glad of my company. She was easy to befriend. On the very first day we met I took a spare key from a tray in the hallway, that must have been left by Pamela. In the beginning a few misplaced items and noises at night were enough to make her wonder if she was going crazy.

It doesn't take much to destroy someone's sanity. My husband taught me that. If you hack away at someone in the same place, again and again, eventually they crack.

Claire was an easier target than I thought. The fault lines were already there.

'Stephanie!'

She's calling me. I hear the desperation in her voice.

I turn to face her. After all these years, it's finally time to make her pay.

CHAPTER 45

When I arrive at the village, I pull over by a pub that backs onto the river.

I force myself out of the car, sick with nerves.

I've never been back here and I can hardly make myself turn down the narrow alleyway towards the river. I feel faint, as if I might collapse on the pavement.

But I have to get to my daughter.

I make myself run down the alleyway alongside the pub, my heart thumping.

As I come out the other end, back into the daylight, I catch sight of the sparkling river.

Memories flood my mind: The bare arm, sticking out of the reeds. The men in uniforms doing mouth-to-mouth. The scream of the police sirens.

I can't bear it. My ears are ringing and I can hardly catch my breath. I can feel myself losing my grip on reality, as the environment around me blurs into one green-blue haze. I stumble and fall to the muddy ground.

I push myself back up, my vision still double. I can't waste any time. I have to get to Olivia.

There's a blurred figure sitting by the riverside.

It must be Stephanie. The trees are bare now and raindrops dance on the water. There's no sunshine, no birds. But I recognise the spot. It's the exact spot where Lily died.

'Stephanie!' I manage to get the words out through tears.

At first I think she hasn't heard me, but then she turns and rises up to greet me, my daughter in her arms.

I reach her side, holding out my hands for my daughter. 'Give her back!'

Stephanie pulls her away.

I tense with fear, my heart racing. What's she going to do to my baby? I imagine Olivia submerged, caught in the reeds. Just like Lily. I can hardly breathe.

'I won't,' she says. As our eyes meet I can't get the thought out of my head that she's still Emma, that she's still my friend. Somehow, I still can't believe Emma would betray me.

But her eyes are harder now, cruel. I remind myself that she's Stephanie. She created 'Emma' just to hurt me.

'You don't deserve Olivia,' she says, echoing the note that came through my door. My heart contracts and I long to hold my daughter.

'You sent the note?' I ask.

'Yes. And I moved the smoke alarm. Did it work, Claire? Did it scare you?'

'I thought you were my friend,' I say.

Stephanie laughs bitterly. 'I thought you were mine. On the helpline. You were the only one I could trust.'

'I'm sorry.' The wind whips round me, blowing the rain into my face and turning my voice into a whisper. I remember how desperate Stephanie seemed on the phone, and guilt engulfs me, a vice around my heart. Back then I was so focused on the story that I couldn't see how cruel I was being. I was supposed to be Stephanie's lifeline, but I took away everything she loved.

Stephanie is lost in her own thoughts. 'You didn't even answer the phone,' she says. 'After Lily died, you just ignored me.'

'I couldn't face you. I was a coward. I'm so sorry.'

'You didn't care.'

I shuffle closer to Olivia. If I can just get a little bit closer, I'll be able to reach out and grab her.

I keep talking.

'I did care about you. I told you to leave him. I was worried about you. I wanted you to be happy.'

'You published the story that destroyed my life. My daughter is dead because of you.'

She's right. What I did was unforgiveable. My body tenses. Even after all this time, I can't believe that I could be so manipulative and cruel.

But I can't let Olivia be punished for my mistakes.

If I reach out now, I might just be able to grab her. But if I lose my balance, we'll both fall into the water below.

I try to distract Stephanie, not knowing what else to do. 'Did you always intend to take her?' I ask. 'From the very beginning?'

Stephanie adjusts Olivia in her arms, shifting her onto the other hip, so once again she's out of my reach.

'I wasn't certain at first. But when I saw how little you cared for her, it was clear I was doing the right thing. The one thing a baby needs was the one thing you couldn't provide. You couldn't love her. You didn't have it in you.'

Her words make me reel. 'I have postnatal depression. I thought you understood.'

Stephanie laughs bitterly. 'Yep. That's you, Claire. Despite having everything, you had the audacity to say you were depressed. Even though you were living the life I wanted. The life you stole from me.'

'I wanted to love her,' I say. Tears free-fall down my face. I look at Olivia's tiny hands peeking out from under her clothes. It's too cold for her. She needs a coat.

'Please give me another chance.'

'I didn't get another chance, Claire, did I? After you published your story I had no chance at all.'

'I'm sorry, Stephanie. I still think about Lily every day. A day doesn't go past when the guilt doesn't eat me up.'

It's true. I've never been able to get Stephanie's daughter out of my head.

'Why did you do it? Why did you set up the helpline? Why did you make me confide in you? You knew I was vulnerable.'

'I couldn't think of anything else,' I say quietly. 'I wanted the story so badly. You never left the house. It was the last roll of the dice. I thought if I set up the helpline, you might confide in me, tell me about your husband.'

She turns to me, her eyes raging. 'And I fell into the trap.'

She steps into the water, holding my baby.

*

Today

The shock of the cold water wakens my senses. I can feel the heaviness in my shoes, in the bottom of my jeans.

I wade in further. I want to get away from Claire, away from everything she reminds me of.

I don't want to think of her. I only want to think of Lily.

I try and imagine her face; her mischievous green eyes, dimpled smile, flowing hair. But the image is static, a photograph.

I squeeze my eyes shut, trying to imagine her laughing and running around. The film in my head jumps and skips. I can't conjure her up like I used to. I can't feel her here.

'Stephanie.'

Claire interrupts me and I squeeze my eyes shut tighter.

'Shut up.'

I stroke Olivia's hair gently and try to speak to Lily. This is the last place she saw, where she took her last breath. I imagine her soul still lingering, waiting for me to come back.

'Lily?' I say.

I want her blessing. I want her to let me restart my life. To live. To be. To care for another baby.

I listen intently for a reply but all I can hear is the sound of the water washing over the stones.

I can feel so many things. Bracing wind, icy water, bitter air. But I can't feel her.

She's gone.

I realise then that there's no point. Because I'm not whole without Lily.

I can't go on like this. I can't live.

CHAPTER 46

Stephanie holds Olivia above the water. She starts to whine as her small body shivers violently. The rain is soaking through her clothes.

'Please,' I say. 'Give her back.'

But Stephanie isn't listening. She wades towards the reeds.

'Is this where they found her?' she asks.

I realise that she doesn't know what I know. She wasn't here. She doesn't know where her daughter was pulled from the river. She doesn't know how hard the paramedics tried to resuscitate her.

'A little further along,' I say.

'Did you see her? Did you see her here?'

'Yes.'

'How did she look?'

I think of how Lily's spirit had already left her. 'She looked at peace.'

Stephanie nods, and pulls apart the reeds, looking at the murky water.

'This is where she took her last breath.'

'They tried to save her, Stephanie. They did mouth-to-mouth, chest compressions. But she was already gone.'

She turns and for a moment I think she's going to wade into the river with Olivia.

But she only looks into the reeds and whispers softly. 'Goodbye, Lily.'

CHAPTER 47

I reach out and try to take Olivia from her, but Stephanie pulls away, wading deeper into the water.

'Olivia's not Lily,' I say. 'She can never replace her.'

Stephanie nods and I think for a moment that she might come back to the riverbank. But she turns away.

'Give her back to me,' I say, softly. 'Please.'

'There's nothing for us here,' Stephanie says, wading deeper. 'Lily always wanted a sister. We can all be together now.'

She's going to drown them both. She can't.

A flush of heat rises through me, despite the bitter cold, and I think I'm going to be sick.

I feel an urgent need to act, to save my daughter, but I'm frozen to the spot, terrified that any sudden movement will force Stephanie further into the river.

'Stephanie. Stop.' The words stumble out through the tears.

But she steps further in.

I jump in beside her, the bitterly cold water shocking my system. Even in the shallows, the current is stronger than it looks. I can see Stephanie's finding it difficult to stay on her feet, her waterlogged jeans dragging her down.

I daren't step closer.

'Please,' I say. 'Please give her back to me.'

'You don't deserve her.'

A wave of pain washes over me. She's right.

'You don't love her. You don't care about her the way I cared about Lily.'

'Don't drown her,' I whisper. 'Please don't drown her.'

I try and grab at Olivia but Stephanie takes a step further back and stumbles in the water. My heart stops as Olivia shifts in her arms and the current threatens to take her, but Stephanie recovers, keeping her grip on her.

'Why shouldn't I?' she shouts through tears. 'You took everything I loved from me. You took my daughter. You stole my future. Lily will never grow up, go to university, find a job. Why should you have that when I can't?'

I hear myself scream as Stephanie struggles to maintain her footing. Soon the current will be too strong for her and Olivia will be swept away.

Olivia is crying now. So is Stephanie. I can hear her sobs wracking through her body.

'Stephanie, I'm sorry,' I say. 'I'm so sorry.'

'It was my fault,' she whispers. 'My fault my daughter died. I shouldn't have told you anything.'

Stephanie chokes on her tears.

'No,' I say. 'I should never have—'

But she's not listening. She's lost in the past, staring down into the murky water that's now up to her chest.

'There's no point. There's nothing to live for.' Her voice is so soft I can barely hear her.

I reach my hand out to her, ice-cold water lapping around my thighs.

'There is,' I say. 'There is.' I remember when I was in her place, ready to give up. I felt so overwhelmed by guilt as I stood on top of the multi-storey car park, staring at the tiny people below going about their day to day lives, as I prepared to jump.

'Why should I believe you? You comforted me before, remember. You told me everything would be all right. You told me to open up to you, to confide in you. And then you betrayed me. You printed it in the paper.'

My head pounds. She's right. It is my fault. It is. I set up the fake helpline and befriended her. I printed that story. It's my fault her daughter died. Now it's my fault my daughter is in danger.

'I'm sorry,' I repeat. It's all I have, but the words sound empty. 'I haven't been able to live with myself.'

Stephanie laughs bitterly.

'But you have though, haven't you? You won a prize for my story, you carried on as normal. And then you had a daughter.' Her eyes flash with anger.

'I didn't carry on as normal, Stephanie.' My head pounds harder, the rush of the river inside me. 'I couldn't. I had a breakdown and left the newspaper. I tried to kill myself. I was where you are now. I wanted to die. After your story was published in the paper, after what happened, I couldn't face it. I couldn't face what I'd done.'

I remember how guilty I'd felt. Empty inside. I couldn't cope. I drank more and more. Friends fell by the wayside as I spiralled out of control. I couldn't sleep at night, the images of Stephanie's drowned daughter haunting me. I ran away. I found myself on the roof of a car park, ready to jump.

'Why didn't you just do it?' she asks bitterly. 'I wish you had died. Why did you have to live and have a daughter?'

'I wanted to end it all. You have no idea how much.' I remember how strong the desire was, how intense. It seemed like the only option.

But Matt had come and stopped me. If only I could do the same for Stephanie.

Stephanie's demeanour changes. She seems intent now, concentrating on my words. She takes a step towards me.

'When?' she asks. 'When did you try to kill yourself?'

'Three years ago. A couple of months after your daughter's death.'

Stephanie is silent as she stares at me, her face blotchy from her tears, her hair wet from the drizzling rain.

'You were sorry?'

'I hated myself for what I'd done. I couldn't forgive myself.'

She pauses for a moment, considering this as I shiver violently in the freezing water.

Then she says quietly, 'Chris killed her, not you.'

I have told myself that a thousand times, tried to believe it is true. But I know that if I hadn't run the story, if I hadn't told Stephanie to leave him, then things might have been different. I have to take responsibility.

'I shouldn't have published the story.'

But Stephanie is immersed in her own thoughts. 'He was the one who took her here. He was the one who drowned her. I thought it was my fault. I'd told you our secrets. I'd tried to leave him. I betrayed him. I knew what he was like. I knew his temper. I just never thought he'd hurt Lily.'

'It wasn't your fault, Stephanie. You couldn't have known what he'd do next.'

She looks at me. 'You couldn't have known either.'

I nod, tears streaming down my face, remembering her daughter being pulled from the water. I'll never forgive myself for the way I behaved, for what I did. But she's right. I wasn't the one who killed Lily. Chris did.

Stephanie looks down at Olivia in her arms. 'Do you love her?' she asks.

And suddenly it's there, the surge of love I've always wanted. I am here, I think. I am here to rescue my daughter. I do care. I'm her mother.

'Yes,' I answer truthfully.

Stephanie hands Olivia over and I wrap her up in my arms. Relief floods me.

She's cold and shivery and her hair sticks to her tiny face. I hug her close to me, warming her up, kissing her again and again.

Stephanie must be even colder, the winter river soaking through her clothes.

'Come back,' I say. 'Please.'

She shakes her head. 'There's nothing for me here. I'll never have what you have.'

She's right. Whatever life I have with Olivia, she will never have it with Lily. She's gone. I swallow, ashamed of my good fortune when I caused Stephanie so much suffering.

'Please,' I say. 'Come back. There are people who can help you.'

Olivia shivers in my arms. I need to get out of the water and get Olivia inside, into the warm.

In the distance, I hear sirens.

'I need to get Olivia inside, Stephanie. She's cold.'

She looks at Olivia, as if realising for the first time what she'd been about to do. 'I didn't want to hurt her,' she says. 'I just wanted to say goodbye.'

'Lily's gone, Stephanie. Please come in. Please.'

Stephanie stares back at the river, at the reeds.

In the silence, the quiet rush of the water seems deafening.

'She's gone,' she says.

Stephanie turns away and takes a step deeper in the river. She pushes off the riverbed, into the central current.

'No!'

There's a split second when she floats, before the current takes her, her body tossing and turning, rolling downstream. She doesn't make a sound.

I cry out, stumbling through the heavy water to the bank. I put Olivia down on the riverside and clamber up after her.

I must get to Stephanie, I must save her. She doesn't deserve to die.

The silence is suddenly filled with noise.

Sirens. Paramedics. Police.

It brings it all back.

The rain intensifies as the wind picks up.

I rush over to the police, nearly slipping on the sodden mud, holding my baby close as I rub her back over and over to warm her up. I tell them that Stephanie has been swept away, that she's further down the river. They mobilise immediately, desperate to save her.

I feel a hand on my arm and turn to see Miriam.

'Are you OK?' she asks.

'Stephanie's gone. She… she went down the river.'

'They'll do everything they can to rescue her.'

'I know.' I also know that sometimes it's not enough. I remember the look in Stephanie's eyes. The desperation for her lost daughter. She didn't want to live without her. I hope, whatever happens, that she finds peace.

Miriam wraps her arms around Olivia and me and then the paramedics put us in an ambulance. As it departs, I squeeze my daughter tight, reflecting on everything. I had Olivia because I felt a gap in my life, an emptiness. When she was born, I couldn't love her because I felt I didn't deserve her. Not after everything I did. I was punishing myself.

But she is innocent of all of this. It's not about whether or not I deserve her. It's about whether she deserves me. And she does. She deserves a mother who's fully present, a mother who loves her.

I promise her that this will be a fresh start for us.

I hold her close to me. Her eyes meet mine. I need to give myself and my daughter a chance.

I do deserve Olivia. I do deserve to be a mother.

CHAPTER 48

Epilogue

3 months later

I stare up at the cottage, its limestone walls so full with promise and potential. The home I thought we'd be happy in.

Ruth's sold the cottage to a family; two parents, two children. She's already recruited the mother for the tennis club. 'A nice family,' she said. I imagine them looking round, deciding which colour they'll paint each room, exclaiming at the huge garden, picturing their kids running free. The sale has made Ruth finish sorting through Pamela's things, and now the rooms are beginning to clear, the cottage seems lighter and airier.

Ruth isn't pleased that Matt and I are back together. I think she'd still prefer him to be with Sarah, although there's no chance of that. They were never having an affair. We're pretty sure it was Stephanie who planted the scarf. And I think "Graham", who I supposedly left the nightclub with, was just another one of Stephanie's creations. But even though my STI tests came back negative, I'll never know for sure what happened that night and that scares me. I've stopped drinking again. This time I hope it's for good.

Matt has finally taken my side against his mother and told her she has to accept me or she'll see less of her granddaughter. That's the last thing Ruth wants. She might not like me, but she loves

Olivia. She wanted us to rent somewhere close by in the local area, but both Matt and I are ready to leave.

We're moving to Oxford, between Matt's surgery and the magazine I'm doing freelance work for in London. The magazine focuses on social issues and has a small, but growing, readership. I won't win any awards this way, but I will get to expose the issues that matter to me, to help people. And that's enough. When I get to Oxford, the first person I'm going to call is Miriam. She rushed to the river to be by my side as soon as I called. She's forgiven me, despite everything. I know I can trust her and I want us to be friends again. I've missed her so much.

To my surprise, Sarah's become a friend too. We've both made mistakes, and I think we understand each other. She even babysits for us occasionally.

I feel awful about what happened to Stephanie. Despite everything, I wanted her to have a second chance. But her body was never found and she was declared dead. Sometimes a sudden noise in the cottage would make me jump and I'd be convinced she was back, watching me. But when I turned around there was no one there. I think I'm just used to that feeling now, constantly being watched. Once we're away from the village, I'll feel safer.

I hold Olivia tightly in my arms, comforting her as she whines. I feel so differently about her now. When she giggles, my heart lifts. When she cries, my heart aches with hers. It's like we're one being, intimately connected. The strength of my feelings has taken me by surprise. I hadn't been able to feel them before. I was numb from everything that happened. But now I'm free. Free to start over again.

Matt puts the final box in the car, and goes around the back to strap Olivia in.

He turns to me, and we look up at the looming cottage together.

'Are you going to miss it?' he asks.

'No,' I say.

'Me neither.'

He embraces me, kissing me full on the lips. It feels like we're defying the house, defying Ruth.

'I can't wait to start again,' I say.

'A fresh start,' he replies. 'A chance to put the past behind us.'

We get into the car and drive away from the cottage for the final time.

A LETTER FROM RUTH

Thank you for choosing to read *The Mother's Mistake*. If you enjoyed it, I'd be very grateful if you could write a review. I'd love to hear what you think, and it makes a huge difference helping new readers to discover one of my books for the first time.

If you want to keep up to date with all my latest releases, just sign up at the following link. Your email address will never be shared and you can unsubscribe at any time.

www.bookouture.com/ruth-heald

I wrote *The Mother's Mistake* when I was on maternity leave. It struck me how motherhood seemed to go hand in hand with both fear and guilt. Fear that something will happen to your child and guilt that you aren't living up to society's ideals of the 'perfect mother'. I think these feelings affect all of us from time to time.

But for many others it's far worse. Over 10 per cent of women suffer from postnatal depression after the birth of a child, and while I was very fortunate not to be affected myself, I saw other confident, capable women struggle with the condition. In my novel, I wanted to explore the universal feelings of guilt and fear for a mother who's already on the edge.

I put Claire in a situation where she was isolated physically and mentally, and the people she thought she could depend on (Matt, her mother-in-law) continuously let her down. Lack of sleep can make anyone question what's real and Claire's never sure if the threat is on the outside or if it's really her own fragile mental health. She feels intense guilt because of her past mistake and believes she doesn't deserve her own child.

I hope you could relate to Claire's journey and that you also felt for Stephanie, who had to live through every mother's worst nightmare. Both women paid a high price for their mistakes. Although Stephanie hated Claire, they were both mothers who tried their best to care for their daughters. And they both couldn't forgive themselves for what happened to Stephanie's daughter, living with an ongoing sense of guilt and shame.

I'm always happy to hear from my readers – you can get in touch on my Facebook page, through Twitter, Goodreads or my website.

Best wishes,
Ruth

 Ruth.Heald

@RJ_Heald

 www.rjheald.com

ACKNOWLEDGEMENTS

Many people have contributed in large and small ways to the production of this book, but the underlying foundation has been my husband, who has supported me in everything I've done, and continues to provide an ever-patient sounding board for all my ideas.

The Mother's Mistake is about mothers and daughters. Although my own mother isn't here to see the novel published, I will always remember her relentless determination and enthusiasm in helping me get the word out about my debut novel, *27: Six Friends, One Year* and I'm forever grateful.

I wrote *The Mother's Mistake* while I was on maternity leave. After a difficult pregnancy, I was lucky to have an easy ride of early parenthood. My daughter has been a source of joy throughout the writing process. I've learnt so much from the delight she takes in the world around her and it's a pleasure to watch her develop and grow.

I'd also like to thank all the family and friends who have supported me in the development of my novel, including those who have advised me on police operations, medicine, social services and psychology, and those who have read chapters of the book and provided feedback.

I'm grateful to my editor Christina Demosthenous, firstly for signing me to Bookouture and secondly for providing such insightful editorial feedback. She has been unfailingly positive and allowed me to push back deadlines when I've been unwell, making the whole process very rewarding and stress-free. Thanks also to the rest of the team at Bookouture, a highly talented group who have provided ongoing help and guidance.

There were many people who helped me on my way to my publishing deal with Bookouture. My online writing group, the Neons, helped me fine-tune the early chapters. My mentor, Claire McGowan, provided invaluable feedback on the book and was an essential guide to the publishing industry. Marco Crivellari kindly read the manuscript at very short notice and gave me extremely useful feedback, drawing on his background in television. Debi Alper provided objective advice on publishing options, which helped me make a decision on which path to take.

And finally thank you to everyone who has taken time out of their lives to read my book. One of the greatest pleasures for me is knowing that there are people out there reading and enjoying my work.

42012205R00214

Printed in Poland
by Amazon Fulfillment
Poland Sp. z o.o., Wrocław